Elisabeth Hyde was
Hampshire, and the
Justice Department.
lege Fiction Award, t

ELISABETH HYDE

# Her Native Colours

This edition published 1994 by
Diamond Books
77–85 Fulham Palace Road
Hammersmith, London W6 8JB

Published by Grafton Books 1987

First published in Great Britain by
Severn House Publishers Limited 1986



Printed and bound in Great Britain

Set in Times

For Pierre
and
For my parents

# 1

Phoebe Martin chose a bad time to tell her ex-husband Rusty that she was taking their son Andrew back East for two weeks. Andrew was going on five, and that Thursday afternoon in early November Rusty Goldblume had spent four hundred dollars on backpacking equipment for him, including a child-sized down sleeping bag rated at minus ten degrees, a miniature backpack, hiking boots, a mess kit, and dark-blue multipocketed shorts. Rusty had planned to take Andrew to Yosemite National Park before the snow began, at the same time Phoebe was planning to take him back East.

'If you're not coming back until the twenty-second, that means I don't get him until Thanksgiving,' Rusty said, pacing back and forth in front of the couch in her living room while she folded a basket of laundry. His tie was loose, his shirt sweat-stained under the arms. Rusty was a public defender. 'You know what it can be like in Yosemite at Thanksgiving?'

Phoebe smoothed out a towel, and waited.

'It can snow up there, Phoebe,' Rusty said. 'I can't take a four-year-old camping in the snow.'

'I hate to break the news,' Phoebe said, 'but they already have two feet of snow in the valley. If you wanted to take him camping you should have taken him in August.' Rusty's mother, Angela, had just given Andrew new overalls, and they had bled in the wash, turning her underwear light blue.

'You haven't been back East in six years,' Rusty said.

'Why do you all of a sudden have to go back on the spur of the moment?'

'Because Molly's getting married on the spur of the moment,' Phoebe replied.

Before Rusty could answer, Andrew, dark haired and already muscular, ran from the bathroom into the living room. He was naked except for a ragged grey T-shirt. 'Daddy!'

'There's my boy,' Rusty said, picking Andrew up and slapping him on the bottom. 'You want to go camping with Daddy? You want to go to the Sierras?'

'What's the Sierras?' said Andrew.

'They're big mountains,' Rusty said, 'with lots of waterfalls and great big boulders.'

'The waterfalls are frozen over at this time of year,' Phoebe said.

Rusty ignored her. 'What happened there?' he asked Andrew, smoothing over a bruise on Andrew's cheek.

'I killed myself,' Andrew said. 'Playing war. Watch, Daddy, like this!' He scrambled out of Rusty's arms and picked up a large heavy book on commercial law from the sofa, then hit himself on the head with it and fell, spread eagled, on to the floor.

'I've really got a lot to do, Rusty,' Phoebe said. 'Don't you have plans for tonight?'

'You're talking about this as though it were final!' Rusty said. 'If I remember the agreement I get him every other weekend. You're violating the agreement, Phoebe.'

'Get up, Andrew,' Phoebe said. 'It's time for your bath.' She went into the bathroom, shut the water off, and dumped a bucket of boats and colourful windup bath toys into the tub. Andrew had names for them all: Racer-boat, Diver-boat; Binky and Duke.

'Where are you getting the money for this trip, anyway?' Rusty demanded. 'Two round trip tickets to

Vermont – did you get a raise or something? Did my mother pay for this?'

Phoebe returned to the living room. 'I found a Halloween special, Rusty,' she said wearily. 'We picked up the tickets on Halloween and Andrew wore a mask and so he gets to fly free.' Andrew also had to wear the mask on the flight, and now Phoebe made a mental note to buy an extra mask in case he lost the first one.

'It's still going to cost you a fortune,' Rusty said.

'Andrew,' Phoebe said. 'Get up. Your tub is ready.'

Andrew rolled his head to one side and crossed his eyes. 'Pretend I'm really dead, Daddy,' he whispered. 'Pretend you have to bury me now.' He rolled his head to the other side.

'Take him back for one week, then,' Rusty said. 'I don't care how long you stay but send him back before the nineteenth.'

'The seats are all booked until the twenty-second,' Phoebe said. 'And besides, do you think I'm about to put Andrew on a cross-country flight by himself?'

'I look pretty dead, don't I,' said Andrew.

Phoebe finished folding the last towel. 'And remember, Andrew's never been back East,' she continued. 'There are a lot of people back there who will want to see him. It's not like I've been able to run over to *my* mother's any time I want: drop in on the Cushmans, run over to the Allens, a family picnic up in Tilden Park before bringing him home to Mummy. Andrew,' she said. 'I'll give you to ten.'

Rusty massaged his eyelids. 'You really picked a good day to tell me this,' he said. 'After sitting through eight hours of prelims I try and relax by going out and buying my kid some camping equipment and then you tell me I can't take him camping. Nice timing, Phoebe, really nice timing.'

Phoebe stacked the clean clothing neatly into the laundry basket. Briefly she wondered if this was staged, if Rusty had found out about her trip from someone else and then gone and bought the camping equipment just to make things difficult for her; but then she scolded herself for looking too hard for maliciousness on Rusty's part. (Though who could say, considering their relationship these days.) She wished he would leave: her head was throbbing. Andrew was never going to take his bath, there was another load of laundry to do, they were out of milk and bread, she had a brief to write for Herb Sullivan before leaving on Tuesday – getting hassled by Rusty tonight was the last thing she needed.

Phoebe decided to switch tactics. 'Why don't you take him to Point Reyes?' she suggested. 'Over Thanksgiving. There won't be any snow at the ocean.'

'It's not the same at Point Reyes,' Rusty complained; 'the guy's almost five and the highest mountain he's ever seen is Mount Tam.' Rusty's concern both puzzled and amused Phoebe; when she and Rusty were married he had never talked about any love for the mountains. In fact Phoebe was sure that the highest mountain Rusty had ever seen was Mount Tam, viewed from the Bay Bridge.

'Up you go, kiddo,' Phoebe said, lifting Andrew and carrying his limp body into the bathroom. She pulled off his T-shirt; he climbed into the tub and wound up Duke, the scuba diver. Duke began kicking his legs, propelling himself around the tub as Andrew fired his water pistol at him.

Back in the living room she crossed her arms. 'Rusty, I have the tickets, I've lucked out with Herb letting me go, my trial's only going to heat up after I get back and so I'm going. I'm sorry. Why don't you take him this weekend?'

‘I’ve already made plans with Shirley,’ Rusty said. Shirley and Rusty had been seeing each other for six months. Shirley was originally from Los Angeles, and presently taught aerobics to pregnant women.

‘Then do it as a favour,’ Phoebe said. ‘I have to write a brief this weekend.’

‘Oh? Now we’re doing each other favours?’

Phoebe ignored him. ‘You don’t even need to take him tomorrow night; I’ll drop him off Saturday on my way into the office.’ She turned a pair of socks. ‘Look, Rusty, this isn’t to rub salt into the wound or anything, but really, you know, it’s your last chance for a while?’

The pained expression returned to Rusty’s face. ‘I want you to know you’ve really screwed up my autumn,’ he said. ‘I have two major trials between Thanksgiving and Christmas, not to mention my normal caseload, and the weekend of the thirteenth was the only time I had to get away. Try turning the tables, Phoebe – what would you say if I walked in and announced I was taking him to Oregon, or Arizona, for two weeks? What would you say then?’

‘Daddy!’ Andrew shouted from the bathroom.

‘Not now, Andrew!’ Rusty shouted back.

‘Daddy, there’s a big bug in the water!’ Andrew exclaimed.

‘I’ll be there in a minute,’ Phoebe called. ‘Play with Binky.’ She turned back to Rusty. ‘If I were in your shoes I’d try and be understanding,’ she said, tiring of the argument. ‘I’d try and think what it would be like for you if we lived in New York, and Angela never got to see Andrew, and your best friend from childhood was getting married out here. All right, I’d say, it screws up my plans, but on the other hand it’s his friend’s wedding and why shouldn’t he have a chance to show off Andrew to *his* family?’

Rusty closed his eyes.

'I think it's time for you to go, don't you?' Phoebe said sweetly. 'Take the hiking equipment back. If you want to buy him a present buy him a new mattress.'

'All right, forget it,' Rusty said, pressing his fingertips to his forehead. 'Go; – stay as long as you want, for all I care.'

'Hey, Mum!' Andrew shouted. 'Look at this!'

'Where are you going?' Phoebe said to Rusty.

'I'm going to say good night to my son,' Rusty said, heading for the bathroom. Just then the vacuum cleaner started its loud whine. Something was different, though; the motor of the ancient machine sounded as though it were choking, and then it stopped.

Phoebe followed Rusty into the bathroom. Andrew was standing on the bath mat, holding the dripping hose of the vacuum cleaner above the tub. Behind him, muddy dirt from the unchanged filter had sprayed out from the back of the machine, splattering the wall.

'Oh Andrew,' Rusty said.

'Oh shit,' Phoebe said, sinking back against the door.

'I got the bug,' Andrew said.

Just why the motor of the vacuum hadn't shorted out, just why Andrew hadn't got electrocuted, remained a mystery. Rusty cleaned up the mess, then helped Andrew into his pyjamas while Phoebe ran another load of laundry. By eight-thirty it was in the dryer, and she suddenly realized that she had forgotten to feed Andrew. Though Andrew hadn't seemed to notice. He and Rusty were now playing Go Fish on the sofa. Phoebe stretched out on the rug in front of the fireplace, waiting for them to finish this round so that Rusty would leave. How much Andrew's growing to resemble Rusty these days, she mused – the same jawline, the same eyebrows forming a straight line across his brow, the same dark curly hair.

'Quit cheating, Andrew,' Rusty said. 'You cheat like that and you're not going to make any friends when you go to school.'

'Do you have any jacks?' Andrew asked.

Rusty plucked a card from his hand and gave it to Andrew, who squealed and placed the set face-side up on the cushion. Phoebe left to remove the clothes from the dryer.

'Hey, you want to have dinner with us?' Andrew was asking Rusty when she returned.

'I was just thinking of dinner.' Phoebe held Rusty's jacket. 'I think it's time for Daddy to leave.'

'I've got an idea,' Rusty said. 'Why don't we all go out and get a pizza? Shirley's working late anyway.'

'I don't think so,' Phoebe said. 'I've got too much to do tonight.'

'Do you have any eights?' Andrew asked.

'Come on, Phoeb,' Rusty said. 'It doesn't mean anything.'

Phoebe bristled. 'It's going on nine,' she said. 'It's past Andrew's bedtime.'

'The kid's gotta eat, Phoebe,' Rusty said. 'Are you feeding him three meals a day?'

'I said, DO YOU HAVE ANY EIGHTS?' Andrew shouted.

Rusty gave him another card.

'I'm winning, Mum,' Andrew said.

'Hey, kiddo, you want to go for a pizza?' Rusty asked.

'Yeah!' Andrew stood up and began jumping on the sofa, his pairs of cards sliding together into a jumble.

'Sofas are for sitting, Andrew,' Phoebe said, but she realized she had no choice: Andrew would never calm down tonight if she said no. Avoiding Rusty's eyes she went in to change her clothes. It was late, and the idea of pizza wasn't a bad one, but she wished she had thought of it on her own, after Rusty had left. Just Andrew and herself. She could have been a lot nicer to the poor kid, wouldn't bitch at him for everything like she did with Rusty here. Look at her tonight: she hardly ever scolded him for jumping on the sofa; it was secondhand and needed the springs tied and a new slipcover anyway. But now, with Rusty, she felt like the type of mother who would slap her child in the grocery store for opening the box of Fruit Loops. The lady with the ugly disposition. Ms Veto. Nothing would go over well tonight: why, Rusty could say he'd take Andrew if she really had so much to do, and she would accuse him of trying to deprive her of time with her son. Christ, she thought, glancing at Molly's wedding invitation on her bureau – he could even tell me to have a good time on the trip and I'd say how can I, we're probably flying on a DC-10 and you think it's going to be easy to go home after all this time? To put on a smile and give Molly a hug and tell her how great she looks, how lucky she is to have such a big house and look at those jars of jam, me I'd *never* find time to make jam.

Phoebe pulled on a pair of baggy trousers and fluffed out her hair – a thick mass of cinnamon-coloured curls – with a wide-pronged African comb. Admit it: you don't really want to go back East. You're nervous about seeing Molly and so you're taking it out on Rusty.

But why? Why are you so nervous?

Phoebe fastened a pair of gold hoop earrings into her lobes and checked her wallet for cash. Go get a pizza. Be nice.

And let Rusty pay. He's the one who suggested it.

To Phoebe's surprise they made it through the dinner without any further squabbling; afterwards Rusty and Andrew played Space Invaders. On the way home they drove by the university. 'Look, that's where Mummy and

Daddy went to law school,' Rusty said to Andrew, pointing out a low, squarish building on the edge of the Berkeley campus.

'Don't remind me,' said Phoebe.

'And that's where Mummy went swimming when you were in her tummy,' Rusty went on, indicating the gymnasium.

'Oh, Rusty,' she said, but couldn't help smiling, remembering how she had felt, bobbing about the pool during her seventh month.

Rusty started up the long hill to her house, and soon she could look out to the broad darkness of the San Francisco Bay, the lights of the city on one side, the dark hills of Marin on the other. Andrew was dozing on her lap, and she wrapped her arms around him, feeling his small stomach bloated from the pizza. How would he react to everyone back home? she wondered. And how would they react to him? Say hello to Aunt Molly, she heard herself prod; say hello to Auntie Bea and Uncle Dave. He can get a little shy in front of strangers, she would probably have to explain; it takes a while to get to know him. Phoebe smiled, and smoothed his hair away from his forehead. It won't be so bad, she consoled herself. It'll be good to see everyone; and it'll be just like old times with Molly.

As Rusty pulled out from a stop sign, his head turned back to the road; he'd been glancing at the two of them. She wished she could talk to him about these apprehensions that were hovering in the back of her mind; she also wished she could let him know that she really *was* sorry for messing up his plans. She wondered what he was thinking right now; perhaps he was wishing that he were going back with them. Just think, she thought; this is how it could have been, the three of us, a family, going out for a pizza on a Thursday night, planning our trip back to Vermont: arguing over how long to stay, whether we should spend a day in Boston, or take a short trip over to the Maine coast.

But then Rusty was parking the car in front of her house; he turned off the ignition and cleared his throat. 'About Christmas,' he started.

'What about Christmas?'

'I know it's your turn to have him this year,' Rusty said, 'but seeing as you're violating the agreement I don't think you should have any problem with my taking him over Christmas.'

Phoebe could have sworn that deep in her stomach the pizza suddenly began to burn. 'A little quid pro quo,' she said. 'Isn't that what you mean?'

Rusty switched the blinker on and off. 'I was just thinking it might be a good time to take him to Colorado, teach him to ski.'

'Oh, I don't care,' Phoebe said wearily. 'I'm not going to get any time off this Christmas anyway.'

'I mean, it's only fair,' Rusty said.

'No it's not,' Phoebe retorted. 'It may be equal but nothing about all this is ever fair.' She gathered together her handbag and Andrew's jacket. 'Are you taking him this weekend?' she inquired. 'Because if you're not, I'll have to line up a sitter.'

'I'll take him,' Rusty said.

'Thank you,' Phoebe said. 'And look, I'll pay you back for the pizza on Saturday, I'm just low on cash tonight.'

'Don't worry about it,' Rusty sighed. 'It was only a couple of bucks.'

'No, I'll pay you,' Phoebe said irritably. As she opened the door Andrew yawned; he stiffened his legs, contorting himself in her lap, then fell limply against her. Phoebe slid out with the boy in her arms, and closed the door without saying good night.

* * *

Molly's wedding invitation had come just a week ago: a hand-painted watercolour of emerald hills and evergreens and royal-blue lakes. Wasn't that just like Molly, Phoebe had mused as she pulled out the card: making her own stationery. It even *looked* ecological. The she had opened it up. *Mary Elizabeth Adams and Nicholas John Ulrich*, she read, *request the pleasure of your company at their wedding, on Sunday, the fourteenth of November, at two o'clock*.

Her first reaction had been that it would be impossible for her to make the trip, in view of the current state of affairs in the Parco-Fields litigation. This large antitrust case, in which her firm represented one of the five defendants, had been going on for several years and was scheduled for trial the following April. As one of the junior associates on the case Phoebe's primary function was to review all documents they received from the plaintiff. 'Captain Document,' Janice, another associate, had nicknamed her; and though Phoebe had already screened twenty-six file cabinets and separated out those worth reading, which amounted to three cabinets, she was falling behind in her work. Every morning she would stack up two feet of documents on the left side of her desk, determined that they would be on the right side, pigeonholed into their proper category, by noon. Often by one o'clock, however, she would be lucky to have skimmed through three inches. ('I'm bored,' she would say over the buzzer to Janice. 'Oh good,' Janice would say. 'Want to go shopping?' 'No,' Phoebe would say, 'no, I'm just so fucking *bored*.') And a week ago one of the partners had asked her about a hot document she had overlooked (he had heard about it from one of the attorneys for the other defendants); he'd been polite about it, but made it clear that her negligence was to be a one-time mistake. Fearful, she had talked with Janice about getting off the case – she felt like she was getting in over her head, didn't want this case to go to trial, wished she were doing something else, even writing research memoranda – but Janice was pessimistic. 'They'll never let you off,' she said. 'Not this close to trial.'

And not only was she behind reviewing documents; several weeks ago a dispute had erupted over who had neglected to turn over what, with both sides accusing the other of holding back information; and because of her role in reviewing documents Phoebe was now in the midst of preparing one of the many cross-motions to compel discovery.

No, Phoebe had thought that night; with all the work she had, with this discovery dispute, there was no way she could take even a week off and go back East for a wedding. Not even Molly's wedding. She was sorry, but she just couldn't. She had worried, though, about Molly's reaction when she tried to explain it: Molly would get angry, Molly would never understand.

'That's all right,' Molly had said, long distance.

Phoebe, prepared for an argument, hadn't known what to say.

'It was a long shot,' Molly said. 'I didn't really think you'd be able to just pick up and leave on such short notice.'

'It's this trial I have,' Phoebe said, feeling compelled to explain. 'I'm just swamped with work – and on top of it I'm in the middle of getting this damn motion filed – '

'Don't worry about it,' Molly said. 'Really.'

'I just don't have any choice,' Phoebe said. 'You wouldn't believe this jerk I'm working for.'

'It's all right, Phoebe,' Molly said. 'Listen, we'll make a toast to you.'

'What about postponing it,' Phoebe joked. 'Get married next May.'

Molly said nothing, and Phoebe felt silly.

'Look, I should go, this is costing you a lot of money,' Molly said.

'Maybe I'll make it back after the trial,' Phoebe said. 'Maybe I'll bring Andrew home for a visit next summer.'

'Sure,' Molly said. 'I'm not going anywhere.'

Strange phone call, Phoebe thought after hanging up; she was unable to tell whether Molly didn't care if she came back in the first place, or whether she did in fact feel let down, and was just trying to cover it up. Probably the latter, she reasoned, remembering how Molly would always bend over backwards to avoid an argument. Sure you can borrow that shirt, she would say back in high school, fully aware of Phoebe's propensity for spilling things; sure you can borrow that book, I'll finish it later. Did you really think that Molly would challenge your decision not to come? Phoebe asked herself. Of course not. She may be pissed, but she's not going to say anything to you about it.

Well, I can't go, even if she is pissed, Phoebe had thought. There's just no way I can swing the time.

But as it would turn out, Phoebe was wrong about that, for the next morning the dispute resolved itself, with the parties suddenly willing to release a few of what they perceived to be relatively harmless documents, in exchange for what they hoped would turn out to be extremely valuable documents. Which made Phoebe's motion to compel a little moot, to say the least.

For a brief moment after hearing the news she thought maybe this would free up enough time for the wedding, but then she reminded herself that it didn't really change anything; she still had all those remaining documents to be reviewed. Still, without the discovery squabble to worry about she now felt this vague obligation to make a last-ditch effort to get the time off. Perhaps she felt as though she owed it to Molly? Ask Herb, she thought. He's sure to say no, but then you'll at least be able to tell Molly you made every effort you could.

So after lunch she went down to Herb's office. His secretary was out; he was in at his desk, reading.

'Herb?'

'Yeah.'

Phoebe ventured into his office. Herb was a heavyset man with prematurely grey hair and eyes the colour of slate. He had removed his jacket but his waistcoat remained buttoned, his deep maroon tie knotted tightly around the starched collar of his white shirt. On his desk an icy-looking glass bulldog weighted down a stack of papers.

'About the fact that we're not going to be filing that motion to compel?' she began.

Herb made some notes in the margin. 'Uh-huh,' he said, without looking up.

'Well, there's this wedding I've been invited to back East, two weeks from now.'

Herb lifted his glance.

'My oldest friend,' she added, and smiled a goofy monkeylike smile.

Herb waited. Little fold lines crossed his waistcoat at each button.

'Well, when I heard about the compromise I thought there might be time for me to go but I know there's a lot to do regardless, so if you think it would be better if I didn't go – '

'Go,' Herb said.

Phoebe blinked.

'Go,' he said. 'Take the time while you can. Things are only going to explode after this; you're not going to see a day's vacation for a long time.'

Phoebe didn't really want to hear that.

'What about that brief, though?' Herb asked. 'The brief for the protective order?'

'I'm working on it,' Phoebe said. 'I'm pretty much through with the research.'

'Just get it to me before you leave,' Herb said.

Phoebe nodded, and turned.

'Hey, Phoebe.'

She turned back.

'I still want to see a draft of this last set of interrogatories right after Thanksgiving,' Herb said.

Phoebe nodded.

'And the documents I'll need for Schein's deposition,' he said. 'I want them by the first. Anything hot?'

Phoebe punched the air. 'I think we're on to some good stuff.'

'All right,' he said warily. 'I just wanted to make sure you weren't going to fall behind.'

'Of course not,' Phoebe said.

'And, Phoebe,' Herb said.

'Yes?'

'Appreciate the trip,' he said. 'I'm giving you a real break by letting you go, you know.'

Herb's secretary, Pearl, had returned to her desk; she wore a permanent frown, as though it had been stamped on her face long ago with a branding iron. Back in her office Phoebe called Molly.

'I thought you had a trial,' Molly said.

'I do,' Phoebe said. 'I guess you could say it's the eye of the hurricane right now.'

'Well then, want to be my maid of honour?'

'Hey, matron of honour,' Phoebe joked. 'Don't forget about Andrew.'

'Speaking of which,' Molly said.

'What?'

'Oh, never mind,' Molly said. 'I'll tell you later.'

That was all a week ago; yet despite having worked things out with Herb, despite having found the Halloween special, Phoebe's misgivings about the trip began to grow. She almost wished Herb would change his mind, that he would march into her office with another rush project: a new motion, say, that would have to be filed the day after Molly's wedding. She tried to tell herself that the misgivings weren't really there; and one night she even got out her old photo album and flipped through the pages with Andrew, pointing out pictures of the old farmhouse, Grammy Louise's flower garden, Dave Adams's beaver pond; of Molly and Phoebe riding bikes, guarding their clubhouse, dressing up for Halloween. ('Do I have to play with those girls?' Andrew had demanded.)

But Rusty was right. She didn't have the money for this trip, even if she had managed to find the Halloween special. In addition to the cross-country flight, there were the tickets from Boston to Burlington, Vermont, which together cost almost as much as the Halloween special. And then there was the matter of a new dress. Phoebe had just charged two woollen suits on an overextended credit card, and a dress for Molly's wedding would probably end up costing over a hundred dollars, plus another hundred for new shoes. But she couldn't wear a suit to a wedding in Vermont: too severe, too professional, too businesslike. (Doesn't *she* look the part, she heard Molly's mother, Bea, remark; all spiffed up in her tailored clothes; I guess she's forgotten how casual we are back here.) Well, maybe she could find a dress on sale. At least Andrew had new overalls and shirts, thanks to Rusty's mother – even if everything did have an alligator or a polo player on its breast. (Losing Angela as a mother-in-law had always given Phoebe a few regrets about the divorce. Both during and after the proceedings she had been oddly neutral, and even now – three years later – she stopped by on a regular basis and kissed Phoebe hello and good-bye and reminded her to go as her guest at the Claremont pool any time she wanted, whether or not she brought Andrew. Once the older woman had even broken down, telling Phoebe that she wished Rusty hadn't blown it, there had never been anyone like her before and he was such a moron, he didn't know a good thing when he had it. 'I shouldn't be saying this,' Angela had cried, 'but you were so good for him, you got him to stop smoking and look at him now, he's back to two packs a day. And the girl he brought home last weekend looked like she hadn't read anything other than movie magazines for the past ten years. She's even from LA!' The Goldblumes were of old San Francisco stock. 'Fullerton! What and I going to do if my son marries a girl from Fullerton! Oh' – Angela had sighed, wiping her eyes – 'make me shut up. Rusty will come through, I guess. But for crying out loud, Phoebe, how is it that *you* managed to do so well? How come *you* didn't go all to pot?'

And Phoebe had said nothing.)

And it wasn't just the money that counselled against the trip; she shouldn't be taking all this time off, despite Herb giving her the go-ahead. He had no idea how far behind she really was. She still had the Schein documents to organize, those interrogatories (hopefully the final set) to be drafted, three new file drawers of documents to be reviewed, and a memorandum on one fine point of commercial law (a subject which she knew nothing about) to be written for another partner. And on top of it all she had been assigned to this year's Christmas Party

Committee. The firm wanted a Hawaiian banquet, and Phoebe was in charge of the leis.

She would take a briefcase of work back East with her, of course, but it would be a token gesture, dead luggage. Every morning she would get up and promise herself an hour before lunch, perhaps while Andrew napped, maybe as the others watched television in the evening – but the work would never get done. Andrew would be clamouring to visit the Big Rock, Barnet's Ledge, the sugarhouse; and her mother would schedule all meals promptly at eight, twelve, and six so that just as she was getting into the work it would be time to eat again. That was the trouble with going home; you had to readjust to someone else's alien schedule, an eerie reminder of being eight or ten, home from school with the flu, *I Love Lucy* and *Mayberry R.F.D.* and *The Real McCoys*, a tray of chicken noodle soup and cinnamon toast and then naptime from one to three.

But ultimately, the bottom line wasn't really her workload, and it wasn't really money. It was Molly, as Phoebe realized earlier that evening while getting ready to go out for a pizza; Molly, her friend since the age of five, when the Adamses had moved into the farmhouse up the dirt road.

'But why?' said Janice, the next afternoon. 'If she was your best friend, then why are you so nervous about seeing her?'

'I don't know why,' Phoebe said.

'Maybe it's just because you don't see her very much these days,' Janice said. 'When was the last time you got together?'

'My wedding,' Phoebe said, and she thought back to that week in April, five and a half years ago, when Molly had flown out to California to be her maid of honour. As a bride-to-be Phoebe had been in a fairly overwrought state much of the time, but still, she had taken a day off and driven Molly up to the wine country so that they could have some time alone, just the two of them; and they spent the day sampling wines and trying to keep from getting drunk by breaking off and wolfing down chunks of a sourdough baguette they kept in the front seat. At the first winery they were a little awkward with one another; it was their first time alone, really, and Phoebe spent most of the time philosophizing – pompously so, she thought now – about the differences between the East Coast versus the West. But at the second winery they loosened up, and began recalling old times in high school, playing hooky and going up to the quarries with a six-pack of beer; and when they pulled into the third winery they didn't even make it to the tasting room before they were laughing about the summer after their junior year in college, when they had shared a room in Stowe and waited tables at a Swiss-style fondue restaurant. 'Remember those goddamn caps we had to wear,' they cried. 'Remember that *asshole* bartender?' They drank enough wine that by late afternoon Molly was insisting on a mud bath at Calistoga; she couldn't return to Vermont, she claimed, without having taken one, and Phoebe, a little surprised to see this side of Molly – after all, it was so very *Californian* to take a mud bath at Calistoga – had given in. They didn't get back to Berkeley until eleven that night, tired, giddy – and hung over.

You had a good enough time with her back then, didn't you? Phoebe asked herself now. Certainly it was good enough that they had continued to write while Phoebe was in law school. Of course, their letters had dwindled of late; in fact, if pressed Phoebe would have had to confess that she hadn't written a letter to anyone since starting work at the firm. But she always remembered to call Molly on her birthday, and vice versa.

So *why* was she so edgy about seeing Molly now, face to face?

'What does she do, back there in Vermont?' Janice was asking.

'She's a schoolteacher,' Phoebe replied, feeling a little defensive, for Molly's sake – but at the same time feeling a little ashamed, for thinking there might be anything to be defensive about. 'She teaches science to tenth graders.'

Janice waited.

'And she does a lot of crafts,' Phoebe said. 'She weaves and knits and I think she also makes quilts and sells them. You know, at those craft fairs they have in the summer.'

Janice nodded, as though Phoebe had provided her with more than enough information about this woman back in Vermont.

'Though I have to say, I don't know how she can stand it,' Phoebe said. 'She's never lived anywhere else in her life, she teaches at the same rinky-dink high school that we both went to – and it's not as though she's stupid, either, it's not as though she couldn't have gone on to graduate school – but for some reason she chooses to settle down five miles from where she grew up and teach *school*?'

Janice frowned.

'I guess I just don't know her any more.' Phoebe sighed. 'That's the problem; and what I *do* know about her – well, how am I going to manage to sound enthusiastic about teaching high school and knitting baby sweaters? And how's it going to look when I start talking about my job as an attorney? She doesn't know it sucks; none of them do back there. To them it's a big deal, and I'm going to look as though I'm bragging.'

'Well, it's no small potatoes,' Janice said, 'but I do know what you mean. I have this friend back in Iowa who's just had her fourth kid. She's into Congoleum. She's into 4-H. She's into weed killer. All I have to do is send her a card postmarked San Francisco and I feel like I'm being condescending,' Janice said sadly. 'Can you imagine what I feel like mentioning Judson and Day?'

Phoebe looked glum.

'Well, listen,' Janice said. 'If you don't have the money and you don't have the time, why don't you just tell her you can't make it?'

'I can't,' Phoebe said flatly. 'Without Herb for me to blame she'll take it as a put-down if I don't go. She made it out to be maid of honour at my wedding on a schoolteacher's salary; how can I tell her I can't afford it when I'm making over forty grand a year?'

'So fudge a little,' Janice said. 'Tell her Herb changed his mind. Quite frankly I'm surprised he hasn't already – what got into him, anyway, to let you go?'

'Damned if I know,' Phoebe said.

'Maybe it's a setup,' Janice said. 'Maybe he's planning to put something in your evaluation about the fact that you took time off when it was given to you instead of insisting on being a martyr.'

Was that what Herb had in mind?

'So?' said Janice.

'So what?'

'So make up a story,' Janice said. 'Tell your friend you've got a deposition all of a sudden.'

But Phoebe shook her head. 'Molly'd know,' she said. 'She'd pick up on my tone of voice, or something. Besides, I should want to go back,' she went on. 'We grew up together. And growing up in East Winslow – well, it wasn't like there were a lot of other kids around; there was my brother, of course, but he was five years older than me, so we never wanted to pal around together – so really, Molly was like a sister to me.' Phoebe sighed. 'I guess I could understand feeling strange if she were someone I'd lost touch with over the years – but it's not like that – '

Janice's telephone buzzed.

'Excuse me,' she told Phoebe. 'I've been expecting the Clapp.'

'You know, I think you're worrying about it far too much,' Janice said as they left the firm that Friday evening.

'I know I am,' Phoebe said.

'Well, then, stop being so analytical about things,' Janice said. 'Your oldest friend's getting married. She's asked you to be her maid of honour. It's going to be a week-long party with food and wine and everybody getting crocked; it's not like she's asked you back to have it out with her.'

'You're right,' Phoebe agreed. 'I'll have a good time. I shouldn't worry so much. 'Night, Linda,' she said to her secretary. ''Night, Stella; 'night, Maureen,' she said to the other secretaries in the pool. 'You all have a good weekend.'

'You too,' Linda said. 'What are you doing?'

'Working,' Phoebe said. 'What else?'

That night, after putting Andrew to bed, Phoebe poured herself a glass of wine and went out on to the balcony. The air was cool, filled with the pungence of eucalyptus, and she leaned against the railing, listening to the distant sound of foghorns. It was soothing to her, that sound, and she began to relax. She and Andrew had a good arrangement, living up here in the hills. The house was a large three-storey stucco, built against the side of a steep hill in the north end of Berkeley. It was owned by a professor at the University, who lived with his wife and three-year-old daughter on the bottom two floors and rented out the top floor to Phoebe, giving her a light, airy living room with a cathedral ceiling, a small kitchen with a breakfast nook, two bedrooms, and a large walk-in closet. It was sparsely furnished, a result of the divorce, and the only artwork in the entire apartment was a print by Miró, one that Andrew had picked out with her this past summer. Having grown up in a cluttered farmhouse with curtains on every window and pictures on every wall, where the ceilings were so low they could almost be touched (because low ceilings conserved heat), and where a slant-roof porch cut off all the light in the kitchen – Phoebe loved the lightness, the airiness, the simplicity of this apartment.

But what made the place was the outdoor balcony, which overlooked the city, the bridges, Mount Tamalpais, and Marin County. On the south side a camellia tree blocked off the neighbours' view, and on sunny weekend afternoons when Rusty had Andrew and she wasn't working, Phoebe would sunbathe in the nude. (*It's Washington's Birthday*, she had written her mother one year, *and I'm sitting out on my balcony without even a bathing suit! What are you doing!?*) The balcony was free of clutter; Andrew's toys were forbidden because a year ago he had dropped a truck over the edge; it had hit the professor's daughter, Marilyn, who was playing below and who, as a result, had to have eight stitches taken.

Janice was right; she was being too analytical. She was letting her apprehensions overshadow everything. Part of it was Molly, of course; but a large part of it was that it had been more than six years since she had been back. (She hadn't intended for it to happen that way; but there she was, pregnant, and then she'd had Andrew, and her mother had insisted it was easier for her to come out

West than for both of them to come back East; and then there was the divorce, when she didn't want to see anyone; and then there was her job.) Who were they all expecting to see, after all this time? Phoebe the lawyer? Phoebe the divorcée? Phoebe the Californian? 'How's the SLA?' Molly's father, Dave, would joke, permanently prejudiced against the West Coast. 'How's Jane Fonda, she causing any more earthquakes these days?' And her own mother would press her to come home for good. 'Why *don't* you move back *East*,' Louise was always saying. 'You should see what they've done to the Boston waterfront. You could get one of those condos right by Faneuil Hall and Andrew could grow up with more of a . . . well, more of a *heritage*, Phoebe.'

'How's Jack?' Phoebe would ask. 'How's his job? How are he and Cindy Ann doing?' Because grandson or no grandson, she wasn't moving back; California was home. Occasionally she would feel a twinge of homesickness, of course; that one afternoon, say, in October, when the Berkeley hills were straw-brown and dry as kindling, and she would remember the maples behind the old farmhouse in East Winslow, violent with crimson, fiery orange and gold. It was then that she would miss the smell of autumn: baskets of apples, pumpkins in the sun, a sweater just out of its mothballs. Or a night in January when she would wake up, unable to remember for a moment where she was, and she would look out of her bedroom window to the streetlamp, expecting to see the flurry of snowflakes but instead seeing nothing but shimmering sheets of northern California winter rain.

Yet those moments were rare. Phoebe liked the anonymity of California, the lack of heritage, as her mother would say. Right after the divorce she had given away all her button-down collar shirts and based her wardrobe around shades of purple. She bought a futon. She snorted cocaine. She took a belly-dance class. She got Rolfed (although by the third session of probing massage she felt strangely ripped off; and she also hurt). And on hot nights in September when the fog stayed out on the ocean, Phoebe and Andrew ate homemade burritos on fresh tortillas from the Mission District out on the balcony, and Phoebe would think of those grim family dinners back East, sitting around the table under the sad overhead light with her mother and Jack, scalloped white china on a blue-checked oilcloth, spoonfuls of mashed potatoes and green beans and slices of stringy meat, all washed down with a glass of room-temperature milk. Phoebe would dip her burrito into the hot sauce. 'Good, huh?' she would mumble to Andrew, stuffing it into her mouth. The closest thing to a heritage she gave Andrew was teaching him songs she had known as a child. 'If Pow-wow couldn't help them he would go to the Medicine Man,' she would chant. 'And he would tell the story, of how it all began.'

'All began,' chorused Andrew.

Didn't you ever want to leave, Molly? she thought now. Try something different? She wondered about Nick, suddenly ashamed that she had never asked Molly much about him. Maybe he was going to go to med school, business school; maybe he would drag her off to Baltimore, Atlanta, Dallas. Fat chance that Molly would ever move away on her own. Six years ago, on that cool morning in August when Phoebe had packed up her Beetle with two suitcases of clothes and one box of linens and a potted Swedish ivy, Molly had sat on the large slab of slate that formed the front porch of the Martin farmhouse, a bandana kerchief tied around her hair, winding a skein of yarn. Molly was about to start teaching at the Barrington Union School; she was supporting herself that summer by knitting Icelandic sweaters. She had her own place in the village of Winslow but came home every weekend. As Phoebe saw it, Molly had watched her with no trace of envy on her face, no sense of I-wish-I-were-going-too, just the usual calm complacency that Phoebe had known for seventeen years. Yet Phoebe, anxious to leave, anxious to make Buffalo that night, nevertheless felt that she was letting her friend down. After all, she wasn't moving to Boston, or New York – she was moving across the country, to the far edge of the continent, the other side of the Rockies.

Downstairs the professor's wife began to practise the piano; she was working out the right hand to a Bach fugue, it sounded like, and she kept repeating the same series of notes, over and over. From her balcony Phoebe looked over to the city. Using the Transamerica tower as a base, she counted over several office buildings to locate her office building; then she counted down to the firm's windows. Of course, it was too far away for her to tell, but Phoebe was sure that the windows on the associates' floors – the Barracks, Phoebe called them – were lit; and those on the partners' floors – the Officers' Club – were dark. She finished her wine, pulling her jacket closely around her. In four days she would be on a plane, wondering whether Andrew would throw a tantrum, whether she had brought enough gum for his ears, whether they would make the connection with US Air. In five days she would probably meet this Nick. And in nine days Molly and Nick would be standing before some minister and she, Phoebe, would be up there in a new dress, handing Molly the ring.

Don't blow it.

# 2

Saturday morning Phoebe was anxious to get to work. Upon waking up she had promised herself she would stop brooding about the trip – there wasn't anything to brood about, as Janice had said; but more importantly there wasn't *time* to brood; she had a brief to write before leaving. So she dropped Andrew off with Rusty before breakfast – Rusty liked to cook in the morning anyway – and drove directly to the office. She had a few more cases she wanted to look up before she actually began drafting Herb's brief, and Saturday mornings were a good time to work in the library: there weren't many other attorneys around, and those who were there had the same goal as she did – getting in and out as quickly as possible.

Phoebe's law firm, Judson and Day, was one of the largest in San Francisco, with a present count of 78 partners and 123 associates. Phoebe had been there three years since graduating from law school. Within her first month she had devised a system for categorizing her fellow associates: there were those who would go for partnership – the Nuts – and those who would leave after three or four years – the Bolts. (The Nuts were clearly in the majority.) Each group had its own set of marked characteristics: Nuts, for instance, chatted with partners on the main set of lifts, while Bolts used the back lifts and kept to themselves. Nuts regularly were asked out on recruiting dinners – usually held at the finest restaurants in the city, where they would spend upwards of eighty dollars per person while glorifying the firm to the candidate; Bolts, disgusted with this deception, begrudgingly went out on one dinner, and afterwards – *if* they were asked again, which they usually weren't, since they failed to give enough of a pep talk to the poor interviewee – became unavailable due to their heavy workload. Nuts had a knack for knowing when to speak at meetings and when to stay quiet; Bolts played it safe by keeping their mouths shut the whole time.

And there were other differences, of course: Nuts buttoned and belted their raincoats neatly; kept their hair trimmed; jogged along the Embarcadero with other members of the firm during lunch hour; got married and stayed married; bought houses out in Orinda; wore rubbers over their wingtips when it rained; remembered the names of the wives of senior partners; and decorated their offices with framed Japanese prints. Bolts, on the other hand, ate with the same people (other Bolts) every day; rented; took midafternoon breaks at nearby video arcades; and only had time to grab a plateful of shrimp and crab from the buffet at the weekly thank-God-it's-Friday-afternoon party before escaping back to their own private office gatherings in the Barracks. Nuts and Bolts were similar in two respects: they all padded their hours, some more, some less; and they all hated Herb Sullivan.

Phoebe, of course, was a Bolt.

Her friend Janice was also a Bolt, and often Phoebe and Janice would spend their lunch hour at the baths on Van Ness – one of the few places where they could be reasonably certain not to run into any other members of the firm, who if they were inclined towards this kind of relaxation would have joined one of the more acceptable and more elaborate health-and-fitness clubs downtown. But there in the privacy of a small redwood-panelled room, Phoebe and Janice would soak themselves in one of the large round tubs, listening to rock music and letting the jets of hot water pulse against the small of their backs as they commiserated with each other. Janice's problem wasn't Herb Sullivan; her problem, for the past two years, had been Francis Clapp, a shy, bumbling Milquetoast of a partner who specialized in wills and trusts. Francis Clapp was the only partner in Judson and Day who practised in this field, and Janice was the only associate assigned to him. Janice, who had accepted the job offer after receiving an explicit promise that she would be assigned to the litigation section, despised that area of law; she had taken a course in wills during law school, but never went to class, and managed a sixty-eight on the exam only by having hand-copied an old *Bar View* outline on the subject the night before. 'Transcription,' she would always claim, 'saved my ass.' Yet although she had made it clear to the partner in charge of assignments that she wanted out – she even emphasized her grade as a sign of her lack of expertise in the area – he was unsympathetic. Janice worried that the longer she worked for Francis Clapp the more likely it was that she would get locked into wills as a speciality field. She was right.

'But look at the bright side,' Phoebe told her one day at the baths. 'You're not working your ass off for Mr Fuckface. Try working for Herb. See what it's like having someone throw your work back in your face when he hasn't even read it.'

'But the guy's so incompetent,' Janice said. 'We went into probate court the other day; Frank turned beet red when it was his turn to talk. I don't think he had even read the will.'

'What did you do?'

'Kept my mouth shut, of course,' Janice said. 'It's not my place to talk in court. Not with this firm.'

Phoebe took a sip of her Calistoga water.

'It's enough to make you want to go back to Iowa and hang out your own shingle,' Janice grumbled.

'I wouldn't go that far,' Phoebe said.

'Well, if I keep working for Frank my career's going to be ruined.'

Phoebe closed her eyes. 'How did a guy like that ever get to be partner?' she wondered aloud.

'Who knows?' Janice said. 'Maybe he slept his way to the top.'

'I still think you have a better deal,' Phoebe said later, drying off. 'When was the last time you had to work on a weekend?'

'I don't know,' Janice said. 'A month or two ago?'

'I work every other goddamn weekend,' Phoebe said. 'Whenever Rusty has Andrew. And I don't screw around during the week, do I? Not like others? I work *hard* all week long and still I have to come in every other weekend for that baboon.'

'Yes, but at least you don't have a problem with your hours,' Janice said. 'I haven't billed more than a thousand.' That was back in August; associates were expected to bill between eighteen hundred and two thousand hours annually (though Nuts usually billed more), and yearly reviews were coming up in November.

'Pad,' Phoebe said. She pointed her toe into her stocking and pulled.

'I already have,' Janice said.

'I'm so fat.' Phoebe sighed. 'Look at this gut.'

Whenever the gloom, the hopelessness of it all, overwhelmed her, Phoebe would spend the morning tinkering with her résumé, which she kept locked in her bottom drawer. It was getting shorter and shorter as she realized the irrelevance of outside interests and activities. This is how Phoebe's résumé currently read:

PHOEBE L. MARTIN

622 Marin
Berkeley, CA 94708
(415)397-9800 (o)
(415)525-2109 (h)

Member, California Bar
Born August 10, 1953

PROFESSIONAL EXPERIENCE

| | |
|---|---|
| 9/79-present | Associate, Judson & Day, San Francisco, CA (antitrust and securities litigation) |
| 6/78-8/78 | Summer Associate, Judson & Day |
| 6/77-8/77 | Legal Extern, Center for Public Advocacy, Oakland, CA |

EDUCATION

University of California School of Law, Berkeley
J.D. 1979
Articles Editor, *California Law Review*

Wellesley College, Wellesley, Massachusetts
B.A. 1976 (political science)
Phi Beta Kappa

PUBLICATIONS

Note, *The Agreement Element of the Sherman Act: An Emerging Distinction Among Contracts, Combinations and Conspiracies?* 66 *Calif. L. Rev.* 193 (1978).

This version of her résumé was about as condensed as Phoebe could manage; it was neat, informative, and perfectly outlined; and it would probably have elicited a number of favourable responses had Phoebe chosen to circulate it among other law firms in the city in search of a new job. But Phoebe never really thought very seriously about leaving Judson and Day; rather, she kept her résumé up to date and ready to go as a symbol of hope, of means, of untapped possibilities – as sort of a one-way ticket to greener professional pastures. It was like having money in the bank, and the mere addition of a new line here, or the deletion of an old line there, seemed to make her job just tolerable enough to get through another day.

Sometimes, too, Phoebe and Janice plotted ways to take out their frustrations with the firm. Janice had a monetary approach: she stayed past seven o'clock as many nights as she could, then went out to dinner with her boyfriend Stu and charged her portion – up to twenty dollars – to the client, along with cab fare. This was a risky business for Janice, given her low number of billable hours, the lack of pressure under which she worked for Francis Clapp, and the fact that most of her clients were individuals for whom soaking up the expense was not as easy as for a large corporation. But Janice liked to play the odds; some weeks she would stay late all five nights, and often she and Stu would just take a bus straight home and cook, and Janice would put in a claim anyway, pocketing the cash. Janice also stole supplies from the firm. She was eventually going to set up her own practice, she said, so she was stocking up on legal pads, pencils, pens, folders, and anything else that wasn't clearly marked with the firm's name. Phoebe pointed out that legal pads and such weren't going to be the big expense in setting up her own firm, but Janice replied that it was more the principle of the matter: she felt *good* when she stole from the firm, she said; she felt vindicated, even if it didn't cost them very much. Besides, she claimed, she had bigger plans: calculators, dictating equipment, a squawk box for her telephone, an IBM Selectric. And Phoebe didn't know if she was kidding or not.

Phoebe's approach was more personal in its vindictiveness: it was aimed directly at Herb. At first she thought of going through his files late on a Saturday night for inculpating documents – records of conversations, for instance, which read in a certain light, would show him proposing to destroy certain damaging documents. This she referred to as the Exposure Plan, and she relished the thought of sending the memos to the State Bar. But Phoebe didn't really know of any specific incidents, and the search could very well be fruitless. Also embarrassing, if anyone saw her going through Herb's files at that hour. Maybe some other associate could explain it away, but not Phoebe. Then she devised the Tip-off Plan: calling the Internal Revenue Service and giving them an anonymous tip that for the past three years one Herbert J. Sullivan had failed to disclose a significant amount of income on his tax returns. And check out those tax shelters he's been claiming, she would add; I think they're just a sham. But this, too, had problems, since for such a plan to trigger an investigation and an audit she assumed she would have to substantiate her tip with some hard evidence. Of which she had none. Ditto the idea of notifying the Securities and Exchange Commission that he was engaging in insider trading on the stock market.

A third plan – the Personals Plan – consisted of placing an ad in one of the weeklies: *Gay white male age 47 seeks same age 20 or under for short-term exploration of heretofore undiscovered delight. Call Herbert J. Sullivan, Esq., at 452-9821 (o) or 544-3389 (h).* This seemed foolproof – she could type out the ad and pay with cash; the only problem she could foresee was having to sign something. But Phoebe knew Herb's wife Cynthia, and the ad could have a ripple effect on Herb's family. While Phoebe wasn't crazy about Cynthia – she was always playing tennis, it seemed, and she had a southern accent – she thought it would be unfair to drag her into this.

Finally she came up with what she thought was a perfect – and completely moral – plan. Herb drove a 1981 Porsche to work every day, commuting in from Marin County. His reputation as a fast driver was well known, and once at a cocktail party he let it slip that in the past year alone he had received three speeding tickets. One more ticket – for anything – and a suspension hearing would be held.

Herb regularly attended the firm's Friday afternoon TG parties, and the few times Phoebe had gone she had noticed Herb consuming quite a bit of wine. He never acted really drunk, but every so often his eyes might glass over, or his tongue might stumble – ever so quickly – over a phrase or two.

One Friday afternoon during her second year, when she had been working for Herb for about eight months, Phoebe convinced Janice to leave her desk, and they went down to the party. The conference room was walled with glass, providing a panoramic view of the San Francisco Bay; colourful sailboats dotted the whitecapped water on this sunny afternoon. Phoebe sipped a glass of wine and filled a plate with cheese, crab legs, cut-up vegetables, and sourdough bread; she had been working straight through the day, and hadn't had time for lunch. She saw Herb over the end of the conference table, and she made her way towards him. His eyes were already a little bleary-rimmed; and for the first time she noticed a thickened, beefy quality to the skin on his face.

'How's it going, Herb?' she said.

Herb looked at her, annoyed.

'Just taking a break from Parco-Fields,' she explained, and showed him her food. 'There's not much time for lunch these days.'

Herb made a face and finished his wine. 'Ridiculous suit,' he said. 'We should have counterclaimed for malicious prosecution. Prince-fix my eye – I'm the one who counselled them to do what they did, what do these guys think I'm going to do, tell my clients to fix prices?' He laughed a mean guffaw, and looked around. The attorneys next to him, a mix of partners and associates, smiled politely and looked into their drinks. Nobody really liked Herb Sullivan.

He turned back to Phoebe. 'This is a pretty good opportunity for you, I'd say. How long have you been with the firm?'

'Two years,' Phoebe replied.

'Not a whole lot of second-year associates get put on such an important case,' Herb told her.

'More wine?' Phoebe asked.

Herb looked into his glass. 'Sure,' he said. 'I'll try some of the Cabernet.'

Phoebe smiled.

When she returned he thanked her. 'You're the one who's looking at all the documents, aren't you?'

'Right-o,' Phoebe said.

Herb squinted 'Read them carefully,' he said. 'You can win or lose a case with a hot document.' Just then another partner pulled Herb aside. Phoebe moved away, but stayed at the party another hour, during which time Herb consumed another two drinks.

As soon as Herb left she hurried up to her office and grabbed her coat. She went out into the reception area by the main set of lifts and sat down in one of the wing chairs, leafing through an issue of *The New Yorker*, pretending to be waiting for someone. In a few minutes Herb came out, his briefcase in one hand, his keys dangling from the other. He walked on by, muttering to himself, oblivious to her.

''Night, Herb,' Phoebe called.

'What?' he said, turning. 'Oh, good night. Don't work too hard this weekend.' He punched the lift button.

'Oh, I'll be in,' Phoebe said cheerfully.

The lift doors opened and Herb walked in. He nodded to her again. As soon as the doors had closed Phoebe hurried back to her office and dialled the California Highway Patrol. 'I'd like to report a drunk driver,' she said. 'California licence plate DJL-888. I just saw the guy heading up 101 towards the Golden Gate.'

'How bad?' the police officer said.

'Oh,' Phoebe said, 'pretty bad.'

Now, on this bright Saturday morning, Phoebe took the back lift up to the thirty-third floor. It was only eight-thirty, but there were already several other associates (Nuts, mostly) at work in the Barracks. She gathered her materials and went down to the library, where a few more Nuts were working at the tables. There didn't seem to be a Bolt in the entire office. Just as well, Phoebe thought; I won't be tempted to talk. She wanted to keep but one thing on her mind today, and that was the brief.

By noon she had finished her research, and it was time to begin writing. Without stopping for lunch she got a fresh legal pad, stacked up the copies of the cases in the order to be discussed, and uncapped a blue flair.

'CAPTION, ETC.,' she wrote in the top centre of the page. 'MEMORANDUM OF POINTS AND AUTHORITIES IN SUPPORT OF DEFENDANT PARCO-FIELDS'S MOTION FOR A PROTECTIVE ORDER.' Then, stuck for words, she went out and got a

Tab from the soft-drink machine. Back at her desk she doodled in the margins, and then wrote, *Introduction*, in the middle of the page. She skipped another few lines and began, *On March 13, 1979 Plaintiff filed this action under Section 1 of the Sherman Act, 15 USC § 1, alleging that the Defendants engaged in price information exchanges constituting an unlawful restraint of trade.* She crossed out 'unlawful,' and continued.

By four o'clock she had composed fifteen pages double-spaced, which she took down to word processing and left in the Urgent box. She returned to her office and spent the next three hours drafting another twelve pages; these, too, she took downstairs to the Urgent box. It was now seven-fifteen. She went into the snack bar and bought a yogurt from the cold-foods machine, returned to her desk, and read the paper. By eight o'clock that evening she had thirteen long pages of a clean, freshly printed brief. She spent the next three hours polishing her language, filling in case cites, conforming everything to the blue book. At eleven-thirty she dropped it all in the Urgent box and left.

As she drove across the Bay Bridge back to Berkeley she thought of the upcoming trip; and now for some reason she found herself looking forward to it. Maybe the fact that you had the brief hanging over your head was affecting your outlook over everything, she thought; and you're not *that* far behind with the documents. Suddenly she wanted very much to see Molly: was she still as skinny as she'd always been? Was her hair still shoulder length, blunt cut, and tipping under at the ends? As a girl Molly had worn her hair long, in two braids tied at the ends with plaid ribbons; and Phoebe remembered the day – they must have been eight, or nine – that she had taken Molly into the bathroom, locked the door, and then, with her mother's kitchen shears, hacked off first one, then the other braid. Molly sat still, unconvinced that Phoebe was doing the right thing yet not stopping her; and Phoebe, coiling the shiny dark plaits into a shoebox, sought to reassure her: she would sell them to a wigmaker in Paris, and they would become millionaires.

Bea never forgave me for that, Phoebe thought, shaking her head and smiling.

And she wanted to see her old bedroom, with its flowered wallpaper, its ripply-glass windows; she wanted to visit the Winslow General Store – did the Poultneys still run it? Did they still sell railroad pants and Keds next to the potatoes and onions? Phoebe thought happily now of the dirt road winding up through the stand of sugar maples, of the smell of apples in the sun. Maybe she would have time for a trip over to the woollen mill in Johnson; perhaps she could bring back a wheel of Cabot cheese, a gallon of maple syrup.

Sunday morning she was out of the house by eight and at her desk by eight forty-five. The fresh draft read like a finely tuned piece of advocacy to her this morning; its organization was logical, its language straightforward, punchy enough to keep the judge awake but quiet enough to get out of the firm with Herb's signature. She was pleased. When something like this went well she forgot how much she hated Judson and Day. She liked practising law, when you came right down to it, and took pride in her work. Maybe it wasn't so bad here after all.

While the word processor made the final set of corrections, Phoebe wandered over to I. Magnin, found it closed, and went into Macy's instead. The store was nearly empty this Sunday afternoon, and with the help of a gaunt, slickly coifed saleswoman Phoebe found two dresses, on sale: one in blue silk and another in a lavender rayon print, each one suitable for both Molly's wedding festivities and the office. She browsed in the gift department, looking for a wedding present for Molly, but the silver and glassware struck her as a bit too formal. Though maybe Molly had changed? Nothing seemed appropriate, though, and Phoebe told herself to check with her mother before buying anything. Maybe Molly needed camping equipment, or a backyard grill. Finally she went over to Eddie Bauer, where she bought turtlenecks, knee socks, and matching fisherman's knit sweaters for Andrew and herself. She returned to the office with her arms full of packages, trying not to add up the debts she had just incurred.

'Where are *you* going?' asked John Dunn, coming out of his office as she walked towards hers. John Dunn was a fourth-year associate, a Harvard graduate, clearly a Nut. John had short brown hair and roundish glasses with pale pink frames; occasionally he smoked a pipe. Sometimes Phoebe could hear him talking on the phone; John Dunn haughtily spoke of '*my* clients,' of '*my* case against so and so.' One night Phoebe had gone out with some friends, and she saw John at a disco. He was trying to dance with a woman who had a jagged green streak running through her hair. Something about her looked familiar, and then Phoebe recognized her as a former Xerox operator at the firm.

'Back East,' Phoebe replied without stopping.

'Where back East?' He followed her into her office, cupping the bowl of his pipe in his palm.

'Vermont,' she said.

'Aaahhh,' he sighed. 'Vermont in autumn. *Incroyable.* My parents have a ski lodge in Killington. They know the owners of the mountain; we always got free ski passes.' He looked thoughtful for a moment. 'I wonder if I could still get them,' he mused. 'I should look into that. Why are you going back East?'

'A wedding,' Phoebe said.

'Aaahh,' John said, tipping his head back and half closing his eyes. 'An autumn wedding, foliage and all. How lovely.'

'Not any more,' Phoebe said. 'The leaves have all dropped. Do you mind?' She pointed to the pipe, and John extinguished it.

'Good friend?'

'Yes,' Phoebe said. 'A very good friend.'

'Aren't you from Vermont? Originally?'

Phoebe sat down and leafed through the fresh draft. 'Yup.'

'Where in Vermont?'

'East Winslow.'

'Huh,' John said. 'Where's that?'

'Up north,' Phoebe said.

'Huh,' John said. 'Never heard of it.'

Phoebe uncapped a red pen. 'Too bad,' she said. 'It's a gorgeous place – though we're not exactly clamouring for visitors,' she added; 'we like it just the way it is.' Nothing like a John Dunn to bring out the old hometown spirit, she thought.

John twisted his head to look at the work on her desk. 'What are you working on?'

'A brief.'

'What for?'

'Protective order.'

'Huh. What case?'

'Parco-Fields.'

'Aaahh,' John said. 'Herb Sullivan?'

'Yup,' Phoebe said.

'My sympathy,' John said.

'Thanks.' Phoebe compared the pages of the old draft to those of the new one, checking to make sure the corrections had been made.

'Didn't the plaintiff just ask for another extension for discovery?'

'Yup.'

John grinned. 'Nothing like a little gratuitous delay,' he said. 'Taken any depositions?'

'Nope.'

'Why not?'

'I don't know.'

'That guy Sullivan,' John said. 'I really feel for you, working for him. Too bad you can't work for Carmichael. I've got a securities case with him. I've taken three depos in the past four months – though unfortunately it looks like things are slowing down for a while. But three depos – not bad, huh?'

'That's great, John,' Phoebe said. She was on page four; so far, so good. She would be able to leave it on Herb's desk tonight.

'Did you *ask* for a depo?' John said.

'Nope.'

'Why not?'

'I don't know.'

'You might want to speak up,' John advised. 'You're never going to get any good work by hiding out in your office.'

Phoebe felt a tingling sensation creep up the back of her neck. She kept on proofing.

'That's how I got to do my first deposition,' John said. 'I just asked Carmichael. He said he hadn't planned on it, but he liked my work and had a lot of confidence in me. That's just what he said. He said, "John, I've got a lot of confidence in you."'

'Great,' Phoebe said.

'It was really incredible,' John said, crossing his arms. 'I got this guy who was stonewalling us all over the place. Every time I asked him if he remembered this document or that document he'd say, "I don't know." And then I'd say, "Are these your initials?" and he'd say, "Possibly," and I'd say, "And you're still saying you don't recognize the document?" and he'd say, "That's right." This went on for five hours. Can you believe it?'

'Incredible,' Phoebe said, squiggling a typo.

'*Five hours!* You know what I finally did?'

'Nope.'

'This is just great,' John said. 'You're going to love this. Are you listening? I threw my pen on to the conference table and said, "I think we might as well call this whole thing off."' John was pacing back and forth in front of Phoebe's desk. 'I said, "This is a waste of time. We'll see you in court with a motion to compel, and we'll seek every sanction in the Federal Rules."' He stopped pacing and leaned forward, palms down on the desk. 'Know what?'

'Nope.'

'The guy started remembering documents. You should have seen Carmichael's face.'

There was another error on page ten.

'I was so high that day,' John said. 'You really should try to get a deposition. It would be good for you. You're awfully quiet for this firm.'

Phoebe stood up. 'Thanks for the advice,' she said. 'Excuse me, I've got to get these changes made.'

'Think about what I said,' John said, following her out of the office. But Phoebe wasn't listening. She was already on her way down to the WANG.

At seven o'clock she skimmed the final version, ran a copy off for herself, and left the original for Herb on Pearl's desk with a note. She drove back to Berkeley and picked Andrew up at Rusty's. Shirley was there, and although she was making piña coladas in the blender that Phoebe and Rusty had received as a wedding present, Phoebe was so elated with the brief being finished –

early, no less – that she accepted a drink and stayed to watch Shirley do her imitation of the very pregnant women in her aerobics class.

In the car she hugged Andrew. 'I missed you!' she said. 'Want to get Chinese food?'

'I don't feel good,' Andrew said. 'I have a stomachache.'

'What did Daddy feed you?'

'Hot dogs,' he said. 'And then him and that lady took me to the merry-go-round and we got popcorn and then we went out and got ice cream.'

As Phoebe tucked him into bed that night she said, 'Guess where you're going to be in three days.'

'Where?'

'At Grammy's.'

'Can we go to her pool?'

'Not Grammy Angela,' Phoebe said. 'Grammy Louise.'

'Who's that?'

'You know who Grammy Louise is. Grammy Louise is my mother. Grammy Louise came here to visit when you were a baby.'

'I don't like Grammy Louise,' Andrew said.

'You know where Grammy Louise lives?' Phoebe continued.

'Disneyland!'

Phoebe shook her head. 'The state of Vermont.'

'I want to go to Disneyland.' He yawned. 'That lady's been to Disneyland.'

'We'll go to Disneyland sometime.' She smoothed the hair back from his forehead. 'You know who else you're going to see back there?'

'Who?'

'My oldest friend,' she said.

'Old like Grammy?'

'No,' Phoebe said, 'old like she was my best friend

even when I was your age, and that's a long time ago. We played together every day. Remember the pictures I showed you?'

'What's her name?'

'Aunt Molly.'

'I don't have any aunts,' Andrew said, closing his eyes.

'Well, you just call her aunt,' Phoebe said, 'since she's my oldest friend. Now, think about the aeroplane. Maybe you can see the pilot's cabin, with all the lights. Maybe he'll give you a badge.' She tried to remember all the other things they gave out to kids on planes, but Andrew had already fallen asleep.

Phoebe spent Monday tying up loose ends before the trip. She expected to stay late that night, as Herb would undoubtedly have changes for her. She waited for him to call, but by two o'clock she hadn't heard from him, so she buzzed his secretary.

'I gave it to him, Ms Martin,' Pearl said. 'At nine o'clock sharp.'

'Is he there now?' she asked.

'He's in a meeting,' Pearl said. 'Do you want me to have him call you when he's through?'

'No,' Phoebe said. 'No, thanks.' She hung up. Maybe he was going to read it this afternoon. She hoped he didn't wait until tonight, though, because that would mean the changes would have to be made tomorrow morning; with an eleven o'clock flight, that was calling it too close. Impossible, in fact. He knows I'm leaving Tuesday, she thought. Then she paused, her hand still on the receiver. At least I think he knows.

Linda poked her head into her doorway. 'I'm running out for a sandwich now,' she said. 'Can I bring you something? Maybe a bagel? A salad from the deli?'

'No thanks,' Phoebe said. 'I'm not really hungry.' She

sat at her desk for another few minutes, then went into Janice's office. Janice was picking off split ends and staring out of her window. The associates' windows looked out over construction on lower Market Street, with sliver-like glimpses of the Bay.

'Don't count on it,' Janice said. 'If you told him last week I doubt he remembered.'

'Should I say something to him?' Phoebe asked. 'I know he'll have changes.'

'I don't know.' Janice made a face. 'It could tick him off. Wait until five.'

But at four o'clock Phoebe went to check her mail, and happened to find the brief rolled up in her mailbox. *This is shit!!!* Herb had scrawled across the top in a red flair. She hurried away and flipped through the pages. *Lousy introduction!* he had scribbled. *More facts!!! What is the law on this point??? Topic sentence!!! Unclear!!! BFD!!! Facts of case??? Any more Ninth Circuit options??? Faulty reasoning!!!* On the last page he had scrawled, *Needs* a lot of work. */s/ HJS*.

Phoebe felt her throat swell. She went into Janice's office and closed the door. 'Janice,' she began, but she couldn't help it; she started to cry.

Janice, who had worked as a support counsellor for battered women before law school, switched into high gear. 'You'll get it done,' she said, her voice firm, her hands flat upon her blotter. 'Don't worry about Andrew; give me your keys and I'll stay with him until you get home tomorrow. You'll have to stay all night, but you'll get it done. Now, stop *crying*. Sullivan is known for pulling this kind of crap, you know that. Phoebe!'

Phoebe covered her face with her hands. Her shoulders shook.

'*Phoebe!* You can't let him get to you like this! He's going to like whatever you give him tomorrow – even if half of it is exactly the same. You know he never reads things carefully, he just likes to make people squirm. Let me see it. Come on, give me the brief.' Phoebe gave her the brief. She flipped through it. 'This is nothing, Phoebe. In fact' – she glanced at the stack of papers on her desk – 'shit, this stuff isn't urgent, I'll get you an all-night WANG operator and then I'll check Lexis and see if there are any more Ninth Circuit opinions. You just write. Okay? Go in your office and *write*.'

'The plane leaves at eleven tomorrow.' Phoebe said, hiccuping. 'If we miss that plane we can't go, I can't get another Halloween special, I can't afford a full-price ticket.' Her eyes were swollen, her cheeks smudged with mascara.

'You're not going to miss that plane,' Janice said. 'Now, here's a Kleenex. Wipe your eyes. Blow your nose. And GO WRITE!'

So Phoebe wrote, and rewrote, and rewrote again. She felt sickish to her stomach, but she kept on going. At two o'clock in the morning she handed a mass of odd-sized pages that had been cut-and-pasted together to her all-night WANG operator; it was such a mess that Phoebe had to sit there beside him and translate, line by line. By four a new draft was printing, and when the sky began to turn grey she was proofing a final version. With Janice's help the brief had been bolstered with a few more citations, but apart from that she couldn't tell if it was what Herb had in mind; it read like gibberish to her, she was so exhausted. She hadn't gone to the bathroom in seven hours, and when she finally tried she was so keyed up that nothing came. At six o'clock she saw two Nuts walking towards their offices, carrying paper cups of coffee.

'What the hell happened to you?' one of them asked.

With shaking hands Phoebe groped for his cup, her

fingers feeling gnarled and clawlike, arthritic as an old woman's.

'Does it bite?' the other one asked.

'Not if you feed it,' the first one said, handing her the cup.

'Sullivan?'

Phoebe's hands shook as she brought the coffee to her lips.

'Guess she can't talk,' the first one said.

'Here.' The second one handed Phoebe a sugary doughnut. 'Eat, woman.'

Phoebe ate.

At nine o'clock she was waiting by Herb's office with the brief. At nine-ten he appeared.

'Oh,' he said. 'It's you.'

'I rewrote the brief,' Phoebe said.

'Jesus,' he said. 'You look like shit.'

Phoebe touched her hand to her hair. She set the brief on the secretary's desk and tucked in her blouse, which was drooping out over her navy-blue skirt. Smudges of mascara remained underneath her eyes. She had forgotten to put her shoes on, and one of her stockings had a large hole in the toe, a long run up the front of her leg. And she suddenly realized that she smelled like a locker room.

'What'd you do, pull an all-nighter?'

Phoebe looked at the floor.

'That was rather stupid. What good are you going to be today if you just pulled an all-nighter?'

'I'm leaving today,' Phoebe said weakly. 'I'm leaving at eleven o'clock. My son and I, you know? My son Andrew?' She was sounding ridiculous.

'Oh, that's right,' he said. 'When'd you say you were coming back?'

'The twenty-second.'

He looked at the brief on the desk.

'You rewrote this thing?' he shouted. Pearl jumped a little in her chair, and frowned at them from over her typewriter.

'What's the matter?' Phoebe asked.

'This is a brief for a protective order!' he shouted. 'We just stipulated to a proposed protective order yesterday afternoon! Where were you?'

'I didn't hear about it,' Phoebe said in a small voice. 'Nobody told me.'

'For Chrissake,' he snapped, 'you expect people to tell you about everything? That's what we mean when we talk about keeping on top of things. Now, how are we going to bill your hours for this?' He turned and unlocked the door to his office. 'Why don't you just go *home*. *Feed* yourself. And take a bath, for crying out loud.'

Phoebe climbed the stairs back up to her office.

'What happened?' Linda asked.

'Phoebe,' Stella said. 'You look terrible.'

'Is it Herb?' Maureen asked. 'What did he do to you this time?'

Phoebe was too tired to answer. In her office she dropped the brief into the wastebasket, slung her jacket over her arm, and walked to the back set of lifts. Down in front of the building several cabs were waiting. Phoebe opened the back door of the nearest one and fell on to the seat.

'East Bay,' she murmured.

'That'll cost you a pretty penny, toots,' the driver said.

'Just give me a receipt,' Phoebe said. Her eyelids drooped, and before they were even on the Bay Bridge she was asleep, her head against the window.

Phoebe and Andrew made the plane, although it was close. Andrew decided at the last minute that he didn't want to go, and Phoebe had to carry him into the car as he hollered for Rusty and beat against her shoulders. Then she realized she had forgotten his gorilla mask, so they had to go back. He quieted down during the ride to the airport, but as she was checking their bags he ran off, and it was ten minutes before she finally spotted him, riding the escalators with his mask on. Several other passengers on the flight were also wearing masks, and they all joked together as they boarded the plane. Andrew had a window seat, and the flight attendant gave him a set of pilot's wings to pin on his shirt.

'Say thank you,' Phoebe said.

'Grrarrhh,' Andrew said, raising his arms at the flight attendant.

'Thank you,' Phoebe said to her.

'And where are you going?' asked the passenger in the next seat, a frail elderly woman who smelled of roses.

'Vermont.' Phoebe smiled politely.

'How exciting!' the woman chirped. 'Visiting family?'

Phoebe nodded.

'Won't you have a good time, then!' the woman said. 'Won't you have fun!'

We'd better, Phoebe thought. After all this we'd *better* have fun.

As they took off Andrew removed his mask and pressed his face to the window, but the fog hadn't yet lifted, and there wasn't much to see. By the time the seat-belt sign went off, Phoebe was dozing, and she felt the light touch of a woman's hand on her shoulder. Ms Martin, Pearl was saying. Mr Sullivan wants to see you in his office tomorrow morning. You'll have to deplane in St Louis and come back. Phoebe saw Herb's secretary frowning above her. She started in her seat.

'Would you care for anything to drink?' the flight attendant was asking. Phoebe ordered a ginger ale for Andrew and, though it was only eleven-thirty, a bottle of wine for herself, and when it was gone she fell into a deep sleep, and didn't even wake up when another flight attendant came by, offering a choice of beef, chicken, or vegetarian lasagna on their ocean-to-ocean service.

# 3

On Saturday afternoon – about the same time that Phoebe was delivering the first half of her brief to the word processor – Molly and her mother, Bea, were upstairs in Molly's former bedroom, pinning together the holes in the old lace dress of her great-grandmother Adams, which Molly planned to wear at the wedding. Bea, a small, perky woman with short dark hair, sat on a stool with her back to the skirted kidney-shaped dressing table. Her fingers worked deftly, easing the torn edges of the dress together; then she removed the last pin from between her lips and wove it through the fabric.

'So she's coming after all,' Bea said. 'Or have there been any more changes since last week?'

'She's coming,' Molly said.

'Turn,' Bea said.

Molly turned.

'Won't that be nice, after what, six years?' Bea said.

'Won't what be nice?'

'Why, Phoebe coming back,' Bea said, 'to be in the wedding!'

'Oh,' Molly said. 'Yes.'

'And what about her little boy,' Bea went on, ' – is she bringing him too?'

'I don't know,' Molly said.

'I hope so,' Bea said. 'Aren't you just dying to see what he's like?'

Molly looked out of the window; her father was stacking firewood between two maple trees with a mathematical precision.

'Aren't you?'

'Oh,' Molly said, 'sure.'

Bea raised her eyebrows and glanced up at her daughter's face, but Molly didn't look back.

'Pull your stomach in,' Bea said.

Molly sucked in her breath, but the fabric only tightened across her chest.

'Dear,' Bea said, leaning back, 'why don't we just go out and buy a new dress? Something new? Something . . . *whole*?'

'I don't need a new dress,' Molly said. She twisted, examining the tear in the waist of the dress. 'If you're pressed for time I'll take this home and patch it myself.'

Bea pursed her lips. 'But what about a slip? Look at that – you can see your underwear right through the lace!'

'What happened to the old slip?'

'Molly, I don't know,' Bea said. 'That dress hasn't been worn in seventy-five years. *Don't!* – move your arms like that,' she sighed; a new tear had just opened up across the shoulder seam.

'Sorry,' Molly said.

'That does it,' Bea said. 'We're going into St Audenbury.'

But Molly glared at her mother. 'I told you, *no new dress*.' She reached around to undo the buttons up the back. I'll be damned if I have to go into some hokey bridal salon this afternoon, she thought, and stand around shivering in front of fourteen mirrors while some painted leather-faced matron fills the room with white dresses and drapes me in yards of taffeta. Besides, she thought, fingering the new tear, it's sort of appropriate, this dress of Grandma Adams, all torn and yellowed. Considering the circumstances.

'And you'll catch your death of cold,' her mother was fretting.

'What?'

'Standing outside in a dress like that! It could snow in the middle of November, you know.'

'So relax, I'll wear my parka.' Molly eased her arms out of the lace sleeves and let the dress fall to the floor in a crumpled heap. At twenty-nine she had the figure of a young boy: flat chested and narrow hipped, with long limbs that still at times moved in directions she hadn't planned. She rarely wore makeup, and left her eyebrows unplucked, so that with her dark-brown hair clipped close to her head there was an unkempt boyishness to her appearance. As she folded up the dress she looked out of the window again, and this time saw the brown-and-white delivery truck from the Winslow General Store, idling in the driveway. 'Looks like your booze is here,' she said.

Bea set the box of pins on the glass top of the dressing table, and stood up. 'Think about it, honey – your father and I'll be more than happy to pay for it, you know.'

'It's not a question of money,' Molly said.

'What about wearing my wedding dress?' Bea suggested. 'It's hanging right in the back of my closet – '

'Mother,' Molly said, 'go tend to the delivery guy.'

I wish she would lay off about the dress, Molly thought when her mother was gone; I wish she would relax about this whole thing. She knew that since the announcement two weeks ago Bea was averaging four hours of sleep a night, or less, worrying about 'the Event,' as she called it. First she had worried about the number of guests, where they would stay, how they would get the invitations out on time; later, whether Poultney's could order enough champagne on such short notice. She had worried about what to wear, whether she should make a dress or just go out and buy it for once because when in heaven's name would she ever have time to sew? ('You never sleep,' Molly reminded her. 'You could make it during the night.') She had worried about the reception: whether everyone would fit into their small living room, where to get enough flowers, and what kind of cake would be the least damaging to everyone's health. ('How about beer and hot dogs?' Molly suggested. 'Makes it easy on all of us.') But when Bea began to worry about Molly and Nick having to pick out flatware and china on such short notice, Molly put her foot down.

'I don't want flatware,' Molly said firmly. 'And I don't want china and I don't want any silver chafing dishes. Oh, please, Mum,' she said as her mother's face clouded over, 'I don't mean it that way; I think all these things you and Daddy have are nice but Nick and I don't *want* that kind of wedding.'

She's going to get her ulcer acting up again, Molly thought, peering out of the window and watching her mother scurrying from the delivery truck to the kitchen porch and back again like a high-strung puppy. All this fuss: over the dress, the food, the champagne – it was exactly why she had never wanted to get married before. The whole process always struck her as such a high-pressure sort of job. No wonder people felt let down the day after: it was as though you just got fired. She didn't know if she could take it, even for the next week: all the planning, all the forced excitement, the buildup, people dropping by in the late afternoon and hugging her, biting their lower lips as they broke into smiles. 'We're so happy for you' was all they could say, looking as though they were about to cry.

'Dear,' Bea would say when they had left, 'couldn't you look a little more enthusiastic?'

We should have eloped, Molly thought; I knew it. In fact she and Nick had discussed the possibility, and Molly had lobbied vehemently for it, but Nick had finally confessed to wanting some public attention over his marriage. 'You don't get any gifts if you elope,' he said.

'What do we care about gifts,' Molly said. 'We've got everything we need.'

'Besides,' he continued, 'you have to think of how they would feel.'

'Who?'

'Molly,' Nick sighed, 'the *parents*.'

So Molly had finally consented, but not without doubts. It would have been so much easier: just get in the car one night and drive to some JP over in Maine and walk in and say the I do's. No dress, no presents, no invitations – just Nick and herself and a cheap bottle of champagne in some wayside motel afterwards, dropping quarters into the Magic Fingers and watching colour TV until the 'Star Spangled Banner' came on.

But Nick was right; her parents would have been crushed if they had eloped. Being an only child had always put an extra burden on Molly – she *had* to sing in the choir, she *had* to attend her college graduation, because Dave and Bea wouldn't have had any other chances at those events. So she had agreed to a wedding, but she warned Nick that her mother would try and make a bigger deal out of it than they wanted.

'She'll want me to have a wedding like Phoebe's wedding,' she told him, 'with two hundred guests and an open bar and a cake four tiers high.'

'Should I wear my zoot suit?' Nick asked.

'And since you can't have that kind of event without months of planning, she's going to hit the roof when we tell her we're going to do it on the spur of the moment,' Molly went on. 'She'll be unbearable.'

'We don't have to rush, you know,' Nick said.

'Yes, we do,' Molly said.

'That's bullshit,' Nick said. 'We're not going to fool anyone.'

Molly said nothing.

To be sure, Bea had been a little taken aback with the news that Molly and Nick wanted to get married on such short notice. They announced it on a Sunday afternoon in late October. Molly didn't know it, but her parents hadn't been speaking to each other for two days. The fight had started Friday night when Dave had refused to attend a local meeting of a nuclear freeze group with Bea, calling her a morbid old lady with nothing to think about but her own death. 'I've got better things to do than sit around writing letters about the bomb to a bunch of Russians,' he had said.

'Like what?' Bea had demanded.

'Like build a new mulch bin! Set out fruit trees! Go look at dairy cows, go look at chickens!' Dave, more concerned about the personal consequences of world food and energy shortages than nuclear war, was aiming for self-sufficiency within the next two years.

'And a lot of good a new mulch bin will do us when Reagan pushes the button,' Bea muttered. The disagreement should have stopped there, but Bea went to the meeting alone and stayed until well past midnight, an act which Dave took as a sign that she was sulking. By the time she returned he'd gone off to sleep in Molly's room with the door closed. Now, two days later, with only a minimum of words between them – 'Are you through eating?' 'Did you plan on using the truck this morning?' – Bea was typing envelopes on the sun porch and Dave was in the living room, looking over mail-order blueprints for a solar heating system. It was an Indian-summer afternoon, the air buttery-warm, the remaining foliage shimmering gold in the afternoon sun. On the

Adamses' front lawn loomed an ancient maple still shedding its yellow leaves; propped against its thickened leathery trunk was the figure of an old woman, stuffed with cotton batting and dressed in a blue calico smock, a red bonnet tied around her featureless head. A basket of apples lay on one side, a trio of pumpkins on the other. Bea's doing.

Molly and Nick went into the house and shed their sweaters.

'Hey, Mum,' Molly said.

Bea peered over the top of her half-glasses.

'Hey, Daddy!' Molly shouted.

'What do you want!' he shouted back.

'Come out on the sun porch! I have something to tell you!'

'Go ahead!' he shouted. 'I can hear!'

Bea looked disgusted.

'Well,' Molly said loudly, taking Nick's arm, 'Nick and I are going to get married.'

Bea leaned back in her chair and looked at the ceiling. 'I don't believe it,' she said, and laughed.

'It's true,' Molly said.

'Pinch me,' Bea said.

Molly pinched her arm.

'I don't believe it,' Bea said.

Dave appeared in the doorway. He had grown more heavyset over the last year, had developed a thickening around the middle that was undisguised by the heavy chamois-cloth shirts he wore. His hair was thinning, and recently the doctor had strengthened the left lens of his glasses. As he stood there he didn't look at Bea, and Bea didn't look at him.

'Holy smokes,' he said.

'We don't want anything fancy,' Molly went on. 'Just a

simple ceremony. I was thinking we could have it up at the sugarhouse.'

'That's fine,' Bea said, 'but were you planning to wait until next spring? It might be difficult to plan a winter wedding up there. That's a long steep hill, honey – how would everyone get up there? Where would everyone sit?'

'We were thinking of having it a little earlier,' Molly said.

'Earlier?'

'November fourteenth, actually,' Nick said.

'*This* November fourteenth?' Bea exclaimed.

'Three weeks from today,' Molly said. 'Like I told you, we don't want anything fancy.'

'Oh, Molly.' Bea closed her eyes.

Dave shrugged. 'That's a Sunday, isn't it? I don't have any plans for that day,' he said. 'Ask your mother what the problem is.'

'What's the problem?' Molly asked.

'Molly,' Bea moaned. 'Do you have any idea how much planning a wedding – even a simple one – takes?'

'We were only thinking of about twenty people,' Molly said.

Dave tabulated costs in his head. 'Sounds good to me,' he said.

'But I could count twenty heads just in the families,' Bea said. 'And that doesn't even include friends!'

Molly looked at Nick.

'Mum,' she said. 'You're not listening. I said, we want a small simple wedding.'

'There's no such thing – unless it's a shotgun wedding.' Bea laughed nervously. 'Is this a shotgun wedding?'

'*Mother*,' Molly said.

Nick went into the kitchen, opened the refrigerator door, and popped open a beer.

'Then why don't you wait a few months?' Bea said. 'Do it during the February thaw.'

'No,' Molly said firmly. 'We're doing it November fourteenth. Think of it as a party. You've given parties for twenty people before; this is no big deal.'

'She says it's no big deal,' Bea said to her typewriter. 'She's getting married and she says it's no big deal.'

Dave finally looked at his wife, exasperated. 'Hey, Bea, knock it off,' he said.

Bea looked up at him.

'You've been wanting her to get married ever since she graduated from college,' he said. 'Now, let yourself enjoy it, huh? Why ruin it for everyone just because she's not going to do it the way you and I did?'

Bea's mouth had dropped open.

'I mean it,' he went on. 'You're spoiling an otherwise joyous occasion. Kids,' he said, 'congratulations.' He slapped Nick on the back and tousled Molly's hair, then returned to the living room to his blueprints.

So Bea had finally accepted the date, but her idea of what constituted a simple wedding differed drastically from Molly's – which was why Molly was now standing calmly in the rosebud-papered eaves of her old bedroom, her wedding dress nearly in shreds a week before the wedding; and why her mother was downstairs chewing Rolaids while pushing the porch furniture aside to make room for the cases of champagne, liquor, and mixers.

Molly decided she'd take the dress home with her and work on it tonight. She had planned on staying with her parents through dinner, but the way her mother was acting she decided she needed an evening to herself. Things were only going to get more hectic. In four days Phoebe was arriving, and next Friday Nick's family, whom she didn't know very well, was due in. She would have to be *on* all the time.

Downstairs she took a grocery bag from the cupboard and stuffed the dress into it.

'Where are you going?' Bea asked. 'I thought you were staying for dinner.'

'I need some time alone.'

Bea smiled. 'I understand,' she said, coming forth and putting her arms around her daughter. 'And I'm sorry for nagging you about the dress, honey. This one will look beautiful on you. Go home and relax. I know just how you feel, the nerves and all. It's a very stressful time for a girl, the week before her wedding.'

But Molly swung herself out from her mother's embrace. 'It's not nerves,' she said. 'I just need some time to myself. Besides, I've got to feed the animals; Nick's going to be late tonight.'

'Are you coming down with a fever?' Bea asked. 'You're flushed, you know.' She touched the back of her hand to Molly's forehead.

'I'm not sick!' Molly said. Suddenly the room began to blur, and the air felt hotter than a day in August. She reached for the edge of the counter, breathing deeply, but sweat began to form on the upper edge of her lip. She hurried into the bathroom.

Bea followed her. 'Sweetie pie,' she said, holding a wet washcloth across the back of Molly's neck as Molly heaved, over and over, into the toilet basin. 'You poor thing. You shouldn't worry so much. We've all been through it.'

Molly retched again.

'Let it come,' Bea said. 'It's the worst set of jitters you'll ever know.'

The dirt road from Molly's parents' house down to Winslow, where she lived, followed a stream, then wound around the willows bordering the Martin property to where it started up a long steep hill. There the open fields ended and a stand of sugar maples began, and near the top of the hill was the old road that led to the abandoned sugarhouse where Molly and Nick planned to be married. Most of the leaves had fallen by this time, leaving a doe-brown carpet throughout the woods, and a thin northern light gave the silver-grey trees a flat, almost chalky quality.

Molly downshifted into second as the hill steepened. She was feeling better now; just as quickly as the nausea had overwhelmed her, it had disappeared. Still, though, she wondered how long she was going to have to put up with this pattern. Would it stop after a few months? Or would it last for the duration? Maybe it was just something you had to get used to?

Molly wished there were someone – a woman – for her to confide in about the pregnancy. As a high school teacher at a small rural school her daily circle of social contacts was limited to the likes of Doris Conran, for instance, the principal, sixty-two and unmarried, taking care of her ailing mother in an old Victorian mansion; Brad Kenshaw, the ninth-grade history teacher, mostly interested in making passes at any available girl or woman or, alternatively, in racing his crumpled-up 1952 Chevy in the stock-car races; Susan Mitchell, a middle-aged matron who had recently returned to teaching after sending her fourth daughter off to Katy Gibbs; and Mrs Welch, an elderly overweight widow who should have retired four years ago but who was kept on because her son presided over the school board. Mrs Welch was deaf in one ear and trembled with a touch of Parkinson's disease. She taught Art. Often in the middle of the morning Molly had to go down to Mrs Welch's classroom to quiet things down. 'We can hear them all the way up on the third floor!' she would shout at Mrs Welch, who would set down the back issue of *Good Housekeeping* that she had checked out of the library, and turn up her hearing aid.

'Say what, honey?' Mrs Welch would burble, and her head would bob about like the decorative dolls that signal to drivers out of the back window of automobiles.

'You have to quiet them down! I can't teach!'

'Children!' Mrs Welch would clap her hands at the classroom of sullen smocked adolescents, the flab under her chin wobbling like the loose wattle-section of a turkey's neck. 'Miss Adams says you have to be quiet!'

The classroom would be as still as a church.

'Is that better?' Mrs Welch would ask; but as soon as Molly left, the old woman would turn down her hearing aid and go back to her magazine, and the noise would begin again.

Molly was fond of her colleagues, she really was; but she was also lonely. Pregnancy aside, what she needed was a woman more her age, someone who wasn't afraid to talk about sex, for instance, without the fear of violating some vague sense of marital privacy. Once, over a sandwich with Susan Mitchell while Brad Kenshaw coached the cheerleading squad, Molly had confided that she thought she and Nick seemed to ebb and flow at opposite times of the day, if Susan knew what she meant, and did Susan ever notice this with Steven? Susan Mitchell had put her sandwich down and wiped her mouth daintily with the calico print napkin that she kept in the top drawer of her desk. Her face had reddened. 'Why, no', she said, wiping her mouth again. 'Why, no, I don't know quite what you mean.'

And now, of course, Molly needed a woman friend even more. Someone who had been through it all before, who could tell her what was normal and what was not. Molly thought she seemed crankier than usual, she thought her face was breaking out more and more and couldn't stop worrying about that night she got so drunk; that was before she'd known and couldn't it have harmed the baby? Later there would be her mother to talk to; but right now she certainly wasn't going to bring it up.

Of course, there was Phoebe. In four days Phoebe would be back – but Phoebe would guess right off that she was pregnant (thus depriving Molly of the chance to tell her something she didn't already know), and then she would go on to offer an overdose of advice: Don't drink, don't smoke, look out for caffeine; iron's good, aspirin's bad, and are you wearing support hose? Molly tightened her grip on the steering wheel as she heard Phoebe's bits and pieces of advice echoing from one end of the country to the other. For some reason she didn't want Phoebe's advice; she wasn't sure why. Maybe because Phoebe could act so knowledgeable about everything?

Maybe. Was there anything Phoebe didn't know about? Was there anything Phoebe hadn't done first? Between the two of them Phoebe had had the first period, the first abortion, the first wedding, the first baby; she had been the first to get her driving licence, the first to get her ears pierced, the first to lose her virginity. (Supposedly; though Molly was never quite sure when it had happened.) Molly felt that, except for the past couple of years, when she'd made so many of her own gains with her weaving, she had been trailing in Phoebe's footsteps ever since they met – not only that, but Phoebe managed to take credit for guiding her, for showing her how to do everything – even if Molly would have figured it out for herself. 'Squat,' Phoebe had said, showing Molly how to insert a tampon, 'it's the best way to get it in. See?'

Not that any of this mattered. Tampons, driving licences, babies: it was all trivia, wasn't it, who did what first? You should be more mature about this, Molly told herself; you shouldn't get so threatened by it. Think of it as Phoebe's need to think she's controlling things. You're just as capable as she is; and so what if she's a lawyer?

But still, it bothered her to think of Phoebe taking credit for teaching her everything. They hadn't told anyone yet, but she and Nick had tentative plans to leave the area, for Nick was thinking of law school (and there again, if you counted Nick as sort of an extension of herself, it would end up with Phoebe having been the first to go to law school!) – and I'll put money on it, Molly thought as she passed the Cutters' dairy farm at the crest of the hill: if we *do* move away, Phoebe will take credit for that too! As though she came home for a quick visit and – *voilà!* – inspired us to leave Vermont!

Molly took a deep breath to counteract the flush of anger that was creeping up her neck. Calm down, she told herself; it's not good for the baby, getting all worked up like this.

At least, I don't think it is. Though maybe it doesn't matter?

Molly didn't know.

Phoebe would know.

You should be in fourth gear, Phoebe would be reminding her right now as the car hit forty miles an hour. You're revving the engine too high.

Winslow was a small town set on the banks of the west branch of the Barrington River. Halfway through the town the river dropped thirty feet, and the sound of the waterfall was such a permanent part of the townspeople's lives that many of them couldn't sleep when they left home; the silence was too disturbing. A nineteenth-century mill by the waterfall had recently been restored; now a health-food restaurant, its large dining-room window overlooked the great mossy water-wheel that churned around and around outside. In the centre of the town was the neatly trimmed village square, bordered by a white crossbeam fence. At one end stood the Baptist church; at the other, a green-and-white gazebo, in which band concerts were given on Sunday evenings in the summer. People would bring picnics on those breezy nights, and spread out blankets on which to lie back, listening to the music underneath the stars.

Molly pulled into the long driveway of the house that she'd been renting for the last four years. Built in the early part of the century, it was painted yellow; its eaves were lined with gingerbread trim, and a wide porch circled the first floor. All around the front yard ran a white picket fence, and behind the house was a large garden and a grazing area for the two sheep that she raised for raw wool. She parked the car; walking up the porch steps she clapped her hands at Butch and Frankie, her Boston terriers, who were waiting for her on the window seat in the kitchen. Butch scooted off the seat and met her at the door, leaping at the shopping bag in her arms.

'Get down, Butch,' Molly said. 'This is my wedding dress, for Pete's sake.' Frankie cocked her head, trembling. 'Out?' Molly held open the door, and Butch ran out to the yard, but Frankie just waddled out to the porch, where she sat shaking amid the cases of empty beer bottles.

It was time for chores, and after setting out food for the dogs Molly went out to the shed to feed the sheep. Then she brought in an armload of wood and stoked the embers in the small woodstove in the kitchen. When the fire was hot enough to turn the dampers down a bit she went into the living room, carefully stepping around the half-finished quilt that covered the floor; she cleared a stack of newspapers from the sofa and sat down to mend the wedding dress.

It was a peaceful hour, quiet except for the logs snapping in the stove, but for Molly tonight this peace was drowned out by the untidiness of her house, as though its clutter were creating its own noisy static in the air. The problem was that though the house was large and Molly had it mostly to herself (for Nick had never officially moved in), she was a packrat, and the house was running out of space. The living room, for example, was stuffy and cramped, furnished with ragged secondhand furniture that she planned to re-cover someday; in one corner was a player piano (minus its rolls of music); in another was an antique organ (minus its bellows). And her kitchen served as a sort of transitional depot for all types of recyclable matter: newspapers, aluminium, glass, and tin; and by the sink was a bucket of mulch-destined rubbish that always smelled. Even her cupboards were running out of space, packed as they were with odd sets of dishes handed down by her grandmother and her mother: wishful heirlooms she didn't much care for but which, coming from family, she couldn't bring herself to discard.

Yet much of what made the house seem so cramped had more to do with ongoing projects and tools of her trade than it did with superfluous junk. The patchwork quilt at her feet, for example: she was tacking on the batting at this point, and no other room had enough floor space on which to spread it out. And the fact that the front hall was occupied by her spinning wheel and a massive eight-harness loom – well, the spinning wheel was temporarily out of the living room so she could work on the quilt; and the loom, a gift from her parents last Christmas, she planned to move into the living room as soon as she found someone to haul away the organ. Molly had a studio, of course; but it was a tiny room off the front hall, and as such it was taken up by her old four-harness loom and her supplies of wool. Baskets of yarn alone made the room difficult to manoeuvre around in; but on top of that she had just received a large order of fleece, which, when she untied the strings from the outside wrapping, had begun expanding, so that the floor of her studio now looked as though an ocean of white wool had rolled in during the night.

Molly knew that every room in the house had to be cleaned out and sorted, that space would be needed for the baby; but she couldn't seem to motivate herself to make those decisions as to what to throw away and what to keep. However, with a baby coming she had to get motivated, she had to get organized. As she mended the wedding dress she wondered what Phoebe would think of the house – Phoebe who had been off living in the city, Phoebe with her sleek urban tastes, Phoebe who probably had white sofas and blond wood and clean cupboards with just one set of contemporary dishes –

Just then she heard Nick's jeep pull into the driveway; she brought the wedding dress into the kitchen and greeted him at the door. Nick was tall, though not much taller than Molly; his red woollen shirt was covered with tiny chips and splinters of wood, and his dark hair was two shades lighter from sawdust. He had a master's degree in American literature; this autumn he was selling firewood for a living.

'Uh-oh,' he said, scrutinizing her face. 'What's the matter?'

'Nothing.' She sat down at the table and continued her mending.

'Yes there is,' he said. 'You're in a bad mood. I can tell.'

'I'm not in a bad mood.'

'Yes you are.'

'No I'm not.'

'Yes you are.'

'Do you want me to be in a bad mood?' Molly asked

him. 'I will if you want. Just keep doing what you're doing and I'll get in a very bad mood.'

Nick went to the refrigerator, took a Molson from the top shelf, and untwisted the top.

'I threw up at my mother's today,' Molly told him, because she didn't want to get into the subject of her feelings about Phoebe, which were quite possibly the root of her bad mood right now.

'So she knows?' Nick said hopefully.

'No,' Molly said. 'She thought it was nerves.'

'Why don't we tell them,' Nick said. 'I'd like to tell my parents – they're going to ask anyway.'

'After Thanksgiving,' Molly said.

'What's the point? They're going to figure it out sooner or later.'

'After Thanksgiving.'

'Your parents aren't stupid,' he said. 'I bet they already know.'

'Maybe they do,' she said, 'but they'd rather nobody acknowledge it. Shit!' Molly had just jabbed her finger with the needle, and instantly the blood had got wicked up into the web of lace she was trying to mend. 'Fucking dress, fucking needle!' She stuffed the dress into the shopping bag and shoved her finger into her mouth.

Nick calmly watched her from the other side of the table. Then he sighed. 'Would you mind telling me what's bothering you now,' he said, 'so that we don't waste an entire evening with you being pissed off and then finally explaining it to me at two in the morning because you can't sleep?'

'I was fine,' Molly said, 'until you came home.'

'Nick,' Molly whispered.

Nick didn't reply.

'Nick,' Molly said. 'Wake up.'

Nick rolled over.

'Nick,' Molly said. 'I can't sleep.'

Nick leaned up on his elbow and looked at the clock. 'It's two o'clock, Molly,' he said.

'It's about Phoebe,' she said.

'*What's* about Phoebe?'

Molly sighed. 'You know what I wish?'

Nick waited.

'I wish she weren't coming.'

'Oh, Christ,' Nick said.

'You know how she told me at first she couldn't make it? Because she had all this work to do?'

'Yeah.'

'And then she called back and said it was the eye of the hurricane or something, and she could make it after all?'

'Yeah.'

'Well, I wish it hadn't changed,' Molly said. 'I was relieved when she said she couldn't come.'

'Why?'

Molly was quiet.

'You have no idea?'

'I *do* have an idea,' Molly said. 'It's just not nice.'

Nick waited.

'She's going to steal the show!' Molly blurted out.

Nick propped up a pillow, and leaned back. 'How?' he said. 'Why?'

'Because she hasn't been back for so long! And now she's coming back, and she's bringing her little kid – God, the way our families were almost related, it's like Andrew's the first grandchild of the Adams-Martin clan – and so everyone's going to be watching *her* and nobody's going to be watching *us*!'

'I thought you didn't want anybody watching us,' Nick said. 'I thought you wanted to elope because you didn't want all these people watching you make the big commitment to me.'

'Well, I'll be damned if Phoebe's going to be the centre of attention during my wedding,' Molly said.

Then she made a face. 'Listen to me,' she said, closing her eyes. 'The things I say, it makes me sick, Nick,' she said. 'I'm such a bitch.'

Nick yawned. 'Why did you ask her back? Why did you ask her to be your maid of honour, if this is how you feel?'

'Because I didn't *know* I'd feel this way,' she said, annoyed. 'And besides, I had to ask her to be my maid of honour. I was hers, don't you remember? She'd never forgive me.'

Nick shrugged. 'Times change, people change,' he said. 'Situations change.'

'And in any event,' she went on, ignoring him, 'who else would I have asked? Susan Mitchell? Doris Conran? Mrs Welch?'

For a while they lay in silence. Then Nick asked, 'What's she like?'

'Who?'

'*Phoebe*.'

'She's gorgeous,' Molly said.

'Oh, come on.'

'No, she is,' Molly said. 'And I don't mean just pretty, I mean gorgeous. Thick auburn hair, beautiful skin – oh, Phoebe never had pimples in high school, Phoebe didn't even own a tube of Clearasil – and of course Phoebe needed a bra by the fifth grade – but then she didn't grow any more, she just stayed that perfect size – '

'Perfect?'

'Well, you know.'

'No,' Nick said. 'I thought you were perfect.'

'Thank you,' Molly said, 'but let's be real.'

Nick shrugged, removed his hand from her breast.

'And she's very smart,' Molly went on, ' – obviously, if she went to law school – '

'Where'd she go to law school?'

'Berkeley.'

'That's a good school.'

'It's all right, I guess.'

'I bet I can't get into Berkeley.'

'Sure you can,' Molly said, turning to him. 'If Phoebe can, you can.'

Nick shrugged. He had taken the Law School Admission Test earlier that autumn, and was awaiting results, convinced that he had not done very well.

'Who does she work for?'

'Some big firm,' Molly said. 'I think she's into making a lot of money.'

'Does she like it?'

'Of course she does, why else would she stay there all this time?'

'Huh,' Nick said.

'Huh what?'

'Huh nothing,' Nick said. 'Just huh.'

Molly sighed. 'It's just that she always makes me feel as though I'm playing second fiddle,' she said. 'Have you ever had a friend who did that to you?'

'No,' Nick said. 'Maybe. I don't know.'

'And she's going to criticize me for everything,' Molly said. 'You just watch.'

# 4

The next morning Molly and Nick loaded up his jeep with rakes, brooms, and baskets, and set off for the sugarhouse. One week from today, Molly thought to herself; one week from today I'll be somebody's wife. No more this-is-my-boyfriend-Nick, she thought, looking at the man she had been involved with for almost six years. Say it. Husband.

'What?'

Molly felt herself flush. 'Just talking to myself.'

With the top up the jeep felt strangely closed in, like a tent with all the flaps shut during a storm. As they headed out of Winslow up the hill towards the dairy farm, Molly thought of what she had said to Nick the night before. I *am* a bitch, she thought. Here my oldest – really, my best friend is coming three thousand miles to be in my wedding and all I can do is get defensive, worry about her stealing the show from me. Oh, well, she thought; better that it come out with Nick, in bed at two in the morning, than with Phoebe.

'I was pretty cranky yesterday,' she said to him, 'wasn't I.'

'It's all right,' he said.

'I was just getting freaked out about Phoebe coming home,' she said. 'I was overreacting.'

'It's all right.'

'I didn't really mean what I said,' Molly told him. 'All that stuff about not wanting her to come back.'

'I know.'

'Because I really do want her in the wedding,' Molly

said. 'Like we've known each other since the age of five, I mean what other friend is more important – '

'Molly,' Nick said, 'take it easy.'

Molly sipped her coffee. 'Just do me a favour?' she asked, after a while.

'What's that?'

'When I'm *in* a bad mood, don't *tell* me I'm in a bad mood?'

Nick took the coffee cup from her, sipped, gave it back.

'Because it just makes matters worse,' she said. 'I hate being analysed.'

And the way Nick looked at her, she knew he wouldn't ever go along with that request.

In a while they reached the turnoff to the sugar bush. The old road, no more than two tracks of matted-down leaves separated by a narrow strip of dried weeds, followed a brook, then headed up a steep hill. Today the sky was overcast; it had rained the night before, and the road was so slippery from the wet foliage that Nick had to put the jeep into four-wheel drive to make it up the hill.

Molly hadn't been up to the sugarhouse in so long that she was surprised to see how badly it had suffered from lack of upkeep. Its grey weathered wood had been eaten away by termites, and the floorboards on the front porch had rotted from lack of paint. Clusters of shingles had fallen off the roof, which in one area sagged from the weight of dead leaves and sticks; and shards of broken glass littered the ground below the windows.

'The place looks haunted,' Nick said. 'Are you sure you want to be married up here?'

Inside the floor was still solid, though, and much of the equipment appeared to be in workable condition. In the far corner were boxes of metal sap-collecting spouts and haphazard stacks of tin buckets; most of the space was taken up by the long, shallow evaporator pans, once used for boiling down the sap. Molly couldn't remember a time when the sugarhouse had been functioning. The property was owned by a retired banker who lived in Florida, and every year Dave had a fit about the uncollected sap. This year, in fact, he was going to propose tapping the bush himself, in exchange for a percentage.

They walked back outside and surveyed the clearing. Without the sun the air was damp and chilly, and Molly remembered what her mother had said yesterday about snow. What if a blizzard blew in during the ceremony? Molly tried not to think about that, and turned her attention instead to planning the ceremony itself. It was going to be short, so they weren't going to arrange for any seating except for a portable lawn chair for Phoebe's grandmother, for Max. Nick thought that they should stand on the porch, with the guests in front of the sugarhouse, but Molly objected; she didn't like the feeling of being up on a pedestal.

'Pedestal?'

'You know,' Molly said. 'With everyone staring at us. What if I trip on the way up the steps? What if you fall through the porch floor?'

Finally they agreed they would just stand in front of the steps, and decorate the porch with pumpkins and baskets of gourds and bunches of Indian corn. Molly began sweeping away the fallen leaves from the porch, while Nick set about picking up the sticks and other debris around the shack. As she worked she recalled coming up here with Phoebe when they were young. One summer – they must have been ten – they had used it as a clubhouse; though Molly couldn't remember the exact purpose of the club, she did recall that they spent most of their time trying to keep Phoebe's brother Jack and his friends away. Until they showed up with cigarettes, of course, at which point Phoebe convinced Molly that the boys could join the club as long as they paid their dues with packs of Marlboros. It all ended when Bea came upon them one afternoon and found her daughter seriously losing a round of strip poker.

'What's so funny?' Nick asked, sitting down beside her on the porch steps.

'Oh yeah?' he said when Molly told him. 'Like how bad were you losing?'

'Nick,' she sighed, 'this is a very painful memory for me. Do you have to press the matter?'

'Like was your shirt off?'

'Oh, yes.'

'And your pants?'

'Oh, yes.'

Nick began kissing her neck. 'God,' he said. 'Tell me more.'

'Nick,' Molly said, laughing, pulling away.

'Really,' he said. 'I love it.' He started unbuttoning her shirt. She gave in, but as Nick spread two blankets on the ground she had this strange feeling of being ten again, of being forced to take off her clothes while down the road her mother's voice, calling her, was lost to the wind.

Phoebe called Molly from Wellesley with the news that she had been accepted at Boalt Hall School of Law on a Saturday afternoon in mid-March, during their senior year. Molly, a geology major at the University of Vermont, was studying for an exam on plate tectonics, and when she hung up the phone she found it hard to concentrate. For one thing, Phoebe's voice sounded different. True, it may have been the connection; true, they didn't talk a lot on the phone but instead wrote long frequent letters; but Phoebe's voice sounded different. A little cockier than usual, and a little condescending, as though she were talking to the Winslow Ladies' Aid rather than her best friend. Hey Phoebe, Molly wanted to say, *I* know where Berkeley is, *I* know it's a good school.

But the phone call was also unsettling for her, because it made her wonder if her own aspirations weren't too low. Already she had accepted the teaching position with the Barrington Union School District, and was looking forward to going back to Vermont's Northeast Kingdom, away from Burlington, away from the University. But perhaps teaching high school was a copout, she had thought. It wasn't as if she'd always wanted to be a teacher, after all; it just seemed to be an easy job that would leave her with time for weaving and quilting, maybe even with enough extra time to start experimenting with natural dyes. But perhaps she should push herself a little more: go on to grad school, get her master's, go into research, teach at a higher level.

But Molly didn't want to do that. She was tired of geology – tired of rocks, tired of data, tired of dusty field trips hammering away at specimens. So grad school in geology was out. She probably had enough of a science background to make a crack at med school; but who wanted to give up all that time – the best years of your life – just to become a doctor? Molly had dated an intern for a while, and she rarely saw him; he would go forty-eight hours without sleep at the hospital, and then come over to her apartment and pass out before they could even make love. He was skinny. He was pale. He chain-smoked, and couldn't carry a conversation. Who in her right mind would want to become a doctor?

Nor did she want to leave Vermont, which she probably would have had to do in order to go to grad school. She hated cities, hated the noise, felt claustrophobic even in

Burlington; perhaps it was memories of living in New York as a toddler, before they moved up to Vermont, and never being able to go outside alone, always feeling as though she were on a leash. And even if she could manage to get accepted at a school that was not located in a large city – well, what area of the country could compare to Vermont? The South was hot and full of snakes; the Mid-west was flat and boring; upstate New York seemed like an imitation of Vermont; the Pacific Northwest had more grey days, she had heard, than Burlington, which by March was usually driving her crazy; and California – well, California was just too weird. Her father had a tendency to go overboard with his opinions, but on the issue of California he was right; it was full of flakes.

And yet, hearing that her friend was going to go to law school out in San Francisco, Molly wondered if perhaps she wasn't being adventurous enough. She was, after all, going to be living just five miles from her parents' home, the home in which she'd grown up. How could she justify that? It certainly looked unadventurous, by objective standards. ('Winslow?' Phoebe had said when Molly had told her. 'You mean, like . . . home? No, no,' she had protested quickly, 'no, I think that's great.')

But Molly hadn't chosen Winslow; if she'd had her druthers she would have taken a teaching job in a town that was at least a toll-call away from her mother. But as it had turned out, the Barrington Union School District had been the only one in Vermont with an opening for a science teacher, and so Molly found herself interviewing one autumn afternoon with her high school principal, Doris Conran: a woman whose very resignation she and Phoebe had called for when Doris vetoed the school library's purchase of a book on Che Guevara. (Though Doris now recalled only Phoebe's role in the attempted ouster; as she said to Molly during a lunch break, 'She was always a troublemaker, that redheaded friend of yours, that Phoebe Martin, and I must say that I wasn't surprised to hear she was a lawyer – because that girl would have argued about the colour of forget-me-nots, if you'd have let her. Though I never imagined she'd be working at a law firm, I thought she'd be out there defending those farmworkers, or Angela Davis, or any one of those, well let's face it, they *are* mostly communists, you know. Well, anyway, Mary' – for the ageing principal had always called Molly by her real name – 'I'm delighted that *you* decided to teach here in Winslow.'

Well, almost, Doris; but not quite.)

Opening her book on plate tectonics again, Molly had wondered how Phoebe would get herself out to California. If she drove, maybe Molly could take the trip with her, and then fly back. It would be in keeping with their tradition of doing something during the summer together, a tradition that had been growing since they'd left Winslow for their separate colleges: backpacking in the Presidential Range one year, lifeguarding on Lake Champlain the next, waiting tables in Stowe after their junior year. And it would be a nice break, she had thought, before starting my job. We could take the northern route, and camp along the way; maybe we could stop off in the Grand Tetons, and do some hiking. But she had held off saying anything to Phoebe until she knew more about her own schedule; and in the meantime she noticed a change in Phoebe's behaviour. They were both home for most of that summer, Phoebe devoting her time to catching up on various history and political science books that contained what she felt would be essential material for her as a law student, Molly getting herself settled down in the village of Winslow, and Molly wasn't sure, but it seemed as though Phoebe was always trying to trip her up over her words – as though she were playing at being a lawyer, practising for her first year of law school by using Molly as a sounding board for her little exercises in debate. And she wasn't even that good at it either. 'That's inconsistent with what you said earlier,' she would accuse Molly, and Molly, knowing that what she had just said was not in fact inconsistent at all, would delicately hint around as to just why it wasn't, hoping that Phoebe wouldn't lose her temper. It began to get on her nerves, this aggressiveness on Phoebe's part, and by mid-July she decided against bringing up the issue of travelling out West with her: she didn't know if she could sit in a Volkswagen, listening to Phoebe on the offensive, for three thousand miles. It was just too damn *exhausting*.

Molly thought about all this as they drove back to Winslow late that afternoon, Nick and herself in his old petrol-smelling red jeep. She had even felt a little relieved when Phoebe finally left towards the end of that summer, despite the fact that she knew their summer tradition would probably die. Yet it was so much easier without Phoebe around to hound her all the time. Molly now wondered what Phoebe had been like in law school. She had seen *The Paper Chase*, like everyone else; and had Phoebe always been prepared for class? Did she always know the facts of the case? Did she prepare those voluminous outlines while studying for exams – and if so, did she share them with a study group? Did she rent a hotel room? Did she know anyone who got so worked up that he attempted suicide?

That evening, while Nick worked on the Sunday crossword, Molly pawed through a box of papers in the downstairs closet.

'What are you doing?' Nick asked. 'You're not cleaning, are you?'

'I'm looking for some letters,' Molly said.

'Letters from who?'

'Phoebe,' Molly said. 'Ah. Here we go.'

*Dear Molly*, Phoebe had written on December fourteenth of her first year. *Finally some time to myself. I am presently nursing a terrible hangover; I had my last exam – contracts – yesterday afternoon, and probably consumed two (?) bottles of wine last night. It was my worst exam; afterwards I sat in the car and just grabbed the steering wheel and screamed until I was hoarse. Pardon the advice, but I mean it, don't (you or anyone) go to law school unless you are really dead keen on being a lawyer.*

*Rusty finishes up tomorrow, with tax. He is really sweating this one, as he never went to class and refuses to buy the tax code, which is out of date as soon as it is published anyway. He's trying to memorize Gilbert's; all he wants, he claims, is a passing grade, though he'll probably pull an A. We are going to celebrate tomorrow night – dinner at the Hunan. And lots of sex! We haven't even seen each other during these past two weeks – I've been hiding out in my library carrel, and he studies at home, and by the time it's midnight both of us are too tired for anything except a peck on the cheek. You'd think we were an old married couple.*

*But overall things are going well; I hope you can meet him soon. Maybe we'll make a trip back East next summer. He is smart (smarter than me, when it comes to law, that's for sure); a bit of a slob; and likes to go biycyling in the wine country, which of course we never have time to do. We fight a lot. And make up a lot too! I've enclosed a picture of us, taken by a friend over in the City; out by the ocean. Very handsome, yes?*

*How's your teaching going? – Love, Phoebe.*

Contracts, tax, Molly thought, slipping the letter back into its envelope – what could be more boring? How had Phoebe managed to stand three years of subjects like that? How would Nick stand it? Maybe she was missing something – maybe once you got into the legal material it became interesting, in its own nitpicky way – but Molly doubted it. What could be drier? And the *time* sacrifice – maybe it wasn't as bad for Phoebe as it had been for her intern friend, but it sounded like she didn't have time for anything but law.

The next letter that Molly opened was large and square, Phoebe's wedding invitation: engraved words on creamy stationery. Inside was a folded note on which Phoebe had written, *We purposely scheduled it during your spring break – because you have to be my maid of honour! I'll call soon, and we can talk about it. XOXOX. PS Being engaged is wonderful!*

Phoebe's wedding. April in California. It was as beautiful as everyone told her it would be, and Molly to her surprise found herself liking California. Or northern California, at least. The hills were a brilliant green, and everywhere you looked there were flowers: fuchsia trees, which she couldn't get over, and poppies growing wild, and flamboyant tropical-looking blossoms cascading down the hills. She could even see living there herself – except for the fact that the city seemed so – well, so Disneyland-ish. Cable cars, sailboats in the Bay, the colourful narrow streets of Chinatown – it was pretty, to be sure, but a little too happily quaint, in her view. Did people ever get in bad moods when they lived in San Francisco? What did they do when they wanted to gripe about the weather? ('They gripe about the fog,' Phoebe told her; 'people hate the fog, especially if they've moved up from LA. Though I like it, the way it moves in so quickly.') Phoebe, of course, loved California, and Molly realized she didn't have much to say in response when Phoebe chattered on and on with her comparisons of California and Vermont. Winters *were* unbearably long and bleak, and black flies *were* a royal pain, and it was true, you never could count on good weather for anything. But at least it gave you something to bitch about. Molly thought to herself; and besides, how could you know about spring fever without living through a Vermont winter? How could you appreciate a fresh April breeze blowing stale air out of rooms just unlocked? Or the smell of mud, of dampness; or the site of a lone purple crocus?

And how, Molly had thought, lifting her champagne glass as Phoebe cut into her wedding cake and the cameras flashed, how would you ever explain any of this to Californians? They were all so convincingly sold on their overdose of beauty.

All told, she had stayed in California for a week that spring. When she returned to Vermont – by then it was the end of April – the snow was gone, and the trees were budding, and Nick, who'd been taking care of the house while she was gone, had already aired out the two bedrooms that she had closed off for the winter. 'Because it's summer!' he explained giddily when she noticed that he had switched from flannel sheets to smooth cotton ones, and put on the summer-weight blanket. And Molly had felt a loss, having missed all this during her one-week stay in California; though she found it hard to explain to Nick, who, after all, just had a bad case of spring fever.

'Mrs Rabbit,' Nick said.

Molly, who hated crossword puzzles, ignored him.

'Six letters.'

Molly opened up another letter.

'Janice,' Nick said. 'God, I'm literate.'

*Dear Molly*, Phoebe wrote – this one dated October tenth, when she would have been about seven months pregnant. *Thanks for the sweater! It's really beautiful – and I'm glad you chose blue; everything else we get seems to be green or yellow. You are truly talented.*

*It arrived at an opportune time, actually: I am so* tired *of being pregnant. I feel like I am losing control over everything – body, school, my relationship with Rusty – you name it. I'm behind in my courses and the bathroom smells and I have zero energy. I am going to breathing classes, which helps; but tonight Rusty said he couldn't go with me because he had to work, so I went by myself, and then came home to find him asleep on the sofa. Pissed me off, though I will admit there was something very satisfying to be lying on the floor doing my exercises all alone. Sometimes it's a bit much seeing all these guys panting and counting and clutching the women's shoulders. I mean come on, let's not overdo it; this thing is going to come out of* me, *not him; it's going to tear up* my *body, not his.*

*I also keep wondering if I am doing the right thing. It's probably the worst possible time in my life to be having a baby, with school and second-year interviews and all. But I guess part of it was wondering what a second abortion would do to me – the doctors tell you it's all right, but you have to wonder about it, getting vacuumed out over and over. You know how fickle opinions can be; one minute they're selling you on the Dalkon shield like it's the greatest invention since the wheel and the next thing you know it's perforating wombs right and left. Chances are nothing would go wrong with just two abortions – but what if?*

*Well, anyway, life goes on. The decision's been made; there's no turning back. I wait and wait and wait and wait. For ever. I am working on a note for law review, and will hopefully get a draft started after the birth – I'm just doing research on it now, spending hours in the library stacking up my neat little piles of coloured index cards with separate legal points on each one. (No you* don't *want to know what it's about.)*

*We moved right before school began – a bigger place, for the baby. Still close to the law school, so I can walk back and forth. It's good exercise. I also swim every day – though I feel like a walrus in the pool, especially next to all those sorority girls who are all legs and no stomach. And yet at the same time I feel like I've got one over on them. I splash around for a little while but spend most of the time kicking at the edge of the pool. Sometimes the baby even kicks with me: the scissor kick? the frog kick? I wonder.*

*I've been interviewing with law firms. Reactions are all over the board – one firm didn't even blink when I waddled in, and I had to hand it to them. Another time, though, my nose began to bleed (my doctor says it's common) as I was telling them where-I-saw-myself-in-five-years, and nobody had a Kleenex, and it was flowing out of both nostrils, and finally I had to run out of the little interview cubicle to the john. My friends thought something very terrible had happened between us in there. No offers yet, but there's still a lot of time, so I'm not too nervous. I can always go back to Public Advocacy, where I worked this past summer, but I think I would like to go with a firm, at least try it for the summer. You do work your ass off, but they pay well, and it (supposedly) keeps more options open. So who's a whore?*

*Again, thanks for the sweater. My regards to Doris. Ha. Ha. Love, Phoebe.*

And soon after that, another letter, written after the birth:

*Dear Molly*, Phoebe wrote on March twenty-sixth. *Well, Rusty has taken Andrew out for a walk in the backpack, and it's the first time I've heard silence since he was born. What a winter! Andrew is bald, noisier than I thought possible for a mass of flesh his size. I had planned on taking him to classes with me but the way he cries I'd be shot. My son, the public nuisance.*

*And things with Rusty aren't so great, these days. Our schedules are completely different, and when we are together all we focus on is Andrew. Is he crying, do you think he's hungry, he just ate how could he be, do you think he's sick, should we call the doctor, is that a rash, for Chrissake do you have to leave the poopy diaper on the floor can't you throw it away.*

*I'm not being fair. It's not so bad; I just need to let off a little steam, I guess. I just finished a near-final edit on my law review note (all 143 pages, triple spaced, including footnotes), and Andrew was up all last night with some mysterious intestinal disease that caused him to scream louder than usual, and Rusty slept through the whole thing. He can sleep through everything, including my nightmares. I keep having these dead baby dreams, where I have given birth to a tiny monkey, two or three inches long; my mother is there, reminding me to bathe it, and I forget how fragile its tiny body is, and end up wringing its neck by scrubbing it briskly between the palms of my hands underneath the kitchen tap. I am a murderess.*

*Oh – one piece of good news is that I got an offer from a firm for next summer: Judson and Day, a pretty good firm here in the city. Rusty will be home studying for the bar, so he can take care of Andrew during the day. Hah. If there's one good thing about both of us being busy, it's that we don't have to worry about my getting pregnant.*

*Not that I'm ever in the mood.*

*Oh, well. Maybe when Andrew gets a little older we'll be able to get away for a weekend, just the two of us – maybe go up to the Russian River, relax, and fall in love again.*

*The pictures I'm sending were taken by Rusty's mother during a trip to Muir Woods. We were going to climb Mt Tam but I was too tired. Look at Andrew smiling (sort of). Look at Rusty smiling (sort of). Look at Phoebe on the verge of crying. Do I look twenty-four? Can you tell how flabby my stomach is? I weigh 149!*

*– Love, P.*

These last two letters troubled Molly. They saddened her, for one thing; she knew the outcome of the story, knew how things were going to turn out with Phoebe and Rusty. There would be no trip to the Russian River, there would be no falling in love again. And Phoebe was trying to sound so glib about everything, as though she had to paint a rosier picture for her friend back East. But the letters also frightened her, in a way, because they brought home to her how different their lives had become. She had had a preview of this feeling during her visit to California for Phoebe's wedding; when Phoebe had talked about law school, her professors, her courses, Molly had had a vague sense that she was losing her friend to an archaic culture. And now, although the letters didn't make it seem all that archaic, they did seem to bring into focus so many of the ways in which she and Phoebe had grown apart. Phoebe interviewing, writing for the law review; Phoebe coping with an infant, arguing with her husband – could she even say that she *knew* Phoebe any more? Here was the woman – the girl – she had grown up with, spent almost every day of her girlhood with, and while it was true that Phoebe was always the first to do things, and Molly was always a little behind, at least they had been on the same track. Now, though, it was as though someone had pulled a lever, so that as Phoebe continued on one track, Molly found herself on another (or vice versa), and the two of them would never quite be going in the same direction.

But why should that frighten you? Molly thought. Isn't that the way it's supposed to happen? You grow up, you grow apart – it doesn't mean you're not friends any more.

But it did frighten her.

The next morning Molly overslept, and didn't have a chance to outline her lecture for the day, which was to be on sedimentary rocks. She decided to show slides, thinking she could make up a narration as she went along, but discovered that the only programme available was an outdated one entitled 'Outcroppings in the Adirondacks: A Look at America's Oldest Rocks.' In lieu of a slide show she babbled off the top of her head, and the students were bored. She felt antsy – antsy for Phoebe to arrive, antsy to get married. At lunch she saw Susan Mitchell and Mrs Welch, their heads together as they laughed and whispered. When they looked up and noticed her, Susan dabbed at her mouth with her calico napkin and Mrs Welch bobbed her head about as though searching for someone. Brad Kenshaw winked at her. Something was up, and she wasn't a part of it. She decided she wasn't hungry, and went for a walk along the river.

Later, back at the house, she undressed and slipped under the covers. She slept soundly until seven. Although she hadn't eaten all day, she still had no appetite; since Nick wouldn't be home until late, she got the bundle of letters and went back to bed. There was one more, written a year later. It was the last letter she had received; once Phoebe started work, correspondence on both ends had dropped off.

*Dear Molly*, Phoebe had written. *Sorry for not writing. How are you? How is teaching? How is Winslow? How is Nick?*

*And how am I? Well, things have been better. The divorce is in high gear, and it's not very pretty; it really brings out the worst in you. I had that table before we were married. That's my grandmother's chair, so what if it was a wedding present? You never even liked that sofa, why does it suddenly mean so much to you? I made those curtains. I bought that rug with birthday money. I lugged that blanket all the way back from Tijuana, you didn't even want to buy it. And I never added anything to my old savings account while we were married, goddammit, it's mine.*

*Luckily I have a good lawyer. She's expensive; my mother calls her my graduation present. Some present! Her name is Frances; she bites. I'd rather this thing be over and done with, but she tells me I'll regret it six months from now if I let Rusty walk off with all the designer sheets, the Cuisinart, the crystal, the silver, etc. Frankly I'd rather have new sheets, but she's bargaining right down to the last pillowcase. So I go along, letting her haggle it out with Rusty's lawyer, and I pay the bills; but at times I'd rather sign away everything just to get rid of the memories.*

*And then of course there's the issue of Andrew. Rusty wants joint custody, and as much as I believe in it theoretically, when it comes to my own child it seems like a bad idea. Am I awful, I wonder? I think Rusty should get him alternate weekends, maybe some time in between, and Frances agrees. I don't know how it will work out. But we need a solution soon; the indecision surrounding our lives has to be felt by him, even if he is only sixteen months. He certainly notices that Daddy isn't here any more. (You should see him; he's got a mess of dark hair now, and knows lots of words, and never shuts up. And talk about a will of his own! Try and get him dressed – try and get him into bed – try and get him to sit still in the grocery cart. And this isn't even the terrible twos!)*

*Speaking of grocery carts I met the Woman last weekend at Safeway. There I was coming up the aisle from frozen foods, and there was Rusty at the dairy case with Her. Then as he started to put a hunk of cheese into the car he turned and saw me. Rusty usually has this sallow-coloured skin but at that point it turned the colour of tomato soup. Then Andrew, who was sitting in my cart, saw Rusty, and of course he started hollering and trying to climb out of the cart and so I had to take him over to his Daddy. Rusty and Andrew did all the talking. She and I just stood there, smiling politely at one another, checking each other out when the other one wasn't looking. She is very tailored, very WASPy, very thin, very chic, obviously childless (I of course still weigh over 140) – but she has pimples on her forehead, and I think she is a little cross-eyed.*

*At least the ice is broken. I'm sure all three of us were wondering when it would happen. I wish them well. My mother thinks it is outrageous, thinks I should be furious (especially since, as it turns out, he was seeing her while I was pregnant); yet my first feeling when Rusty told me he was having an affair was one of relief. The only explanation I had was that now there was an objective reason to end it. I used to lie in bed at nights when he was presumably working and wonder how a judge would react if I got up and said, I don't know, I just don't like him any more, Your Honour; he bugs me. He can never admit when he's wrong and I hate the way he eats one thing at a time from his plate, the way he lets beer foam sit in his moustache and I also hate for your further information the way he leaves his fucking pubic hairs on the bar of soap. Why can't he pick them off? Welcome to the world, the judge would say; next case? But when your husband is screwing around on you, judges listen. They call it no-fault divorce, but they're wrong. Even in California nobody likes an adulterer.*

*And yet this is certainly not to say it was his fault. If it hadn't been Rusty who was screwing around it might have been me, if I looked a little better; who knows?*

*I have to run. I'd invite you out for a visit this summer but I'll be studying for the Bar. A real drag. The Bar Review people tell you not to worry if you're in the top half of Berkeley – you'll pass, they say, unless you're going through a divorce, ha ha. If they only knew. But maybe it will be settled by then (July 23–25 – pray for me!) and all we'll squabbling about is which dentist Andrew should go to.*

*Say hi to Nick – Love, Phoebe.*

There was that glibness again. Molly wondered if Phoebe was still bitter about things, if she was down on marriage these days. How did she feel about Molly getting married, anyway – was she sceptical? Protective? Or maybe envious? And would they be able to talk about it? Molly hoped she would get over this defensiveness she'd been feeling, get rid of this chip on her shoulder; she wanted to be able to open up to Phoebe, to fill that void in her life and have a good long talk, the way old friends should.

Outside a storm had begun, and tiny beads of raindrops spun dotted lines on the windowpane by her bed. Butch and Frankie appeared in the doorway; Molly patted the quilt and the dogs leapt up, curling around one another at the foot of the bed, snorting themselves into a dream. Molly pulled the covers closely around her. By the time Nick let himself in, she was asleep, the dogs at her feet, the letters in a pile on his side of the bed. He set them on the floor and slid in beside her, wrapping his arms around her waist.

'Maybe we should fix her up with Leo,' Nick said the next evening. Leo was one of Nick's friends from college who now worked for a senator on Capitol Hill. Leo was going to be the best man,

'I think that could be risky,' Molly said.

'It'd only be for the weekend,' Nick said. 'They've got a lot in common, you know. Both lawyers, and Leo went through a divorce himself five years ago. He has a little girl.'

Molly worked the needle in and out of the torn lace sleeve of the wedding dress. She didn't know if it was ever going to be wearable, and wondered if she should just wear jeans instead. 'I don't know,' she said. 'What's Leo like?'

Nick was about to respond, but suddenly Butch started racing around the kitchen and barking at the back door. 'What is it, Butch?' Molly said, but Butch kept barking furiously. Molly stood up and went over to the door. 'Hello?' she said, walking out on to the porch. 'Who's there?'

It took a minute for her eyes to adjust, but then she saw a small masked figure standing at the bottom of the steps, wearing overalls and an old quilted parka with fur around the hood. Mittens dangled from elastic straps that had been clipped on to the cuffs. She stared at the boy, and the boy stared back. He started to raise his arms as if to scare her, but then suddenly he tore off his mask and ran down the driveway.

'I don't like that lady!' he bellowed.

Then Molly saw another figure squatting at the end of the driveway, arms extended. The boy collided against her.

'You have to like that lady,' Phoebe said, standing up. 'That's your Aunt Molly.'

# 5

They were on time.

Phoebe leaned over and tightened Andrew's seat belt; there was no sense waking him up until they had landed. She wondered who would be there to meet them: Louise, of course, but also maybe Jack and Cindy Ann? Maybe Molly too? She imagined the two-hour ride back to Winslow going just like that, with everyone jabbering nonstop: Molly talking about Nick and the wedding plans, Jack and Cindy Ann filling her in on their house, Louise asking about work, the apartment, Andrew's paediatrician.

Phoebe took a comb from her bag and ran it lightly over Andrew's hair, then dabbed at the corners of his mouth with her napkin.

'Awful cute little tyke,' said the elderly woman next to her, leaning forward. 'Awful awful.'

Phoebe smiled. Yes, he was.

'I can see the family resemblance too,' the woman said. 'He's got your nose – though I'm sure that's what everyone says.'

Phoebe nodded, looking again at Andrew's face. People had always said that Andrew looked like Rusty, but the woman was right – the boy did have her nose. It made her wonder if perhaps it was because Andrew was growing up in the midst of Rusty's family that people said he looked like a Goldblume; maybe next to Jack and her mother, next to pictures of her father, people would finally see the resemblance.

Phoebe smiled, and kissed the top of his head. He was

a knockout, no doubt about it. He was going to bowl them over.

When the plane had taxied to a stop and the lights came on, Phoebe gathered up her bags from beneath the two seats; Andrew, groggy from his nap, ground his fists into his eyes and and insisted that she carry him off the plane. That meant carrying, in one hand, a small suitcase, her briefcase, and a shopping bag full of toys and books and loaves of sourdough bread, so that she could hoist Andrew on to her hip; but she managed, because at this point she didn't want a fussy child. Not with everyone in her family waiting there to meet them. First impressions and all that.

Phoebe clumsily made her way down the aisle, past the smiling flight attendants, down the steep steps, and across the pavement to the waiting room.

Louise wasn't there.

Phoebe continued to smile and scan the crowd; she edged past the expectant faces to where she could set her bags down, and looked around again, still smiling. Maybe her mother had ducked into the ladies' room? Maybe she had got the gates mixed up? She gave Andrew another hoist – she rarely carried him any more, and for good reason, she realized as her shoulder began to ache – and looked around again. Still no Louise.

Phoebe set Andrew down. He began to whine. 'Andrew, I can't keep holding you, you're too heavy,' she said. Andrew broke into a cry, clutching at her legs. Where was her mother?

'Come on, you carry my briefcase, we'll go get our suitcases,' she said, untangling his arms and picking up the other two bags herself.

But then Andrew began to shriek; when she reached for his hand he snatched it away and dropped to the floor, thrashing about and screaming, his cheek pressed against the airport carpet. Other travellers glared at her; to avoid their hostile looks she worked at keeping a smile of anticipation on her face, turning her head eagerly in first one direction and then another, as though it were perfectly normal that she be stranded at the Burlington airport at eight o'clock with two bags, a briefcase, and a four-year-old bent on throwing his annual temper tantrum.

'I'm leaving, Andrew,' she finally said.

Andrew screamed louder.

'I'm going to get our luggage,' she told him, impressed with how calm she sounded. 'Would you prefer to stay here on the floor?'

Andrew screamed even louder. Phoebe smiled, looked out of the window, pretended to search the parking lot. She thought he was going to burst something internally.

'Okay, Andrew,' she said furiously. 'I'm leaving now,' she said.

'Phoebe?'

She turned.

'Welcome home, Phoebe darling!' her mother exclaimed, wrapping her arms around her. 'Welcome *home*, honeybunch!'

Louise, it turned out, had been held up in traffic. As they collected the baggage Phoebe realized that nobody else had come over with her, and she tried not to show her disappointment. 'Where's Jack tonight?' she asked lightly, as they headed out of Burlington.

'Oh, he and Cindy Ann went to Joe-Ray's,' Louise said, and it took Phoebe a couple of seconds to recall the tavern by the river in a neighbouring village. Wasn't Joe-Ray's the place that served minors? Wasn't that where they had gone during high school? 'Tuesday's the night one of their friends plays the guitar and they wouldn't miss it for the world,' Louise told her.

'Oh,' Phoebe said.

'But they'll be up for supper tomorrow night,' Louise went on. 'Along with Max, and I thought you might like to have Molly up too.'

'Sure,' Phoebe said. 'How's she doing, anyway – is she getting nervous about the wedding?'

'Mum,' said Andrew from the back seat.

'Just a minute,' Phoebe said. 'I'm talking to Grammy.'

'What did you want to say, lambykins?' Louise asked, and Andrew's head appeared on the edge of the seat between the two women.

'Where's Daddy?' Andrew asked.

'Daddy's home,' Phoebe said. 'You know that.'

'Let's go over to his house,' Andrew said.

'Andrew,' Phoebe said, 'Daddy's house is a long way away now. Why don't you put your head down and take a nap.'

'I'm not tired,' said Andrew.

'Then why don't you just listen for a while,' Phoebe said. 'Grammy and I are talking.'

'Grammy,' Andrew said.

'What is it, honeybunch?' Louise said.

'I eat rubbish, you know,' Andrew said.

'Andrew,' Phoebe said, growing irritated. 'You shut your eyes now.'

Andrew flopped back against the seat.

'So what kind of a wedding is this going to be?' Phoebe asked. 'Are there going to be a lot of people?'

'Last I heard it was only going to be family and close friends,' Louise said. 'Though with Bea planning things you never know how many people will show up.'

'Grammy,' said Andrew.

'What is it, sweetie pie?'

'Did you come visit when I was a baby?'

'That's right,' Louise said. 'All you did was cry.'

'No I didn't *cry*,' Andrew said.

'Oh yes you did,' Louise said. 'I hardly slept a wink.'

'Andrew,' Phoebe said, 'if I let you come up front and put your head in my lap will you take a nap?'

Andrew scooted over the seat and flopped down, nestling his head against her stomach.

'What do you think of Nick,' Phoebe said. 'Do you like him?'

'Nick's having trouble finding himself, I think,' Louise said. 'Don't tell Molly I said that, but he doesn't seem to be able to figure out what he wants to do. For a while he was teaching over at Goddard, just one class, but they cancelled the class and now he's cutting firewood. He's drifting,' Louise said.

'Are they going to stay in Molly's house?' Phoebe asked. 'Or do they have plans to move?'

Louise frowned. 'Oh, they'll stay put for the time being, I'm sure,' she said. 'I don't know why they'd move. Molly's got that lovely old house down by the river, and if I were them I'd try to buy it. After all, it'd be a great place for the baby.'

'Baby,' Phoebe said blankly.

'Molly didn't tell you?'

Phoebe frowned.

'Oh, dear,' Louise said.

'Molly's *preg*nant?'

'Molly's pregnant.'

Phoebe fell silent. 'Like how far along?' she asked, after a while.

'Not far,' Louise said. 'In fact let me warn you, nobody's supposed to know about it – she's probably planning to make a timely announcement after the wedding.'

'You mean she's trying to keep it a secret? Oh,

brother,' Phoebe said. 'How do you know she's pregnant, anyway?'

'Oh, it's obvious just looking at her,' Louise said. 'And plus she's always throwing up. Besides, Phoebe,' her mother went on, 'when a girl get married on three weeks' notice it doesn't take very much.'

Hearing that, Phoebe suddenly felt incredibly stupid: how could she not have suspected anything? Molly getting married on the spur of the moment – of course she would be pregnant. But then she thought, Wait a minute – that's a fairly archaic perspective. Nobody bothered getting married now just because of a pregnancy – why should she have jumped to the conclusion that Molly would be pregnant? Hasty weddings didn't mean anything these days.

'It doesn't have to mean she's pregnant,' Phoebe argued. 'It could mean a lot of things, maybe they just want it over and done with, maybe they don't want to make a big deal out of things, maybe – '

'Believe me,' Louise said. 'She's pregnant.'

'Mum,' said Andrew. 'How much longer?'

'Not long,' Phoebe said. 'We're almost there.'

By the time they pulled into the driveway of the farmhouse it was ten; and Louise, an early riser, was ready for bed, she said apologetically. But Andrew was now wide awake, due to his long nap on the plane and the time change (because for them it was only seven o'clock), and Phoebe, who was herself keyed up, suddenly did not want to wait until the next day to see Molly. 'Come on,' she said. 'Let's go surprise Aunt Molly.'

'I don't like Aunt Molly,' Andrew said.

'You don't know Aunt Molly,' Phoebe said. 'Look, you can wear your gorilla mask and play a trick on her!'

Phoebe's first impression when she saw Molly was that her friend had lost too much weight. Molly had always been thin – she could eat and eat and eat and never gain weight, Phoebe thought, remembering how Molly would finish everyone's discarded sandwiches in grade school; but now she seemed gaunt, unhealthy – especially for someone who was pregnant. Plus she had cut all her hair off – a pixie cut, almost – and it would have looked all right if whoever had cut it had not gone so short on the bangs.

God, she thought; you are so critical!

'You look terrific!' she said gaily, giving Molly another hug. 'Your hair looks great that way.'

'So does yours,' Molly said. 'You never told me you got it cut – I thought I was doing something original for once.'

'Andrew,' Phoebe said, turning around, 'come on and meet your Uncle Nick.'

'*Uncle* Nick?' Molly said. 'Where do you get this aunt-and-uncle bit, Phoebe?'

'Wellll . . . you are, in a way,' Phoebe said. 'Hey, Andrew, you can see Molly's dogs too.'

'I don't want to see her dogs,' said Andrew, lingering behind. 'I want to go home.'

'Come on,' Phoebe said, holding out her hand. 'Let's go get warm.'

Andrew lowered his eyes, then pulled his mask back down and caught her hand in his.

'Look who's here,' said Molly to Nick, once inside the kitchen. Nick stood up and extended his hand; Phoebe shook it, feeling a little too businesslike, as though she were meeting one of the attorneys on the other side of a lawsuit. But she liked Nick's face; he looked like Molly's type: studious and thoughtful, but with a rough edge from northern elements.

'And what's the gorilla's name?' asked Nick, kneeling down to Andrew's level.

Andrew regarded Nick with distrust.

'That's Nick, honey,' Phoebe said. 'Tell Nick your name.'

Andrew said nothing.

'Want to look at this magazine with me?' Nick said, reaching for a copy of *National Geographic*.

'No,' Andrew said. 'I want to go home.'

'We won't stay too long,' Phoebe promised him. She looked about the kitchen: open shelves lined with their jars of whole grains and pastas and dried beans, bunches of herbs hanging in the window, a half-finished, knubby-looking sweater on the kitchen table. 'Molly, this place is lovely,' she said. 'It looks so homey, so lived in.'

'Thanks,' said Molly.

'Well? Aren't you going to give me a tour?' Phoebe demanded.

'Go ahead,' Nick told them. 'I want to show Andrew something. Hey, Andrew,' he said, 'watch.' He pulled his chair over to the stove, and Andrew looked on as Nick played with the dampers, the fire roaring up from within. 'Quite a contraption, isn't it?'

Andrew watched Nick silently, then held out his hands to catch the warmth. Phoebe slipped out of the room, holding up two crossed fingers. 'Amazing,' she said to Molly, shaking her head. 'Andrew is usually so shy with strangers – wow!' she exclaimed as they entered the front hall. 'Does this work?' She gave Molly's spinning wheel a slight turn. The wood was old and waxy-looking, light coloured, and felt as warm and smooth as worn leather.

'Sure it works,' Molly said.

'Do you use it?'

Molly smiled. 'Of course.'

'You mean you spin your own wool?'

'Not all of it,' Molly said. 'I usually buy my warp wool and use my handspun wool for the weft.'

'Like where do you get wool to spin?' Phoebe said. 'I can't believe you spin your own wool.'

'From my sheep,' Molly said.

'Your sheep?'

'It doesn't make too much sense financially,' Molly admitted. 'But it's nice to do things from start to finish.'

Phoebe shook her head. 'You really get back to basics, don't you?'

Molly shrugged modestly.

'And this,' Phoebe said, indicating the loom. 'I take it this isn't for decoration.'

'Actually I haven't had the chance to use it very much,' Molly said. 'My parents gave it to me last Christmas. It's an eight-harness,' she said proudly.

Phoebe wondered what that signified.

'So that I can get into more complicated pattern weaving,' Molly explained.

'Aaahhh,' Phoebe said, nodding, still not really understanding but not wanting to press for more of an explanation. 'And what are you working on these days?' she went on. 'Are you doing shawls? Or table mats? Didn't you say you were getting into rugs?'

Molly frowned. 'That must have been a while back,' she said. 'Actually, I've been doing a lot of wall hangings – in fact I just sold a piece to a lodge over in Stowe.'

'Molly, that's wonderful!' Phoebe exclaimed. 'That's very impressive!'

But Molly didn't seem to want to wait around for any more praise. 'Come on, I'll show you the studio.' She continued down the hall, and Phoebe followed. 'Of course I've got so spread out that the whole house is a studio,' Molly said over her shoulder, 'but this is the official studio.'

'Very helpful for the IRS,' Phoebe agreed.

'IRS?'

‘For tax purposes,’ Phoebe said. ‘You do take a deduction, don’t you?’

Molly looked amused. ‘With my income?’ She switched on the light and Phoebe glanced about at this room that was going as an unclaimed tax deduction. Densely wound spools of yarn filled the shelves that had been built into one wall: autumn brick tones, twiny blues and greens, royal hues of purple, and, on the bottom shelf, peppery blends of taupes and greys and browns and whites. In the middle of the room stood Molly’s other loom; and scattered about the floor were fluffy piles of raw fleece and baskets of what looked to Phoebe like skeins of mohair. All across the far wall Molly had tacked up various woven samples; and on the wall near the door hung a collection of brushlike tools with bent wire teeth that Phoebe remembered from grammar-school history books. Carding tools? Is that what they were called?

‘What do you think?’ Molly was asking.

Phoebe looked; Molly had unrolled a wide woven hanging from a wooden dowel. It first seemed to be an abstract design; only when Phoebe stepped back a few feet was she able to recognize the furry overlapping arcs of greens and blues as the gentle hills between the two farmhouses up in East Winslow, the hills that her bedroom window overlooked.

‘Molly,’ she breathed. It was a beautiful piece of work, no doubt.

‘Do you like it?’

‘It’s gorgeous. You really made this?’

‘Do you want it?’

Phoebe gave her a cautious look, not wanting to say anything unless she was sure she understood what Molly was offering.

‘Really, go ahead,’ Molly said. ‘I owe you at least three birthday presents.’

Phoebe took the hanging and held it up against the wall. She was stumped for words, because the cold hard truth was that she didn't really like it. Oh, from what minimal knowledge she had in this area she knew it was a very skilfully done piece of art; but, well, she would have liked to see it hanging on somebody else's wall. Not hers.

And yet she had to like it. Molly had made it. Molly had given it to her.

'It's just so beautiful,' she said, not knowing what else to say. 'How long did it take you to do this?'

'Oh, maybe a couple of weeks,' Molly said. 'Off and on.'

Phoebe tried to think of other questions to ask, but a second problem had just arisen: suddenly all she could think about was the terrible fact that in the turmoil of getting the brief written for Herb she had neglected to buy Molly a wedding present. Anything she bought here would be obviously local and obviously an afterthought. Molly had just outdone her.

'It's really beautiful,' she said once again.

'Okay, okay,' Molly said, laughing. 'Enough already!'

Phoebe was relieved to return to the kitchen, where she found Andrew sitting on Nick's lap, turning the pages of the *National Geographic*. 'Look, Andrew,' she said, showing him the hanging, 'look what Aunt Molly gave us.'

'*Aunt* Molly,' Molly said to Nick, shaking her head and giving Phoebe an affectionate nudge. 'The girl just won't drop this aunt-and-uncle bit.'

'Hey, wait until you have a kid,' Phoebe joked, then stopped, suddenly realizing what she had just said. She looked at Molly, who was looking at Nick, who was looking at Molly.

'I was going to get to that,' Molly said to Phoebe.

'The answer is yes,' Nick said.

'Next June,' Molly said. 'Do you think I show?'

'Of course you show,' Nick told her. 'That's how Phoebe knew.'

'Is that how you knew?' Molly asked.

'Molly,' Phoebe said, 'when somebody tells you she's getting married on three weeks' notice it doesn't take very much.' She hated the false teasing note in her voice; and yet to be honest she actually felt a little hurt that Molly had kept the pregnancy a secret until now. Why hadn't she told her over the phone, two weeks ago? And what if Phoebe hadn't slipped just now – when *would* Molly have told her the news?

'See?' Nick was saying. 'I told you we might as well tell people. Everyone's probably guessing anyway, just like Phoebe did.'

'Well, I don't *want* to tell people yet,' Molly said, and Phoebe detected a snippish note to her voice. So this was an issue of contention between them, Phoebe thought. She herself agreed with Nick, of course; if her mother knew, then everyone in town probably knew; apparently in rural Vermont hasty marriages still meant but one thing. However, the last thing she wanted to do on her first night back was to gang up with Nick against Molly, and so instead she said, 'I imagine the wedding itself seems beside the point?'

'For the most part,' said Molly.

'Molly wanted to elope,' said Nick. 'Can you believe that?'

Molly shrugged. 'I'd just as soon it be over and done with,' she said flatly. 'I really don't care so much about making a big deal over things.'

'I can understand that,' Phoebe said. 'How are you feeling? Do you get sick a lot?'

'Oh, it's not too bad,' Molly said.

'She throws up once a day,' Nick said. 'Around four.'

'It'll pass,' Phoebe said. 'Are you tired?'

'Actually, yes,' Molly said.

'She only sleeps about fifteen hours a day,' Nick said. 'That'll pass too,' Phoebe said. 'When I was pregnant I could hardly stay awake during classes. Then as things wore on it wasn't staying awake that was the problem; I had to leave class to go to the bathroom all the time.'

While they were talking Andrew had climbed down from Nick's lap, and now he tugged at Phoebe's arm. 'Sing "Ten Little Indians,"' he said.

'Not now, Andrew,' Phoebe said.

'We'll sing it tomorrow,' Molly said.

'I don't want *you* to sing it,' Andrew said. 'I want my *mum* to sing it.' He dropped his head into Phoebe's lap.

'What about drinking?' Phoebe asked. 'Have you given that up?'

'Oh yes,' Molly said. 'Alcohol and caffeine and everything else. I know all about it.'

'Speaking of drinking,' Nick said, 'how about a beer?'

Phoebe felt she should decline; Andrew was getting restless, and she should be leaving soon. Besides, thus far things were going pretty well with Molly; and perhaps it was better to quit while they were ahead on this first night back, go home, get a good night's rest.

But Nick had already uncapped two Molsons, and was handing her a bottle. She had to stay a little longer.

'Andrew,' Molly said. 'Want a cookie?'

Andrew shook his head.

'A hermit?' Molly said. 'Or a snickerdoodle?'

Andrew shook his head again.

'So tell me,' Phoebe said, sitting down on a stool, 'how's your teaching going these days?'

'Oh, that,' Molly scoffed. 'It still brings home the paycheque, but that's about it.'

'What about Mrs Welch,' Phoebe asked, 'is she still teaching art?'

'Oh yes,' Molly said. 'She gets as far as the colour wheel and then turns the kids loose on their own.'

'I can write with my toes,' Andrew said. 'Watch!'

'Andrew,' Phoebe said, 'put your shoes back on. And who was that guy,' she said to Molly, 'that lech who always asked if you needed a nickel whenever you were going to the girls' room?'

'Brad Kenshaw,' Molly said.

'That's right,' Phoebe said. 'And he's still there? God, that place doesn't change, does it. What about Doris, how's Doris?'

'Doris always has something to complain about, I guess,' Molly said. 'This autumn it's her mother.'

How do you stand it? Phoebe wanted to ask. Aren't you going crazy, working day in and day out with a group like that? Herb Sullivan and John Dunn aren't the greatest, but at least I have Janice.

But Phoebe didn't ask Molly that question; instead she said, 'Do you remember the time Doris followed us up the river and caught us smoking dope? We were so out of it, all we could do was laugh in her face and she didn't even know what was going on.'

Molly had begun to chuckle. 'Not only that,' she added, 'but remember that letter she wrote to our parents, telling them how we were smoking cigarettes and they'd better have a talk with us? Remember that?'

'Do I,' Phoebe said. 'I still have this guilt complex for having deceived my mother. She showed me the letter and asked if I was smoking, and I said, smoking what? And she said, smoking *cigarettes*, obviously, I trust you do not smoke *marijuana*. And so I said, "No, Mum, I'm not smoking cigarettes – "'

'Mum,' Andrew whispered.

'I'm talking to Molly,' Phoebe said. 'Say excuse me if you have to interrupt.'

'Mum,' he whispered, this time a little more urgently, 'I have to go to the *bath*room.'

'Down the hall,' Molly told her. 'After the studio.'

Phoebe excused herself, and led Andrew out of the kitchen, past the loom and the spinning wheel and into the bathroom, which was almost as large as the kitchen itself. Against one wall stood a large commode, with towels on its shelves and dried flowers in a vase on top; by the window was an old rocking chair. Phoebe would have loved to have a bathroom like this, and for a second she imagined taking long baths with, oh, whomever (for Phoebe had hopes; she would fall in love again) in this long solid bathtub with its claw feet and porcelain handles. Outside a blizzard would rage, and they would add more hot water, nestling back, V'd against each other as the heat crept up their thighs.

'Wash your hands,' she said to Andrew. 'Isn't this fun, visiting Aunt Molly and Uncle Nick?' But her voice betrayed a certain exhaustion of cheer, and here, alone in the bathroom, she questioned how well the visit was really going. Oh, they were getting along, of course – but wasn't there some tension in the air? Maybe not; maybe she was looking too hard for this tension, after her conversation with Janice back at the law firm. Dammit, Phoebe, you don't always have to be looking on the dark side, you know. You could be optimistic, for once.

And yet she did sense tension. Like when she had asked Molly about her spinning – hadn't she act overly enthusiastic, as though trying to cover up whatever perplexity she was feeling over what Molly was doing with her life? Between that and the way she'd responded to the gift of the wall hanging she felt as though she had continually been putting her foot in her mouth; Molly would have been a fool not to pick up on this. On the other hand she didn't feel as though she was entirely at fault for whatever tension did exist – for Molly hadn't made any effort to find out about her job, about Judson and Day, about whether she liked practising law. Perhaps Molly thought that it was a subject that should be delved into more deeply, later – but still, didn't she merit a few perfunctory questions tonight? ('You look like shit,' echoed Herb's voice. 'Go take a bath.' Phoebe shuddered. Maybe it was just as well that Molly hadn't asked her about Judson and Day.)

Phoebe reflected back on their last conversation. They seemed to do best when they talked about old times together, she realized, and she recalled again their day together long ago, up in the wine country; then, they had finally relaxed when they started reminiscing. But that wasn't all they could talk about as adults, was it? Why, of course not – look, they had talked about the pregnancy. (Though it seemed a little stiff – not like two twenty-nine-year-old women talking about female concerns but rather like two children, out of their league.)

Phoebe wasn't sure what to think. Be patient, she told herself as a bottom-line piece of advice. You're probably tired, and it's the first night back. Give it a little more time.

Out in the kitchen she gathered together Andrew's mask, his jacket, her handbag, the wall hanging. 'We're going to run,' she told Molly. 'If I keep him up any later tomorrow's going to be a killer.'

'Thanks for coming down,' Molly said.

'Thanks for the wall hanging!' Phoebe exclaimed. 'Oh – my mother's invited Jack and Cindy Ann to dinner tomorrow night,' she said. 'You want to come up too? Both of you?'

'I can't make it,' Nick said. 'But you go, Molly.'

‘Come up in the late afternoon,’ Phoebe said. ‘We can take a walk down to the beaver pond; I promised Andrew that’s the first thing we’d do.’

‘All right,’ Molly said. ‘And thanks again for coming down.’

‘But I don’t want her to go to the beaver pond with us,’ Andrew said as they got in the car. ‘I just want me and *you* to go to the beaver pond.’

‘Andrew, honey,’ Phoebe said, ‘be nice?’

That night the temperature dropped below freezing; Phoebe, who went to sleep with her bedroom window open, was vaguely conscious of shivering all night long. She woke up at dawn with her legs drawn up, the faded pink-and-yellow patchwork quilt pulled snugly up around her neck. Her nose was cold and her breath formed a cloud in the crisp morning air. Outside a light frost had crystallized the fields, turning them into a brittle silver sea; and down in the far meadow a smoky mist hung over the beaver pond.

Phoebe drew the covers more tightly around her neck, hoping to slip back into an early-morning dream, dreading that first cold step on to the bare wood floor. But she was wide awake now, and her eyes fell upon Molly’s wall hanging, which she had draped over the rocking chair by the window the night before, perhaps as a way of getting used to it. What didn’t she like about it? Its lines were simple, it was really quite elegant – but it was the colour, she realized; the green was edging towards a shade of avocado that reminded her of sad hotel lobbies. Not only that but it would also clash with the dusty blues and pinks of her own living room. And of course as a gift from her oldest friend she would feel compelled to hang it up in a prominent place, as though that would reinforce any bond that she had been afraid might be splitting. Damn, she thought – I *like* my Miró print, I don't want to replace it with this wall hanging. Even if it is by Molly, and even if it is in good taste. Then she frowned inwardly with shame. Aren't we grateful, she thought. Aren't we appreciative.

She thought back to her reunion with Molly the night before. This morning, alone in her bed and well rested, she was inclined to think that apart from her reaction to the wall hanging (which hopefully was not as obvious to Molly as she had originally thought), the visit was off to a good start. Sure, it could have been a little less frenetically cheerful, but they would calm down. And although there might have been some tension, a bit of groping around for the right subject, Phoebe was certain that it would snap and they would be able to be as intimate about the things that really mattered to them today, approaching thirty, as they'd been as little girls, and then as teenagers, when nothing was hidden from the other, when every single daily development of body and mind was pooled for collective dissection. She had known Molly through and through back then, and vice versa; a few years apart could never erase such a history.

Relax, Phoebe told herself. You're still you, and Molly's still Molly. And if you operate on that assumption everything will fall into place.

Her room was directly over the kitchen, and from downstairs came the heavy banging of stove lids as her mother started a fire in the cookstove. Shortly afterwards Andrew appeared; she let him climb up into the high double bed with her, and they cuddled together until the smell of coffee and almonds drifted up through the circular iron heating grate.

'Want to get up?'

'No,' said Andrew. 'It's too cold.'

'Come on,' Phoebe said. 'It'll be warm down in the

kitchen.' Though we could use a little heat up here, she thought, wondering with vague annoyance if her mother had turned on the furnace for the winter yet.

Their leisurely breakfast that morning would have continued into the lunch hour, but at eleven o'clock Bea Adams rapped on the back door. Molly's mother wore a striped sweater and stretchy-looking jeans; she presented Louise with an irregularly shaped loaf of grainy-looking bread. 'I'm cleaning out my freezer for the wedding food,' she explained. (Phoebe, finishing up her third piece of Sara Lee coffee cake, immediately felt guilty. She knew what Bea's loaves contained – soy flour, potatoes, wheat germ, bran – and she didn't want to hear a lecture on the need for more roughage in her diet.)

Bea had come down to enlist Phoebe's help in carrying off a surprise shower for Molly. Here was the plan (Phoebe cut herself another piece of coffee cake at this point): She – Bea – would offer to babysit for Andrew on Thursday afternoon so that Phoebe and Molly could have some time alone together. At four o'clock she would call with the news that Andrew had fallen and cut his head; the wound was not bad, she would say, but he's screaming like the dickens for his mother and won't let me near him. Then she would tell Molly that she had found the slip to the wedding dress, and so Molly should also come up, to try the whole outfit on. And Phoebe was to make sure that Molly did indeed come along.

Phoebe thought a surprise shower for Molly was a terrible idea. True, she didn't know Molly very well these days; but one thing that had come across quite clearly last night was that with the pregnancy Molly was not up for all the trappings of a formal wedding.

'I don't know,' she said, wondering how much she could disclose without mentioning the pregnancy to Bea, who, according to everyone so far, wasn't supposed to know. 'I got the feeling last night that she doesn't really want a lot of fuss.'

'That's what Molly says,' Bea said. 'But when she walks into the living room and sees all of us there, all the presents, all the food – she'll be tickled pink!'

'I don't know if it'll go over the way you think it will,' Phoebe said, envisioning a sun-drenched dining room with white linen and silver candlesticks, chafing dishes steaming with creamed *things* to be spooned out over frozen patty shells, packages wrapped with wedding-bell paper. Not Molly's kind of event, not at all.

'It's not going to be a big affair, Phoebe,' Bea said, obviously irritated. 'It's going to be a very modest little party, right in keeping with the wedding.'

'How many people?'

Bea slipped on her glasses and scanned the list. 'There's the three of us plus Cindy Ann,' she said, 'then the girls from the school, Norma Welch and Susan Mitchell and hopefully Doris Conran. Oh, and I promised Ida Poultney, she's been wanting to be in on something.'

Phoebe still couldn't manage to look very excited.

'Oh, Phoebe, a wedding isn't a wedding without a shower!' Bea exclaimed.

'I had a shower,' Phoebe remarked. 'A lot of good it did me.'

Bea frowned, and raised her eyebrows.

'Look, I don't mean to put a damper on things,' Phoebe said. 'It's just that, oh, I don't know, surprise showers don't seem to be Molly's thing; surprise showers go with big formal weddings and – am I making any sense at all?'

But a look of disapproval had spread over Bea's face. 'This is a special time for Molly,' she told Phoebe. 'I know it may bring up some difficult memories for you, Phoebe, but you shouldn't let that spoil it for Molly.'

'It's hardly a question of difficult memories,' Phoebe

retorted. 'My own marriage is water over the dam, and believe me, I'm not shedding any tears about it any more.'

Bea continued to purse her lips, and didn't break her gaze. Phoebe felt as though she were six years old, and Bea were trying to get her to admit to having trampled down the flower bed, having taken the raisins from the pantry.

'I just think the shower's a bad idea,' Phoebe said. 'That's it. I've stated my case. I just think it's a bad idea.'

As soon as Bea left, Phoebe turned to her mother. 'How could she say that!' she exclaimed. 'Thinking that I don't want Molly to have a shower because I can't stand the memory of my own, like I'm some kind of basket-case divorcée? What kind of a person does she think I am, anyway?'

'Calm down, Phoebe,' Louise said.

'Jesus! If that were the problem do you think I'd have come back East for the wedding? Hell no, I'd have sent her a leftover fondue pot and wished her all the best!'

'Calm down, honey,' Louise said.

Phoebe shook her head. 'You watch,' she said. 'Tomorrow afternoon we'll all be sitting around stuffing ourselves with cake and Molly'll be in the bathroom throwing up. And everyone will be making like they haven't the fucking faintest idea of what's going on. We ought to just tell Bea,' Phoebe said. 'Then she might see things my way.'

'Phoebe,' Louise warned. 'Don't rock the boat. Bea is not the most open-minded woman in the world.'

'Well what does she think, her daughter's still a virgin? At twenty-nine?'

'Phoebe,' Louise said, 'Bea comes from a minister's family.'

'So what?' Phoebe exclaimed. 'She's living in the dark

ages if she can't accept her daughter getting pregnant first and married second.'

As she poured herself a cup of coffee Andrew walked into the kitchen wearing a blue bowl on his head, upside down. 'Look at this, Mum!' he said, just as the bowl slid off his head and crashed to the floor, shattering.

Sudden fury mushroomed up in Phoebe's head, bright and white. She grabbed his hand, whipped him around, and spanked the seat of his trousers.

'Oh, Phoebe, it's all right,' Louise said, frowning, 'it's just a dish – '

'I told you not to touch Grammy's special dishes!' Phoebe said, dragging him down the hall to the living room, where she pushed him down on the sofa. 'Now you stay there until I tell you it's okay to get up. I don't want to hear a *peep* out of you, do you understand?'

Andrew glared at her.

'I said DO YOU UNDERSTAND!' Phoebe yelled.

Andrew kept glaring at her; she turned and stomped back to the kitchen. 'Jet lag,' she said, lifting her coffee cup with shaking hands. 'He'll be better tomorrow.'

Louise knitted her brow.

Suddenly Phoebe's eyes stung with tears, and though she blinked rapidly they spilled out on to her cheeks. She cupped her hand to her brow. 'I'm a terrible mother,' she cried.

'Oh, Phoebe, you're just tired yourself,' Louise said.

'No, I am, I'm an awful mother,' Phoebe cried. 'I hate myself and I hate my job and I should never have come back East, this was all a big mistake. I don't have time for this trip and I don't want to be here, all I manage to do is make trouble, I'm sure everyone would just as soon I hadn't come.'

'That's not true, Phoebe,' Louise said. 'You know that's not true.'

But Phoebe felt as though she had alienated everyone at this point: certainly Bea, perhaps Molly, and now even her own child. She wanted to run, to be home alone on her balcony listening to the foghorns – but of course without having to go into Judson and Day the next morning. Which made it a ridiculous hope: because if she wasn't in Vermont enjoying herself at Molly's wedding festivities, she should be back in her office, reading documents, catching up on the rest of her work –

Oh, crap, Phoebe thought. You don't know *where* you want to be right now.

'Let me ask you something,' Louise said. 'May I ask you something?'

'What?' Phoebe said glumly.

'Are you dating anyone these days?'

*Dating* anyone? Oh, for heaven's sake. 'No, Mother,' Phoebe said. 'I'm not dating anyone, I'm not involved with anyone. I'm too busy to get involved with anyone.'

Louise gave a knowing smile. 'One is never too busy to get involved.'

'Hah,' said Phoebe. 'Tell that to the partner who reviews my billable hours. When you're doing litigation you don't have time even to fantasize about getting involved.' She told her mother about the all-nighter she had spent, rewriting the brief for Herb.

'You mean you didn't go home at all?' Louise demanded. 'With no dinner? No sleep? Honey, you can't work like that!'

Phoebe gave a wry laugh. 'I haven't got much choice, Mum,' she said.

'Then no wonder you're exhausted.' Louise adjusted the curls across Phoebe's forehead. 'Wouldn't it be different practising in a place like Burlington?' she said. 'Wouldn't the pressure be a lot less?'

Her mother's suggestion was so predictable that Phoebe

almost had to laugh to herself: she had baited her own trap and walked right into it. But she didn't laugh. She was too depressed to laugh. 'No, Mum,' she said. 'I'm not moving back. You know that. I do not now nor will I ever want to practise law in Burlington, Vermont.'

'Then forget Burlington,' Louise said quickly. 'What about Boston? Maybe now's the time,' she said. 'You really ought to give it a chance.'

Phoebe held up her hand. 'Mother,' she said tightly, 'I live in California now. I'm a member of the California bar. I like California. Now lay off the Boston bit!'

Louise stood up and began loading the dishwasher. Good going, Phoebe told herself; now you've alienated your mother too. She watched her mother silently wiping off the countertop, noticed the curve in her shoulders, the wisps of grey in her hair that suddenly seemed so prominent. Her mother was getting old. She could have high blood pressure, a stroke, a heart attack. Phoebe felt her stomach quicken as she realized how far away she would be if anything like that happened. Or worse; and she thought of Andrew growing up with only a vague recollection of this East Coast grandmother whom he had seen but twice in his life before she died. Tell me about your mother, he would say to her at twenty-five; what was she like? How old was I when we went back there? Didn't she have this big iron cookstove in the kitchen?

And yet what was she to do? Move back East, give everything up, just to be nearer her family?

'I'm sorry,' she said. 'I've just been under a lot of pressure, I'm a little snappy these days.'

'That's all right,' Louise said, and Phoebe marvelled at her mother's willingness to forgive so quickly. 'But take a nap this afternnon, for heaven's sake; don't let yourself ruin this entire visit just because you're overworked and overtired. Working all through the night,' she said, shaking her head. 'As though you were in college!'

'Molly's coming up this afternoon,' Phoebe said. 'We're going to take Andrew down to the beaver pond.'

'Then you tell Molly to take Andrew by herself,' Louise said. 'You're staying here and getting some rest. Or you're going to be a wreck for dinner tonight.'

Just then Andrew appeared in the doorway, clutching Binky, his orange rubber duck. With eyes cast downward he went over to Phoebe and put his head in her lap, murmuring into her crotch.

'He says he's sorry.' Phoebe stroked his head. 'He's tired, I'm tired. I'm sorry too,' she told him.

'It was just an old bowl anyway,' Louise said.

'Old bowl, right,' Phoebe said. 'It was Wedgwood.'

Andrew picked his head up. 'I was in a car crash once,' he told Louise. 'My dad doesn't let me drive but when I'm five I get to drive an aircraft.'

'Oh,' said Louise, '*my*.'

From her bed Phoebe could see Molly and her own red-jacketed son slowly making their way down through the field towards the beaver pond. The sky had clouded over, muting the late-autumn colours of the hills to gentle heathery shades of mauves, of shadowy blues and sagelike greens; looking out Phoebe thought of tweeds, of heavy grey sweaters flecked with brown and smelling of lanolin. These fields belonged to Molly's father, and she recalled the summer that Dave had hired Molly and herself to help with the haying. Her shoulders grew strong and broad that summer from sinking hooks into the bales of hay, hoisting them on to the lifts that chugged them from the wagon up to the second storey of the barn; she also went from a 34B to 36C, and credited it all to the job, though Molly, who had lifted at least as many bales as she, was still wearing her Gro-With-U stretch bra (and even that Bea had frowned upon as a waste of money).

By now Molly and Andrew had disappeared over the crest of the second hill, and Phoebe lay back against the pillow. She was glad, actually, for the time to herself, even if she didn't sleep; she felt she needed to be alone for a while. (After all, she was used to having a lot of time alone; she spent so much of her day at her desk, reading documents.) Yet she was relieved that her mother had assumed the blame for her not going, because she didn't want to risk offending Molly. 'Call me an ogre, I don't care,' Louise had said when Molly arrived. 'My daughter's got to have a nap or she'll eat us alive tonight.' Phoebe had rolled her eyes, smiled, shrugged helplessly. Molly had laughed, and leaned down to zip Andrew's jacket.

Out in the shed Louise was splitting wood; every few seconds came the quick clip of the axe. Her hair may be getting grey, and her shoulders may be a little stooped, but she certainly doesn't act like she's getting old, Phoebe thought. And after she'd chopped enough wood for the evening she would repair the toaster, which had broken just that morning; and then she would sit down with some mending, and then she might go out and fix the gutter that was falling off. Her mother was a whiz at everything around the house, in Phoebe's view; she could install a lock, rewire lamps, cane chairs, dewarp a drop-leaf table. She knew about plumbing, how to fix a water hammer, what to do when the pipes froze on the first of January, or when the toilet tank wouldn't stop running. She even knew about cars, tune-ups, oil changes. Unlike Phoebe, who panicked when handed a screwdriver; who had thrown away the coffee grinder when it just didn't *go* one morning; who had paid a woman two hundred dollars to recane three chairs.

It put her to shame, what her mother could do and she couldn't.

You could learn, she told herself. Maybe you could get her to show you how to rewire a lamp, say – or teach you the basics in electrical repair. The you could fix things around the house.

Who are you kidding? That's about as likely as your learning to weave from Molly. You're not a handywoman and you're not a craftswoman. And that's never going to change.

She wondered if any beavers would be out. She would have to go down to the pond herself; it would be so peaceful down there at this time of year, the steely grey water surrounded by birches and maples, balsam and spruce, its edges lined with cattails and rushes and reeds. She remembered the magic of the reeds as a child, their hollow cores, their serrated snapping-off points; they had always seemed to hold a music she was unable to hear.

Phoebe closed her eyes. Tonight Jack and Cindy Ann will be here. Along with Max. And Molly. Your mother will cook a nice dinner, and you'll make toasts: to Molly and Nick getting married, to Andrew's first visit to the East. Now fall asleep. When you wake up, you will be gald to see them all, and they will all be glad to see you. You won't have to try so hard. Everything will mesh.

# 6

Phoebe's older brother Jack and his wife, Cindy Ann, had been high-school sweethearts. He'd kept her picture on top of his bureau; she'd worn his knuckly class ring on a ribbon around her neck. Phoebe and Molly, then in grade school but newly informed on the reproductive process, had speculated endlessly on whether Jack and Cindy Ann were *doing it*. Of course they're *doing it*, Phoebe would insist (though at that age she had a hard time actually visualizing the act); they've been going out for two years, he's got a drawer full of those things, how could they not be *doing it*?

As it would turn out, Jack and Cindy Ann *had* in fact been doing it, because near the end of her senior year Cindy Ann became pregnant. In the midst of arranging for a wedding she lost the baby, but Jack insisted on going through with the marriage that summer; they were in love, and so they might as well marry sooner rather than later. That ten-week pregnancy would be the only one Cindy Ann would ever know; while over the course of many years she and Jack would faithfully make love regularly on her fertile days, nothing would ever take to the womb. Just a few years ago, though, they had finally put their names on an adoption list, and their arguments now resolved around whether to hold out for a healthy white infant (Jack's preference), or whether, as Cindy Ann was urging, to 'open up their options a little more.'

Phoebe was shocked when she saw Cindy Ann that Wednesday afternoon. From the yearly Christmas photos she knew her sister-in-law had gained a little weight, but nobody had warned her it would be so much. Cindy Ann weighed over two hundred pounds, Phoebe estimated: now how could she have let herself go like that? (There you go again! Criticizing everyone you see!) Tonight Cindy Ann was wearing a giant red tent dress with Argyle knee socks and flip-flop clogs, and Phoebe must not have controlled her expression, because Cindy Ann made a quick comment about a glandular deficiency, and hastily turned her attention to Andrew. 'Did you ride in an *aircraft*?' she asked. 'Did you go way up in the *air*?'

Her brother Jack, who was a state trooper, had changed in a different way. Phoebe had never been very close to him; as children their age difference had always seemed insurmountable despite the fact that they'd grown up in such an isolated area; and by the time they were old enough for a five-year difference to become irrelevant – well, Jack was married and off patrolling Interstate 89, and Phoebe was down at Wellesley getting stoned and protesting the war. The last time she'd seen him was before leaving for the West. In those six years her brother's face had become more angular, and his hair had thinned out a little; but as they hugged, Phoebe picked up on another, more subtle change: he smelled different. He smelled like a mixture of household cleaners: Bab-o, Lestoil, maybe a little carpet shampoo; and because of this he smelled older to Phoebe than he should have, more alien, in fact; no longer just like her older brother but like someone approaching a sad middle age: a man with a prefab house, and an obese wife, and a history of infertility.

'Long time no see,' said Jack, stepping back and grinning.

'No kidding,' Phoebe said.

'You don't look like a lawyer,' he said.

'You don't look like a cop,' she said.

'He's not just a cop,' Cindy Ann said. 'He's a *state* cop.'

'Well, you don't look like a state cop either,' Phoebe said.

Jack grinned again, and gave his head a shake. 'Still getting in that last word,' he said. 'Haven't changed a bit.'

Jack and Cindy Ann had picked up Max from the nursing home on their way up to the house, and so right away Louise removed her apron and herded everyone into the living room to line up on the sofa so that Molly could take a picture of the entire family – four generations, Max kept pointing out – together at last.

'Commere, Andy,' Cindy Ann said, 'Come sit on ole Cindy Ann's lap for the picture.'

'Is my wig okay?' Max asked. 'Does my hair show?'

'You look fine,' said Phoebe.

'You gotta take the lens cap off,' Jack told Molly.

'I know that,' said Molly. She took the lens cap off.

'Ole Cindy Ann'll cry if you don't sit on her lap, Andy,' Cindy Ann said.

'Something's burning,' Max said. 'Do I smell something burning or is it just me?'

'Boo hoo,' Cindy Ann said. 'Look what you're making ole Cindy Ann do, Andy; ole Cindy Ann's crying now cuz you won't sit on her lap.'

For heaven's sake, thought Phoebe; is this going to go on all night?

'Okay,' Molly said, 'ready on three.'

Andrew climbed on to Phoebe's lap and buried his face against her shoulder.

'One, two, *three*!'

'The flash didn't go off,' Jack said. 'You have to turn the flash on.'

'I know that,' Molly said. She turned the flash on.

'Look at the camera, honey,' Phoebe whispered to Andrew. 'Just for one second.'

'Ready on three,' Molly said. 'One, two, three!'

Phoebe blinked.

'There!' Louise said, rising. 'Now, if it doesn't come out we'll just have to get you back here at Christmastime, Phoebe.'

'It'll come out,' Phoebe said. 'I'm sure it'll come out.'

Along with her dessert – a chocolate banana supreme cake made from a variety of mixes – Cindy Ann had brought a gallon jug of Carlo Rossi Chablis; and though it was not Phoebe's favourite brand (there you go again; you are such a snob!) she poured herself a large glass and began setting the table with Molly while Jack took Andrew out to his police car and turned on the siren and the flashing lights. As they laid out plates and silverware Molly told Phoebe that after visiting the beaver pond ('No beavers,' she said, 'though Andrew'll try and tell you he saw one'; and Phoebe detected a note of authority in Molly's voice that irked her: she didn't like hearing someone else predict what her child would try and do), they went up to the Adamses' house.

'Daddy's wild about Andrew,' Molly said. 'He even invited him up tomorrow afternoon, to help him work in the garden.'

So Bea was going ahead with the shower plans. Phoebe wondered if she should give Molly some advance warning. Maybe later, she thought. Maybe tomorrow afternoon, before Bea makes her preplanned phone call. You owe it to her.

'Tell me more about this trial you're working on,' Molly said. 'Who are you suing?'

'No one,' Phoebe said. 'They're suing us.'

'Who's us?'

'The price-fixers,' Phoebe said. 'The bad guys. You

know, the guys I was never going to be caught dead representing?'

Molly began folding napkins. 'So what do you do,' she said. 'Do you go to court? Do you argue strategy with the other lawyers?'

'I read documents,' Phoebe said.

'Oh,' Molly said. 'Well,' she said, after a few seconds, 'that must be pretty interesting.'

'And sometimes I write briefs,' Phoebe said. 'But mostly I read documents.'

'Huh,' Molly said.

Phoebe gave a wry laugh. 'Sounds pretty bleak, doesn't it.'

'I don't know,' Molly said. 'Maybe the documents are interesting.'

But it did sound bleak; it sounded terribly bleak, reading documents and preparing for depositions; and Molly was just being polite. Phoebe thought back to John Dunn advising her to take a deposition. As things stood now her role was to organize the relevant documents for Herb and back him up while he asked the questions during the deposition; but maybe John was right, maybe she should try and ask the questions herself. Phoebe had always assumed that taking a deposition was the last thing she wanted to do: going on the record, pretending to be in command, trying to coerce and intimidate some guy twenty years her senior into answering questions that he had no intention of answering: it was terrifying to her. But maybe that was the wrong attitude: after all, she'd gone to Berkeley, she'd done law review; she was as competent as anyone else, certainly as competent as John Dunn. If she could draft deposition outlines for Herb, there was no reason why she couldn't ask the questions herself. It was all a matter of self-confidence.

Which Phoebe, at this point in her career, was lacking.

She wondered how Herb would react if she asked him if she could take one of the upcoming depositions. Herb, I've been thinking, she would say, I'd like to have a shot at a deposition – Hah. He'd never let you do it, she thought, not after you pulled that stunt by writing the brief for the protective order when they'd already stipulated to the underlying issue. You don't keep on top of things, Herb would reply; how're you going to handle a deposition when you can't even keep yourself up to date with what's happening on the case?

Well why don't you give me a chance, Herb, she thought, suddenly angry: a real chance, rather than judging me by some fluke mishap where you go and negotiate on your own and then expect me to find out about it. I'm not an investigator, I'm a lawyer. I do my work. And I do it *well*.

For the most part.

'What's the matter?' Molly asked.

Phoebe realized she had been scowling at the dried flower arrangement in the centre of the table.

'Nothing,' she said, because she didn't want to go into it: at this point she didn't know how to begin to explain the frustrations of her job to someone who had never spent a day at her law firm, nor come into contact with Herb Sullivan. Even if she and Molly could completely relax with one another tonight, even if that good long catching-up talk were possible, where would she start? With Herb? The Nuts and Bolts? The all-nighters, the weekend hours?

Just then Louise came in with a platter of ham, followed by Cindy Ann, who set a casserole of scalloped potatoes down on the table.

'Looks good,' Phoebe said to her mother; but Molly had clapped her hand to her mouth, and her eyes were darting from the floor to the window and back to the floor again.

'Are you all right, Molly?' Louise asked.

Molly gave a quick nod.

'You sure?' Phoebe asked.

Molly hurried out of the dining room.

'What's wrong with her?' said Jack, coming in with Andrew.

'Nerves,' said Louise, casting a warning glance at Phoebe, who rolled her eyes.

'You remember,' Cindy Ann said, poking her husband's stomach. 'You told me you threw up *five* times the night before our wedding!'

Max was having difficulties with a man named Julian who lived down the hall. Julian was a pest: in the past month he had gone through a quart of her bourbon and hadn't made one move towards replacing it. 'Nothing but a big mooch,' Max said during dinner; 'and not only that, but now he's following me into the dining room and doesn't let me talk to anyone else at the table.'

'He has a crush on you, Mother,' Louise said.

'I don't have to go to bed early tonight,' Andrew announced.

'Little boys shouldn't interrupt,' Max said. 'My children never interrupted.'

'Finish your ham, Andrew,' Phoebe said. 'If you finish your ham you can stay up until eight-thirty.' The longer he stayed up the easier it would be to put him to bed; she hoped to get him into his pyjamas right after dinner and let him stay up until he fell asleep, to avoid any squabble over the matter.

'Peek-a-boo!' Cindy Ann sang, splaying her fingers over her eyes. 'I-see-you!'

'I've lost my train of thought now,' Max said. 'I forgot where I was.'

Just then Molly returned to the table. Her face was pale, and damp tendrils of hair curled against her temples. Phoebe tried to catch her eye, but Molly seemed intent on dishing out healthy-looking portions of food.

'How's your house?' Phoebe asked her brother. When Jack had finished police school he and Cindy Ann had bought a prefabricated house and installed it on a thistle-covered acre of land nearby. In her annual Christmas box Cindy Ann always enclosed a snapshot, and year after year the pose never changed: Jack and Cindy Ann cuddling on their love seat with Geronimo, their German shepherd, lapping at the air by their knees. Over the years the photos had shown numerous changes in the decor: an orange-and-yellow shag rug, heavy green drapes, a bold flowered slipcover for the love seat. Phoebe was not looking forward to visiting them; she imagined the house had a tired, sour smell from a lack of fresh air and light, since Cindy Ann religiously kept the drapes pulled to protect her slipcovers. Besides, every year Cindy Ann seemed to have taken up a new hobby – découpage, stained glass, macramé – making doodads, Louise said, because she couldn't make a baby – and Phoebe would have to admire her handiwork (which in Phoebe's view was void of any artistic merit) and envy her for having the time for such projects. You're so lucky, was what she would have to say; I wish I had time for crafts. When that was the last thing she wanted.

Now Jack said, 'The house is sinking.'

'That's right,' Cindy Ann said, swallowing. 'Can you believe it? That piece of property they sold us is just a bog!'

'It's the sewer,' Jack said. 'The sewer's leaking all over the place.'

'Grammy,' said Andrew.

'It makes me so angry I could cry.' Cindy Ann swallowed again. 'All the flowers I planted died, and then I went to the bathroom one day and the toilet didn't flush right, and then Jack took a good look at the bedroom wall and said, "Cindy Ann, this house is sinking." Isn't that just what you said, Jack?'

Phoebe shook her head sympathetically.

'Maybe Phoebe can help,' Louise said. 'Can't they sue somebody, Phoebe?'

Phoebe picked a string bean off Andrew's plate and ate it. 'Maybe,' she said. 'I'm not very good with property law.'

'Seems to me that they should be able to at least sue the man who sold them the lot,' Louise said. 'That's just common sense.'

'As a matter of fact he did tell us there was nothing wrong with the land,' Cindy Ann said. 'He told us there was good drainage, he told us we'd never have any trouble with the sewer system. Remember, Jack? Remember him saying that?'

Molly cut a piece of ham, brought it up to her mouth, set it back down.

'Do you know where the deed is?' Phoebe asked. 'You could look at the deed and see what kind of warranties he made. You might have some kind of a cause of action, though I'm not too sure; like I said, I wasn't very good at property law.'

'I'll check the deed,' Jack said. 'There may have been some other papers too.'

'Grammy,' said Andrew.

'Speaking of legal problems we should ask Phoebe about Muffet,' Cindy Ann said. 'Tell Phoebe about Muffet, Jack.'

'You tell her, honey,' Jack said. 'You tell stories better than me.'

'Muffet Downey?' said Molly.

'That's right,' Jack said.

'I like Muffet,' Molly said. 'Muffet's cute.'

'Who,' Phoebe said, 'is Muffet?'

'Muffet's the Downeys' Irish setter,' Cindy Ann said. 'He's really just a puppy, and last summer Joey – that's the Downeys' little boy – was walking Muffet by our house and he threw a stick for Muffet and it landed in my zinnias – this was before they started dying from the leaking sewer. Anyway, the zinnias were full of yellow jackets and when the stick landed in the zinnias the yellow jackets came after me!'

'Ouch,' said Phoebe.

'*Grammy*,' said Andrew.

'You're darn tootin' it was ouch,' Cindy Ann declared, 'but that's not all, I was carrying this vase I had just painted out to the car and when I got stung of course I dropped the vase and it shattered all to pieces.'

'It was a nice one too,' said Jack. 'I liked that vase.'

'So did I,' said Cindy Ann. 'Anyway: shouldn't the Downeys pay me for my vase?'

Phoebe cut Andrew's ham into tinier chunks. 'Well, this is interesting,' she said, 'because the question here is whether it was foreseeable to the little boy – or maybe even to his mother, when she let him take Muffet for a walk – anyway, whether it was foreseeable that throwing the stick into the flower bed would result in your dropping the vase.'

Cindy Ann frowned.

'It's a question of proximate cause, you see,' Phoebe explained. 'Was it reasonably foreseeable that there would be yellow jackets where he threw the stick? That the yellow jackets would sting you instead of him, that you would drop the vase?'

Molly pushed her string beans about on her plate.

'And then there's the issue of damages,' Phoebe went on. 'Was it just any old vase? Or was it a valuable handcrafted vase?'

'But all I want to know is, shouldn't they *pay*,' Cindy Ann said.

'I think they should,' Molly said. 'I think it's black and white.'

'It was a beautiful vase,' Jack said. 'I think it was worth quite a lot. You never know who might have paid a lot of money for that vase. These people, they come up from New York, they love that kind of stuff, handcrafted gizmos and all.'

'Maybe you should just ask the Downeys to pay for it,' Molly said.

'I did,' Cindy Ann said. 'Mrs Downey said no, they'd rather just get rid of Muffet.'

'Oh, no!' exclaimed Molly.

'And I don't want them to get rid of Muffet,' Cindy Ann said. 'I like Muffet. I just don't like getting stung and dropping my vase when Muffet chases after a stick.'

'Well,' Phoebe said. 'I don't know what you should do. But it's an interesting tort question.'

Molly yawned.

'*Grammy!*' said Andrew.

'Yes, honeybunch,' Louise replied.

Andrew looked around at all the expectant faces at the table. 'I don't like ham,' he said in a small voice.

'One more bite,' Phoebe said, 'and then you can be excused.' Andrew speared a small piece of the pink meat, popped it into his mouth, and washed it down with the rest of his milk.

'My children always belonged to the clean-plate club,'

Max remarked as Andrew climbed down from his chair. 'Throwing away food was like throwing away pennies.'

'He's usually pretty good,' Phoebe said. 'He's keyed up.'

'See you later, alligator,' Cindy Ann said.

Andrew stared at her.

'Say, "In a while, crocodile!"' Cindy Ann said, smiling.

'Do I have to say that, Mum?' he said.

'No,' Phoebe said. 'You can be excused now.'

'Here, I'll finish his plate,' Cindy Ann said; 'no sense letting it go to waste.' But there wasn't much left, and soon it was time for Cindy Ann's dessert, which Phoebe didn't have room for but which she dutifully ate. They spent the rest of the evening in the living room playing hearts. Phoebe tried to shoot the moon, and neither Molly nor Jack nor Cindy Ann could stop her.

'Hasn't changed a bit, has she,' Jack said to Molly, grinning. 'Always shooting the moon, always putting up a string of hotels on Boardwalk.'

Well, all right, Phoebe thought later that evening; maybe I did get a little competitive about the game. She recalled the long rainy summer afternoons when she and Molly and Jack too – forced by the bad weather to play with his little sister – would set up the Monopoly board in front of the fireplace. Molly would go broke within an hour, leaving Jack and Phoebe to compete for houses and hotels, for Park Place and Atlantic Avenue. And Phoebe would consistently manage to land her tiny hatpiece on all the right spaces. (Of course, look who's the property owner now, Phoebe wanted to point out to her brother; your land may have a sewage problem but at least it's yours.) But so I was competitive; so what? At least I made things a little more interesting tonight; nobody else took the initiative. Besides, the game was going to go on for ever at the rate we were playing.

And anyway – it's *not* true that I haven't changed a bit, she wanted to say to her brother – and to Molly, too, and Louise, and Bea, to anyone back here who thought they really knew her. I'm different now, she wanted to say. I've gone through a divorce; I work for a man who constantly undermines my confidence; things aren't coming as easily as they used to; and I *never* get the last word on anything, Jack! How can you tell me I haven't changed a bit?

Yet hadn't she been afraid it would be this way, that they would be inclined to see in her the girl she used to be and not the woman she had become? Wasn't it because of this, in fact, that she had chosen to stay out in California? There were no roles she had to feel locked into when living so far away from her past; she was free to be as strong or as weak, as optimistic or as pessimistic, as she wanted. Back here in Vermont, though – well, Phoebe had a terrible feeling that as soon as she saw Doris Conran, for instance, she would revert to being sixteen again: angry, rebellious, defiant; the know-it-all who wore her black armbands religiously, who tried so hard to make sure that everything she did was so consistently left wing, consistently cynical. Phoebe had stopped smoking when she was pregnant, but she was sure that tomorrow afternoon at the shower she would want to light up again, merely to flaunt it in Doris Conran's face. Winslow just brought out the worst in her.

(Which is probably why you're not very partial to the wall hanging, she realized, glancing at Molly's tapestry, which still lay draped over her rocking chair. It was like receiving a *Vermont Life* calendar: pretty scenes of changing seasons that somehow sought to trap you once again.)

As Phoebe undressed for bed she wondered if perhaps she wasn't making the same mistake, failing to update her own image of everyone back here – locking them into old roles, viewing them as though they, too, hadn't changed a bit. Of course with Jack it was difficult to gauge the extent of any real change, since she doubted whether she had ever known him very well in the first place. But what about Molly – whom she'd once known better than anyone? How had Molly changed? And how willing was she, Phoebe, to reacquaint herself with a new Molly? Maybe she wasn't giving Molly a chance; maybe she was still bent on seeing her as the shy one, the deferential one, the friend who would always listen as Phoebe tried to come up with a solution to everything. (What a burden that had been, after all.) Yet in these last six years Molly, too, must have moulted; she'd fallen in love, she was struggling to sell her artwork, she'd decided to have a child – but how did it all add up to an adult woman?

Phoebe recalled their conversation last night, when she had drawn Molly into reminiscing about the teachers at the high school. 'God, that place doesn't change!' she had said. So yes, in a way she, like Jack, was guilty of perpetuating a few outdated images: of the teachers at the high school, if not of Molly herself. Phoebe suddenly wondered if their tendency – or rather, *her* tendency – to slip so readily into reminiscing wasn't perhaps indicative of an underlying ambivalency: for although she claimed to want to move away from that territory, maybe she was in fact afraid of what she might encounter if they were to open up. Maybe she wouldn't be able to understand the woman Molly had become; maybe she wouldn't even *like* Molly.

Phoebe buttoned the back of her nightgown, frowning. It troubled her, of course, to think that she might not like the woman Molly had become; but it troubled her, too, that she might be choosing to play it safe by reminiscing, for it made everything seem so superficial between them. And yet the idea of asking Molly the questions that were really on her mind – Don't you feel constricted, living in your hometown? Don't you want to break away from all these preconceived notions of who you are? And how on earth is it possible to deal with someone like Doris Conran as an adult, a professional, a peer? – asking these questions seemed unthinkable. She might have been able to ask them of a new acquaintance, with whom she shared no history; but to Molly they were sure to come off as condescending – and who was *she*, anyway, to come down on her friend for staying here in Winslow? What she should be focusing on, simply, was not how Molly could possibly stand living in her hometown, and not old times, either, but rather whether her friend was happy. Whether it was really working out, trying to separate creative activity from income-producing activity. Did she ever wish she'd gone on with geology instead? As a child, Phoebe recalled, Molly had wanted to become an astronomer; her room was filled with star charts, and one Christmas she received a telescope, which she aimed out of her bedroom window, charging her parents ten cents to look at the moon. Then she had decided that it wasn't stars but rather cells that she wanted to study, and for her thirteenth birthday she received a microscope, which she also set up in her room, spending long hours preparing slides with strands of hair, or smears of blood, or the fragile peelings of sunburned skin.

Funny the way we both had such glamorous aspirations, she mused (putting aside for the moment the issue of how Molly had changed, and how clumsy she felt, trying to understand those changes). She herself had aspired to become a ballerina, and then an anthropologist. Had anyone ever told her she would become a lawyer when she grew up, she would have scoffed at the ida. Lawyers were a dusty sort; they worked over storefronts in St Audenbury with Venetian blinds in the windows and dark lacquered moulding around the doorways and long dim greenish halls leading to dirty drinking fountains. Their faces were pale, their glasses unpolished; they needed fresh air and sunlight. Who would volunteer for such a life?

Well? she asked herself. Do you like it, now that you're a member of that dusty profession? Judson and Day aside, Herb Sullivan aside: if you had to do it all over again, would you have chosen this line of work?

She would.

Sure it got a little dry at times; sure the hours were long; sure it left her with little time for Andrew, or outside interests. But the underlying issues, they were challenging to her, they really were. Even Cindy Ann's problem with Muffet Downey: she could have gone on and on at the dinner table about that routine kind of issue. (Though I probably came off as a real John Dunn, she thought, a little embarrassed. I probably came off as a real show-off. Oh, well.) And she like the process of legal reasoning. Sometimes a particular line of argument would seem so foolproof, so tight, so unassailable; and she would think about it and think about it and think about it until she thought it was not possible to think about it any more, and then it would come to her: what precisely it was that was wrong with the argument. And she would sit back and smile, and realize that, yes, she *had* grown; despite the boredom, despite the fear, despite the knots in her stomach when Herb buzzed her – her mind was working one notch higher than it had been the day before. It was exhilarating, in its own methodical way, and she liked surprising herself, proving to herself that she could do it.

Phoebe went in and checked on Andrew; he was lying flat on his back, arms flung above his head. He does look a little like Jack, she thought, leaning over to kiss him; maybe even like the image of her own father, whom she had never had a chance to know. She was Andrew's age when he died, and she could remember that day so clearly: a hot summer afternoon, beads of sweat collecting on a pitcher of lemonade, a blue-black fly buzzing frantically against an oily strip of yellow flypaper. 'Jack and Phoebe,' her mother had said, 'your father's been in an accident. He's not going to be coming home again.'

What memories from early childhood would Andrew be able to recall, she wondered, tucking the covers around him. Day care? His parents shuffling him from one house to the other, squabbling endlessly? A plane trip to Vermont, where his mother spanked him for breaking a dish? Or Grammy Louise stoking her woodstove, far away, in a house that was never quite warm enough?

That night she found herself unable to sleep; finally around midnight she tiptoed down to the kitchen and dialled Janice's number. A Wednesday night: she might be out to dinner with Stu, but maybe she'd be home.

Janice was drunk. 'I'm so glad you called,' she said giddily. 'You're not going to believe this, Phoebe, you're going to die.'

'What?'

'It's Frank,' said Janice. 'I'm telling you, you're going to die.'

'Francis Clapp?'

'That's right,' Janice said. 'Francis Clapp had a heart attack!'

Phoebe stared at the stack of bills on the telephone table.

'And you know where it happened?'

'Where?'

'Room seven twenty-one at the Hyatt.'

'Don't tell me,' Phoebe said.

'You got it,' Janice said. 'Julianna was right by his side.' Julianna was Francis Clapp's secretary, a plump dark-haired woman with a small berry-coloured mouth and painted nails to match.

'He's all right now,' Janice went on; 'he's out of intensive care but rumour has it that the firm is pressuring him to leave. Seeing as nobody really liked him anyway, this gives them a great excuse.'

Phoebe thought of forty-five-year-old Francis Clapp, his gangly limbs too long for his suits, the pasty dough texture of his face, the drawn-out monotony of his voice. Hellllowww, Phooeeebee, he would drone, pouring milk into his tea. How are things with Parco-Fieeeeelds? Not exactly your prime candidate for a heart attack, not at that age. Then she thought of Herb Sullivan, his torso thickened with steak, prime rib, shrimp, and crab, the boozy redness of his eyes, the long vein that stood out on his forehead when he flew into one of his frequent frenzies –

'You do realize what this means, don't you?' Janice was saying.

'What?'

'Phoebe! No more wills! No more probate! I'm free, finished with all this necrophilia!'

'Janice – '

'I mean, is it litigation time or is it litigation time?'

'Janice, get a hold of yourself.'

'I am. Stu – over here – I'll take a little more of

that, thank you very much. We're having kiwi daiquiris, Phoebe; wish you could be here.'

'Janice, I hate to break this to you, but just because Frank's out of the picture doesn't mean the wills are going to go away.'

'Of course it does. He's the only one who does this kind of work. All his clients will go with him.'

'I don't think so, Janice. It wasn't Frank Clapp they liked, it was Judson and Day. Even if some of them go, there will still be the ones who'll want to stay on with a big-name firm.'

Janice was silent.

'You're the only one now,' Phoebe said. 'They'll stick some partner on to oversee your work but you're the only one who knows what's going on. You're the expert.'

Janice was still silent.

'Maybe I'm wrong,' Phoebe said, 'but I wouldn't get your hopes up. Besides, what if they make you work for Herb?'

'It'd be better than wills,' Janice said.

'Wrong,' Phoebe said. 'Wrong, wrong, wrong.'

When Janice spoke again her voice was flat. 'Well, so much for celebration,' she said. 'I shouldn't be getting drunk on a work night anyway.'

'I guess I threw a damper on things,' Phoebe said. 'I'm sorry.'

'Yeah, well,' said Janice. 'Jesus, it's depressing.'

Phoebe tried to think of something that would cheer her friend up. 'It's not that bad,' she said; 'I mean, it's not as if we have to stay there – hell, we could phone in our resignations tomorrow and go open up an office in Oakland!'

'Ha ha,' said Janice. 'Very funny, Phoebe.'

But though Phoebe meant it somewhat as a joke, there

was an element of hope, of possibility, in what she was saying. 'It's not *that* off the wall,' she said.

'Come on, Phoebe,' Janice scoffed.

'Really,' Phoebe said. 'You've always said you wanted to set up your own firm – we could do it together.'

'It's too soon,' Janice said dully. 'I haven't found a squawk box yet.'

'But the longer we stay, the more we cement a connection between law and Judson and Day,' Phoebe said. 'I don't hate law, do you? I just hate the firm.'

'And so you think we should go out on our own, now, at the ripe old age of twenty-nine, three years out of law school. Okay, tell me this,' Janice said. 'How would we set up an office? How would we get clients? How would we even pay ourselves?'

'I don't know,' Phoebe said. 'But we could figure it out. We're not stupid.'

'Sure, we'll figure it out while we're sitting alone in some slum of an office down in the Tenderloin,' Janice said, 'looking out of our windows at skin-flick joints and wondering how to pay the rent. We'll be right next to Grand Central Sauna and we won't even be able to afford to go.'

Phoebe tried to respond, but the optimistic fever needed to counteract Janice's despondency was cooling. She wasn't really serious about this idea, anyway – at least she didn't think she was; it was just an attempt to make Janice feel better. And she wasn't even succeeding at that. She wanted to go to bed.

'Look,' Janice said. 'I appreciate the effort. Any other time and I'd probably think it was a great idea. Right now, though, nothing's going to go over well. Dashed expectations, you know?'

'I know,' Phoebe said. 'It was just a joke, anyway.'

'How's the visit going? How are things with your friend Molly?'

'All right,' said Phoebe cautiously. 'Though it's kind of hard to know where to begin, you know? I seem to divide my time between rehashing old times with her or else gushing over her work – neither of which gets us very far. But thumbs up,' she said. 'We're going to spend tomorrow afternoon together. Oh, by the way, she's pregnant.'

'No kidding,' Janice said. 'Why didn't she tell you that before?'

'I don't know,' Phoebe said, defensive now, for this was still a sore point for her. 'She probably wanted to tell me in person.' Except that she never actually told you, she reminded herself; you went und blurted it out.

'And how's Andrew doing?'

'Other than breaking my mother's Wedgwood, fine,' said Phoebe. 'Everybody's wild about him – tomorrow he's going to spend the day with Molly's parents.'

'Give him a hug,' said Janice. 'Give him a big kiss for me.'

'I will.'

'And thanks for calling,' Janice said. 'I miss you. It's lonely in the office. I even had lunch with John Dunn yesterday.'

Phoebe laughed.

'Oh it was *fun*,' Janice drawled. 'We talked about ripeness and standing. Those are big issues in the case he's working on.'

'*His* case, you mean.'

'Right,' Janicc said. 'John Dunn's case. Well, guess I'll get some sleep so I can dig into all those wills bright and early tomorrow morning.'

'Think about what I said, though,' Phoebe said. 'In terms of the long run, you know? It might not be such a joke. We could be name partners. Martin and Williams, Williams and Martin – either way, it sounds good.'

'How about Will-Mar,' said Janice, 'or Mar-Will. That way we could open up a trailer resort if it doesn't work out. Mar-Will Vistas,' she said. 'Will-Mar Estates.'

Phoebe's second morning was not nearly as leisurely as the first; her mother was busy baking for Molly's shower, and so to get out of her way Phoebe set Andrew up at the dining-room table with old newspapers and finger-paints, and sat down to read a memorandum she had brought along from the office. But before she had even finished the introduction Dave Adams was knocking at the door. Bea had kicked him out so she could clean up for the shower, he explained, and he wondered if Andrew could come up and help him with the garden now instead of waiting until the afternoon.

Just then Andrew appeared in the doorway.

'Hi there, champ,' Dave said.

'I'm fingerpainting,' Andrew said. He held up his hands, which glistened red.

'Mr Adams – '

'Uncle Dave,' said Dave. 'Please.'

'Uncle Dave wants you to come up and help him in the garden,' Phoebe said. 'Would you like to help him in the garden?'

'I'm making a jogger,' Andrew said. He wiggled his fingers.

'Really, I just got him set up with the paints,' Phoebe said. 'How about if I bring him up in another hour?'

'Sure,' said Dave. 'See you then, tiger.'

Despite Phoebe's advice the shower was still on for four o'clock. Doris Conran had switched to a Definite, so there were going to be nine women in all – nine too many, in Phoebe's view. But the plans had solidified:

presents had been bought and wrapped; food was being prepared. Susan Mitchell, for instance, was bringing her ham croquettes; Ida Poultney had made tomato aspic; and Cindy Ann was baking a chocolate Cool Whip cake.

Cindy Ann, in fact, could hardly wait for the shower. The night before she had taken Phoebe aside to show her the guest towels she had embroidered for Molly: they were sunshine yellow, with large army-green *U*'s, for Ulrich, at one end, bordered with orange squiggles. 'They're gorgeous,' Phoebe had said, wondering if she had ever seen anything more hideous; 'you really have a knack for handiwork, Cindy Ann.' 'Oh, it's easy,' Cindy Ann had laughed; 'any dummy can do it!' 'Not me,' Phoebe had declared; 'the day I pick up an embroidery needle is the day I die.' And naturally after saying it she felt terrible: because once again she had managed to turn a compliment into an insult. All Cindy Ann had to know was that Phoebe *couldn't* embroider; yet Phoebe had to go and make it appear as though she didn't think very much of people who *could*. Why couldn't you have just complimented her and let it go at that? she thought angrily. Why were you so bent upon shoving your values down her throat? For once can't you grant these people their due?

Later that morning she and Andrew walked up to the Adamses' house. Dave was out in the garden. He had changed into an old grey sweatshirt and jeans, and he wore an orange hunting cap backwards on his head, the brim sloping down his neck. He'd been hoeing over a row of green onions that had grown too large and then died with a succession of frosts. Phoebe could still smell them, their pungency diluted with the smell of freshly turned earth. The rest of the garden had been harvested long ago, except for a few scattered pumpkins and butternut squash; behind Dave stood several rows of cornstalks, dead-brown and brittle, their leaves crackling whenever the wind picked up.

'Hey there, champ,' Dave said, continuing with his work. 'How about giving me a hand?'

Andrew lowered his head.

'Go ahead, honey,' Phoebe said. 'It's fun working in the garden.'

'I don't want to work in his garden,' Andrew said. 'I want to go with you and visit that *girl*.'

'Oh, but your mum wants some time alone with Molly,' Dave said. 'Your mum and Mary Elizabeth want to sit around and drink coffee and yak it up this afternoon, girl talk, just the two of them. Here,' he said, and he pulled from his pocked a small orange cap that said JOHN DEERE in black on the front. Andrew hesitated, then walked over and put it on backwards, his bangs sticking out unevenly from the front. He looked from Dave to Phoebe, then back to Dave again, and rubbed his chest.

'You collect the onions I've already dug up,' Dave told him. 'Put them over there in the straw basket. What do you say, champ?'

Andrew looked back at Phoebe, who nodded; then he squatted and spread his hands around in the dirt, sifting it in his fingers. She wondered if he would do the work or whether he would just horse around; but it wasn't long before Andrew was stumbling across the soft damp earth, his arms full of the long celery-coloured stems with their fringed white bulbs, clumps of dirt raining from the roots as he shook them over the basket before letting them fall.

'He should have a nap from one to three!' she called out to Dave. Then she turned and left them together. She resented Bea's plan more than ever right now, wished she weren't being prised away from her child. After all, part of the reason for the trip was to give her some extra time with him. Damn Bea and her silly shower, her silly concocted plot for getting Molly up to the house. And damn *you*, she scolded herself, for not putting your foot down; even if you didn't tell Bea just *why* the shower was such a lousy idea, you could have at least forced her to come up with a different scheme so that you didn't have to be apart from Andrew.

But that wasn't written into the script. As it was, she and Molly were to have their little chunk of time together. Which she would have been looking forward to, except for the fact that Bea was forcing it upon them. Phoebe resented Bea structuring her vacation; this bossy treatment, designed to serve Bea's purposes more than anyone else's (now we're going to pick blueberries, girls; now we're going to hunt for wild asparagus, won't that be fun) only fuelled a matching childlike belligerence in Phoebe, a surliness that she hoped she could check before the afternoon visit. Hi, Molly, she heard herself say as she walked into Molly's basil-scented kitchen. I'm here so we can yak it up now, just the two of us. Come on; let's have ourselves a little girl-talk, right now. You first.

# 7

'That was nice of you,' Nick said.

Molly sprinkled Comet into the toilet bowl.

'I didn't know you were planning to give her that wall hanging,' he said. 'When did you decide to do that?'

'Right on the spot,' Molly said.

'That was really nice,' Nick said. 'That was the one that took you all summer to do, wasn't it?'

'Yes.'

'Do you think she appreciated it?'

Molly swabbed the brush around and around the bowl. 'You know what I wish?' she said. 'I wish someone would explain why it's always me who notices when the bathroom needs to be cleaned. Why don't *you* ever notice it? Why don't *you* ever walk in and say, Oh, gee, this bathroom smells, whaddya know, I guess it's time to clean the bathroom.'

'She must have appreciated it,' Nick said, answering his own question. 'I like Phoebe, you know?'

'I like Phoebe too,' Molly said.

'No, really, from everything you told me about her, I thought she'd be some know-it-all wanting to tell us all about her lawyering.'

Molly thought back to the dinner the night before. 'Well she does have a know-it-all side to her, you just haven't seen it yet. You should have heard her last night. Cindy Ann asked her one simple question and Phoebe went off about something that made no sense at all. As a lawyer she sure knows how to complicate things.'

Nick sat down on the edge of the tub. 'Well, I think

she's nice,' he said. 'And her little boy's a riot, don't you think?'

'Oh, he's a charmer,' Molly said.

'What's the matter?' Nick said. 'What don't you like about him?'

'I said he was a charmer,' Molly said. 'Don't put words into my mouth.'

'Okay, boss.'

'All right, I'm sorry but I have to admit she's been pissing me off!' Molly said. 'I wrote her about my sheep three years ago and Tuesday night it was like she'd never read the letter. And then launching into those remember-when stories: "Remember that guy who was always asking us if we needed a nickel?" "Remember Doris catching us smoking dope?" Why can't she ask me something relevant, like what it's like to teach at the same school you went to as a kid?'

'That's a tough question,' Nick said. 'What *is* it like?'

'It sucks,' Molly said. 'You know that.'

'Okay, so Phoebe's probably a little reluctant to ask you that,' Nick said. 'She's probably afraid it could come out the wrong way.'

'Why are you so reasonable?' Molly sighed. 'Why are you so mature?'

Nick held out his hands, shrugged, smiled at the window, as though behind it sat an audience of fans.

Molly flushed the toilet. 'All I can say is, I wish she'd quit treating me with kid gloves. If all this visit turns out to be is Phoebe either sheltering my ego or lapsing into remember-whens . . .' She broke off, and shook her head.

'You can change that,' Nick said. 'You can ask her about her job.'

'I certainly tried last night,' Molly said. 'I asked her about her work, and my God, lemme tell you!'

'What?'

'Oh, it sounds awful!' she exclaimed. 'I didn't say anything but it sounds absolutely deadly! You know what she does after seven years of higher education? She reads documents.' She was scrubbing the basin now, and stopped to look up at him. He was standing with one foot on the rocking chair, arms folded across his chest. She handed him the can of Comet. 'Here,' she said. 'You can at least do the bathtub instead of just standing there. It's your parents, not mine, who are coming to visit.'

'Cranky cranky,' Nick said.

Molly continued to scrub away at the porcelain. 'Also I would like to point out how one of the first things she did was to give me a lecture about alcohol and caffeine. Did you hear her? She learns I'm pregnant and within the next breath it's do this, do that.'

'I don't think that's what she was trying to say,' Nick said. 'I think she was just trying to get a dialogue going. She's been pregnant too; it's one of the few things you guys have in common these days.'

'Don't argue with me, Nick,' Molly said. 'I have a sixth sense for knowing when Phoebe's climbing into the driver's seat.'

'This doesn't come off,' Nick said.

'What doesn't come off?'

'This,' he said, pointing to a rust stain.

'It does too,' she lied. 'It comes off when I'm cleaning the tub.'

Nick scowled and sprinkled more Comet on to the stain.

'Plus I know she disapproves of my not telling anyone about being pregnant,' Molly said. 'It was written all over her face. She just didn't want to overtly jump on me the first night back.'

'Jesus,' said Nick, 'we certainly are hostile, aren't we?'

Molly sighed, and wrung out the sponge. 'I'm not hostile, not really,' she said. 'I'm just frustrated right now. Phoebe isn't telling me what she thinks of me, and I'm not telling her what I think of her. Like I have no idea why she's spending her life in such a miserable profession! And I don't know where to begin to talk to her about it. The best thing for us to talk about right now is raising children, and I'll probably be too defensive to even talk about that. I just can't deal with her *advice*, you know?'

'I'd actually like to talk to her about the law firm,' Nick said. 'I'd like to hear what it's really like there.'

'Oh no, you wouldn't,' Molly said. 'It would depress you so much that you'd never go to law school.'

'It beats cutting firewood.'

'Sure,' Molly said, 'but only because it pays better. Now,' she said, 'why don't you help me move the organ out to the back porch.'

'Why?'

'I want to get rid of it,' she said. 'This house has got too junky.'

'Leave it for later,' he said. 'I've got to go to work.' It was Veterans Day, but the legal holiday that had given Molly the day off did not extend to woodcutters. Nick put on a woollen shirt-jacket and kissed her good-bye. 'Don't let this whole visit go by with your defences up,' he said. 'You'll only feel terrible afterwards.'

Molly tightened the corners of her mouth; but she knew Nick was right; she would have to get over this defensiveness. Grow up, she told herself. Get rid of this chip on your shoulder.

After Nick left she fixed herself a second breakfast: a yogurt shake, two pieces of toast, leftover drumsticks – her appetite was back this morning – and thought of things that she and Phoebe could talk about. I *will* make more of an effort, she thought; after all, Phoebe's making an effort: it was sweet of her, really, to make the arrangements for the two of us to spend the afternoon together today. So. How about kids? If I could get over my defensiveness about Phoebe always doing everything ahead of me, we could talk about Andrew, she thought. He's a cute kid – a little bit of a whiner, perhaps, but smart: that you could tell right off. What was it like bringing him up alone? Did she miss him, having to be away from him all day long? Was she thinking about schools, whether he should go to summer camp, or take up a musical instrument?

And we could always talk about being pregnant. If you'd only let her, Molly scolded herself, she'd probably be able to give you a lot of reassurance. God, the way you've been bitching at Nick these days it's a wonder he still wants to marry you. Had Phoebe been so bitchy? ('Are you tired?' 'Do you get sick a lot?' Phoebe's questions echoed through her mind, and she was ashamed that she hadn't taken that opportunity to open up to her friend. Nick was right. She had to give her more of a chance.)

Of course, if we talked about my being pregnant it would probably lead to her asking me why I'm not announcing it until after the wedding. Molly wondered if she would be able to explain it to a sceptical Phoebe: that it wasn't a question of upsetting her parents – hell, they knew that Nick practically lived at her house, that he kept his tiny three-room apartment over the post office only because the rent was so cheap and he was too lazy to move his things. No, it was because if she went and announced the pregnancy now, everyone would think that it was the only reason they were getting married. And as much as Molly swore up and down that other people's opinions didn't matter, it bothered her to think that her parents might view this as some kind of forced marriage. Is this a shotgun wedding? her mother had asked that Sunday afternoon back in October; and while Bea probably would have bent over backwards to make like it didn't matter to her, deep down it would. A shotgun marriage was a shotgun marriage, whether it was 1950 or 1980. And no matter how much they liked Nick, he would always be the guy who knocked up their daughter and had to be dragged to the altar.

Would Phoebe understand?

Maybe. But nevertheless Phoebe would undoubtedly argue with her: she would point out that everybody had already put two and two together anyway. And Molly knew that; but why did everything have to be brought out into the open nowadays? Molly didn't think that her approach was old-fashioned; she thought it was discreet. Why, half the women in Winslow had probably been in her shoes; but nobody said anything about it; they just went and got married and the baby came a little early and that was that. So why did it have to be any different now? Besides, it was nobody's business yet anyway – she was only in her second month, and a lot of people waited until they were after the danger point before telling everyone. Why should she be obliged to announce it prematurely, just because they weren't married?

And of course they could talk about why she had suddenly decided to have a baby.

Not that it had been planned. It just happened, due to a complex web of hairline cracks in a diaphragm she had neglected to inspect in front of a light bulb. Until the test results came back, of course – at which point Molly, baffled to hear that she was pregnant, stretched the rubber dome between her thumbs and watched it split and crackle apart like a sun-chapped bathing cap.

'What now?' Nick asked.

'I want to keep it,' she confessed.

Nick was silent.

'What about you?' Molly asked. 'What do you want to do?'

Nick stayed silent for a long time. Then he shook his head, and broke into a boyish smile. 'I want to keep it too,' he said. 'I can't believe I feel this way, but I do.'

'So,' said Molly. 'You want to get married?'

'Oh, for crying out loud!' Nick said. 'Couldn't you at least wait and let me do the asking?'

'I just want to know,' said Molly.

'Well, yes,' said Nick.

'Well, good,' said Molly. 'But I don't want to take your name,' she added.

'What about the child, though?' said Nick. 'The child will have my name, won't it?'

'All right,' Molly said. 'As long as we put my name in the middle. John Adams Ulrich,' she said. 'Sounds all right, doesn't it? Mary Adams Ulrich?'

But why had she wanted to keep it, this unplanned, unscheduled baby? Well, as she saw it there was no reason not to keep it. She was twenty-nine, soon to reach the decade of increasing risks. She was in good shape, a little on the thin side perhaps, but none the less fit. She was employed; she had a good income, a good health plan (though Nick getting accepted at a faraway law school could certainly change that). But most of all, she was ready.

Ready and also a bit relieved, for she had had an abortion back in college, and since then she had always wondered if it had damaged her insides. It was as Phoebe had said: they tell you it's all right, but you have to wonder about it, getting cleaned out like that.

She had been a sophomore at the time. He was a long-haired bearded drifter named Ira, a twenty-five-year-old draft evader who lived out of a backpack and happened to find Molly's dormitory a convenient hostel, a warm place to get out of the cold. The first night he set up camp in the lounge, where Molly found him smoking a joint and playing Gershwin on the piano. Within two days Sally, Molly's roommate, had moved out and Ira had moved in, bringing with him sacks of various granolas and a collection of Grateful Dead albums. Ira also brought crabs, which, given his philosophy of freedom, quickly spread throughout the dorm. But Molly forgave him. He was kind, he was gentle, he had no place to live, he needed her. It was a long harsh winter that year; and as it dragged on Molly thought spring would never come. Late in March she also began thinking that her period would never come; by the time she had the test she was two months pregnant, and the doctor advised a quick decision. When Molly returned to the dorm to discuss it with Ira, she found not Ira but Sally, unpacking her clothes. On her bed was a letter, which in Ira's roundabout way attempted to say good-bye, and told her to keep the Dead records as a memento. Peace.

Since it was a university community Molly easily located a clinic, one that would perform the abortion as quickly and as efficiently as a tooth extraction. Molly checked in on the designated morning, stomach empty, womb full, in the company of other women all sharing the same mixed-up sense of impatience, fear, urgency, and determined resignation: women all on hold. She was given a robe and a bonnet, both in the same sterile blue-green tissue. Because she'd never had this done before, she requested a general anaesthetic, despite the doctor's advice that it would be both unnecessary and more dangerous. But Molly wanted to be sure that she felt absolutely nothing. She lay back on the table, knees up, heels in the stirrups, the doctor's head between her legs, the anaesthesiologist by her side. 'I'm very nervous,' she told him, feeling her bones begin to vibrate.

'Relax,' he said. 'Do you like to ski?'

Afterwards, in the recovery room, she expected to feel an unfathomable sense of loss, regret, guilt; expected to feel as though she had made the wrong decision, to want to turn back the clocks. But as she stared at a vase of plastic purple irises Molly felt only relief. It was over. There was no longer any opportunity to change her mind; as her father would have said, it was water over the dam. She drank her grape juice and ate her crackers and forbade herself to think about two things. The first was Ira, and where he had gone, and why he had left. The second was the date the nurse had written down on the top of her chart, a now moot delivery date sometime towards the end of the following October.

She had never really regretted it; but still, she had always harboured a fear that it would come back to haunt her. She would think of that one grade-school teacher, Lily was her name, who couldn't seem to get pregnant. Lily had become obsessed, and the obsession had grown out of control, a germless infection spreading from the womb to the mind until the mere sight of a pregnant woman would fill Lily with a bitter and envious anger: anger at herself, at the world, at the unfairness of getting stuck with faulty parts. And she would think of Cindy Ann; while Cindy Ann seemed to have accepted it with less anger than Lily, still you would catch her pausing before the storefront displays of infantwear; you would find the mail-order catalogues in her kitchen readily opening to pictures of bassinets, playpens, nursing bras, expressers. And so Molly was relieved to find out that she still worked, that she wasn't going to have to focus on right days and not-so-right days, on temperatures and positions, on the option and danger of fertility drugs.

She had never told Nick about her experience; she knew she should have told him, but she had never wanted to dredge up the details. She considered her affair with Ira to be a mistake, a big one, and she didn't want to start remembering things she had happily forgotten: the granola crumbs in his beard, for instance, or his long unclipped toenails. It was hard enough to hear the Grateful Dead; the chords of their music, the pedal steel, the harmony of their voices, left in her mouth a thick, vaguely bitter taste, like home-brewed beer. But she wished she had said something to Nick; the omission now seemed more a lie, and she carried with her a flicker of guilt and a lighthearted promise that she would let it slip, offhandedly, at the right moment. Not that it was any big deal, but he should know.

So she and Phoebe had a lot of things to talk about that afternoon. Molly spent the rest of the morning cleaning house. She packed up old clothes for Goodwill (some, like a long Indian-print jumper, seemed too out of style even for charity; but she rationalized that someone might be able to use the fabric for something else); she tied together bundles of newspapers; she even finished tacking on the batting to the quilt, and gently rolled it up, then brought it upstairs to the guest room, where she laid it neatly along one wall.

Back in the living room her clogs echoed on the bare pine floor; she suddenly had a vision of what the room could be like without the useless overbearing organ, and she wanted it out now. She didn't want to wait for Nick, she didn't even want to wait for Phoebe. In the back hall she found a smaller rug, just a little bit larger than the base of the organ; this she spread on the floor in front of the instrument. Lifting in turn each of the four corners of the organ, she kicked the rug underneath, evening it out with her toes so that the organ's full weight rested on the rug. Then, edging around to its back, she began toiling against the mass of ornate wood, inching her way towards the kitchen, prickling with sweat underneath a wool sweater. By the time she had edged it over the small step from the kitchen to the back porch her whole body was tingling from the muscle strain. She shoved the organ off to the side, then went back inside and sank down on to the sofa, her heart pounding.

But the job was done. She observed with satisfaction how much space was freed up; if they got rid of the player piano, too, they would have room not only for her new loom but also for the infant gear they would inevitably acquire. They could put a playpen where the organ had been, a swing, a Johnny Jump Up. She could hear the song of a windup mobile, the wobbly music of a topsy-turvy ball. Nick could build a cradle, and she could weave throughout the day, lulling the baby to sleep with the gentle thumping rhythm of her loom as she threw the shuttle, hand to hand, beating the weft into place.

Throw and catch, firmly beat,
Hold the beater, change the feet.

Molly was still lying on the couch when Phoebe arrived. She was wearing her new fisherman's knit sweater, with rust-coloured corduroy trousers that matched her hair; large gold hoops hung from her earlobes, and her cheeks were flushed from the cold November air.

'I'm a little early,' she said as Molly met her on the back porch. 'Your father wanted Andrew to help him in the garden this morning. Where did that come from?' she said, looking at the organ.

'Oh, that,' Molly said. 'I just moved it out of the living room. Come on in and take a look; it really changes things.'

'You moved it? You and who else?'

Molly held up her arm and flexed her bicep.

Phoebe stared. 'Molly,' she said. 'You're pregnant. What are you doing, moving something as heavy as an organ?'

Molly bristled. Here it comes, she thought, bracing herself for the first of a series of lectures.

No, wait. You are going to make a real effort today, remember?

'I guess that was pretty stupid, wasn't it,' she said lightly. 'Oh, well. Nothing to do about it now.'

'Yes there is, from now on you take it easy,' Phoebe said, putting an arm around her shoulders and giving an affectionate hug. 'Give that little kid a break.'

Yes ma'am, Molly wanted to say. Anything else, ma'am? Though Phoebe was right. It *was* stupid for her to have moved the organ; why couldn't she have been more patient? When Nick found out what she had done he would explode.

In the meantime Phoebe had wandered over to the backyard garden area. 'This is huge!' she exclaimed. 'You could grow enough food in this garden to feed an army!'

Now, what am I supposed to say to that? Molly wondered.

'What did you grow?' Phoebe called out. 'Come over here and show me what went where.'

Molly went over to the ploughed-up garden area. It wasn't huge, it was a normal-sized garden; any Vermonter would have known that. Phoebe'd been living in the city for too long.

'Did you grow corn?' Phoebe asked.

'Sure.'

'God, I'd give anything for fresh sweet corn! Did you grow courgettes?'

'Oh, sure.' Of course I grew courgettes. Everybody grows courgettes. Everybody grows too *much* courgettes.

'What about tomatoes? Did you grow them too?'

Molly smiled and nodded.

'I tried growing tomatoes,' Phoebe told her. 'They never even blossomed. You'll have to sit down and give me some good tips on growing tomatoes. I just can't do it, you know? I've got such a brown thumb.'

Molly debated offering Phoebe sympathy: A brown thumb, what a shame! I'm so sorry! Oh, all right, maybe that was going overboard, but Molly had no idea how to get a conversation going when Phoebe seemed intent upon babbling on and on about brown thumbs and blossomless tomatoes. What was she supposed to do, move right into the subject of her pregnancy as though it were the next logical step in this general discussion of fertility?

But Molly didn't have to dwell upon this, because Phoebe had now wandered over to the sheep's pen and was leaning against the fence. 'What are their names?' she called back.

'They don't have names,' Molly said, joining her.

'Why not?'

'I don't know.' Molly shrugged. 'I never got around to naming them; they're just "the sheep."'

'Oh, well, then,' Phoebe said, and she reached out to pat their woolly heads, 'hi there, sheep.'

But the two sheep turned around, almost as one unit, and backed their dung-crusted hind sides towards the fence. Phoebe stepped back.

'They're not very social,' Molly said. 'They've had diarrhoea all autumn.'

'Ah,' said Phoebe, and she dug her hands into her pockets. (Goddamn right they're not very social, she was thinking. Fucking *unsanitary* is what they are.)

They headed back to the house. 'So you have the day off today,' Phoebe remarked. 'It must be nice, a teacher's schedule – Christmas vacations, spring breaks, summers off – what's it like, having all that time?'

And Molly, who up until now had been wondering when Phoebe would ask something substantial, was stunned by this question.

'I *don't* have a lot of time,' she finally said. 'When I'm not teaching I'm weaving.' She knew it was a harsh, clipped response – Phoebe didn't even try to answer – yet didn't Phoebe know that she was a craftswoman first and a teacher second? What did she think, that her weaving was a hobby, filler-work, something with which to while away the hours until *suppertime*?

Molly frowned inwardly. This afternoon's visit was getting off to a very bad start. Phoebe's litany of factual questions had been excusable the first night – after all, everyone who visited the house asked about the looms, about the spinning wheel – but today her questions were either incredibly trivial (how to grow tomatoes, for Pete's sake) or insulting. And thus far she herself wasn't taking much of an initiative to nudge the conversation along, certainly not by dropping these flat one-liner answers designed to cover up her anger. (Maybe Phoebe didn't know how important her weaving was? Maybe Molly had never spelled it out for her?) In any event they seemed to be having an enormous difficulty finding something to talk about; and Molly began to begrudge a certain limited merit to the remember-when conversations she had complained about to Nick: for without them, they seemed to be two strangers, searching blindly for that elusive common thread.

Maybe we should get away from the house, Molly thought. Some people, after all, were ill suited at being guests – they became nervous, started making off-the-wall statements, asking ridiculous questions – and perhaps Phoebe was one of them: perhaps she didn't know quite how to act on Molly's turf. This explanation seemed both comforting and rational to Molly; after all, she didn't recall them running into this problem out in California, five years ago; and she couldn't believe that since then they had both undergone such enormous changes that every potential conversation was doomed to splinter off into disjointed fragments.

Neutral territory. That's what they needed.

'Look,' she said, 'I've got a couple of cases of beer bottles to cash in at Poultney's – want to help me take them back?'

Phoebe readily agreed; in fact, she wanted to pick up some maple syrup, she said, and so they loaded up Louise's car with cases of empty Molson bottles – or rather Phoebe did the loading while Molly gathered together the bags of old clothes, which they would drop off at the Goodwill dumpster. As she brought the bags out to the car she made yet another pledge to herself: she would try to be more open, try to take the intitiative; and hopefully Phoebe would stop asking these ridiculous questions. Maybe they would reminisce, okay, but maybe they wouldn't; maybe they'd move on to the subject of pregnancy, and Phoebe could tell her what to expect –

Oh, please. Make me talkative. Make me cheerful. And make me . . . laid back.

As Phoebe would say.

Carl Poultney came out and met them on the store porch. He was wearing a blue-and-white-striped railroad hat and soft worn overalls; as soon as Phoebe and Molly stepped out of the car he came down, removed his hat, and pumped Phoebe's hand, pulling her forward and puckering his lips to plant a kiss on her cheek. 'Just missed your little one!' he exclaimed in his flat New England drawl.

'Andrew?' said Phoebe, smiling.

'That's right – he and Dave come in here just ten minutes ago. Cute bo-wee, that little one, isn't he, Molly!'

'Oh, he's a heartbreaker,' Molly said, and smiled at Phoebe. Phoebe smiled back.

'How's the wedding plans coming, Molly?' Carl said. 'Molly's getting married this weekend,' he told Phoebe.

'I know,' Phoebe said. 'I'm going to be her maid of honour.'

'Why of course!' Carl said. He frowned and shook his head. 'Now I knew that, *course* I knew that, who else would be her maid of honour. Hey,' he said to Phoebe, 'how's the law business these days? They let you lady lawyers do everything the boys do?'

Phoebe dug her hands into her back pockets, and Molly sympathized with her; predictable as his question might have been, it was nevertheless dead end, and she knew she herself would have had a hard time figuring out how to respond.

But Phoebe managed a tactful reply, 'Everything and more,' she said, smiling at the ground.

'You know, we've got ourselves a new lady lawyer right over in St Audenbury,' Carl said. 'Oh, she's a crackerjack, isn't she, Molly!'

'Sure is,' said Molly. She had met the woman at one of her mother's nuclear freeze meetings; everyone else was dressed casually, but this woman wore a navy-blue suit with a cream-coloured blouse adorned at the neck with a droopy maroon bow tie. And burgundy pumps to match her handbag. Bea told her that the woman was only a few years older than Molly, but Molly thought that with her dowdy clothes she looked middle-aged, matronly. She wondered if Phoebe dressed in a similar uniform.

'You ought to go over and introduce yourself,' Carl was saying to Phoebe. 'Who knows, maybe someday you'll want to come back, and the two of you could have your own office together.'

Phoebe kept smiling at the ground. 'Maybe,' she said.

Just then a sandy-haired young man in a beat-up leather jacket came out of the store, carrying in his arms a box of groceries. It was Duncan Crane, a relative newcomer to the area who had bought the Caleb camp down at Barnet's Pond. Molly had met him briefly at one of the band concerts last summer; what she knew about him came mostly from Bea, who had become better acquainted with him through her nuclear freeze group. He was from Philadelphia, or Baltimore, Molly couldn't remember which; and he was winterizing the Caleb camp, to make it his year-round residence. He was also, according to Bea, a practising member of the dowsing society over in Danville.

Now Duncan grinned at Molly. 'Big weekend, or so I hear from your mother.'

Molly smiled. 'I think I'll be glad when this "big weekend" is over,' she said.

'Oh Christ, enjoy it,' Duncan said. 'You're only going to do it once, right?'

Molly laughed.

'Actually, I'm glad to run into you,' Duncan said. 'Tell Nick I have to talk to him next week.'

'About what?'

'About getting some work,' Duncan said. 'Dollars are running low these days. Speaking of which, I paid my bill, Carl, so you can get a good night's sleep tonight.'

'How are things out at the camp?' Molly asked.

'Pretty good, pretty good,' Duncan said. 'Though I

could use a couple of extra weeks of Indian summer, if anyone's selling them.' He hoisted the box of groceries up against his hip, and looked at Phoebe. 'And this must be the old friend who's going to be in the wedding?'

'Oh,' said Molly. 'This is my friend Phoebe.'

'Phoebe's from California!' Carl exclaimed. 'Not only that, but she's a lawyer!'

'Whoa,' Duncan said. 'Guess I better watch what I say. I'll bet you find things pretty different around here,' he said to her.

Phoebe shrugged. 'Not really,' she said. 'It all looks just about the same to me.'

'Not if you saw the Caleb place, you wouldn't say that!' Carl exclaimed. 'Duncan here's changed the whole insides around, insulated it for the winter – you find any more of those noxious rays in the house?' he asked, giving Molly and Phoebe a quick wink. 'Duncan's one of them dowsers,' he told Phoebe. 'Soon's he moved into the camp he said the bedroom was full of what he calls these noxious rays, he can't sleep, he says, kept waking up with a backache until he finally just moved the bed right into the kitchen up against the sink. Isn't that what you told me, Duncan?'

'Don't knock it, Carl,' Duncan said.

'I ain't knocking it!' Carl said, winking again at Phoebe. 'Just because it's a bunch of malarkey doesn't mean I'm out to knock it.'

Duncan shrugged, and carried the groceries down the steps to his Scout, where he slid the box across the front seat. 'By the way, Carl – you going to be getting any more weather stripping in?'

'Nope – but I'm driving over to Burlington on Saturday; you want me to pick some up?'

Duncan climbed up into the driver's seat, slammed his door, and started the engine.

'You're not going to Burlington this Saturday,' he told Carl.

'What are you talking about?' Carl demanded.

'Snow's coming,' Duncan said.

'*Snow?* Ho, it's not going to snow this Saturday, it's been way too warm. Where'd you get this idea, anyway, your willow stick?'

'Five bucks,' Duncan said.

'I don't gamble,' Carl grumbled. 'Just tell me how much weather stripping you need and I'll get it for you.'

'Enough for the back door,' Duncan said. 'But if you can't get it don't worry, I'll pick it up in St Audie on Monday.

'And don't forget to pass the message on to Nick,' he told Molly. 'If I don't get a job I won't be able to keep paying my grocery bills to Carl here.' He grinned at Carl.

Carl, however, was looking on edge, and as Duncan drove off he worked his jaw, as though wanting to put that last part of the conversation behind him. Molly, herself a sceptic on the issue of dowsing, nevertheless wondered if perhaps Carl had already lost a number of non-monetary bets with Duncan on this subject. And she also began to worry about the possibility of a snowstorm. 'Come on,' she said. 'Let's get these beer bottles taken care of.'

Phoebe, however, was watching Duncan's Scout make the turn up the hill towards East Winslow. 'He's really fixing up the Caleb camp?'

'So he says,' Molly replied.

'There isn't much to fix up, is there?' Phoebe said. 'As I recall it was just about falling down – and that was ten years ago.'

'I don't know,' Molly said. 'Ask my mother, she gets a week-by-week account at her antinuke meetings. Actually, I think she has a crush on Duncan,' she told Phoebe.

'He's always borrowing some tool or another from Daddy and when he comes by she insists on filling him up with her bran muffins and oatmeal cakes and wheat-germ biscuits.'

'Huh,' Phoebe said.

From the curious tone in Phoebe's voice it occurred to Molly that her friend might be interested in seeing more of Duncan during her visit. She thought back to Nick's proposal that they fix Phoebe up with Leo, his friend from DC. As between Duncan and Leo, Molly would have predicted that Phoebe would have a better time with Leo; he was a lawyer, after all, and worked in a large city, and had gone through a divorce. But who could say?

'Duncan's a nice guy,' Molly said. 'If you'd like to see more of him maybe we could do something, all four of us, next week – '

Phoebe laughed. 'A double date, is that what you're saying? Oh, no, I have enough on my schedule for the next week; I came home to see you, not to get fixed up with someone. Now, go on inside and let me take care of the beer bottles.'

Molly felt herself bristle again. I wasn't suggesting a *date*, she wanted to say. You don't have to act as though I'm trying to marry you off. She left Phoebe to unload the bottles and went inside, where the air was warm and damp from a pan of water vaporizing on a potbelly stove; the smell of boiled chicked and onions drifted out from the Poultneys' two-room apartment at the back. Behind the counter, tending the cash register, sat old Ida Poultney, dressed up today in a rose-coloured skirt and matching cardigan, a string of pinkish pearls looped around her neck. Her hair, tinted silver-blue, was freshly waved, and a cluster of silver grapes gleamed from each earlobe. Ida stared when she saw Molly, for she had in her lap a lace doily she was trying to finish for Molly's shower that afternoon; quickly she thrust the handiwork under the counter.

'You look nice, Ida,' Molly remarked. 'What are you all dressed up for?'

Ida nervously twisted her pearls. 'Oh, this old thing,' she said, and her voice trailed off as she fingered the keys on the cash register.

Molly shrugged. It was none of her business anyway.

'Say hello to Phoebe Martin, Ida,' Carl said.

'Hello, Mrs Poultney,' Phoebe said.

Ida stared at her from behind the counter. 'Why, I know what's different,' she finally said. 'You've cut your hair all off!'

'Do you like it?' Phoebe said. 'I cut it when I started work.'

'I do like it, I do. Tell me!' – and Ida leaned forward eagerly – 'is California really like they say it is? Is it really summer all the time?'

'Summer and hot tubs and avocado trees growing in your backyard,' said Molly cheerfully. 'All you have to do is say Walt Disney and the sun shines.' Phoebe glanced at her curiously, and Molly looked away. It was just a joke.

'We get a lot of rain in January,' Phoebe said. 'But no snow. No blizzards. It's nice.'

'Imagine that, Carl,' Ida said, sitting back. 'No snow! I'm dreading it,' she said to Phoebe. 'I'm just dreading it this year. I don't know how I'm going to get through. And Carl wanting to keep the thermostat turned down so low it makes my bones ache just thinking about it.'

'I like the snow,' Carl said. 'I like the seasons.'

'Me too,' said Molly. 'I'd hate to have it warm and sunny all year round; I need a few cold months to make me appreciate spring.'

'I could do without winter,' said Phoebe. 'I could do without March in Vermont.'

'I actually love March,' Molly philosophized. 'The sap's running – and there's such anticipation in the air!'

'Well, I'm with you, Ida,' Phoebe said, looking at Molly again; but Molly turned away. The smell of boiled chicken had suddenly brought a queasiness to her throat – though it was a bit early in the day for her usual bout of nausea. She opened the rounded old refrigerator in which the Poultneys kept their produce, and held her face into the coolness, pretending to look for something to buy. Inside were five anaemic tomatoes, three bleached heads of iceberg lettuce, and a flaccid-looking cucumber.

'I think Texas would be nice too,' Ida went on. 'Do you watch *Dallas*?'

'Oh, yeah,' Phoebe said. '*Dallas* is great.'

Molly stood up and clamped the door shut. '*You* watch *Dallas*?'

'Hey,' Phoebe said. 'It's not so bad.'

'Oh, God,' Molly couldn't help saying.

'You should see her,' Carl Poultney said of his wife. 'Friday nights it's like the band concerts in the summer-time, you can't pry her loose from the Sony.'

'It keeps me warm,' Ida said, drawing herself up. 'I pretend I'm down there on the ranch, sitting in the sunshine.'

'Hogwash,' Carl said.

'And *Dynasty* too – don't you like looking at all those rich people?' Ida went on. 'I watch the show and pretend I live where they live. I pretend I drive their cars. I pretend I have butlers and swimming pools and diamond brooches. Wouldn't you love to be one of them?'

Phoebe laughed.

'Don't you watch those shows, Molly?' Ida asked.

'No, Ida,' Molly replied. 'I don't have time to watch

*Dallas*. Or *Dynasty*. Or *Howdy Doody*, for that matter. I usually try and get some reading down in the evening.'

Phoebe raised her eyebrows, and looked around the store. 'I actually came in here for some maple syrup,' she said. 'Andrew's never had the real stuff.'

'Never had the real stuff!' Carl exclaimed. 'You mean you let him pour that Log Cabin junk on his pancakes?'

Phoebe smiled sheepishly; Carl Poultney shook his head, trudged into the storeroom, and returned with a gallon-sized can. 'You tell him ole Grampa Carl sent this up for him. Cutest boy I ever saw,' he said. 'Just too bad he don't get to grow up in Vermont.'

Out in the car Phoebe asked. 'Are you feeling all right?'

'I'm fine,' Molly said, though a strange feeling had settled into her abdomen. 'Do you know where the Goodwill box is? Take a right. Follow this road.'

'You seemed a little touchy in there,' Phoebe ventured. 'What do you have against *Dallas*?'

'I think it's a waste of time, frankly,' Molly said.

'Not when you've been busting ass all week,' Phoebe said. 'It helps you wind down. In *my* experience,' she added hastily.

Molly shrugged. They were driving along the river now, where everything – sky, trees, water – was a leaden grey; and Molly again felt very discouraged. Every pledge to try and get along with Phoebe seemed to be followed by disaster: back at the house, here at the store . . . it just wasn't working. Much of it was her fault – if she wasn't failing to take the initative, she was making comments like that one about the hot tubs and avocado trees, for instance – but to be honest, the more she saw of Phoebe the less she liked. *Dallas? Dynasty?* To wind down from a day reading *documents*? Molly opened the window for some air as a dull but distinct and all-too-familiar ache spread through her abdomen; her insides suddenly felt heavy, as though weighted down by chains. Someone tightened the chains, and she brought her knees up to the dashboard.

'Well, anyway,' Phoebe said. 'That was nice of him to give me the syrup, wasn't it? Though he really made a dig at the end, about Andrew not growing up in Vermont. Such *chauvinism*. I tell you, if one more person pressures me to move back I'm going to scream.'

Molly folded her arms across her stomach. Something wasn't right. 'He didn't mean anything by it,' she said. 'He was just making conversation.'

'Oh, no,' Phoebe said. 'I know pressure when I hear it.'

Don't flatter yourself, Molly couldn't help thinking as the chains tightened even more. Nobody cares if you live in California or Timbuktu, for heaven's sake. She lowered her knees and stretched out her legs, gently kneading her stomach.

And then she suddenly realized that all this attention she'd been focusing on her relationship with Phoebe was a misdirected effort right now; suddenly it was all beside the point.

'Phoebe.'

'Did I miss the turnoff?'

'Forget Goodwill,' Molly said. 'I want to go home.'

'Are you sure you're feeling all right?' Phoebe said. 'Are you going to be sick again?'

'I don't think that's the problem,' Molly said. 'To tell the truth.'

# 8

Phoebe had been having a hard time controlling her temper. All right, so her question about Molly's teaching schedule, about all the spare time it gave her, had come out a little wrong. But did Molly have to get so upset? Was she so insecure that she had to jump on Phoebe for not acknowledging her as a weaver every time she opened her mouth? Phoebe *knew* Molly spent her extra time weaving, and spinning, and quilting; all she was trying to do with that question was to get away from the subject of vegetables and on to the subject of whether Molly was indeed happy. And so what if she hadn't phrased the question as sensitively as she might have – was Molly going to hold that against her for the rest of the day, for the rest of the visit? Did all her thoughts have to be perfectly expressed just because she was a lawyer?

Phoebe thought Molly had been unfair; and she was trying to soothe her temper and formulate a way to broach the subject again – very tactfully, of course, because she didn't want to offend Molly a second time – when Molly directed her to turn the car around. All right, Phoebe thought; I'll turn around; we can go back to your house and we can talk about it in your kitchen rather than in the car. It's getting time for Bea to call anyway.

But the way Molly half walked, half ran into the house without closing the car door, Phoebe quickly realized that number one, something was very wrong; and number two, whatever it was, it was going to supersede any attempts to delve into whether or not Molly was happy back here in Vermont. She yanked up the emergency brake and hurried after her friend, through the kitchen and into the bathroom, where Molly was sitting on the toilet. As Phoebe stood there Molly drew the wad of toilet paper out from between her thighs, and the two of them stared at the blot of brownish-red.

'Ira,' Molly whispered.

'What are you talking about?' said Phoebe. Her own voice suddenly sounded small and faraway, not the way it should have sounded when her friend was starting to miscarry and no one else was around. 'What are you talking about,' she said, louder now, and she planted her hands on her hips. 'Come on, get up, you should go lie down.'

'I'm being punished,' Molly said. 'Fucking Ira.'

'Come on,' Phoebe said, still trying to make her voice sound more in control, commanding, reassuring. 'Let's go into the living room.'

'Don't tell me what to do!' Molly screamed, and Phoebe drew back. 'I'm losing my baby down the toilet and for once don't you tell me what to do!'

Phoebe swallowed.

Molly pressed another wad of tissue to her crotch and inspected it. 'Oh God!' she cried. 'It *is* coming out, it's coming out and I can't stop it!'

'It's all right,' Phoebe said. 'Look, can you stand up? Can you just keep pressing with the toilet paper?' Oh, what a silly thing to say, what a silly *silly* thing to say.

But Molly had straightened up; with her pants down around her knees she let Phoebe lead her into the living room, clutching the wad of tissue against her crotch as though hoping that there might be something to what Phoebe had said. In the living room Phoebe helped her down on to the sofa, then ran upstairs and pulled the top quilt off Molly's bed, ran back down, and spread it over Molly.

'Who's your doctor?'

'Dr Frankel,' Molly said. 'Fucking son of a bitch wasn't worth it,' she said; 'why did I ever get involved with such an asshole?'

'Where's his number?'

'On the bulletin board,' Molly said. 'And it's a she.'

As Phoebe dialled the St Audenbury clinic she glanced at the clock; it was twenty to four. She thought of Bea's living room bustling with the shower-happy ladies, the food, the presents, the decorations.

The clinic line answered.

'Dr Frankel, please, it's an emergency,' Phoebe said.

'Dr Frankel's off duty,' the receptionist said.

'Dr Frankel's off duty,' Phoebe told Molly.

'Figures,' Molly said. 'Who's taking her calls?'

'Who's taking her calls?' Phoebe inquired.

'Dr Milton,' the receptionist said.

'Dr Milton,' Phoebe told Molly.

'Oh, wonderful,' Molly said to the ceiling. 'That old idiot.'

'May I tell him who's calling?' the receptionist said.

'I'm calling for a friend,' Phoebe said. 'Her name is Molly Adams.'

'One moment, please,' and Phoebe heard a click as the receptionist put her on hold. She looked at Molly, who was watching her with narrowed eyes. Phoebe looked back at the telephone. They weren't reminiscing right now, that was for sure.

'We don't seem to have a record on a Molly Adams,' the receptionist was saying.

'What do you mean, you don't have a record on her? You have to have a record on her.'

'Mary Elizabeth,' Molly said. 'They probably don't know me as Molly.'

'Mary Elizabeth,' Phoebe said.

'One moment, please.' Again the receptionist put her on hold. 'Mary Elizabeth Adams, of Winslow?' she said when she had reconnected them.

'Yes.'

'Dr Milton will have to call her back,' she said. 'He's seeing a patient right now.'

'But this is an emergency!'

'And what is the nature of the emergency?'

'She's losing her baby!' Phoebe yelled.

'Oh, God,' Molly moaned. 'I really am, aren't I? That's what's happening, isn't it?'

Phoebe closed her eyes, and turned away from Molly. 'I mean she's bleeding,' she said quietly. 'She's not supposed to be bleeding.'

'One moment, please,' the woman said, and for the third time Phoebe heard the line click. She waited, drumming her fingers on the phone book.

'Hello?' Dr Milton said in a thin tenorish voice.

'Yes, hello!'

'Now, Mrs Watkins tells me that Mary Elizabeth may be having a problem with the pregnancy?'

'She's started to bleed,' Phoebe said carefully. 'A little.'

'And what colour it it?'

'Brown,' Phoebe said. 'Brownish-red.'

'And does she have any cramps?'

'Do you have cramps?'

'Some,' Molly said.

'Some cramps,' Phoebe reported.

'And how bad are they?'

'How bad?'

'Not too,' Molly said.

'Not too bad,' Phoebe said.

‘And are there any clots?’

‘Any clots?’

‘No,’ Molly said. ‘I didn’t see any.’ She pulled her hand up from her crotch and inspected the wad again. ‘No clots.’

‘No clots,’ Phoebe said.

‘Well, then, I wouldn’t worry just yet,’ Dr Milton said cheerfully. ‘Is she lying down?’

‘Yes,’ Phoebe said.

‘Keep her there,’ Dr Milton said. ‘Really, it’s nothing to worry about. Call me, though, if the cramps get worse, or if the bleeding doesn’t stop, or if it does begin to clot. And if she passes any unusual tissue, save it for me.’

‘Save it?’

‘Why not,’ the doctor said cheerfully. ‘Just put it in the refrigerator.’

Phoebe hung up the phone. ‘He said not to worry. He said wait and see, and call him if you begin to clot.’

‘I told you he was an idiot,’ Molly said. ‘Take two aspirin and call me in the morning. Oh *God*, I don’t believe this is happening!’

‘It’s not happening yet,’ Phoebe said. ‘Don’t jump to conclusions.’ On a bookshelf by the telephone table she spotted a women’s health collective handbook; she flipped through its pages, searching for a section on miscarriage.

‘Isn’t there anything I can do?’

‘He said just wait.’ There it was: ‘Miscarriage (Natural Abortion).’ ‘Listen to this,’ she said, and began to read. ‘“If bleeding does begin there is always uncertainty. The pregnancy might or might not continue.” Did you hear that? It’s just uncertainty. You haven’t lost the baby yet. Chances are you’re going to be all right.’

‘They didn’t say “chances are,” Phoebe. They said “might.”’

Phoebe didn’t know what to say. She was running out

of consolations. This had happened to a friend of hers at Berkeley, a little bit of staining, but it had turned into a full-bodied flow, and the woman had indeed lost the child. Phoebe didn't know what else she could say to make Molly feel better. Right now she wanted facts, hard cold statistics. She wanted to know how many women spotted, how many times the spots carried out their threats; whether it was more likely in the second month than in the first, or the third; whether it was more common, really, in women who had had a previous abortion.

'I want to talk to Dr Frankel,' Molly said. 'Call Dr Frankel.'

'She's off duty, though,' Phoebe said.

'So call her at home,' Molly said. 'That guy Milton doesn't know jack shit.'

Phoebe dialled Dr Frankel at home.

'Now bring me the phone,' Molly said.

Phoebe brought her the phone.

'Fucking Ira,' Molly said to the ceiling as she waited for an answer. 'Fucking son of a bitch.'

'Molly,' Phoebe said. 'Ira has nothing to do with this.'

'As if you know,' Molly said. 'Dr Phoebe on abortion.'

Phoebe swallowed again. Molly's just upset, she told herself. She's not out to hurt you, she's just upset.

Then Molly started. 'Oh, Dr Frankel, this is Molly Adams, I'm sorry to bother you – ' And then her face contorted up like a child's. She lay back on the pillow and pressed her hand over her eyes, unable to hold back the tears. Phoebe turned away.

'I'm bleeding,' Molly finally managed to say in a wavering voice. 'I think I'm losing the baby.'

Phoebe looked at her watch. It was ten to four. She wondered what she would say to Bea when Bea called. Maybe Molly would give in and let her tell Bea what was really going on? And yet she certainly didn't want to press the matter, not at this point, not when Molly had just screamed at her for telling her what to do.

'No intercourse,' Molly repeated. 'Anything else?' She snapped her fingers and scribbled into the air, and Phoebe brought her a pad and pencil.

'And that's where you'll be this weekend,' Molly said, writing. 'Thank you, you're wonderful. Oh yes you are.' She hung up and curled into a ball again, knitting her brow, as though listening closely for telling sounds from within. After a while she began to rock back and forth.

'It'll stop.' Phoebe sat down beside her. 'Just lie quietly. It'll stop.'

'I can't help thinking about it,' said Molly. 'I keep thinking it's my own fault.'

'It's not your fault,' Phoebe said. 'This happens all the time.'

'Did it happen to you?'

Phoebe looked away. 'No.' Though I didn't go around moving organs in the second month, she wanted to say.

Molly continued to rock.

'Are you cramping?'

Molly shook her head.

'Are you chilly?'

Molly shook her head again.

'Do you want something to drink? Something to eat?'

Molly continued to shake her head.

'How's the bleeding?'

Molly drew the tissue up from between her legs. There were no fresh spots. 'Oh please,' she said. 'Oh please.'

Just then the kitchen door opened, and Nick walked in. He went straight to the refrigerator and got a Molson, then came into the living room as the two women stared up at him from the couch.

'Sick again?' he said. 'What a bummer. I'll be glad when this stage is over.'

'It's my fault,' Molly said miserably. 'He wasn't worth it. I'm messed up for good just because of that son of a bitch.'

'What are you talking about?'

'Ira,' Molly said.

'Ira?'

'Ira. Ira got me pregnant. I had an abortion, a long time ago. I should have told you.'

Nick looked at Phoebe, confused.

'I can't even remember his last name,' Molly was saying. 'He had a beard.'

'Molly started to bleed a little, just spotting, really,' Phoebe said, standing up so that he could sit down beside her. 'But she's going to be all right.'

'Bleed?'

'It's my fault,' Molly said.

Nick sat down. 'You mean the baby?'

Molly nodded, and closed her eyes. 'Tell me you love me.'

'I love you.'

'Tell me you need me.'

'I need you.'

'Oh, Jesus' – and she shook her head – 'Jesus, I'm scared.'

Nick looked at Phoebe. 'What happened?'

Phoebe was waiting for the phone to ring. Fuck it, she thought. Just go unplug it. Tell Molly what's going on.

'What happened, Phoebe?' Nick said again.

'She started to bleed, but it doesn't really mean anything. The doctor said for her to stay lying down.'

'Bleed?' he said. 'You mean like in miscarriage?'

'Like in miscarriage,' Molly said. 'Oh, what a shitty day.'

And it was right then – four o'clock on the dot – that the phone rang. Phoebe flinched. What was she going to say?

'I'm not home.' Molly sighed. 'Take a message. Unless it's Dr Frankel; I'll talk to her.'

Phoebe hovered by the phone. 'I should have told you earlier,' she started nervously.

'Told me what? Nick, you want to answer the phone?'

'This is going to be your mother,' Phoebe said, her hand on the receiver as it rang for the fourth time. 'Calling to get you up the house for the shower.'

'Shower?'

'I couldn't stop her,' Phoebe said. 'I tried, but I couldn't.'

'*Shower?*'

Nick looked down.

'Did you know?' Molly demanded of him.

Nick took a swallow of beer.

'Oh Christ,' Molly said.

The phone continued to ring.

'Don't answer it!' Molly said. 'What are you going to say?'

Nick stood up and clutched at his scalp. 'Tell her the fucking truth!' he bellowed. 'Tell her you're pregnant!'

'Don't shout,' Molly said calmly. 'Let it ring, Phoebe.'

Phoebe let it ring. After ten rings it stopped. Bea was going to kill her.

'Now,' Molly said. 'Tell me what's going on.'

Phoebe told her everything. 'I tried to explain to her that it wouldn't be a good idea,' she said. 'She wouldn't listen, though.'

'It's really no big deal,' Nick said. 'If you were feeling okay it might actually have been fun.'

'Nick,' said Molly, 'you are really a moron.'

Nick set his jaw.

'Ida Poultney,' Molly said. 'That's why she was all dressed up, that's why she got so nervous when I walked into the store.'

For a while nobody said anything.

'How are you feeling?' Nick finally asked.

'Like a piece of shit,' Molly told him.

'She's going to call back,' Phoebe said. 'What should I say?'

'Let me answer it,' Nick said. 'I'll tell her the truth.'

'Give me a break, Nick,' Molly said. 'Huh?'

Nick shrugged.

And as expected the phone began to ring again. Phoebe put her hand on the receiver.

'Make something up,' Molly said, 'But make it good. You're a lawyer, you ought to be able to come up with a good line.'

On the second ring Phoebe picked up the phone.

'Molly?' Bea's voice was gay, light, controlled.

'No,' Phoebe replied carefully. 'It's Phoebe.' From the couch Molly eyed her suspiciously, her head elevated on the pillow.

'We're all set,' Bea confided, her voice low, as though Molly might hear. 'It's all *perfect*. Remember now, Andrew's had an accident and wants you, but you both have to come up.'

'We're not coming,' Phoebe said. 'There's a problem.'

'You're telling me,' Nick said.

Molly held up her hand to quiet him.

'We can't make it,' Phoebe said.

'Phoebe!' Bea hissed. 'Watch what you say! She's going to know we're planning something!'

'She already knows,' Phoebe said. 'I had to tell her, Bea. She's sick.'

'Sick?'

'Yes,' said Phoebe. 'She's sick.'

'What's wrong?'

Phoebe twisted the cord between her fingers. 'Cramps,' she finally said.

'Oh, phooey!' Bea exclaimed. 'Tell her to come on up and put the heating pad on them. Tell her I've got some brandy.'

'I don't think it'll help,' Phoebe said. 'They're pretty bad.'

'Hey,' Nick said. 'Where'd the organ go?'

'Out on the porch,' Molly said.

'Who moved it?' said Nick.

'Let me talk to her,' Bea was saying.

Phoebe raised her eyebrows at Molly and pointed to the receiver. Molly shook her head.

'She's really not feeling so hot,' Phoebe said.

'Phoebe, there are six people in the living room waiting for her,' Bea said, and Phoebe imagined the woman's lips crinkling together, her nostrils flaring. And there was a part of her that took satisfaction in messing up Bea's plans – if you could put aside the underlying reason, of course.

'She's doubled over,' Phoebe said. 'I don't think she want to move from the couch.'

'Oh, for crying out loud,' Bea said.

Nick was staring at the empty space in the corner. 'Did you and Phoebe move it?'

'No,' Molly told him. 'I put it on a rug and pushed it myself.'

'What's wrong with tomorrow?' Phoebe said to Bea. 'The food will last an extra day, won't it?'

'You guys can have it tomorrow,' Molly said, crossing her arms, 'but I'm not going.'

Nick had been staring at Molly; now he went out to the porch.

'We *can't* have it tomorrow,' Bea said. 'All my *other*

guests are arriving tomorrow. I'm putting on a dinner for eleven *people* tomorrow.'

'Then why don't you just enjoy the party yourselves, Bea,' Phoebe said wearily. 'Eat the food and save the presents.'

'Is she really in pain?' Bea was concerned now. 'Maybe she should see a doctor.'

'She'll be all right,' Phoebe said. 'She just needs to rest.'

'Hold on,' Bea said. There was a lapse of noise, then Bea came on again. 'Cindy Ann said that if it really hurts it might be endometriosis. She should see a doctor.'

'I think she'll be all right,' Phoebe said. 'I don't think it's endometriosis.'

'It could be,' Bea said. 'You never know. It's very hard to diagnose.'

Phoebe wanted to get off the phone. 'Maybe you're right,' she said. 'Maybe she does have endometriosis. I'll pass the word on. I'll tell her to see a doctor.'

'Because it can really make things difficult if she wants to have a baby later on,' Bea said.

'Okay, Bea,' Phoebe said. 'I'll tell her. How's Andrew doing, anyway?'

'Andrew's *fine*. Dave took him out to the Big Rock. You should see them together – Dave thinks he's nineteen again.'

'I'm going to hang up now,' Phoebe told her. 'Say hello to everyone.'

Molly waved at Phoebe.

'Molly says hello too,' Phoebe said.

As she hung up Nick came back from the porch. 'Do you realize how much that thing weighs?' he said. 'That thing weighs like three hundred pounds. Why didn't you wait for me?'

'How are you feeling?' Phoebe said.

'The same,' Molly said.

'It's stopping,' Phoebe said. 'See? You'll be all right. It must have been quite a scene up there,' she said cheerfully.

'Why didn't you wait for *me*, Molly?' Nick demanded.

'Can you imagine all those ladies?' Phoebe hurriedly went on, because she didn't want Nick to say out loud what everyone already knew. 'It's sort of funny when you think about it, all of them sitting there with their sherry – '

But Nick went ahead and said it. 'That's what brought on the bleeding,' he announced. 'It was nothing to do with this Ira guy, Molly; you shouldn't have moved the organ.'

Molly levelled a bitter, nearly unforgiving look at him – almost as damning, Phoebe would later realize, as the look she herself had given Rusty four years ago when he told her he'd been having an affair.

'No shit,' Molly said.

'That was so stupid!' Nick shouted, clutching fists of air. 'Why didn't you wait?'

'Why don't you see if you can rub it in some more,' Molly said. 'Are you trying to make me feel as bad as possible?'

'*No*,' Nick cried, 'I just don't understand why you didn't *wait*, it's our *baby* in there!' He stomped out to the kitchen and got another beer. Then the door slammed, and they heard his boots, heavy on the porch steps.

'What a mess,' Molly said. 'What a fucking mess.'

Phoebe stood by the phone, not knowing quite what to do. Molly was right. It *was* a mess, and Phoebe felt helpless to come up with the words that would make it any less so.

'Tell me a story,' Molly said.

'What kind of story?'

'Any story. I don't want to think, I'm afraid to let myself start thinking. Just tell me a story. "The Three Bears." "Rapunzel." "Peter and the Wolf," anything. What does Andrew like?'

'"Bad Mousie,"' Phoebe said. 'It's his favourite.'

Molly sighed. 'Tell me about Bad Mousie,' she said, and closed her eyes. 'Who was Bad Mousie? What did he do that was so bad?'

# 9

Molly was sleeping. Nick was gone. The phone was off the hook. Phoebe sat at Molly's kitchen table, waiting, listening, looking around the room at Molly's things to try to piece together the person Molly had become over the last six years. Coloured glass bottles on the windowsill, cast iron pans hanging on one wall, a beat-up copper tub by the woodstove, filled with kindling. Not much to go on. She tiptoed into Molly's studio and stood beside the loom, fingering a handful of oily fleece, smelling it, running her palm over the threads of a tightly rolled warp. She tried to feel Molly's drive, tried to imagine Molly getting up early on a Saturday morning, putting out of her mind all thoughts of school, sitting down at her spinning wheel with a basket of fleece by her feet and gradually filling the spindle with fuzzy white thread. Or maybe she would use that quiet time to wind a new warp.

She was about to leave when she noticed a half-finished watercolour, curling at the edges and tacked to the back of the door. It was a picture of a clean unfurnished room, a blue room whose windows looked over a blue, blue sea. Molly had painted it, Phoebe knew that instinctively; and she wondered what had inspired the painting. Was this a place that Molly, from her inland home in Vermont, longed to be? Or was it insignificant – just an old spot, Molly might say with a shrug, just something that popped into my mind, I don't know why.

But why the unfurnished room? Why the ocean?

And as she stood looking at this painting, the mystery

surrounding her old childhood friend seemed more overwhelming than ever. She recalled telling Janice a week ago that she didn't know Molly any more, and that what she *did* know, she didn't understand. But when she'd said it, she'd had no idea what an understatement it would turn out to be. For two days she'd been trying – granted, somewhat clumsily – to reacquaint herself with Molly; but it wasn't working. She couldn't ignore her bafflement over how Molly could stand living here in Winslow; and since she didn't dare to talk to her about it, they were at a standstill, and she saw no way out. There was something more than just the initial awkwardness between two old friends getting together after a long time; their friendship felt permanently stunted, like a plant deprived for too long of its proper nutrients. Would they ever be close again? Maybe. But then again, maybe it was too late.

And Phoebe felt guilty, as though it were her fault. Her own mother had a friend from girlhood who came to visit every three or four years; and when they got together they laughed and cried and talked about everything imaginable, not just old times but everything: blood pressure and sex and wartime and children, oh, the never-ending problem of their children. They scribbled out recipes and traded sewing short cuts; they smoked; and they brought out old letters to read and reread. They talked about the way things used to be but they also talked about the way things were for them now. What efforts had her mother made, to nurture that friendship for so many years, to keep it up to date, that Phoebe had already overlooked?

She had even felt awkward – awkward! – with Molly this afternoon, with Molly's fright, with the biological details of the potential miscarriage: clotting and cramps and the colour of the blood. She thought back to the graphic discussions she'd had with women friends in college, law school, her pregnant-women's group; she was not nearly as close with them as she'd once been with Molly, yet they would all talk freely about their trich infections, or about their abortions, that terrible moment of the suction; or about how to manoeuvre their lovemaking efforts during the ninth month. So why had she felt so awkward with Molly? Why would she have found it much easier if it were Janice, say, who had started to bleed? Nothing made sense any more.

She wished Nick would come back. His jeep was still in the driveway, so he couldn't have gone too far; but it had been three hours now since he had stomped out of the house. Phoebe wanted to go home; she had barely seen Andrew at all today – why, at this rate she might as well be back in Berkeley dropping him off at day care. And this was her last chance to spend a lot of time with him, for a while. When she got back to California she was going to be overwhelmed with work; there would be many evenings, many weekends, when she would have to stay late at the office, preparing for depositions, organizing documents, drafting page after page of interrogatories. (You have to admit there's something to be said for Molly's type of work, Phoebe thought. Molly will never be this frazzled; her job at the schhool, her weaving, will never cut into her time with her child.) And besides, now Rusty was wanting him for Christmas, and she didn't have much of an argument against it, not after getting him for these two weeks. She thought of Andrew on his first pair of skis, zipped up in a red snowsuit, a pair of thirty-dollar down mittens on his hands, knee-high blue plastic ski boots the likes of which would have made her old leather lace-ups feel like a pair of slippers. There would be nothing stopping him. She smiled, thinking of him struggling to keep the T-bar down, dangling his skis high on a chairlift.

But then she thought of how she would miss out on it all, and resented Rusty for being the one to take him skiing for the first time. By the time she got her chance it would all be old hat.

'Hey, Frankie, come on up, Frankie.'

Phoebe returned to the living room. Molly had propped herself up on the couch and was kneading Frankie's neck as the dog lay curled beside her. Her face looked wan, but her eyes were alert.

'You're awake,' Phoebe said. 'How do you feel?'

'Good,' said Molly. 'Better.'

'Stay where you are,' Phoebe said. 'Do you want some tea? Some toast?'

Molly shook her head.

'Where's Nick?' she asked, after a while.

'I don't know,' Phoebe said. 'His jeep's here, though.'

'Maybe he went over to his apartment,' Molly said. 'Could you call his apartment?'

Phoebe dialled the number, but Nick wasn't there.

'Call Joe-Ray's, then,' Molly said. 'See if he's at Joe-Ray's.'

But Nick wasn't at Joe-Ray's either. They hadn't seen him for a week. Phoebe hung up and waited, not knowing what to do next. Her recognition of the distance between them suddenly seemed transparent, which embarrassed her: she felt as though Molly had been reading over her shoulder as she wrote down terrible confessions.

'I'm sorry for yelling at you,' Molly said suddenly.

Phoebe coloured. 'You didn't yell at me.'

'You're right,' Molly said. 'I screamed at you. Well, I'm sorry. I have this tendency to get pretty defensive these days.'

'No, no,' Phoebe said, frowning. 'I *was* sort of ordering you around. But I didn't know what else to do.'

'Well,' said Molly. 'I'm sorry.'

Don't apologize, Phoebe wanted to beg. You shouldn't have to apologize.

After another silence Molly smiled. 'That Andrew,' she said. 'He's really something.'

Phoebe was both touched and surprised by this. It was the first time Molly had said anything about Andrew, except when Carl Poultney forced her into it.

'What's it like,' Molly asked, 'dealing with the divorce and all? Like has Andrew adjusted?'

Had Andrew adjusted? Andrew didn't know anything else. And Andrew got more Häagen-Dazs ice cream cones, more rides on the merry-go-round, more trips to the Oakland zoo, than any other kid in the East Bay. To facilitate weekend transfers Andrew had two of everything: two tricycles, two pairs of Nikes, two toothbrushes, two teddy bears. But had Andrew adjusted?

'I don't know,' she said, and she was eager to speculate on the matter, not so much because she thought she could come up with an answer but because suddenly here was a real conversation beginning; but then Nick burst in through the front door, rushing straight to Molly's side.

'I'm so sorry,' he said, sitting down and clasping her hands in his. 'I'm so sorry. You're not going to lose the baby, I know you're not; you're going to be all right. I never should have said what I said, I'm so sorry.'

'But it *was* stupid of me,' Molly said, and her eyes filled with tears. 'I just wasn't thinking, and I wanted the room cleaned out, I didn't want to wait for you, I wanted it done right *then*.'

Phoebe had the feeling she was very shortly going to be in the way – if she wasn't already. 'I think I'll take off,' she said.

'Thanks for staying here,' Nick said to her. 'I shouldn't have left like that.'

'Yes, you should have,' Molly told him. 'I would have stomped out, too, if you'd done something that dumb.'

'My parents are coming in tomorrow,' Nick said to Phoebe. 'I really want you to meet them.'

'Sure,' Phoebe said. 'I'll be around.' She left, assuring herself they could pick up on the whole question of Andrew, and what it was like, raising him alone, tomorrow.

When she got home Andrew met her at the back door. He was wearing a red, white, and blue Montreal Canadiens hockey shirt, and was biting on a pair of bright-red wax lips. Phoebe swept him up into her arms and made smacking noises against his neck. 'Where'd you get the shirt?' she said, removing the wax lips.

'That man bought it for me,' he said.

'Uncle Dave,' Phoebe said. 'Don't call him "that man."'

'Uncle Dave,' Andrew said. 'But I don't like that lady. She made me eat green soup.'

'That was homemade broccoli soup,' Dave said. He was sitting slouched at the kitchen table, drinking a beer. Strands of hair had fallen across his forehead, and triangular pockets of flesh dipped beneath his eyes.

'How'd it go?' Phoebe asked him. 'You look tired.'

'Nah,' said Dave, finishing his beer 'Tell your mother what we did all day,' he said to Andrew.

'We went to the Big Rock,' Andrew said.

'And of course he wanted to get up to the top,' Dave said. The top of the Big Rock was nearly inaccessible; Phoebe remembered trying to scale the massive granite face as a child, and only making it as far as the crevice halfway up. 'And we had a little altercation over that – I said no because I was afraid he was going to fall and I didn't want to take any chances.'

'So I screamed,' Andrew said. 'And then he let me go to the top.'

'Andrew, it's not polite to scream,' Phoebe said. 'Did he really scream at you?' she asked Dave. 'I'm sorry.'

'Oh, nothing much happened,' Dave said. 'Like I said, we just had a little squabble over the matter, but anyway,' he continued hastily, 'then I thought, oh, hell, we can manage, the two of us, we can do it – there's such a thing as being overly cautious – and when we finally got up there you should have seen the kid, it was like he was on top of Mount Everest.'

'And look what,' said Andrew. 'Look what else he bought me!' He reached into a small paper bag and released a handful of penny candy on to the table: licorice ropes, Tootsie Pops, fireballs, bubblegum, Smarties, and a wiggly black Magic Walking Spider.

Dave gave her a sheepish smile, and shrugged.

'Want some?' Andrew began to tear open a packet of Lik-M-Aid, but Phoebe prised it from his fingers.

'Hey,' he said, 'Daddy told me I could have it tonight.'

'Don't give me that line,' Phoebe said. 'Maybe it works at home but not when we're at Grammy Louise's.'

'Oh, Phoebe, I'm glad you're home,' said Louise from the doorway. 'Rusty called to talk to Andrew. He said to say hello. Also' – and her mother reached for a piece of paper by the telephone – 'a woman called for a Herbert Sullivan? Is that his name? He's having trouble finding some papers for the . . . Shy deposition? I didn't quite get the name.'

Phoebe was puzzled. Herb called her? At home? About the documents for Robert Schein's deposition? Oh, no. Her chest tightened as she thought of Herb searching her office, for the documents were a mess. Phoebe was supposed to have got a paralegal to help her organize everything, but she found it difficult to call upon a paralegal for such tedious work, and as a result the documents lay in various unidentified illogical stacks on her floor, her credenza, the windowsill, the L of her desk. Some of them possibly even had coffee rings on them. When Phoebe started working for Herb another associate had told her, from experience, that Herb was meticulous about organization; he liked his documents colour-coded, tabulated, and filed in three-ring binders for easy access. Phoebe had brushed off his comments because he was a Nut, but she wished now that she had got organized from the beginning. She had planned on doing it when she got back, but if Herb was going through her office right now, all hell would break loose.

'What's wrong?' her mother asked.

'Can I have the Smarties before I go to bed?' Andrew asked. 'I won't get a cavity.'

Phoebe nodded absently. 'Did he want me to call him back today?'

'It's after five-thirty out there,' Louise said. 'Don't you think he's left for the day?'

Phoebe wondered if her mother could even imagine a twelve- or fourteen-hour workday. After Dave left she put Andrew to bed, then went down to use the kitchen phone. It was now almost six, California time. While Herb might have gone home already, at least she could go on record as having returned his call.

But her hopes of not having to deal with him tonight dissolved when she heard his voice. She thought of an electric drill, and held the phone away from her ear. So much for vacations, she thought. So much for getting away from it all.

'Yeah, Phoebe – where are all those hot documents you told me about?' Herb said. 'We're going to do Schein a little ahead of schedule. You said you had some good stuff on him. I need it this weekend.'

Phoebe swallowed. 'It's a little hard for me to describe,' she said. 'How about if I have the paralegal get the documents to you tomorrow?' Her mind was already racing. She could call Janice. Janice would hunt for the Schein documents. Janice would dig. Don't let me down, Janice; not now; you can't let me down.

'I don't care; as long as I get them by tomorrow,' Herb was saying.

'What happened?'

'What do you mean, what happened?'

Read, none of your business, Phoebe thought, but she wanted to turn the conversation away from the documents. 'I thought we weren't going to depose Schein until mid-December.'

'Ah, Christmas plans, something like that, he's going to Tahiti or God knows where with his family so he wants to have us do it right now and I said sure why not.'

'When's the deposition scheduled?'

'Next week,' Herb said. 'I'm getting someone else to help me out.'

Phoebe wondered if she was supposed to offer to go back. Maybe this could be her big chance; maybe she could talk Herb into letting her take the deposition. What are you, crazy? On such short notice? she heard Herb say. No, this was not the time to push for a deposition. Besides, what about her vacation? What about Molly's wedding? What about her time with Andrew?'

'It's all the same to me,' Herb was saying. 'You, Joe Schmoe, it won't make any difference as long as I have someone to back me up. Look, I have to run. Get me those documents by tomorrow. Hey, what do they say, anyway?'

At this point Phoebe heard her other voice take over, her professional voice. 'Some good statements on the mismanagement issue,' was what her professional voice was saying. 'In one memo he talks about how some vice-president said they'd be going down the tubes if they didn't get somebody better in marketing.' It was true. There was such a document, somewhere.

'Hey hey, that's what I like to hear,' Herb said, and now Phoebe thought of the cartoon with the evil spider, about to devour the fly in her web. 'Let me tell you,' Herb said, 'this guy's going to wish they'd never brought this lawsuit when I get through with him.'

'Yeah,' Phoebe said.

'Talk to you later,' Herb said.

'Yeah,' Phoebe said.

She hung up the phone, tingling all over. Okay, first things first. Get a paralegal, fast. In case Herb – by some off-the-wall chance – decides to go looking for him, her, whoever it's going to be. Then call Janice, and get her to start going through the stacks of documents in your office. Phoebe had an idea some of the Schein documents might be on the credenza. Or maybe those were the Miller documents?

Without thinking whom she might ask to serve as a paralegal on this mess, she dialled the main number of the firm. As the receptionist went home at five-thirty, she had to wait for several minutes before one of the attorneys finally answered; and whoever it was, it was clear that he was annoyed with her persistence. When he finally figured out how to transfer her to the chief of paralegals, she realized how ridiculous, how disorganized, how unprofessional, she was going to sound. She would have to get someone she could trust. But whom? Phoebe had never worked with any of the paralegals before. She was actually intimidated by them; many seemed to know the legal system and court procedures far better than the attorneys themselves. Who was that paralegal Janice worked with? It was some guy: Charlie? Buddy? *Ernie*. That was it.

When the chief of paralegals answered Phoebe had to spell her name; she couldn't recall having spoken with the chief of paralegals before.

'There's no Ernie working for us,' the woman said coldly.

Oh, please, Phoebe thought. Please make it easy for me. You don't know what I'm going through; you don't have any *idea*.

'Maybe you mean Eddie,' the woman offered. 'Eddie Sorenson?'

'That's it. Is he available?'

'When?'

'Now.'

'Oh no you don't,' the chief said. 'He's got another case that's going to trial next week.'

'It won't take him more than a couple of minutes,' Phoebe said. 'He just has to get some documents to one of the partners.'

'Getting documents to a partner means more than ten minutes' work,' the chief said.

'Not this time,' Phoebe said. 'The documents are all together. I just need him to deliver them down to the partner. And then he can start working on the case full-time when I get back.'

'Back? Where are you?'

'Vermont.'

'I thought you were calling from upstairs,' the chief said. 'Quite frankly this is very confusing.'

'It's sort of an emergency,' Phoebe said. 'I'll explain it later. Just tell me: can I have him?'

'Jesus Christ,' the chief muttered. 'The things we have to deal with.'

Eddie Sorenson grasped the situation immediately. 'Herb Sullivan?' he crooned, a brassy edge to his voice. 'You poor baby. When does he want them?'

'Tomorrow,' Phoebe said. 'Look, you don't have to do anything except bring them down to him. He thinks there's already a paralegal on the case. There isn't. I never got one.'

'You moron,' Eddie said. 'What's the matter with you?'

Phoebe said nothing.

'Okay, so where are the documents?'

'Oh, you don't have to bother looking for them. They're all in my office. You know Janice Williams? She'll get them together.'

'I don't mind,' said Eddie. 'That's what I'm here for.'

'No no, that's all right,' Phoebe said quickly. She didn't want Eddie going into her office; her disorganization could give him a bad first impression. Then she almost had to laugh: as if he currently thought she was organized!

'One more thing,' Phoebe confessed. 'If Herb comes looking for you, you've been on the case all along. Just tell him you'll get him the documents tomorrow. You can be firm with him.'

'Oh, I'll be firm with Herb,' Eddie said. 'Partners know better than to push paralegals around.'

Phoebe smiled. She liked this Eddie Sorenson, and now she felt a little foolish; for if she had got in touch with him two months ago, the documents would all be colour-coded by now.

Feeling somewhat calmer, she had Eddie switch her to Janice's extension; but Janice didn't answer. Phoebe hung up and called Janice at home, but there was no answer there either. The fear began to grip at her stomach again, so she poured herself a glass of wine. Her head was spinning. Some vacation.

She took the wine upstairs and crawled into bed; she would try Janice later tonight. Lying there with the light on, unable to concentrate on a novel, she wondered how Molly was doing, whether the bleeding had started up again. She tried to blot out that moment in Molly's studio, when all seemed so lost between them; instead she thought of Molly and Nick upstairs in their bed, talking into the night, comforting each other, making plans for their life together. Maybe you are a little envious, she thought; after all, Molly has Nick; Molly has control over her time. And you? All you've got is Herb Sullivan hounding you for a document three thousand miles away. And another six months of all-nighters.

Around eleven she tried Janice once more; still no answer. Try again tomorrow, she told herself. Go get some sleep. But Phoebe didn't sleep very well that night. Too hot under the quilt, she dreamed she was at a firm picnic, and they were all playing softball. Herb was pitching, and when it was her turn he switched from slow pitch to fast, the ball spinning forward so fast that she froze in its path, unable to move.

Janice still didn't answer when Phoebe called her at home again as early as she dared Friday morning. She then called the firm.

'Janice is on leave,' her secretary said. 'With Frank gone she had a little free time, so she went up to Inverness with her boyfriend.'

'Did she leave a number?' Phoebe asked anxiously, though she wondered what good it would do, as she needed the documents today. But she took down the name and number of the lodge, just in case. She hung up and realized that it was Eddie who would have to find the documents. He wouldn't have to find all of them, but he would have to find the mismanagement memo.

'The place is sort of a mess,' she told him sheepishly. 'You may have trouble just walking around.'

'Tell me exactly what I'm looking for.'

'Anything that pertains to Robert Schein,' Phoebe said, and she spelled out the name for him.

'Got it,' Eddie said. 'Any idea as to where they might be?'

'Try the credenza,' Phoebe said. 'If they're not there then try the windowsill.' That was a blatant lie. She had no idea where the documents were.

'You have my number,' Phoebe said. 'Call if you have any questions; I'll be here all day.'

'Take it easy, babes,' Eddie said. 'If I find them I find them. If I don't I don't. The guy's not going to die without the documents.'

'No but I will,' Phoebe said. 'You don't know Herb.'

'I *do* know Herb, and Herb knows me. He's a pussycat.'

Phoebe spent the early afternoon playing Go Fish with Andrew. As he plucked cards, one by one, from her hand she told her mother about Molly's bleeding. Louise showed no surprise, and Phoebe wondered if all the women at the shower had guessed what the problem was. She wondered if even Cindy Ann knew, Cindy Ann with her advice about endometriosis.

Louise said it was indeed common. 'I even bled a little when I was carrying you,' she said.

Phoebe thought she should give Molly a call and tell her exactly that. 'You'll put her mind at ease,' she said.

'You tell her,' Louise said. 'I'm not supposed to know.'

Phoebe hit the table. 'Jesus! When is this bullshit going to end!'

'When Molly's been married a month,' Louise replied.

In the middle of the afternoon Molly called. The bleeding had completely stopped, she reported happily. She was still in bed. Nick was a doll. He had cooked her breakfast and then gone out and bought her a bunch of trashy magazines. Then he had taken the rug to the dump and swept off the porch, washed the dishes, vacuumed the whole house, fluffed up the pillows on the sofa, and scrubbed the bathroom floor. 'His parents are due in today,' she explained.

'Phoebe?' she said.

Phoebe started.

'Is something the matter?' Molly said. 'You're not angry at me for yelling at you, are you?'

'Of course not,' Phoebe said. And she told Molly about the potential disaster with the documents.

'Why don't you just explain it to him?' Molly said. 'Tell him the truth.'

Phoebe shook her head. 'I can't tell him the truth.' She shouldn't have expected Molly to understand; nobody back here would ever be able to understand.

'But all you'd be telling him is that you got a little disorganized,' Molly said. 'What's wrong with being a little disorganized?'

'Everything,' Phoebe replied. 'It's not how well you think, it's how well you *appear* to think. Organized lawyers look smart. Disorganized lawyers look dumb.'

'Oh,' said Molly.

'Look, I shouldn't tie up the line,' Phoebe sighed. 'My paralegal might be trying to call.'

'Okay,' Molly said. 'Good luck. I hope it all works out.'

But when Eddie finally called late in the afternoon, he did not have good news. He had gone through all the documents in her office, but hadn't found anything on Schein. Phoebe tried desperately to think of other places where she might have put the documents. Had she given them to her secretary? Had she maybe filed them? Perhaps she was farther ahead in the game, more organized, than she remembered? She told Eddie to look through her second file drawer, and then to check with her secretary. 'I'm really sorry,' she said. 'I hate to put you through this.'

'I've been through worse,' Eddie said. 'And relax. So I don't find the documents. Herb'll scream and holler and in a week he'll have forgotten all about it. Believe me. I've worked with him before. He's a pussycat.'

Phoebe wanted to believe him, but she couldn't. And in her state of worry Eddie's cockiness was beginning to grate. He had to find the memo Schein had written on mismanagement. It actually was a good document, particularly on the issue of damages, for if the defendants could establish that much of the plaintiff's losses were due to its mismanagement or inefficiency, it would be hard for the plaintiff to recover treble damages, regardless of any price-fixing conspiracy. The damages are just too speculative, the court could say.

(And for a brief moment she marvelled over her concern. Haven't you come a long way, she thought. Look at you, you're actually concerned about preventing some corporation from getting slapped with treble damages.)

Did I lose the memo? she wondered.

Does it even exist? Maybe I just imagined it; the rest of the documents were so boring, maybe I invented it in my mind as the type of document I wished I would find.

But no; she remembered it clearly. There were even four bold, healthy sets of initials on it. What she feared was that it was so hot she had put it in a special place, and then forgotten where.

Half an hour later Eddie called again to say that he had found a stack of documents under her desk, the top one of which was a memo from R.L. Schein. Phoebe couldn't remember what that stack was, or why it was under her desk; but she had Eddie read her the memos. The hot memo wasn't there, though, and the others were essentially useless; Schein was talking about management in general. Along with the hot memo, those documents might possibly tie the knot in the defence, but standing alone they were as innocent as thank-you notes.

'You want me to give him these?' Eddie asked.

'I don't know,' Phoebe said. 'What kind of a mood is he in?'

'Definitely premenstrual, sorry to say,' Eddie said. 'But don't let it worry you. Whoops, there goes your buzzer, wait a sec.' He put Phoebe on hold. 'Speak of the devil,' he said after a brief cutoff. 'Herr Sullivan wants the documents right now.'

'*Shit*.'

'Tell you what,' Eddie said. 'I could type up a document log right now and backdate it and include a description of that memo you're so worried about. That way we can blame it on him. He won't notice it's not there in the stack until tomorrow, hopefully; and then I'll tell him that according to the document log it was in the stack *I* gave him so therefore *he* must have lost it.'

Phoebe was a little taken aback by this proposal. It was out-and-out forgery – of a document log, sure; but *still*.

'Don't get me wrong,' Eddie said. 'I wouldn't do this to anyone but Herb Sullivan.'

'I think that's pushing it,' Phoebe said, 'even if it is Herb we're dealing with. Besides, I don't know the date it was written, or any of the other stuff you have to put in a document log.'

'Whatever you say, boss,' Eddie said. 'You want me to give him this stack?'

Phoebe sighed. 'Go ahead,' she said. 'I haven't got any choice. Look, you go home for the weekend, this is my problem. Go home and relax.'

'Who's gonna relax?' Eddie said. 'I've got a trial next week.'

* * *

Phoebe hadn't been able to eat much all day long, and she watched her mother preparing dinner with little appetite. It was now five-fifteen. She thought of Herb going to the TG party, piercing shrimp with a toothpick, downing his glasses of Napa Valley Chardonnay. Maybe he wouldn't go through Eddie's stack before he left, and Janice could get into the office early tomorrow to look for the memo. By the time he noticed it was missing, Janice would have found it.

And if worse came to worst she herself would go back and look for it. Other lawyers flew cross-country and back in a day; so could she.

But at five-thirty the phone ran again. It was Herb, of course.

'Oh yes, Herb,' Phoebe said. 'How are you?'

'Where's that document you were talking about?' he said. 'Eddie gave me this stack and there's nothing in here on mismanagement.'

'No?' Phoebe said. 'Are you sure?'

'Sure I'm sure. What happened? Where'd it go?'

'Gee,' said Phoebe. 'It should be there.'

'Well, it's not,' Herb snapped.

Phoebe said nothing.

'Look, I need that document!' Herb said. 'We're doing Schein next week and I need that document! Don't we have a copy around here somewhere? Don't we have a document log? Where are the originals kept?'

Phoebe couldn't bring herself to tell him that it was possible that he might very well be holding the originals in his lap. She just wasn't an organizer, and to Herb – to most attorneys, in fact, and for good reason – organization was of primary importance. She didn't know what to say to him. She needed another minute to think. 'Excuse me,' she said to Herb, and she put her hand over the mouthpiece and turned towards the stove. 'Andrew honey, I'll be with you in just a second.' Louise, washing lettuce at the sink, gave her a queer look, for Andrew was out in the living room, playing with the Lincoln Logs. 'I'll be with you just as soon as I'm off the phone, honey. Excuse me,' she said to Herb. 'Now about the document – '

'Just find it, Phoebe,' Herb said. 'But I want it by Sunday.' The phone line clicked, and Phoebe replaced the receiver gingerly, as though it would help placate Herb. She stared at the floor.

'What was that all about?' Louise said.

Phoebe continued to stare at the floor.

'Phoebe?' said Louise. 'Phoebe, what's the matter?'

Phoebe just shook her head. She had no idea what she was going to do next. What an unbelievable mess this visit – this *vacation* – was turning out to be. She had come back to be in her oldest friend's wedding, and was finding herself not in the midst of a happy reunion but rather facing the possibility that her friendship with Molly had withered away during these years of change to nothing but a cold common history of a shared childhood. And now, on top of that, all that she hated about her job at Judson and Day – working for Herb, organizing his documents – was about to explode in her face.

What an unbelievable mess.

# 10

'I'm trying,' Molly said. 'I really am trying.'

'How?' said Nick.

'I asked her about Andrew,' Molly said. 'I asked her if he'd adjusted to the divorce.'

'And?'

'And then you came home,' Molly said. 'So she didn't have a chance to respond.'

'That was sort of a weird question,' Nick said. 'Why didn't you ask her something about herself?'

'Like what?'

'Like how she feels about – what's his name?'

'Rusty?'

'Yeah – or whether she's involved with anyone else. Do you even know whether she's seeing anyone these days?'

'No,' Molly admitted.

'Aren't you curious?'

'I guess so,' Molly said.

'Or ask her how she manages being a single mother with her job,' Nick said. 'I'd be interested in knowing how she manages to raise a kid while busting ass at a job like hers.'

Molly bristled. The note of admiration in Nick's voice was unmistakable, and she suddenly wondered if Nick thought that she should be doing what Phoebe was doing. Or something more along those lines. Maybe Nick was wishing she would take on a different career, something more up to date, more urban, than teaching school and weaving: something like broadcast journalism, say, or a career in advertising. Maybe he had a secret wish that she would get her MBA; they would team up with their degrees and make a fortune. Remember those days back in Vermont? they would say, sitting in their penthouse overlooking Central Park. Remember the garden? Remember the bathtub? Remember never having any money for a vacation?

But Molly couldn't really see it. And she hoped Nick couldn't, either, though it was such an unsettling idea that she didn't even want to bring it up with him.

'I'm just interested,' Nick was saying. 'I think it must be pretty hard for her, trying to become a good attorney and also find time for her child.'

'Maybe.'

'What – you *don't* think it's so hard?'

'I didn't say that,' Molly said. 'It probably *is* hard.' Though she wondered how much Phoebe really disliked that strung-out feeling. Phoebe had never been able to do much of anything unless it was under pressure, and Molly had an idea that Phoebe liked being able to say that she had *no* time for this and *no* time for that and how was she *ever* going to get everything done on time! (She would.) When Phoebe had told her about the document problem earlier that afternoon, her voice sounded frazzled, but it also sounded more exuberant than it had since she'd arrived back here in Vermont. Molly imagined that Phoebe couldn't survive without having to confront more than the average daily dose of hassle.

'Well, anyway,' Nick said. 'I'm glad you're trying.'

'Don't get too glad,' Molly said. 'I also screamed at her not to boss me around.'

'When?'

'When I started to bleed.'

'Why?'

'Because she *was* bossing me around!' Molly sputtered, angry again. 'She was acting like she was in total control, as if she knew exactly what was going on!'

Nick frowned.

'She was,' Molly said. 'And I wish she'd knock it off. You just wait – she'll probably tell me how to put your ring on in the middle of the ceremony.'

Nick continued to frown.

'Two more days,' said Molly. 'You sure you don't want out?'

'No.'

'No-you-don't-want-out?'

'No,' Nick said. 'No-I'm-not-sure.'

Molly looked at him.

'But I'm mostly sure,' he said. 'Same as you.'

The wedding guests arrived in staggered lots that Friday afternoon. First came the Ulrichs, from New York, in their burgundy BMW: Elaine so underweight that in her drapey raw silk suit she looked like an orphan child in grown-up's clothes; Stan, carefully casual in corduroy slacks and a LaCoste V-neck sweater; and Stan's father Matthew, or Bubbah, who wore a red sports jacket with blue madras pants and hobbled about with a walnut cane. With his bushy white hair and moustache he reminded Molly of Mark Twain. Then came Nick's two college friends, Mary Jo and Leo, both congressional aides in Washington, DC; they arrived in a rented Gremlin, puffy and overdressed on this unseasonably warm afternoon in their down parkas, eagerly scanning the clouds for signs of a temperature change, an early snowfall. The last to arrive were Bea's parents; they had flown up from Pompano Beach, permanently sunburned, withered as dried apricots. Ben Colby stepped out of the rented Buick wearing his white buck shoes, and swung an imaginary golf club in the air. 'Who's ready to tee off?' he shouted as Natalie waited for him to open her door.

Dusk fell upon them early that afternoon, and they gathered in the Adamses' living room, where Dave had already lit a fire. From above the mantel a six-point buck that Dave had shot several years ago gazed over their heads; Stan, it turned out, was originally from northern Maine, and hunted elk, and so he and Dave talked about rifles and scopes, about the advantages of reloading cartridges.

Molly had always liked her future father-in-law; he bore an uncanny resemblance to Nick, so much so that she sometimes even felt a little embarrassed in his company, as though she knew too much about his private self. With Elaine, however, she had never had any kind of a rapport. Nick's mother was distinctly a city person; she chain-smoked cigarillos, stretching all the tendons in her emaciated throat whenever she inhaled; and she never stopped talking in her abrasive grainy voice. Molly wouldn't have minded her ceaseless chatter if every so often she had had the courtesy to stop and inquire about her (How's your weaving going, Molly? And did I hear you just sold another wall hanging?); but all she wanted to talk about tonight was the price of real estate on the Upper West Side, the relationship of interest rates to the solvency of the timber industry, the unrealistic optimism of solar energy enthusiasts. At that point Molly grew edgy, for her father was convinced that solar energy was the only solution to Vermont's energy problem, and he was thinking of solarizing the sun porch this next summer, a kind of test run before popping up the entire roof over their bedroom. Molly, feeling protective towards her father's values, wanted to argue with Elaine, but she didn't have a chance, because by now Elaine had turned to the subject of drug dealers on the Lower East Side, she liked to shop on the Lower East Side, in fact she'd bought the silk suit there for half of what it would have cost in Saks, but having read a recent article on how a few blocks from the shopping district it was full of drug dealers she was, well, a little reluctant to go down there. (Later, as she jabbered away during dinner, Molly found herself staring vacantly at Elaine's mouth. At first she wondered whether Nick's mother had cancer, she had grown so thin since the last visit; but then she realized that Elaine just never stopped talking long enough to eat, to fuel her voice box. She was running on reserve all the time, and the reserve was running out.)

'Where's the maid of honour?' Leo asked. 'If I'm going to be the best man I'd better get to know the maid of honour.'

'That's right,' Bea said. 'Where is Phoebe, anyway?'

Molly realized that in all the confusion of yesterday's near miscarriage she had forgotten to invite Phoebe to the dinner tonight.

'You did mention it to her, didn't you?' Bea said.

'I forgot,' Molly said. 'I'm sorry.'

'Well go call her right now,' Bea said. 'I've got a place all set for her!'

'Want me to call her?' Nick said.

'Want me to call her?' Leo said at the same time.

'I'll call her,' Molly said.

'Dinner?' said Phoebe after Molly had apologized for the last-minute invitation.

'I forgot to mention it,' Molly said. 'Things got so mixed up yesterday afternoon.'

'I can't,' Phoebe said. 'Really, thanks, but I can't.'

'Why not?'

Phoebe sighed.

'Come on up,' Molly said, thinking that getting together with Phoebe in the jovial atmosphere of a pre-wedding feast might be just what they needed. 'It's rack of lamb and baked Alaska.'

'Thanks,' Phoebe said, 'but I have to figure out what to do about this document mess.'

'On a Friday night? What can you do about it on a Friday night?'

'I have no idea.' Phoebe's voice sounded dull, discouraged.

'Oh, come on,' Molly said. 'It'll help you take your mind off things. And you have to meet Leo. He's a lawyer too; he works on Capitol Hill. Hey – maybe Leo can help!'

'I don't think so,' Phoebe said. She gave another long sigh. 'I wouldn't be very good company tonight anyway.'

By now Molly was growing annoyed; this was the beginning of her wedding weekend and apparently Phoebe was going to throw a damper on everything because of some trivial mixup back in California. She thought Phoebe was making a mountain out of a molehill, frankly; but if that were the case, then so be it: let her stay home and mope. She certainly didn't want Phoebe spoiling everyone else's good time tonight.

'Okay, then,' Molly said. 'Have fun figuring it all out.' She hung up and went back to the living room.

'Well?' said Bea.

'She's busy,' Molly said. 'She says she has to work.'

'Work!' cried Bea. 'On a Friday night?'

Molly shrugged.

'I'll talk to her,' said Leo. 'I know how it is. Sometimes you think what it is you're working on just can't wait. Where does she work?'

'Some firm,' Molly said. 'Look – why don't we start a round of champagne?'

'A big firm?' said Leo.

'I don't know,' said Molly.

'Yes,' said Nick.

'No wonder, then,' said Leo. 'They can really run you through the grist mill at some of those places. I had a friend who got called back from the Bahamas – he was on his honeymoon! – because some partner wanted him to cite-check a brief.'

'No!' Nick exclaimed.

'I kid you not.' Leo was solemn. 'Let me call her. I know how to handle this.'

But in a few minutes Leo came back from the phone in a huff.

'No luck?' said Bea.

'I don't know what I said,' Leo said, 'but something sure ticked her off.'

'I say we forget about it,' Molly said. 'Let Phoebe deal with it tonight so she'll relax for the rest of the weekend. Come on, let's have some bubblies.'

So Dave set about untwisting the wire from a bottle of champagne. He tilted its neck towards the ceiling and thumbed up the cork; it gave a big pop! and hit the buck on its neck. When everyone had a glass (although Molly wasn't drinking, she took one so as not to raise any eyebrows; she would trade glasses with Nick as soon as he had drained his), Stan proposed the first toast. 'To the bride and groom,' he said with the magic of Nick's voice. 'May they have a long and happy life together.'

'A long and *prolific* life,' said Bubbah. 'I'm waiting for that fourth generation, you know.'

'To my new son,' said Bea, hugging Nick.

'To my new daughter!' cried Elaine.

'To old friends tying the knot,' said Mary Jo.

'*À votre santé*,' Leo proclaimed.

As the wedding guests sat down to Bea's rack of lamb, Phoebe was making reservations on a Saturday-afternoon flight to San Francisco, with a red-eye back East at midnight. Just in case she didn't reach Janice, or Janice couldn't get back to the city to look for the memo. With a couple of Valium and a good pair of earplugs she could manage to sleep on the red-eye so that she wouldn't be too burned out for Molly's wedding, assuming there were no screaming babies. The round-trip ticket came to more than twice the Halloween special, but she reminded herself that it was probably tax deductible. Besides, if she didn't reach Janice she had no choice. Someone had to find the memo.

Phoebe tried calling the Inverness Lodge three times within an hour, and the switchboard operator grew annoyed. Finally Phoebe resorted to telling her there'd been a death in the family.

'We'll do everything we can,' the operator said quickly.

'Thank you,' Phoebe said.

When Louise heard that Phoebe was planning to fly to San Francisco and back in one day, she was dumbfounded.

'There's no other option,' Phoebe said. 'I created this mess, I have to clean it up.'

'Hey Mum, pretend I'm E.T.,' said Andrew.

Phoebe looked at him and nodded.

'What's so important about one little memo?' Cindy Ann said. She had come up to watch *Dallas* with them because Jack was on duty, and she had brought along her needlepoint, a pink-and-green sampler that read, *A Little Bit of Cookin's Like a Little Bit of Lovin'*.

'In that one little memo the plaintiff is talking about how its company was going out of business regardless of what my clients did,' Phoebe said. 'That doesn't make it very easy for the plaintiff to recover treble damages.' Listening to her own legalese she wondered why she was even bothering to try and explain the document's significance; Cindy Ann didn't know anything about anti-trust law.

But that didn't seem to matter to her sister-in-law. 'If it's so important why don't you just show it to a judge?' Cindy Ann said, cutting a piece of pink silky thread. 'Why are you guys even bothering with a disposition?'

Oh, honestly, thought Phoebe.

'Phoebe, I say no,' Louise said. 'I'm putting my foot down.'

'You can't,' Phoebe said. 'If I don't reach Janice I have to go and find the memo. It's as simple as that.'

'Get someone else on the case to find it!' Louise said. 'What's the use of having a litigation team if you can't count on the players when the chips are down?'

'They counted on me,' Phoebe said glumly. 'This is all my doing.'

'Mum,' said Andrew, 'pretend you're the little girl and I'm E.T. and you're scared of me.'

Phoebe looked at him and nodded again.

'Act *scared*, Mum!'

'Not now, Andrew,' Phoebe said. 'I've got too much on my mind to act scared.'

'Why don't you just call up the company who wrote it and ask them for another copy?' Cindy Ann suggested. 'Tell them you'll pay for it. I bet you could get it for a lot less than it'll cost you to fly out there and back.'

Phoebe couldn't help staring at her. Cindy Ann had no idea what she was proposing. Calling the clients rather than their attorneys, and offering in essence a bribe –

'Who says you'll find it, anyway?' Louise demanded. 'What if it's not there? Then you'll have made the whole trip for nothing. Then what?'

'Then I'm unemployed,' Phoebe said. 'Then I throw pots.'

'Oh, knock it off,' Louise said. 'They're not going to fire you for losing one document.'

'You don't know Herb,' Phoebe said. 'And it's not just any old document, it's the smoking gun. Do you understand what a smoking gun is?'

Louise pursed her lips.

'Boy, this guy sounds like a real son of a you-know-what,' Cindy Ann remarked.

Thank you, Phoebe thought. Thank you, Cindy Ann.

'Pretend I'm the dog in E.T.,' Andrew said. He got down on his knees and began to sniff at Phoebe's leg. 'Pretend *you're* E.T. and I'm scared of *you*! Come on, Mum, make your neck long!'

'I'll make my neck long,' Cindy Ann said. 'I'll pretend I'm E.T.!'

'I don't want *you* to be E.T.,' Andrew said. 'I want my *mum* to be E.T.' He dropped back on all fours and sniffed around the woodstove.

'Phoebe, you're acting irrationally,' Louise said. 'You've been with the firm three years. They need you. They're not going to fire you for this.'

'Want to bet?'

'I want you to get on the phone right now,' Louise said. 'Get on the phone and tell them they'll just have to reschedule the deposition. You'll find the document when you get back and then they can take it.'

'It doesn't work that way,' Phoebe said. 'I'm an associate.'

'You're a lawyer!'

'I'm an *associate*, Mother!' Phoebe snapped. 'I read documents. Document readers don't reschedule depositions.'

'Well, I'm sorry,' Louise said. 'I'm your mother, and I'm not letting you go. You'll run yourself ragged. If I have to, I'll call this man Harry myself, I'll tell him to blame it on me if he doesn't have the memo when he needs it.'

'You wouldn't,' Phoebe said.

'Try me,' Louise said.

'How come you're working for such a creep, anyway?' Cindy Ann said. 'Why don't you just switch partners and work for someone nice?'

Phoebe pinched the bridge of her nose. Calm yourself, she thought; these people shouldn't be expected to understand how law firms work. Cindy Ann has probably never dealt with a lawyer, and as for your mother, the only law firm she's familiar with is that one small practice in St Audenbury: two partners, one secretary, an IBM Selectric, and access to the court library. They have no idea.

Andrew pawed at her leg; he was carrying one of Louise's Wallabees between his teeth. 'Andrew, take that out,' she said, 'you can play dog but don't put Grammy's dirty old shoes in your mouth. Excuse me,' she said, 'but I have to try Janice again.' She left them in the kitchen and could hear their voices, hushed and urgent, as she tried the Inverness Lodge for the fourth time. Still no answer in Janice's room. It was no use now; she might as well wait until morning. But even then, what was the chance that she could rely on Janice to get down to the city and find the document in time for her to cancel her flight? Slim. Very slim. She would be on a plane tomorrow.

She went over her flight schedule, assuming she didn't reach Janice. She would arrive in San Francisco at five, and go straight to the firm. Hopefully it would be relatively deserted, and she would make a complete sweep of her office, even check the offices of the other Parco-Fields associates in case she had left it on someone's desk. (Though she knew that was unlikely; the other associates were all Nuts, all on the other side of the fence, and she'd always had as little to do with them as possible.)

And if she didn't find the memo at the firm, she would go back to Berkeley and search her house. It might take some time but she would find the memo. Even if it meant missing Molly's wedding. It wouldn't be the worst thing that could happen, after all; in its own way it might even be preferable, given the way nothing was clicking between them. Sure, call it avoiding the issue; but who wanted a blowup?

Back in the kitchen Miss Ellie was trying to settle an argument between J.R. and Bobby.

'She's too nice,' Cindy Ann said. 'She's always too nice to them.'

'I'll cancel her plane reservations if I have to,' Louise was saying. 'She's lost her senses.'

'Oh Miss Ellie,' Cindy Ann sighed. 'Why don't you just shoot those two boys!'

The next morning Nick got up before Molly and started frying bacon because his parents and Bubbah, along with Mary Jo and Leo, were coming over for breakfast. They had all taken rooms at the nearby Winslow Inn, the town's one historic landmark, built of white clapboards, with low ceilings and a large slate fireplace in the dining room. This weekend, except for a few out-of-state hunters here for opening day of deer season, the five of them had the place to themselves.

By now Molly had gone for thirty-six hours without any further bleeding, but to play it safe she was still trying to remain off her feet as much as possible. Nevertheless she and Nick were feeling jubilant. Nick made a pitcher of Bloody Marys, pouring her a tall glass before adding the vodka. She lay on the couch and imagined she was in a hammock in their backyard; it was June, and the baby was lying across her stomach, and she was sipping iced tea and smelling roses and finding animal shapes in the clouds.

She wondered if Phoebe had managed to resolve her problem at the law firm since they had spoken last night. I guess I really *don't* understand what it's like, she thought. Here was Phoebe, who had always been so defiant towards authority (for instance, with Doris Conran, or with the Girl Scout troop leader, or the choir director, or their Sunday-school teacher) – and she was close to having a nervous breakdown because some attorney who happened to have a little more seniority needed a document. Why was she so terrified of her superiors now? What had happened to the old Phoebe, the girl who in high school refused to take her finals in protest over the invasion of Cambodia? Go ahead, expel me, Phoebe had said to Doris Conran, who did indeed expel her, until Louise made a few well-placed and apologetic phone calls. Yet maybe that wasn't the right analogy; maybe things weren't so black and white for Phoebe any more. Maybe there were no more Doris Conrans to be defied, only a vague hierarchy, with Phoebe near the bottom and this partner demanding his document near the top.

Molly didn't know.

But this was certainly a side of Phoebe she'd never seen. Molly wondered what would happen if Phoebe just called this attorney and said, Look, *you* deal with this, my friend (my best friend? Would Phoebe say that at this point?) is getting married tomorrow and it's very important to me (was it?) and to my friend (was it?) that I be able to take part in the wedding festivities. How would that go over? Was the marriage of one's oldest friend important enough to let you get away with putting your foot down and saying, *No*, you will have to do without me right now? Or did it have to be something dramatic: a death in the family, say, or a debilitating accident?

In the kitchen Nick was breaking eggs into a large bowl. 'What if you were working for a big firm and you were under this deadline and the kid and I were in a car accident,' Molly said. 'Would you put your foot down?'

Nick turned and gave her a bewildered look. 'What kind of a question is *that*?'

'I was just thinking,' Molly said, 'you know, with Phoebe having to deal with this problem at work all of a sudden . . . I wonder if you'll ever be in that boat.'

'Let's not cross our bridges, Molly,' said Nick. 'I haven't even got into law school yet.'

Molly was silent.

'I don't want to be a lawyer's wife,' she announced after a while.

'You won't,' replied Nick. 'You'll be an artist who's married to a guy who practises law.'

'Don't play with words,' Molly said. 'I don't want you to be tied to your job like Phoebe is.'

'I won't.'

'How do you know?'

'I don't know,' said Nick. 'But I just can't see it.'

Molly shook her head ruefully. 'I bet that's what all first-year law students say. *I'm* not going to get sucked into that rat race; not *me*, buster; I'm going to keep my life balanced, save time for the wife and kid, take a vacation every six months, and continue to read good literature.'

Nick went back to beating the eggs.

'I just don't want you to get caught up the way she's caught up,' said Molly. 'You know?'

* * *

Mary Jo and Elaine arrived early. Mary Jo was wearing jeans, Elaine an aqua warm-up suit. From the sofa Molly politely asked Elaine if she had been for a run.

'Well I woke up and opened the window just a crack to see how cold it was and decided it was warm enough to run so I got all dressed and told Stan I was going and on my way out of the door there was Mary Jo and she was going for a walk along the river so there went the jogging idea but it was absolutely beautiful out there! Abso*lut*ely beautiful! Wasn't it, Mary Jo!'

'Sure was,' Mary Jo said. She was watching Nick slice up a loaf of bread. 'Boy, have you come a long way.'

'You should taste my Stroganoff,' Nick said. 'Have a Bloody Mary.'

Mary Jo poured two Bloody Marys, for Elaine and herself. 'Refill?' she called in to Molly, but Molly shook her head. She carefully lifted herself from the sofa, and joined them in the kitchen.

Elaine was leaning against the hutch. 'You know, once you're past the danger period you'll be able to get all the exercise you want, the doctors are saying it's good for you and even Jane Fonda has a book on it now, I'll get it for you, you stay in shape right up until the baby comes and she even tells you what to do afterwards.' Elaine stirred her drink with a stalk of celery. 'But right now you just take it easy.'

Molly stared at her.

Nick had stopped slicing the bread. He closed his eyes.

Mary Jo cleared her throat. 'Excuse me,' she said. 'I think I left something back at the inn.'

Nick opened his eyes and looked at Molly. 'She asked me,' he said. 'I couldn't help it.'

Molly said nothing.

'Don't tell me,' Elaine said, her wrist to her forehead. 'Don't tell me I said something I wasn't supposed to say.'

'You did,' Nick said.

'Oh dear,' Elaine said.

'I told you last night, Mother, Molly doesn't want people to know until after we're married. I told you but as usual you weren't listening.'

'Oh dear,' Elaine said.

Molly sat down on the kitchen chair, not looking at either of them.

'Well Molly, I don't see any point in making such a big deal over it, it's not as though I'm going to rush up to the farmhouse and spread the gospel, I may be a blabbermouth but I'm not that bad, I'm just very pleased for you and I'm glad to be one of the first to know, it's a very happy occasion for us, Bubbah especially, he's tickled pink, he doesn't have any great-grandchildren, this will be the first.'

Molly was getting tired just listening to her.

'My mother won't say anything,' Nick said. 'Not after this. Will you, Mother.'

Molly raised her hands and let them drop into her lap. 'Oh, fuck it,' she said. 'Who cares.'

'Maybe I should leave you two alone for a while,' Elaine said. 'I think I'll go see how Stan is doing.' She zipped up her jogging jacket. 'Very frankly though I don't think this is anything to ruin the wedding over,' she added on her way out the door.

Nick said, 'I'm sorry. I told her it wasn't common knowledge. She doesn't listen.'

Molly was silent. 'She's right,' she finally said. 'I shouldn't get so upset over it. I don't blame you for telling her. Jesus, she talks so fast she'd have put the words in your mouth anyway.'

'I should have known she wouldn't keep her mouth shut,' Nick said. 'If Father'd been here he would have cut her off.'

'It's water over the dam,' Molly said. 'Don't worry.'

Nick looked at her, puzzled.

'You and Phoebe are right, this whole thing is ludicrous. We've got more important things to worry about than what my parents are going to think. Christ, me jumping up and clearing the table last night and doing the dishes just so my mother wouldn't wonder if anything was weird. I've got a baby to worry about; screw this charade.'

Nick smiled.

'I mean it,' Molly said. 'And if they think I'm dragging you kicking and screaming to the altar, then too bad.'

# 11

Later that morning it began to snow. The first flakes seemed to come from nowhere, but then suddenly the air filled with a great white fury that blew in all directions. Visibility was so poor that you couldn't even see from the Martin farmhouse to the Adamses', and within half an hour the fields were white, although the dead-brown grass poked through the thin blanket, a stubby reminder that it was, indeed, only November. Still, the contours of the stone wall along the dirt road began to meld together as the snow collected on its granitey surface, and a set of dark tyre tracks quickly disappeared as the storm continued. Winter was near.

If Phoebe hadn't been so concerned about road conditions, about making it to the Burlington airport on time, she would have been moved by the storm, by its blustering dizziness and simultaneous tranquillity, something that winter rains off an angry Pacific Ocean never gave her. If she'd been less preoccupied she would have closed her eyes and smelled wet wool drying over a hot woodstove, heard the crunch of snow tyres after a January blizzard, the stamping of boots on the porch steps; she might even have recalled the icy shock of a handful of snow being stuffed down her collar from behind by her older brother.

But Phoebe didn't have time to smell or hear or feel any of that; she was angry with the storm, with the snow that was quickly piling up on the road. This would only give her mother more of an argument against her going back to California; why, for all Phoebe knew, Louise might not even have put snow tyres on the car at this early date. Damn Vermont, damn its icy roads. And she didn't even have any boots or hats or gloves with her!

She opened her briefcase, removed some books, and began repacking it with a change of underwear, socks, toiletries. As she snapped it shut Andrew appeared in the doorway. From the time he had got up that morning he had been fidgety, clingy, unable to entertain himself. She had successively given him the Lincoln Logs, Pegity, Tinker Toys, and the Etch-A-Sketch to play with, but nothing had kept his attention for more than fifteen minutes.

'Mum,' he said now, 'what can I *do*?'

'Why don't you look at a picture book?' she suggested. 'Grammy has lots of *Babars*.'

'I don't like *Babar*,' Andrew said.

'You liked *Babar* when Daddy read it to you,' Phoebe said. 'That was all you could talk about.'

'Well, I don't like it any more,' Andrew said. He bent his top half across the mattress and tried to roll his torso towards the foot of the bed by twisting around and around. 'I wish I could go over to Daddy's,' he said.

'You can't, Andrew,' Phoebe said. 'You can't go over to Daddy's until after next week.'

'How long's after-next-week?'

'Not long,' Phoebe said. 'Why don't you go play with Grammy's dominoes?'

'I don't know how to play dominoes,' Andrew said.

'Andrew, do me a favour and stop whining?' Phoebe said. 'You've been whining all morning long.' This is Herb's fault, she thought. If it weren't for Herb I'd have more time to spend with Andrew and he wouldn't have to whine so much.

Andrew now lay with his face down on the mattress.

'Andrew,' she said, 'stand up, I have to talk to you about something.'

'I can hear you,' he said in a muffled voice. 'Hey – pretend you've tied me up and I can't move so I have to stay like this for ever.'

'Andrew,' Phoebe said, 'I have to go away tonight but I'll be back tomorrow.'

Andrew picked his head up. 'Where are you going?'

'I have to go into the office,' she said, and realized she was making it sound as though this were just another Saturday and she were going across the Bay Bridge into the City.

'How come I don't get to go to Daddy's, then?' he demanded.

'You know why,' she said lightly, but she hated herself for trying to paint it so simply. His intuitions were telling him that something unusual was happening, and she had no right to make him feel mistaken. Something unusual *was* happening.

'Daddy's a long ways away,' she said.

'So's your office.'

'That's right,' she said, 'and I wouldn't be going back unless I absolutely had to.'

'How come you have to go back?'

Because I fucked up, Phoebe came close to saying. Because my ass is on the line. 'Because I lost something,' she told him, 'and nobody else can find it.'

'How come I can't go back with you?' Andrew said. 'How come I have to stay here?'

'Because I'm just going back for a short time,' Phoebe said. 'And besides, I can't afford to take you.'

'I don't want to stay here,' Andrew said. 'I hate this place.'

'No you don't,' Phoebe said. 'You had a good time

with Mr Adams yesterday. Maybe you can go visit him again.'

'I don't want to visit him,' Andrew said. 'I told you, I don't like that lady up there, she makes me eat brown bread.'

Phoebe sat down on the bed and pulled him on to her lap. 'I'll bring you a present,' she offered.

'What?'

'What would you like?'

'Nothing,' he said. 'I want to go with you.'

By now Phoebe was beginning to wish she had just told him she was going to spend the afternoon and evening with Molly again. She had felt she owed it to him to tell him the truth – out of a sense of guilt, probably, guilt for having to put her job ahead of everything else once again – but obviously she had overestimated Andrew's ability to just accept the news with no fuss. Of course he would put up a fuss!

'I'll make it up to you,' she said. 'We'll have some special time, just the two of us, when I get back. Maybe we can drive over to New Hampshire, and you can see the Old Man of the Mountains – how about that?'

Andrew shrugged.

'Or we could go over to Stowe,' she suggested. 'We could see the ski area over there.'

'Not if the storm keeps up,' Louise said.

Phoebe looked up.

'The roads are glare ice,' her mother said from the doorway. 'I barely made it up the hill from Winslow. You're not going anywhere today.'

'I have to,' Phoebe said.

Louise shrugged. 'Well, it beats me how you're going to get to the airport, because you're not driving *my* car.'

Phoebe looked out of the window; the storm was

blowing sideways. Her mother was right; no one would be able to go anywhere today. Not right now, at least.

So she was snowbound. What now?

'Did you reach your friend Janet?' Louise asked.

'It's Janice,' Phoebe said, 'and no, I didn't.'

'Try her again.'

'It's not going to help,' Phoebe said.

'Why not?'

'She won't be able to find it,' Phoebe said irritably. 'There are a million places it could be.' She looked out of the window again. Wasn't that a brightening in the sky? Wasn't the storm letting up? If it did, perhaps she should just take Andrew and go home for good, skip the wedding, call it an aborted trip and reschedule it for next summer. They could fly back tonight, and tomorrow morning she could be at the office, and Andrew could be with Rusty. Just as he wanted.

'You might as well unpack your suitcase, or your briefcase, if that's what you were going to take,' Louise said. 'You're not leaving this house.' She turned to go downstairs, then turned back. 'You did check your briefcase, didn't you? The document you're looking for wouldn't by any chance be in your briefcase?'

'I already checked, Mother,' Phoebe lied. 'It's not in there.' Wouldn't that be ironic, she thought, if all the time it was right in front of her eyes. But as soon as Louise left she went through all her folders – because it was certainly possible that she had put it in her briefcase – and yet the memo wasn't there either.

Snowbound.

Well, there wasn't much that Herb could say about that.

Except to fire her for having lost the memo in the first place.

'You go get *Babar*,' Phoebe said to Andrew. 'Get *Babar and the Wully-Wully* and I'll read it to you.'

'Are you going to stay here?' Andrew said.

'No,' Phoebe said.

'Grammy said you couldn't go,' Andrew said.

'Well, Grammy's not my boss any more,' Phoebe said. 'Now go find the book.'

But while she was waiting for Andrew she heard an engine sputtering in the driveway; as she looked out Molly climbed out of Nick's jeep. She wore a puffy red down parka and high rubber-toed L.L. Bean boots; on her head a knitted grey helmet-style hat flapped loosely about her ears. Bending forward against the wind she made her way through the drifts and up the steps to the kitchen porch.

What was Molly doing here? Why wasn't she with Nick? Phoebe didn't really want to see Molly right now; Molly would side with Louise about the trip, and together the two of them would badger her about the need to keep things in the proper perspective, the memo was sure to turn up and Herb could do without it anyway. And Phoebe didn't know if she could hold her temper today.

'Phoebe! Molly's here!'

Phoebe didn't reply. She could lock herself in the bathroom and turn on the shower (not a bad idea; the house, as usual, was freezing this morning), or pretend she wasn't feeling well.

But while she was trying to figure out how to avoid Molly, she heard Molly's footsteps padding up the stairs. In another moment her friend appeared in the doorway. She had taken off her boots; on her feet were variegated ski socks, blotchy with colour.

'Where's Nick?' Phoebe asked.

'Elaine wanted to go tobogganing,' Molly said. 'I didn't think it'd be a good idea for me.'

'That's wise,' Phoebe agreed. (Wise? Who was she trying to sound like, using a word like *wise*?) 'How's the baby, anyway? Any more bleeding?'

'Nope,' Molly said. 'Dry as July.'

'Ah,' Phoebe said. 'Good.'

'So,' she said after a while, 'what's up?'

'I just thought maybe we could spend some more time together,' Molly said, 'but I hear you still haven't cleared up that document mess.'

'It's not a mess,' Phoebe said tightly. 'I just misplaced it.'

'Okay,' said Molly. 'So it's not a mess. We missed you at dinner last night,' she said. 'All of us except Leo, that is. What did you say to him?'

'Nothing,' Phoebe said. 'He told me he knew what I was going through and I said he didn't know what I was going through, nobody back here knows what I'm going through but thank you very much for the advice.' She didn't tell Molly that she had also told Leo that no lawyer who'd spent his entire career as a senatorial aide on Capitol Hill had any right to offer her advice on how to deal with a senior partner at a large law firm, and that he could take his advice and shove it. 'Why?' said Phoebe. 'Was he upset?'

'Not really upset, I guess,' Molly said. 'But he spent the rest of the night blabbing on and on about bills and committees and hearings, monopolizing the conversation.'

'Well, then,' Phoebe said, and she gave Molly a compacted smile, 'I'm not so sorry I missed the dinner. I spend enough time with people like Leo back in San Francisco, I can do without them here in Vermont.'

Molly didn't smile back.

'Look, I should tell you, there's a strong possibility I'm not going to be here tomorrow,' Phoebe said, fixing her gaze on a knot in the pine floor. 'I have to fly back to look for the document and I may not be able to make it back here in time.'

Molly raised her eyebrows.

'I hope you don't mind,' Phoebe said. 'Like I was really touched' – (touched? Where are you getting this formality!) – 'that you wanted me to be your maid of honour but I'm just not sure it's going to work out, not with this document being lost. Professional responsibilities and all that.'

Molly said nothing.

'Who knows, maybe it'll turn up this morning, maybe my paralegal will find it, but I thought I should let you know, give you some advance warning, something like that.

'Maybe Cindy Ann could hand you the ring,' Phoebe went on, wishing Molly would say something. 'Or my mother, maybe? Do you really need a maid of honour, anyway?'

Molly unpopped the snaps to her parka, one by one.

'Look, I'm sorry,' Phoebe said, panicking. 'But if I don't get this document to Herb I might as well kiss that job good-bye and then where would I be after three years, all that work for nothing – '

But Molly interrupted her. 'You're glad you're going, aren't you?'

Phoebe kept focusing on the knot in the floorboard, and fought to prevent her brow from furrowing. She had wished Molly would say something, but certainly not what Molly had just said. This was *not* the time for a blowup.

'Not just glad but relieved,' Molly went on. 'You didn't want to be in my wedding, you didn't even want to come back here, did you?'

'If I didn't want to come back do you think I would have knocked myself out trying to get my work done in time?' Phoebe exclaimed. 'Do you think I would have screwed up the custody agreement? Do you think I would have spent all this money?'

'Sure.'

'*Sure?*'

'Sure,' Molly said. 'What else could you do? Say no? Say no to Molly and offend her? Molly back there in Vermont whose feelings would have been hurt if the hotshot lawyer friend from her childhood didn't have time to make it back for her wedding?'

Phoebe wished Andrew would come back with his book. She had a feeling that terrible things were about to be said, radioactive words that would never break down no matter how many apologies were made.

'Well, to tell you the truth, I'd be relieved if you went back,' Molly announced. 'I'd rather have the wedding with Phoebe on a plane than with Phoebe beside me freaking out about her Important Memorandum and making everyone in the room oh-so-aware of the oh-so-earth-shattering professional demands on her life.'

For a moment Phoebe was stunned. 'Well then, so would I,' she finally said. 'Far be it from me to want to intrude on someone else's good time, especially when that someone else happens to be a little jealous.'

'*Jealous?* Of what?'

'Of me, of what I've done with my life!'

'Which is?'

'Which is more than what you've done with yours,' Phoebe said angrily. 'You're wasting your life, teaching high school out here in the sticks, ten miles from Mummy and Daddy, and justifying it all by knitting baby bonnets and weaving some kind of trinket every now and then. Fibre arts – isn't that what you call it these days? Sure it's nice, but come on, when are you going to really do something, break away from your past, get out and make something of yourself! Look at you – you're twenty-nine and you've never lived anywhere but Vermont!'

'Ah,' said Molly. 'Then why don't you tell me how to make something of myself. You always told me how to do everything else, anyway – '

'I never told you how to do things, why do you keep making that accusation!'

'Because it's true,' Molly snapped.

'It is not,' Phoebe said. 'I was just taking the initiative because you wouldn't.'

And for a split second Molly's eyes flashed about the room, then landed back on Phoebe, as though she had lost and then regained an inner balance. 'Maybe I didn't take the initiative,' she said, 'but it's not all that simple, Phoebe; there was always the assumption that your way was better – so that every chance you got you were telling me how to run my life, just like you're doing now. Well? Go ahead, tell me how to stop wasting my life. Should I go to law school, like you? Get a job with a firm and dress like a nun so I can run myself ragged helping corporations stay out of trouble? That sounds like a real improvement, boy – tell me how!'

Phoebe set her jaw.

'And while you're at it you could also tell me how to structure my workday so I have a few minutes in the evening – maybe – to read a page or two to my kid. Huh? Or how to schedule a vacation so that my boss is screaming at me long distance? Or how to get a good job that lets me read documents all day long? I mean, hey, that sounds really thrilling, I bet you go home every night and say, *Boy* I feel fulfilled, *boy* it's great to put in a good ole twelve-hour day at the office, *boy* I learned a lot from that boss of mine. Really, Phoebe: you're the one who's always on top of things: tell me how to *do* something with my life!'

Molly's words cut deep. Not that Molly was telling her anything startlingly new – on the contrary, during the course of this vacation it was becoming all too clear to Phoebe just how great were the costs of her job at Judson and Day. Yet it was one thing to hear her own conscience whispering this message in her ear – and quite another to hear her girlhood friend decrying her whole life. Maybe Molly was right, maybe it was *she* who was wasting *her* life; but the vicious tone in her friend's voice added a frightening bite to the truth; and as a result Phoebe's inclination was to bristle and fight back, in order to prevent herself from getting swallowed up into a hole that was even deeper and blacker than she'd ever imagined.

But she didn't bristle, and she didn't fight back. Instead, she just shook her head, saddened by the echo of Molly's last words. 'If you think I'm on top of things, then you don't understand very much about me,' she said.

'And you don't understand anything about me, Phoebe,' Molly said flatly. 'You come back here after six years of your whoop-te-do lawyer's life in California and presume that you still know everything about me, just because we used to be best friends. You waltz in through the door and act like you've never left, like you're still my other half. Well, come on, Phoebe – do you really think I've been on hold since the day you left? Do you really think you know who I am?'

And Phoebe, who had been trying ever since the night she arrived to find the right way to reacquaint herself with Molly, suddenly saw that she had taken the wrong approach, that all her attempts to act breezy and cheerful and nonchalantly friendly, in the hopes that it would bypass the awkwardness of getting reacquainted, had boomeranged. Don't ask Molly how she stands it, living in Winslow, she had repeatedly warned herself; it'll come off as condescending. But by censoring that question and opting instead for cheerful chatter, she had actually created more of a gulf; by sheltering Molly from what was really on her mind she had cheated them out of acknowledging to one another a necessary period of estrangement.

Well, there was no way to avoid that acknowledgement any longer. Phoebe knew, of course, that Molly hadn't been *on hold* all this time (just as she herself hadn't) – clearly, Molly was a lot more self-assured, a lot more confident than she used to be – but Phoebe finally allowed that one question that she had kept buried beneath all the smiles and all the reminiscences to surface: What had Molly gone through that could compare with what she had gone through? Phoebe turned her head but she couldn't avoid the ugliness of the truth: for she realized that even if she and Molly could be friends again and even if Molly were to share with her a long and complex list of all the hopes and disappointments and fears and triumphs that had moulded her over the past six years, it would never measure up to Phoebe's list in her eyes. Admit it: you *do* think you're better than she is, Phoebe thought. You think you're smarter, and more ambitious, and stronger, and more capable than she is: because you broke away, and she didn't. Maybe you do have to deal with people like Herb, maybe it is a pretty hectic way to spend your life: but deep down inside you think you're a better person for trying to cope with it all.

'Mum,' said Andrew from the doorway. 'I can't find *Babar*.'

Molly moved aside for Andrew to come in, and Phoebe thought she detected a haughtiness in the way Molly looked at him, as though Andrew were living proof of everything that was wrong, in Molly's view, with Phoebe's life. By way of defence Phoebe hoisted Andrew up on to her lap and enveloped him in her arms. She nuzzled her nose against his hair, smelling its sweetness. She didn't have anything else to say. Part of her felt there were more accusations to be hurled back and forth, part of her wanted Molly to start screaming and grabbing at her hair and slapping her so that she could do the same, an all-out catfight, until both of them were clutching at each other with tears and laughter and forgiveness; but another part of her knew that such a scene was not going to happen. Maybe there was too much reserve built into them both, reserve that would permit them to go *this* far with the accusations but no farther; but maybe, too, they both knew that there was too much of a risk involved. What if it didn't lead to forgiveness? What then?

And yet, what now?

'Mum, sing "Mairzy Doats,"' said Andrew.

'Not now, honey,' said Phoebe. Molly had dug her hands into her pockets and was staring at the whiteness blowing outside.

'But I don't remember how it goes, Mum,' said Andrew.

'Mares eat oats and does eat oats,' Phoebe said. What was Molly thinking now?

'A kittley divey doo, wooden you,' sang Andrew. 'Is that how it goes, Mum?'

'I wish you hadn't come back,' Molly said, not looking at her.

Phoebe said nothing, just set her chin on Andrew's head.

'I wish you hadn't come back, you know?' Molly said. 'Then we could have gone on thinking nothing had changed, thinking we were still best friends. But we're not, are we,' she continued, as though Phoebe weren't there in the same room with her. 'I just wonder what we'd think of each other if we met, today, for the first time.'

* * *

Phoebe sat on her bed, knees together, hands clasped in her lap, and watched the red jeep lose its colour as it headed through the storm towards the Adamses' house. Arcs of snow had collected in the corners of the window-panes, and every so often the curtains wafted from a gust of wind outside. Out in California Rusty and Shirley would be going to a bakery in T-shirts and sandals; Janice and Stu would be running through the eucalyptus groves in the Presidio; Herb might be playing a round of tennis over in Tiburon before going into the office.

Stop feeling sorry for yourself, she thought. Look at the bright side of this visit.

But she couldn't see the bright side.

The jeep turned into the Adamses' driveway, and Phoebe could just barely make out Molly's figure, still bending with the wind, making her way from the jeep to the back door. She wondered if Molly was feeling as heavyhearted as she herself was feeling right now; and if so, would she be able to pep up her spirits to match Bea's? Or maybe she was feeling triumphant (uncomfortably so?) for having finally got off her chest not only what she thought of Phoebe's situation – that it was a sad waste of talent and energy – but also what she had been feeling about their relationship all these lost years. 'You've always been telling me how to do everything,' she had said to Phoebe; 'you've always operated from the assumption that your way was better.' Well? It was true, wasn't it? And she recalled urging Molly to climb a little higher in the maple tree, to coedit the school paper with her, to apply to out-of-state colleges with her. Call it taking the initiative, Phoebe thought; call it just a way of suggesting things, call it whatever you want – but it all boiled down to her always telling Molly what to do: because her way was supposedly better.

Phoebe lay back and pulled the quilt up around her,

wanting to hide from her life. Above the bed a pear-shaped watermark stained the ceiling, and on the wall beside her the blue-flowered wallpaper was curling at the seam. She peeled it back; underneath a large maroon rose bloomed on a tired, ivory-coloured background. Old-ladyish paper. Vaguely she could remember a time when the entire room bloomed with those gaudy roses; she would trace them with her finger before falling asleep, while in the next room Jack would be tapping out Morse-code messages to no one in particular. Then, as a birthday present, she was allowed to pick out new wallpaper, and she remembered the excitement of choosing, the lingering smell of paste and paint, and then to her surprise the strange and alien light that filled the room when all the roses – which suddenly in her memory had grown fuller and deeper, more beautiful than ever – had been covered up. And once again Phoebe felt that same hollow loneliness creeping over her, that same empty loss that had kept her from falling asleep that first night in the new room long ago; it was as though the walls of another room, somewhere, had just been papered over with a foreign pattern, against her will, stealing her roses and changing for ever the space and light of familiar surroundings.

# 12

Because of the storm everyone agreed that the wedding should be held at the Adamses' house rather than up at the sugar bush. Everyone but Elaine, that is. 'A sugarhouse where they make maple syrup?' she exclaimed. 'Oh, let's go ahead and have it up there anyway! We could put Molly on a sled, she wouldn't have to hike up there, wouldn't that be wild!'

'Mother,' said Nick. It was midafternoon; the Ulrichs had returned from their tobogganing outing and Nick was brewing tea while Molly sat in a rocking chair trying to keep herself from getting annoyed over the numerous mittens, boots, socks, hats, and scarves that her guests had scattered about her kitchen floor.

'I've just never *seen* a real live sugarhouse,' Elaine continued.

'Mother, come on,' Nick said.

'Well if the wedding doesn't take place up there we'll have to go up on our own and see it, now *there's* an idea, *that's* what we should do in March, Stan, go maple sugaring, wouldn't our friends be *green*!'

Molly sighed.

'Feel okay?' Nick asked.

Molly nodded.

'Brrr!' Elaine said. 'Don't you just love coming in out of a blizzard? Doesn't it just make you feel so . . . so *robust*!'

'Here we go,' Nick said. 'Drink up.' He handed Molly a mug of tea and tried to catch her eye, but she merely gave him a quick smile and kissed the rim of her mug.

She wished all the guests would leave so that she and Nick could crawl into bed together and she could tell him what had happened that morning. She had been holding back a good cry ever since she left Phoebe sitting with Andrew on the edge of the bed; and she didn't want to hold it back any longer.

Her desire to be left alone must have been apparent, because as soon as everyone had finished the tea Stan suggested that they clear out and give the bride and groom a little time to themselves before the big day. Molly gave him a grateful smile. She wondered how a man as sensitive as Stan could have hooked up with such a goon.

'What's wrong?' Nick asked when everyone had left. 'Is it your mother? Did she get upset when you told her you were pregnant?'

'I wish it were that simple,' Molly said. 'No, my mother wasn't even surprised; she said she'd had an idea I was pregnant all along. How about that?'

'Then what's the matter?' Nick said.

Molly unfolded her legs and put her feet on the floor, right into a puddle of melting snow. She lifted them back up, hugged her knees to her chest, and began to rock back and forth.

'I had a fight with Phoebe,' she said. She felt a lump growing in her throat, and swallowed it back so that she could tell Nick what had happened.

'Oh, no,' he said, when she had finished. 'Dressing like a *nun*?'

'Well she told me I was *boring*,' Molly said angrily.

'Boring?'

'Just about,' Molly said. 'And isn't she the one who's boring? She can't talk about anything but her job all the time – she's got so narrow-minded. Do you think she's read a novel in the last year? No – the only thing she does for fun is watch *Dallas*!'

Nick did not reply, and Molly, who was beginning to feel as though she had made this accusation one too many times, gave a long deep sigh.

'Do you think maybe this was a good thing?' Nick said. 'Perhaps you both needed to clear the air.'

'It didn't clear the air,' Molly said. 'It wasn't that kind of a fight. I just don't think we have anything in common any more, that's what I think it boils down to. Maybe we don't even *like* each other any more.'

Nick was silent.

'You know, I never thought the visit would turn out like this,' Molly said, staring at the floor as she continued to rock. 'Oh, I know I was pretty defensive about seeing her, and I thought things would be a little awkward at first, but I also thought it would change and we'd be just the way were were when we were kids. She really *was* my closest friend, you know,' she said. 'I looked up to her too. Maybe she was always telling me what to do, maybe she had to leave in order to let me grow up – but she was like an older sister to me, always there to help me out, to push me, to make me feel good about myself.'

She closed her eyes. 'Once when we were ten or so I had to give a piano recital. I was petrified. I hated the idea of performing in front of people. But my piano teacher told me I had to do it, my parents told me I had to do it, everybody told me I had to do it. The recital was at the church, in the auditorium, and when I walked out on to the stage and sat down at the piano I froze. I couldn't remember the song I was supposed to play. Nothing. Not the melody, not even the first note.

'And then I looked out into the audience, because I didn't know what else to do; and there was Phoebe sitting in the front row. Phoebe was smiling.' Molly smiled to herself, remembering that moment, Phoebe with her red hair in a ponytail, her green jumper, her black patent leather shoes. 'She kept on smiling, and then she gave a little nod, and I realized she believed in me, you know? She believed that I could do it. And I did it.'

Nick raised his eyebrows, brought his mug to his lips.

'I really loved her that afternoon,' Molly said.

As it turned out the storm didn't last as long as expected; by late afternoon the wind had died down and the flakes were clumping together, drifting down slowly, like torn bits of paper.

At this point Phoebe had made her mind up to change her entire flight schedule and take Andrew home with her. When her mother asked, she told her that she and Molly had had a slight argument, nothing major but yes, Louise was right, things weren't as close between them as one would have expected. 'I don't know why,' she said; 'I guess we're just not getting along these days.' Louise had frowned and pursed her lips. 'That will change,' she said. 'Give it time.'

As Phoebe sat down to call the airlines, however, the phone rang; it was Janice, calling from Inverness.

'Don't you ever do that again!' she snapped.

'What?'

'Telling the operator there'd been a death in the family! For Chrissake, Phoebe, do you have any idea what I went through before I was able to put two and two together?'

'I'm sorry,' Phoebe said. 'I wasn't thinking.'

'Well?'

'Well what?'

'Why'd you call?'

Phoebe realized that Janice knew nothing about the document problem. She related the sequence of events to her, the deposition getting moved up, Eddie not finding the documents, Herb calling back to ask about the mismanagement memo.

'What are you going to do?' asked Janice.

'I'm coming back,' Phoebe said. 'I'm getting a flight out tomorrow morning.'

'Do you think you'll find it?'

'I have to,' Phoebe said. 'It has to be somewhere.'

'Maybe John Dunn stole it,' Janice said. 'Maybe he's afraid you're going to make partner and he isn't.'

'John Dunn may be out to lunch but he's not that stupid,' Phoebe said. 'He knows where I rank in that firm.'

Janice was silent for a couple of seconds. 'Wait a minute,' she said suddenly. 'If you're leaving tomorrow you're going to miss the wedding.'

'Well, that's the breaks,' Phoebe said.

'But you're supposed to be her maid of honour!'

Phoebe wanted to talk to Janice at length about her feelings towards Molly, about what they had said and what had happened to their friendship; but not over the phone. 'I have no choice,' she said. 'Herb's going to be in the office tomorrow, and the deposition's scheduled for Tuesday, I think. I have to come back.'

'I'll go down and look for it,' Janice offered. 'You want me to search your office?'

'No – that's okay,' Phoebe said hastily. 'You'll never find it, I'm sure.'

'I'd be glad to help,' Janice said.

'No, really,' Phoebe said, because right now she didn't want any excuse that would allow her to stay through the wedding. It was a cop-out, to be sure; the more responsible approach would have been to take advantage of Janice's offer and stay back there in Vermont, giving herself time to try mending things with Molly. But Phoebe was not only afraid that there might not be anything left to mend but also emotionally exhausted, and in a way was looking forward to the more simplistic, black-and-white problem of finding the document and dealing with Herb. 'Thanks,' she said, 'but it's not necessary.'

'Want me to pick you up at the airport?'

'No, thanks,' Phoebe said. 'My car's already there.'

'Why don't you and Andrew come over for dinner tomorrow night, then,' Janice suggested. 'I'll make potstickers.'

'Let's leave it open,' Phoebe said. 'I may be working.'

'You know, I'm sorry all this is happening,' Janice said. 'But I have to admit, I'll be glad to have you back a little early. I had no one to talk to, no one to let down my guard with while you were gone. It's a lonely place to be, you know? Even with other Bolts, it's just not the same without you.'

Phoebe was touched by the intimacy in Janice's words; and she, too, had been missing Janice, would have liked to spend the afternoon at the baths with her, talking, confiding, searching for a more reassuring perspective on just where and how Molly fitted into her life these days. Yet this intimacy painfully underscored the contrast between these two friendships right now. Here she was, feeling much closer, much more at ease, with this woman from Iowa whom she had known for just three years, than she was with her oldest friend from childhood. Such a simple realization; but it also made her a little wary, because she couldn't help but wonder whether she and Janice were also bound to outgrow one another. Say they left the firm, and went their separate ways: would they, too, get together for a weekend years from now, and run out of things to say after the first cup of coffee?

Phoebe stayed at the phone after hanging up, because she wanted to get in touch with both Rusty and Herb before the day was over; Rusty so that he could arrange his schedule to take Andrew tomorrow, and Herb so that he would know that she was coming back. She finally reached Rusty at his office; and when he asked why she was coming back early she merely told him that things had heated up with Parco-Fields. But that was too vague for Rusty; he wanted to know whether the judge had cut short discovery, whether they'd been assigned a pretrial conference date, whether Phoebe was going to be putting on a witness –

'I have to come back because I lost a document,' she said flatly. 'And please don't remind me how disorganized I am; I *know* how disorganized I am.'

'It's that important?'

'It's that important.'

'It can't be,' Rusty said. 'One document'll never make or break a case.'

'Tell that to Herb,' Phoebe said. 'Anyway, you'll be home?'

'Sure I'll be home,' Rusty said. 'Gee, it's too bad you've got to cut your vacation short.'

'That's life,' Phoebe said. 'That's law.'

'Not necessarily,' Rusty said.

Herb did not answer his extension. Actually that's not so surprising, she told herself; if he's planning to work on Sunday there's no compelling reason for him to be in the office on a Saturday afternoon. Still, though, she wanted to reach him so that tomorrow morning when he went into his office and didn't find the document on his desk he wouldn't think she was just ignoring the issue. So she dialled the main number of the firm; she would ask whoever answered to check the conference room, or the firm's cafeteria, to see if he was in.

As it turned out, John Dunn answered the phone.

'Hey, Phoebe, how's it going?' he said. 'How are things back there in old Vermont?'

'Just wonderful,' Phoebe said. 'Look, I'm trying to find Herb Sullivan, do you know if he's in?'

'He's come and gone,' John said. 'Hey, guess what.'

'Could you leave him a message?' said Phoebe. 'Could you tell him I'm coming back tomorrow?'

'Sure,' said John. 'Guess what, though.'

'And tell him I'll probably be able to get into the office by noon,' Phoebe said. 'I'm catching an early-morning flight.'

'No prob,' said John. 'But guess what.'

'What?' Phoebe finally said.

'Guess who just got assigned to Parco-Fields.'

Phoebe frowned.

'That's right,' John said. 'Yours truly.'

Phoebe didn't know what to say.

'Bad news, *oui*? Herb comes into my office yesterday at seven – like get this, he doesn't even go through the managing partner – and says, "We gotta get ready for a deposition next week, we're short on staff, what are you working on these days?" And I say, "Well, I'm working with Carmichael on that securities case" – and before I can go any further he says, "You're on, read these." And he throws down a bunch of documents.'

Andrew was biting air as he cut a page of scribbles out of his colouring book at the kitchen table.

'Like what did I do wrong?' John sighed. 'What grievous error did I commit to get myself assigned to *Sullivan*?'

'Does this mean you're the one who's preparing for the Schein deposition?' Phoebe asked.

'Oh, yeah,' John said. 'I can't wait to hear him respond to that mismanagement memo; we're going to cream him on that one.'

'The what?'

'You know, you read it, the memo where he talks all about the company's financial problems – a pretty hot doc if I do say so myself.'

'How'd you get that memo?'

John sucked in his breath. 'Was *that* the one you lost?'

Phoebe said nothing.

'Because Sullivan was pissed as hell! He said there was an incredibly hot document that you lost and he had to spend an hour going through your office looking for it – was that the one?'

John was kidding. Herb found the memo? By going through her office? Phoebe was beginning to wish that she hadn't made this phone call.

'God, Phoebe, you really have to get a little more organized if you're going to do litigation,' John told her. 'A document like that, you shouldn't misplace it.'

Phoebe looked at the ceiling.

'But we can work on that later, I've got a great system for organization that I'll explain to you,' John said.

'Terrific,' Phoebe said. 'Thanks.'

'*De rien*,' John said. 'Glad to help out. You know, I have an idea you and I are going to be practically living together for the next six months. Which reminds me – isn't Eddie Sorenson the paralegal on this case?'

'That's right.'

'Shit.'

'What's wrong with Eddie?'

'Nothing,' John said. 'He's just a little too cocky for his own good sometimes.'

'I like Eddie,' Phoebe said. 'Eddie knows his stuff.'

John snorted. 'Well, I can put up with him, I guess. But it's his attitude that bothers me, you know? Like he doesn't know his own place.'

Phoebe was silent.

'Anyway,' John said. 'What was that message you wanted me to pass on to Herb?'

Phoebe looked outside. Dusk had settled over the snow-covered fields, and up at the Adamses' house a floodlight illuminated the cars in the driveway. Inside Molly and Nick and Bea and Dave and all the other guests of the wedding would be gathering in the living rooms, warming themselves by the fire, proposing toasts and telling intimate tales about the bride and groom: anecdotes from their childhoods, their college years, forgotten *faux pas*; and Molly and Nick would be laughing, protesting, then finally admitting to hidden character flaws as everyone sought to outdo the others with a better tale. Oh, the stories *she* could tell: Molly at fifteen, learning to drive during mud season, sinking the back wheels of Louise's new car into a foot of muck; Molly at ten, insisting on practising her trumpet on the school bus in order to make the school band (she didn't); oh, and get *this*, Molly at seven, trying to call Khrushchev to tell him about the bomb –

'Something about coming back tomorrow?' said John. 'Something about an early-morning flight?'

'There's no message,' Phoebe said. She hugged the phone to her ear as she taped Andrew's scribbles on to the refrigerator door.

'But I thought – didn't you say – '

'I changed my mind.'

'I can appreciate that,' John said. 'No prob.'

'And, John,' said Phoebe.

'Yeah?'

'As for Schein?'

'Yeah?'

'Do him in,' Phoebe said.

'Atta girl,' John said. 'That's the old firm spirit.'

* * *

Which is not to say that Phoebe suddenly knew how to patch things up with Molly. She didn't. She didn't even know if they were patchable. But in learning from John Dunn that he'd been assigned to the Schein deposition, that Herb had finally found the mismanagement memo in her office (where had he found it, anyway? and how clear had it been to him that nothing had been logged in, or colour-coordinated, or filed in the preferred three-ring binders for easy access? And why couldn't he have let her know!) she realized just how expendable she really was. There was no need for her to go back. Sure, if the issue had arisen Herb would have claimed that of course she was indeed irreplaceable, but look: it wasn't true. Not only had Herb found the memo, but John Dunn himself, pumped up with the enthusiasm of being on a major case, would probably manage to cull together more newly discovered hot documents in this one weekend than she'd been able to find over the past year. Documents would *become* hot in the hands of John Dunn; obnoxious as he might be, nevertheless he was a born advocate, and could turn seemingly innocuous statements into damning evidence. Conclusively damning evidence.

*We're going to be living together for the next six months.* Phoebe tried to envision not one all-nighter, not two, but a dreary succession of endless days and nights spent listening to John telling her how to organize documents, how to prep a witness, how to get a business record into evidence. (Just in case, he would say, grilling her on the Federal Rules of Evidence. You gotta be prepared, look like you know your stuff just in case Herb suddenly decides to give you a witness. Did you ever take a trial advocacy course? Civil or criminal? And how'd you do in evidence? Just think of it! John would cry, suddenly delirious with excitement; this is federal fucking court!) Phoebe saw them setting up camp in one of the conference rooms, working around the clock, bleary eyed, living off Chinese take-out food and catching catnaps at odd hours. She wondered if she would be able to stand up to John if she disagreed with him – on a particular line of argument, say, or the significance of a particular excerpt from a deposition. It would be difficult; not only was he a year ahead of her, but his perception of her work habits had just been tainted by this missing document fiasco. And she couldn't blame him for thinking of her as less competent than himself, because she never should have lost that memo. Still, though, she couldn't let him take over and treat her like some kind of little sister. So he *did* know how to organize documents, so he *had* already taken a few depositions, so he *had* gone to Harvard. So what?

Phoebe wondered what Molly would say upon learning that Phoebe would in fact be here for the wedding. Would Molly resort to politeness, and apologize for the things she had said? (And was she sorry? Was Phoebe? Was being sorry appropriate?) Or would she skip the apologies and remain aloof? Phoebe tried to imagine The Moment: the moment during the wedding ceremony when Molly would turn to her for the ring. What would their eyes say to one another at that moment, after all that they had said – and all, too, that they had not been able to say? Would their eyes even meet?

Of course they would. Regardless of the chasm between their present lives, they would always share that core of their childhood, growing up together in Vermont. And though she wasn't sure she ought to trust it, Phoebe at this point had a bit of faith that this common core would somehow make it easier for them, would somehow allow them to gloss over the hurt, the embarrassment, in order to get through Molly's wedding.

'Lookit, Mum,' said Andrew. By twisting both knobs

on the Etch A Sketch he had created an atomic tangle of graphite fuzz.

'That's good, honey,' she said. 'What is it?'

'It's you,' he said.

'Oh,' she said. 'Thank you.'

Andrew nodded, then held the drawing machine upside down and shook it to erase the picture. 'Now I'm making a picture of my dad – lookit, Mum; *lookit*!'

'Yes,' she said. 'I can see.'

She wished she hadn't accused Molly of being jealous of her. It was such an ugly accusation, after all; and besides, based on what Molly had been able to glimpse of Phoebe's life, how could Molly possibly have been jealous? What was there to be jealous about? The prestige of being a lawyer? What prestige? Maybe Carl Poultney was impressed, with all his notions of lady lawyers; but not Molly; all Molly could see was the fact that here she was supposedly on vacation and her problems had followed her East like some kind of a job-related trade wind. Not to mention the fact that she never had any time to spend with Andrew. Phoebe realized that with the trial coming up in May an entire half year was going to pass in which Andrew would be spending most of his time with Rusty. He would lose his first tooth. He would learn to ride a bike. He would outgrow many of his toys, possibly would even be able to get to sleep without Binky. And she would miss it all, under the guise of getting litigation experience. Yes, I've had a trial, she would be able to say. And maybe: Yes, I've taken depositions, yes, I've cross-examined witnesses, yes I feel quite comfortable introducing documents into evidence. (*Very* unlikely, but maybe.)

But was it worth it?

* * *

They had another family dinner that night, with everyone but Max. Louise was looking smug because she thought that since Phoebe had ultimately decided against going back she, Louise, must have finally pounded some sense into her daughter's head. Cindy Ann appeared to have gained a few more pounds; Jack was worried about road conditions; and Andrew, as was becoming his habit during this visit, claimed to have developed a stomachache as soon as Louise dished out his plate.

'You're fine,' Phoebe told him. 'You just ate too many cheese-and-crackers.'

'But Mum,' Andrew whined, 'I *hurt*.'

'Eat your pot roast, Andrew,' Phoebe said, 'or you can't have any dessert. Grammy made apple Betty.'

'I don't like apple Betty.'

'It's the same as apple crisp,' Phoebe said, 'which you love. Now *eat*.'

'Zoom zoom zoom,' said Cindy Ann, flying her fork towards her mouth. 'Yum yum yum.'

Andrew squirmed in his seat.

'Would you send him back next summer for a visit?' Cindy Ann said. 'I'd love to take him for a couple of weeks, if I could.'

'Thanks,' said Phoebe, 'that's nice of you but – '

'How would you like that, Andy?' Cindy Ann said. 'Come visit ole Aunt Cindy Ann and Uncle Jack next summer? Ride on a hay truck? Play in the garden?'

Get stung by yellow jackets? 'That's sweet of you,' Phoebe said, 'but next summer I'm hoping to be able to take some time off with him myself.'

'Oh?' said Louise. 'What do you think you'll do?'

'I'm not sure,' Phoebe said. 'But if all goes well with this trial I should have a little extra time. Maybe we'll go to Disneyland,' she said. 'Maybe we'll get up into Yosemite.'

'What about Christmas, then?' Cindy Ann said. 'Bring him back for Christmas. Oh!' she cried. 'We could all go pick out a tree and trim it with cranberries and popcorn and Andrew could hang up Jack's old stocking and in the morning – what are you asking Santy Claus to bring you this Christmas, Andrew honeybunch?'

'There is no Santa Claus,' Andrew said.

'Now, who told you that,' Cindy Ann said lightly, looking a little nervous, as though Phoebe might hold her responsible for Andrew's lack of belief just because she had brought the subject up.

But all this time Phoebe was shaking her head. 'Rusty's got him this Christmas,' she explained. 'Thanks, but maybe some other year.'

'I thought it was your turn,' Louise said. 'Didn't Rusty have him last year?'

Phoebe nodded. 'But I broke the custody agreement by bringing him back here, and so Rusty's getting him again this Christmas.' She shrugged. 'It doesn't matter; I'm going to have to work anyway.'

'On Christmas!' Cindy Ann shrieked. 'You're going to work on Christmas *Day*?'

'Maybe not on Christmas morning,' Phoebe said, 'but I'm not going to get much of a break this year.'

Cindy Ann shook her head in disbelief. 'Working on Christmas!' she said. 'Doesn't it – ' She stopped suddenly, then picked up her knife and fork and sawed intently at her meat.

'What were you going to say?' Phoebe asked.

Cindy Ann just shook her head.

'What?' Phoebe said.

Cindy Ann frowned. She lifted her glass of wine, but set it down without drinking. 'Well, I don't mean any offence,' she said, her eyes on the basket of rolls, 'and I think you have a terrific job, I mean you're a lawyer –

and of course part of this is due to the fact that, you know, you and Rusty are, well . . .'

'Divorced,' Phoebe offered.

'Divorced,' Cindy Ann admitted. She paused again, as though reconsidering her words. Then she looked at Phoebe. 'But doesn't it bother you that you're not going to be able to be with Andrew on Christmas Day?'

Phoebe didn't reply. She was about to say, yes, of course it bothered her; but suddenly her mind clouded over with a vision of Rusty and Andrew in some condo at Vail, the father and son littering the sunken living room with ribbons and wrapping paper, trying out a new video game, while in the kitchenette Shirley slid a frozen coffee cake into the microwave. All this, while she would be up on the thirty-third floor of her office building, hard at work in the Barracks.

'I said the wrong thing,' Cindy Ann said.

'No, you didn't,' Phoebe said. 'Of course it bothers me.'

'But then . . .'

Phoebe waited.

'Well, why don't you *do* something about it!' Cindy Ann said.

'Honey,' warned Jack.

But Phoebe continued to wait.

'I'm sorry,' said Cindy Ann 'But people kept saying to me, If you can't have your own baby, stop moaning and groaning about it and get yourselves on an adoption list. So I did. And now I look at you with that beautiful little boy and it kills me. Do you know what I would *give*? Yet there you are, working so hard you can't even spend Christmas with him!'

Phoebe twirled her glass of wine.

'I'm sorry,' Cindy Ann said. 'I know it's not your fault.'

'Don't be sorry,' Phoebe said. 'You didn't say anything I didn't already know.'

Cindy Ann sighed, and looked at Andrew. 'One of these days,' she said to no one in particular. 'One of these days that phone's going to ring and they're going to tell me that a baby boy or a baby girl's been born and the papers are all ready to be signed.' She sighed again, and stood up to clear the table. 'And that day's going to be the happiest day of my life.'

Cindy Ann's words echoed painfully through Phoebe's mind as she helped Andrew get ready for bed that night. In fact, in the context of what Molly had said earlier that day, Phoebe felt a little as though she were in the middle of a firing zone, with everyone hurling accusations at her from all directions. But now, instead of fighting back, Phoebe was beginning to feel a bit defeated, a bit resigned to a more honest assessment of her situation. Of course it bothers me that I won't be spending Christmas with him, she thought, watching Andrew arrange and rearrange Binky, Stumpy, and Duke on his pillow. So why don't I do something about it?

What *can* I do about it?

Quit, said a voice within her, a voice that contained an odd blend of Cindy Ann's passion, Louise's matter-of-factness, and Molly's disdain, all at once. Quit, said the voice; go back and send out your résumé and as soon us you get another job give them two weeks' notice; and when their mouths drop, when they look at you in disbelief and stutter that you can't leave them in the lurch like this, four months before trial – be polite but firm. Oh, sure, you'll hear a lot of rubbish about how unprofessional this is (and maybe it is, from their perspective – but not from yours); and you'll hear a lot of accusations as to how you're screwing up the case (which is not true;

they'll get along fine without you, once the shock wears off, which it will, give or take a week or two). But don't let it get to you. It's your life.

Go ahead, the voice said, taunting her; go ahead and say it. I resign. Say it, Phoebe. Two words, three syllables, a very simple sentence. I resign.

But Phoebe couldn't say it. The voice was right on one point, of course – they would get along fine without her, just as they had managed to find that document without her. But the voice was a little too quick to dismiss the unprofessionalism aspect. A few years ago, about the time that Phoebe was beginning her taxonomy of all the associates at Judson and Day as either Nuts or Bolts, a senior associate who was best known for having organized the firm's softball team (clearly a Nut, in Phoebe's analysis, since anyone willing to devote leisure time to anything firm-oriented had to be going for partner) abruptly resigned. Howard Grossman's untimely announcement in general shocked the firm and in particular infuriated the staff of the case on which he'd been working full time, a case scheduled for trial the following month. No matter that he had the proverbial once-in-a-lifetime opportunity to get in on a partnership at the name-partner level – he had deserted the team at a critical moment. And the team was not about to forgive him, either. Even the Bolts on the team, whom one might have expected to have cared just a little bit less, or even to have taken some glee in Grossman's desertion, as a sort of vicarious sabotage, were unrelenting in their bitterness. 'I don't care if he had a chance to be fucking president of General Motors,' one associate (now reputedly the co-owner of a fresh pasta store in Seattle) had fumed to Phoebe. 'He's the only one who knew anything about electronic funds transfer. You know who's gotta learn about electronic funds transfer now in two short weeks? Yeah, *me*!' They managed to get through the trial without Howard, of course (though they lost the case, and while a lot of excuses were offered, the most frequent target of blame was Howard himself); but whenever Howard Grossman's name came up around the coffee machine a collective shudder would pass through the group, and eyes would meet in knowing acknowledgement of an unpardonable sin. In fact, his abrupt departure gave birth to a catch-all slogan for any move that put an unfair burden on one's colleagues. 'Pulling a Grossman,' it was said of someone who left the firm, like Howard, without giving sufficient notice; or of someone who scheduled minor surgery at an inopportune time; or even, by the more hard-hearted, of someone whose relative chose the wrong time to die.

And for all her bitterness towards Judson and Day, towards Herb Sullivan, for all her disdain towards so many of her fellow associates, Phoebe did not want to go down in the firm's history as having pulled a Grossman. Whether it was out of a sense of moral obligation to the Parco-Fields staff (who would manage without her, but for whom the days would run a little bit later into the night while they absorbed her work), or simply for the sake of her own self-image, she wasn't quite sure – maybe a little bit of both – but she wanted to leave with a clean slate.

She couldn't quit, not right now; she would have to stick it out, through the trial at least. But then what? So she could resign next June, say, in good conscience – what would she do after that? She thought back to her telephone conversation with Janice, and her half-joking suggestion that they leave to set up their own practice. Was that really feasible? What were her options?

At this point Phoebe's mind drew a blank. She could imagine handing in her resignation; she could imagine cleaning out her office; she could even imagine her farewell party, with its silly speeches and the inevitable presentation of some funereal jade desk set. But she had no idea what kind of a job she would want to be walking into the next morning.

Later that evening, after Jack and Cindy Ann had left, after Andrew was in bed, Louise found Phoebe alone in the living room, going through an old photo album.

'Where was this taken?' Phoebe asked, showing Louise a cracked black-and-white picture of Phoebe, Molly, and Jack lined up on a picnic table.

'Lake Willoughby,' Louise answered. 'Don't you remember, that was the time you drank the wasp.'

Phoebe examined the picture more closely; sure enough, her upper lip was swollen, distorted, as though caught in the bend of a wavy mirror. She recalled the sweet cold fizz of the Orange Crush, suddenly followed by a piercing fire that didn't stop even when her mother had slapped the wasp off her lip.

'By the way, did you let Molly know you've had a change of plans?' Louise asked.

'Not yet.'

'When are you going to?'

'Tomorrow,' Phoebe said. 'They've got their own party going on right now; I don't want to disturb them.'

'I don't think you'd be disturbing them,' Louise said. 'I think they probably planned to include you originally.'

Phoebe turned the page. There was another picture of Molly and herself, squatting in a sandbox, packing sand into plastic buckets while off to the side a woman's pedal-pushered legs sunned themselves on the grass.

'Give her a call,' Louise said. 'If she knew you weren't on your way back to California she'd ask you up. Come on; give her a call.'

Phoebe didn't reply. Obviously she had to let Molly

know that she would be here for the wedding tomorrow, but she couldn't bring herself to make that call; she didn't know what she would say, nor did she know how Molly would respond. 'I wish you hadn't come back,' Molly had said; so for all she knew maybe Molly no longer wanted her to be in the wedding. Maybe she had already found someone else to take her place.

If only it were last Tuesday again, she thought, and she were driving Andrew down to Winslow, about to surprise Aunt Molly. If only this visit could begin over again.

'I'm tired,' she said to her mother. 'I'm tired and it's late. I'll catch her early tomorrow morning, when both of us are fresh.'

Louise was silent for a moment, then said, 'It was more than just a little bit of a disagreement, wasn't it?'

'Let me put it to you this way,' Phoebe said dryly. 'I don't think either of us will be jumping for joy over the thought of spending the rest of my so-called vacation together.' She could have continued in that tone, but the sulky sarcasm in her voice irritated her – she sounded like a thirteen-year-old, seeking out a little gratuitous sympathy. So she began over again, and tried to give her mother a more thoughtful explanation of what had gone on between Molly and herself earlier that day. Of course, her own perception of Molly, and of what Molly was doing, or not doing, with her life touched upon a sensitive issue, because Phoebe couldn't very well describe how she felt without making it clear that in her view a lifetime in Winslow was, well, the pits; and by putting down Winslow she was, in effect, putting down her mother. Nevertheless she went ahead and said what she felt, gambling on her mother's forgiveness and assuming that in any event her mother probably knew how she felt about Winslow, given her vehement refusals to move back.

As Phoebe talked, Louise sat against the arm of the sofa, one elegant hand patiently angled on top of the other against the brownish tweed of her slacks. She listened, and she forgave; because while Louise did yearn to have Phoebe and Andrew living nearby, she understood Phoebe's need to live in California; after all, she herself had grown up in Rochester, New York, and moving to Winslow at the outset of her ill-fated marriage had given her the same sense of liberation from her childhood self that moving to California had given Phoebe. So that whenever Phoebe slipped – when she referred to Winslow, for example, as 'a narrow-minded WASPy community of bigots, excuse me' – Louise let a smile form in the corners of her mouth. Because it was in large part true, and while she could forgive this town for its faults, she was proud that her daughter couldn't.

'Anyway,' Phoebe sighed, 'after I explained to her how she was wasting her life, she explained to me how I was wasting mine.'

Louise straightened up indignantly. 'Wasting your life!' she exclaimed, and gave a short angry laugh. 'That has to be one of the more ludicrous accusations I've heard in a while! Someone who by the age of twenty-nine not only has her law degree and is practising at one of the most prestigious law firms on the West Coast but on top of it all is managing on her own to bring up a beautiful little boy – I'd like to know what else Molly thinks you ought to be doing with your life so as *not* to be wasting it!'

But Phoebe was shaking her head. 'Mum,' she said, 'I know what you think; I know how it looks to you. But listen. There are a million and one twenty-nine-year-olds out there with law degrees; and my work at the firm, let's face it, it's nothing more than advanced cut-and-paste, twelve hours a day, seven days a week. And as for Andrew,' she continued without giving her mother a chance to interrupt, 'my ex-husband and his girlfriend deserve as much credit for raising him as I do, since I never have any time to spend with him.'

'Well, whatever picture you want to paint of your life, it's still not a waste,' Louise said. 'Maybe everything isn't coming up roses but at least you're out there trying.'

'Sure I'm trying,' Phoebe said, and she recalled that moment in the midst of their outburst that morning, when she had forced herself to admit that she felt superior to Molly, for having broken away, for having tried. But did she really feel better than Molly? Or was she just keeping her defences up, afraid to see through Molly's eyes just how bleak her life as a lawyer really was, afraid to admit just how much was missing? And was Winslow really such a bad place that it needed to be escaped from? Maybe *she* was the bigot, the narrow-minded one, for her refusal to see how the town and its people had changed from the way everything and everyone had looked to her as a child. Something kept Molly here, something that Phoebe wasn't privy to; and it had to be something more than just the pastoral countryside and an annual frenzy of spring fever. But what? What was Molly on to, that she was missing?

'Sure I'm trying,' Phoebe said again, leaning forward and glumly resting her elbows against her thighs. 'But who's better off?'

Phoebe awoke to the sound of rain the next morning. Wasn't that supposed to bring bad luck, she thought – rain on the day of your wedding? Then she thought back to her own wedding day, a long-ago day in April during which the sun sparkled off the Bay and clothed the surrounding hills in an emerald suede. Maybe it's the other way around, she thought; for a sunny day certainly hadn't blessed her marriage.

After two very strong cups of coffee she went into Louise's room to phone Molly in private. She had considered just driving down to Winslow and arriving at Molly's door unannounced, but had decided that such informality would be inappropriate right now.

Molly, however, was not at home.

'She spent the night at her parents',' Nick told her. 'You know, like the groom isn't supposed to see the bride the morning of her wedding and all that. But what are you doing here? I thought you had to go back to California.'

'Things changed,' Phoebe said, not wanting to go into it in detail with him. 'I guess I'm going to be here after all.'

'No kidding,' said Nick. 'That's great.'

Phoebe wondered how much Molly had told him about their encounter the day before. Nick did not strike her as a glossing-over sort, and if Molly had told him everything, Phoebe didn't think that he would so blithely say, 'That's great,' upon hearing that she was in fact staying. Maybe Molly had kept it to herself?

'Go on up and tell Molly,' Nick said. 'She's probably taking one of those prenuptial baths, or getting dressed. Go on up,' he urged her. 'If you're lucky Bea'll give you a sawdust muffin.'

Phoebe smiled.

'Hey, I'm glad you're sticking around – we have to talk later on,' Nick said. 'I've been meaning to catch you but there hasn't been a lot of time.'

'Talk?' said Phoebe nervously. About what – Molly?

'I'm going to apply to law school,' Nick said.

'You are?'

'I guess so,' Nick said. 'I just got my board scores.'

Phoebe wondered if she should ask how he had done.

'I think I did okay,' Nick confessed. 'Better than expected, anyway.'

'That's great, Nick,' Phoebe said. 'I don't know what I can tell you, but I'll be glad to talk about it with you.'

'Maybe I'll catch you after the ceremony,' he said. 'Or maybe sometime next week, when everything calms down. Now, if you'll excuse me I think I'm going to pour myself another drink.'

As it turned out, Molly wasn't taking a bath, nor was she getting dressed. When Phoebe knocked at the back door of the Adamses' house, Molly was coming out of the woodshed, carrying a bundle of kindling in one arm. She wore a green-and-black heavy wool hunting shirt over the heirloom wedding gown, with her duck-toed L.L. Bean boots, unlaced, catching against the scalloped lacy edge of the dress. Noticing Phoebe she raised her eyebrows and smiled faintly, but the guarded shadow that quickly passed across her face made Phoebe wish that she had telephoned first, as she had originally planned, if only to spare Molly from being caught unawares.

'So,' Molly said. 'I guess you didn't have to go back after all.'

'My boss found the document,' Phoebe explained. 'It was in my office all along.'

'You must have felt pretty relieved,' Molly said.

'Sort of,' Phoebe said, although at no point during her conversation with John Dunn had she ever felt relief. A diminishing of anxiety, perhaps, but never relief.

'Come on inside,' Molly said, and Phoebe, suddenly remembering Molly's condition, reached out for the bundle of kindling. But Molly cocked an eyebrow and gave a half-smile of bemusement. 'It's not exactly heavy,' she reminded Phoebe. They went inside, through the kitchen, where a bib-aproned Bea was furiously scraping some kind of a yellowish beany-looking spread from her Cuisinart into a silver serving dish, and into the living room. Molly set the kindling on the hearth and took the woollen shirt off. Gingerly she sat down on the floor, tucking her legs underneath herself; then she began crumpling up balls of paper and placing them on the bed of ashes.

Phoebe knelt down beside her and removed her jacket, taking great care in folding its sleeves and laying it over the arm of a black-and-gold Windsor chair near the fireplace. She sensed a new politeness to Molly's demeanour, one that seemed a little bit battered, as though it stemmed not from inner wariness of Phoebe but from the same emotional exhaustion that Phoebe had been feeling.

Finally Phoebe spoke. 'I'm sorry about yesterday,' she began. 'I guess I ended up saying a lot of things I shouldn't have said.' She was going to say, a lot of things I didn't mean, but she couldn't: because she *had* meant them; she just wished she hadn't said them.

'I'm sorry too,' Molly said. She sat back on her heels and raised her eyebrows, as though reconsidering something, then began making a log cabin out of the kindling sticks.

'Do you want to talk about it any more?' Phoebe asked.

'Not really,' Molly said. 'Do you?'

No, Phoebe realized; no, I don't. Not now, anyway. I need to mull over what you said, but if I mull it over with you I'll only get defensive; I'll polarize; I'll see things one-sidedly – and I don't want to do that.

'To tell you the truth, I don't really want to talk about it right now, either,' she said, 'though maybe later . . .' She left off; then – and this took a good deal of resolve on her part, because it was so naked an admission – she cautiously added, 'Not that you didn't give me a lot to think about.' She felt her face flush as she said it, and hoped that Molly wouldn't take her words and throw them back at her in a new and even harsher elaboration on yesterday's lecture.

But Molly lapsed into another long silence, as though she were even a little embarrassed by Phoebe's admission. Neither of them spoke for a while; then Molly said, 'Could you put a couple of logs on? They're too heavy for me.'

Phoebe fitted three logs closely together on top of the kindling.

'Better move them a little,' Molly ventured. 'You have to create more of a draught.'

Phoebe leaned forward and shifted the logs about, only to knock apart the house of kindling. Molly didn't say anything; but with two swift stabs of an iron poker she rearranged the wood so that when she set a match to the paper the fire caught, hot and crackly. Phoebe sat back and hugged her knees to her chest, watching the flames curl around the logs, acutely aware of Molly's basic fire-building capabilities and her own clumsiness at the simple task.

'I guess I have a lot of mixed feelings about it all,' Molly said after a while. 'Like I don't know where things stand.'

Phoebe nodded.

'And I feel like it may take a little time to sort things out,' Molly said.

Phoebe nodded again.

Together they continued to watch the fire silently, and Phoebe felt her skin tighten from the heat. Alternative topics of conversation seemed to shrivel on her tongue.

'Hey,' she said, after a while, 'I hear Nick's thinking of going to law school.'

Molly smiled. 'So you talked to him this morning,' she

said, and the air in the room seemed to thin out as this new focus took hold. 'That's right,' she said. 'He just got his board scores yesterday; he's pretty excited.'

'Where does he want to go?' Phoebe asked.

Molly shrugged. 'I don't know, really,' she said. 'Maybe Yale, maybe Stanford.'

'How do you feel about that?' Phoebe asked.

'About what?'

'About moving away.' Was it all right to ask that? Or was that a forbidden topic? Was Molly going to think that Phoebe was now telling her how to feel: prodding her to admit that she might like to get away from Vermont?

But Molly just shrugged. 'I'll adapt.'

Phoebe looked back at the fire.

'As long as it's not UCLA,' Molly said flatly. 'I can live anywhere but Los Angeles.'

Phoebe could understand that; she wouldn't want to live in Los Angeles herself. But what if Nick made it into Stanford, or Berkeley – what would it be like, to have her childhood friend move so near? Would they feel compelled to get together regularly, to meet for lunch once a week? And how would Janice and Molly get along? Phoebe feared that she would have to become a go-between, not just between her two friends but between her past and her present. Would she ever gracefully merge the two?

Don't jump the gun, she told herself. Nick could get into some hotshot East Coast school. Maybe they'll end up in New York or Washington, maybe Boston. Who could predict?

'Now *there's* a picture for you!'

Molly and Phoebe turned simultaneously; in the doorway to the kitchen stood Bea, dressed for the wedding in a white blouse and a long blue quilted skirt banded at the waist with a green sash.

'The bride with her maid of honour,' Bea said, aiming her Kodak Instamatic at them, 'two hours before the wedding.' She snapped one picture then recocked the camera for a second shot. 'Oh, come on now, girls – *smile*!'

# 13

If it felt as if the air had just begun to thin out a little once Molly and Phoebe moved on to the subject of Nick's plans for law school, then Bea's interruption came upon them like a gust of wind from the outside. They had both been choosing their words so gingerly, so cautiously, in order to avoid offending one another, and to have Bea suddenly burst in with her camera, jovially demanding smiles as they sat struggling with their fragile conversation – well, it made everything seem a little silly. And then, instead of just snapping a few pictures and leaving them alone to slip back into their tentative fumblings in front of the fireplace, Bea put them to work setting up the living room for the wedding reception – for even though Molly had continued to insist upon a no-frills affair, there was still furniture to be moved about, flowers to be arranged, the dining-room table to be set up buffet-style. ('Honey,' Bea had said to Molly earlier that morning as she polished a silver chafing dish to a hard shine, 'there's no other way to keep the food warm. And we're not using plastic cups or paper plates. Now scoot.')

Molly in particular was relieved to be interrupted by her mother (even though Bea, upon noticing the L.L. Bean boots, pressed her once again to try on the beige pumps that she had dug out of the back of her closet; and Molly, for whom the idea of wearing *any* colour pumps, let alone beige, was as foreign as it would have been for Nick, decided to put an end to her mother's badgering by telling her mother that her feet were killing her, the boots were the only things she could wear in comfort, so lay off with the pumps bit). As for her relief, it wasn't so much that Molly was finding it too awkward to work out a conversation with Phoebe; rather it was that this whole issue of where Nick would be applying to law school was an issue that she wanted to be talking about with Nick – and no one else. Up until now, she realized, his plans for law school had seemed as casually removed from their quiet life together in Winslow as their buying a house; sure, it was something he might do, in the future, depending on his board scores – just as buying a house was something they might consider later on, sometime when they had a little more money, depending on interest rates and the need for a tax break. But then yesterday afternoon she had stopped at the post office to pick up the mail, and there it was, the thin white envelope from ETS that Nick had been waiting for; and when he had opened it up and glanced at the results, the expression on his face told her immediately that this idea of law school was no longer something that *might* happen. It was *going* to happen.

And how would that translate into where they would be living, a year from now? Molly wondered, loading up a tray with wineglasses. They hadn't had much of a chance to talk about it yesterday afternoon, because they'd had to be up at the farmhouse for drinks by five; and then, after dinner, Nick had insisted that his bride-to-be spend the night at her parents' house. (Molly, who thought it was another stupid ritual, was too tired to resist, especially when Elaine joined in with Nick, babbling about what a wonderful little touch of tradition that would add.) But as she carried the tray of wineglasses into the dining room and began setting them out on the heavy linen tablecloth, Molly found herself wishing that she and Nick could have the day to themselves, to go through the catalogue of law schools a little more carefully and talk about where they might want to live. She didn't know what had been running through his mind since he'd received his scores; all she knew was that although he had a chance at Yale (his first choice) and Stanford (his second), to play it safe he would probably have to apply to a dozen or more law schools, all over the country. But where would he apply? And what if he didn't get into his top choices, and it turned out that he was willing to move anywhere – Georgia, say, or Texas – for the sake of the better ranked law school? What if he presented her with a choice between Pittsburgh and Cleveland, between Chicago and Los Angeles? Molly tried to imagine selling quilts out of some student apartment in the middle of LA. Would they even know what quilts were *for* in southern California?

At that point Bea bustled back in with a basket of orange, warty-looking gourds, which she set on the table as a centrepiece; then she drew back the curtains to the long French windows behind the table. Outside it was still drizzling, and with the curtains back a cool, blue-grey light filled the room. All but a few traces of yesterday's snow had melted, but still, that sudden storm had stripped the fields of their autumn lustre. In another month the earth beneath these fields would be frozen solid, and they would be covered over with snow; but right now they looked cold, boggy, in limbo. Here and there the dark shadow of a lone evergreen shifted in the wind; and out in the distance, near the edge of the woods, a hunter's scarlet jacket moved through the brush like an alien animal.

What will it really be like to leave? she wondered, looking out upon these fields that were so familiar to her. Maybe all this time I've been too stubborn, too close minded about living anywhere else; maybe I've been too chauvinistic about Vermont. There have to be other areas of the country that are just as nice, she thought; and if it turns out we have to live in the city, so what; we can always get out to the country on weekends. (Though she remembered Phoebe's law-school letters, and wondered if Nick would even allow himself weekends away from the law library.) And actually, maybe living in a city wouldn't be so bad. She thought back to the height of Phoebe's outburst the day before. 'You're wasting your life out here in the sticks!' Phoebe had said, and Molly suddenly had a frightening image of herself at sixty-five, sitting in Ida Poultney's rocking chair behind the cash register of the Winslow General Store, knitting away, hoisting herself up every so often to trudge over to the Franklin stove in her sensible tie-up walking shoes and shove another log into the fire. What do you want for suppah, tonight, Nick, she would drawl, trudging back, reaching up to push the hairpin deeper into her tiny knotted bun. How about some of them green beans you put up last summah, Nick would drawl back as he finished stocking the shelves with cans of Dinty Moore. Done up with mushroom soup and a can of onion rings? she would ask. Yup, he would reply, long's you don't put too many of 'em on top, them onion rings give me gas.

Is that where she'd been headed? Destined to become another one of those old-timer Yankees who never ventured out of the state, who bragged about having slept in the same bed every single night for the last fifty years? Who ordered sturdy practical clothes, season after season, year after year, from a sporting goods catalogue? Why not? If it weren't for Nick going to law school, what would prevent it? She'd never lived anywhere else, she had no right to identify with those other Vermonters, those farmhouse renovators who during at least one period in their pasts had lived a more urban sort of life and then chosen to reject it in favour of the tranquillity of

Vermont. She was a twenty-nine-year-old Ida Poultney, a hick, a local, a country bumpkin, living under the illusion that she knew what was out there and didn't want anything to do with it – while really it was just fear of the unknown that kept her here.

Just then a distant gunshot cracked across the fields, followed by a rumbling echo that rolled about in the air. All over the state the woods would be full of those red-jacketed hunters, the air full of their gunshot. God, she thought – I might even end up as some kind of a redneck hunter, drooling all year long over the thought of deer season. I'd join the NRA, probably would even take my kid to target practice, get him comfortable with the butt of a rifle pressed against his shoulder as early as possible so that the three of us, Nick and me and our little a redneck kid, could hit the woods on opening day and fill the freezer with venison.

'Now *there's* a nervous-looking bride if I ever saw one!' Bea, pausing by the table with her arms crossed, shook her head affectionately. 'What do you think, Phoebe, have you ever seen such a bundle of nerves?'

Phoebe looked up from the table, where she was arranging the silverware in orderly, reachable rows in front of the stack of plates. 'Hmmm,' she murmured, but she didn't say anything else; she raised her eyebrows at Molly as if to apologize for another one of Bea's left-field intrusions.

'You're excused, honeybunch,' Bea said, giving Molly a hug. 'Phoebe and I'll finish setting things up. You run along upstairs and take a rest to settle those butterflies in your stomach.'

Butterflies, thought Molly on her way upstairs, trying to erase that horrific redneck vision of herself. I wish. A sense of urgency was rapidly overwhelming her, and though she couldn't really put her finger on exactly what it was due to, she did know it didn't have very much to do with the wedding itself. Wedding butterflies, she thought. Now *that* would have been easy to deal with.

'Come up,' Molly said. 'Right now.'

'But I'm not even dressed,' Nick said.

'Then get dressed,' Molly said. 'I have to talk to you.' She was pacing from her mother's nightstand over to the window and back again, dangling the phone from two fingers, but now she sat down on the bed, so that downstairs her mother wouldn't hear her footsteps and start wondering why Molly wasn't lying down to get rid of those bridal butterflies that Bea was sure were flying around in Molly's stomach.

'But we're getting married in two hours,' Nick said. 'I'm not supposed to lay eyes on you before the ceremony.'

'Cut the crap, Nick,' Molly said. 'We're not exactly having a traditional wedding, you know. Get up here.'

Nick hiccuped.

'I'll be in my room,' Molly said. 'Okay?'

'Nick,' she said when he didn't reply. 'I really need to talk to you. What's the matter?'

'Why can't you talk to me after the wedding?'

'BECAUSE I NEED TO TALK TO YOU RIGHT NOW!' Molly shouted.

'All right, all right,' Nick said, and gave a sigh. 'I just don't know if I ought to be driving.'

'Why?'

'Well, uh,' Nick said. 'Jack Daniel's,' Nick said.

'Oh, terrific,' Molly said. 'That's just terrific, Nick.'

'I woke up feeling a little nervous,' Nick said. 'Aren't you a little nervous?'

Molly sighed. Of course she was a little nervous. And she wasn't really angry with Nick for getting drunk on the morning of the wedding; she was just jealous – for she herself could certainly have used a shot of Jack Daniel's right now.

'All right,' she said. 'I'll come down there. Don't go anywhere.'

'I'm not going anywhere,' Nick said. 'What is it you have to talk about all of a sudden?'

'My life,' Molly said. She hung up, went downstairs, put on the green-and-black woollen hunting shirt, slipped out of the back door, got into her mother's Saab, and zoomed off down the dirt road, past the Martin farmhouse, through the sugar bush, up over the crest by the dairy farm, and then down the long steep hill into Winslow. She was driving too fast, and she knew it, but there wasn't a lot of time.

Nick met her at the back door with a patient silly smile on his face. 'Okay,' he said. 'Here I am. What did you want to talk about?'

Molly didn't answer; she left him by the back door and went directly up to the bedroom, where she threw off the woollen hunting jacket, unbuttoned the wedding dress, and let it fall to the floor. When she was completely undressed she climbed in between the sheets. Nick was watching her from the doorway. 'Get undressed,' she told him. He obeyed her, and climbed in beside her, slipping his arm across her stomach. 'No sex,' she warned him. 'The doctor said.'

'I wasn't trying to have sex,' Nick said, exasperated, lying back and clasping his hands behind his head on the pillow. 'I was just snuggling. Now, will you please tell me what is going on?'

'Nick,' she said, and suddenly there were what her mother called butterflies in her stomach, swarms of them, ugly choking moth-like creatures fluttering up against the back of her throat. 'Nick,' she said, 'what am I going to do next year?'

'Is that what's bothering you?'

'That's enough,' Molly said. 'What am I going to do?'

'Have a baby,' Nick said.

'Big deal,' Molly said. 'What else am I going to do?'

'I don't know, Molly,' Nick said. 'Do what you've always done. Weave. Make quilts. Knit sweaters. Teach school, if we need the money, which we probably will. Why should it be any different from this year?'

Molly shook her head. She wished she knew why, but she didn't; she only knew that it was going to be different, very different.

'We have to talk,' she said to him.

'We *are* talking,' Nick said.

'We have to talk about where we want to live,' Molly said.

'That may be interesting,' Nick said, 'but it may not be relevant.'

'Why not?'

Nick shrugged. 'Where we live is going to depend more upon the decisions of various admissions committees than upon where we think we want to be.'

Molly turned and looked at him. 'You mean you'd go anywhere?'

'Well, maybe not anywhere,' Nick said. 'But we're only talking about three years.'

'That's right!' Molly exclaimed. 'And three years is a long enough time that I think we should eliminate some places!'

'Like where?'

'I don't know, like Georgia,' Molly said. 'Or Texas, or LA.'

'There are some good schools in LA, Molly,' Nick said. 'You can't write them off just because you don't want to move to southern California.'

'I can too,' Molly said. 'This isn't just your decision,

you know; there are others involved – namely, a wife and a kid.'

'The kid doesn't care where it's going to be,' Nick said. 'And if it's just you . . .' He left off in midsentence.

'If it's just me *what*?'

Nick lifted himself up on his elbow. 'Well, frankly, you really don't have any right to a veto.'

'Why not?' she said, holding back the fury that was building up within her.

'Because your needs are more flexible than mine,' he said. 'You can weave anywhere in the country, but I can't just set up a law school wherever we decide's the best place to live, which from your perspective is probably right here in Winslow. And I'm not going to settle for some piss-ass law school just because it's in a place that you like,' he said, his voice tightening, 'if I can go to a good school that happens to be in a place you don't like!'

Hot tears stung her eyes to hear the sharpness in his words. All along she had thought she was being so conciliatory by opening up to the idea of moving away from Vermont – after all, until this autumn she had refused to even consider the idea. Yet she now realized how much more of a conciliation was going to be required on her part: she would have to be open to moving just about anywhere. And justifiably so, for it wasn't like she was in a job market that limited their options; as Nick pointed out, she could set up her loom anywhere. Nick was right; she had no right to a veto.

And stop feeling sorry for yourself! she thought angrily. What's the problem? You're not being asked to choke off the Great Career and make do with slim pickings in a new town. Now, if you were in Phoebe's shoes, if you'd invested a chunk of your life at a law firm like Judson and Day, it might be a little different; then you could ask that he choose a law school nearby, or at least where you could find a comparable job. But you're not in Phoebe's shoes, and supposedly you're glad not to be. Aren't you? Put aside the teaching, since that's just a way to bring in some money; with respect to your craftwork, you're your own boss, you're not tied to an institution, with all its hierarchies; you have more freedom than she does. You're lucky.

Yet Molly wasn't feeling very lucky as she lay there beside Nick, listening to this lecture that was running through her mind. Somewhere out there, someone was stacking up accomplishments, and she was coming up short. Truly, what had she accomplished over the years as she built her little nest in the wilds of Vermont? Well, she could knit complicated sweater patterns with her eyes closed, practically. But so could Ida Poultney; the only difference was that Ida knitted her sweaters out of acrylic yarns in dime-store shades of lime-green and fluorescent red, while Molly (the purist) knitted hers out of lanolin-smelling Canadian wool. In natural-dye colours. And she made quilts; but in all honesty she was getting rather tired of stitching all those tiny scraps of fabric into Star-of-Bethlehem patterns – and besides, they were never warm enough; you always needed a down coverlet on top of the bed anyway. And then, of course, she wove. Once upon a time she had fancied herself making her entire living by weaving beautiful wall hangings on commission; but let's face it, the piece they bought over in Stowe was the first piece she had sold in two years. When you figured out the hourly rate it was downright ridiculous. And besides, her work wasn't even that good; she was seeking clean sparse lines in her designs, yet what was coming off the loom continually struck her as cluttered, gimmicky, trite. If she wanted to make money from her weaving she should sit down and crank out a stack of early-American-style bedspreads, blue-and-white geometric designs that would end up on some four-poster bed in some country-style home in Westchester, New York. Just the type of creativity she'd always aspired to.

Thus, on the day of her wedding, Molly managed to convince herself that over the past six years she had accomplished absolutely nothing. She had, in the words of her oldest friend, been wasting her life out in the sticks, making little fibre-arts trinkets while the rest of the world went to law school.

'Look, I'm sorry for snapping, I'm probably a little jumpy today,' Nick said. 'It's really not so bad; I'm sure we can come up with a list of schools that'll include a couple of long shots, a couple of sure bets, and chances are we'll find some places that both of us wouldn't mind spending three years. I'm not dying to go live in Georgia, either, you know.'

Molly didn't answer.

'Or Texas,' he continued. 'If you want, we'll cross the University of Texas right off the list. Right now. How about that. Will that make you feel better?'

Molly stared at the woven hanging that faced them from the wall opposite the bed. It was a recent piece, winter woods, done in muted taupes and greys, with scarlet accents. When she had finished it she was proud of its quiet sense of balance; but now the taupes and greys seemed dead, the scarlet vulgar. Suck-ass piece of shit, she thought.

'Let's make a list,' Nick suggested. 'Okay? We'll make a list of places we'd like to live, and we'll come up with law schools to correspond. Now take Boston.

'There's a lot going on, it's not as overwhelming as New York and we could get up here on weekends – what do you think?'

But Molly wasn't listening. She pressed her forearm over her eyes, as though it would keep back the tears.

'All right, we can scratch Boston,' Nick said anxiously, leaning up on his elbow and fingering a strand of hair behind her ear. 'Really, we'll work something out – just don't cry, Molly, it's our wedding day – please? Please don't cry?'

Bea was worried. 'I don't understand why she just took off like that!' she fumed to Phoebe. They were in the kitchen, arranging platters of food: waxy Goudas, scooped out and refilled with a blend of nuts and cheeses; an oily-looking flatbread studded with garlic and rosemary; rounds of Brie stuffed with green peppercorns.

(Not one platter of junk food? Phoebe thought. Not even a few Doritos?)

'I understand if she's a little nervous,' Bea went on, 'but you don't just take off like that without letting anyone know where you're going.'

'She's probably down in Winslow,' Phoebe said. 'She probably wanted to connect with Nick.' (How do *you* know? a voice within her demanded. With the way things are right now, what makes you an authority on Molly's motives?)

'Of course she's down in Winslow,' Bea scoffed. 'Ida Poultney called up and said that Molly was driving that car like there was no tomorrow – why, Carl was coming up the road in his Scout and she almost ran him right off into the ditch, Ida said!'

'Hmmmm,' Phoebe said.

'I tell you, if that girl's going to have a baby she better grow up and not go tearing off in someone else's car at the drop of a hat.' Bea pushed back a strand of hair. 'Do you think we need more vegetables? More carrots, perhaps?'

Phoebe looked at the carved-out pumpkin that Bea had filled with alternating clusters of carrots, celery, green-pepper strips, and cauliflower buds. There were enough vegetables in there, Phoebe thought, to take care of everyone's vitamin, mineral, and roughage requirements for the next year. 'I think that'll last us,' she told Bea. 'And if we run out I'll chop up some more.' As she spoke she happened to look out of the kitchen window; down by the Big Rock a man in a red jacket carefully walked a straight line towards the stand of willows. At first she presumed it was another hunter, but then she saw that instead of a gun he was aiming two shining metal rods straight ahead. 'What's that guy doing?'

Bea followed Phoebe's gaze, squinting, then chuckled. 'That,' she said, 'is our local dowser, Duncan Crane. Have you met Duncan?'

'Briefly,' Phoebe said.

'Duncan is looking for a hunting knife he claims his father lost on our property forty years ago. I told him if he finds it I'll join the dowsing society myself. Actually I'd love for him to find it,' Bea mused, 'because it might shut my husband up; whenever the subject arises Dave starts complaining about the lack of hard scientific evidence and what can I say? I don't have any hard evidence, *Duncan* doesn't have any hard evidence but who really knows? So many people are doing it – and they can't all be crazy.'

Phoebe watched as Duncan turned abruptly and headed towards the underbrush surrounding the Big Rock. An odd one, to be sure. Where was he from? What had brought him to a place like Winslow? And did he really think he was going to find a hunting knife that someone had lost forty years ago – with two metal rods?

'Back to Molly,' Bea said. 'Do you think it's something more than getting married? That tiff you girls had – what was that all about?'

Phoebe turned her thoughts away from Duncan, away from his dowsing, and back to Molly, to their tiff, as Bea put it. But Phoebe didn't want to go into it with Bea; Bea could be so moralistic about things, and not that Phoebe couldn't take criticism on the way she was living her life but the last thing she wanted was a lecture from Bea Adams. Besides, Phoebe thought, it's none of her business.

She tried to use her lawyering skills to come up with a nonanswer, but she wasn't quick enough.

'Molly told me it had something to do with your flying back to California for that problem you had,' Bea went on. She glanced at Phoebe, as though giving Phoebe an opportunity to correct her, but when Phoebe didn't answer she turned back to the mushroom caps she was stuffing. 'Though it seems to me, I don't mean to pry or anything, but I haven't seen the two of you giggling like you used to. Is anything wrong?'

Phoebe tried to make her laugh sound confident, as though there were the simplest of explanations for it all. 'Oh, I've had a lot on my mind with work and all,' she said. 'I haven't felt much like giggling with anyone these days.' She smiled cheerfully at Bea, who was carefully watching her over the top edge of her glasses. Bea turned back to her mushrooms, unpersuaded.

Well, for Pete's sake, Phoebe thought; this is between Molly and me. Now, I've already gone over it with *my* mother, and if Molly didn't want to talk about it with you, then I'm not going to. Besides, no way am I going to tell you how I told your daughter that she's wasting her life and then have to wait around for you to point out in how many ways I'm wasting mine! Not that I'm wasting it!

'I think I better go change now,' she said abruptly. 'Do you think you can manage?'

Bea's face lost its look of reproach; she glanced at her watch, and the worry lines deepened in her brow. 'Maybe I should call down there,' she said. 'Maybe she's having trouble with the baby again.'

'Why don't you give her another fifteen minutes,' Phoebe suggested. 'If she's not back by that point then you can call and see what's up.'

'She just doesn't act like a twenty-nine-year-old!' Bea fretted. 'She just hasn't ever grown up!'

And Phoebe didn't think it was the time, or the place, to correct her.

As Phoebe opened the door to leave she met Duncan Crane standing on the stoop, hand poised, ready to knock.

'Well well well,' he said. 'Howdy howdy.'

'Hi,' said Phoebe. 'Any luck?'

'Nope. Wrong field, I'm beginning to think.'

'Ah.'

'Hey, you people want to laugh, it's fine with me,' Duncan said.

'I wasn't laughing,' Phoebe said.

'Yes you were,' Duncan said. 'I could tell by your aura.'

Oh, honestly, thought Phoebe.

'Is Bea around?' he asked. 'Oh, there you are – good morning!'

'Not good morning,' Bea said, wiping her hands on her apron. 'Good afternoon. I had a feeling you'd show up here after tromping around in the fields – did you find anything?'

'Not yet,' Duncan said.

Bea winked at Phoebe. 'I can give you just one cup of tea,' she said to Duncan, 'but then I'll have to chase you out because the wedding's starting in less than an hour – '

Duncan held up his hand. 'I can't stay,' he said. 'I was just wondering if I could borrow your chain saw – mine busted on me this morning right in the middle of a log.'

'I thought those damn things were indestructible,' Bea said. 'Yes, I'm sure it's no problem; wait right here.' She disappeared down the basement stairs, leaving Phoebe and Duncan in the front hall together.

'So: how's the visit going?' Duncan asked.

'Oh, fine, fine,' Phoebe lied.

'How long are you here for, anyway?'

'Just another week,' Phoebe told him. 'Then it's back to the grind.'

'Too bad,' Duncan said. 'If you stuck around a few more weeks we might get some real snow.'

And it suddenly occurred to Phoebe that Duncan's weather prediction had come true. If Carl Poultney had taken him up on the bet, Duncan would have had five dollars' worth of groceries coming to him.

'Well, a longer visit's out of the question,' Phoebe said. 'I shouldn't have even taken these two weeks off, with the amount of work I have.'

'What kind of law do you practise?'

'Litigation,' she replied. 'I've got a big trial coming up in April.'

Duncan counted on his fingers.

'That's five months from now,' he said.

'Five short months,' Phoebe said. 'You wouldn't believe how much there is to be done.'

Duncan smiled; a network of tiny lines branched from the corners of his eyes. 'I guess I wouldn't,' he said.

Phoebe switched subjects, because she had just flashed upon her office, with its stacks of documents, half-written memos, unfiled briefs; and the last thing she wanted to think about today was her job. 'I think it's great that you're fixing up the Caleb place,' she said. 'You know,

Molly and I used to play down there when we were kids – there was a rope hanging from a branch out over the water, and we always used to see who could cannonball the farthest from the shoreline.'

'And who won?'

'Me, usually,' Phoebe admitted.

'I know the rope,' Duncan said. 'It's still hanging there, though I wouldn't feel too secure putting my weight on it.'

'Isn't there a lot of work to be done?' Phoebe asked. 'I seem to remember the place as just about falling down.'

'Hell, no!' Duncan said. 'The foundation's great, the supports are all solid, it's just a matter of new windows and a little insulation and at some point a new floor – oh, terrific, you're such a sweetheart,' he said as Bea appeared, lugging the chain saw in both hands. He took it from her, then turned back to Phoebe. 'You ought to come down and see the place while you're here,' he said. 'If only for old times' sake.'

'Thanks,' Phoebe said. 'I'm probably going to be pretty busy next week, though.'

'Well, I'm always there. Tell Dave I'll get this back to him as soon as I get mine fixed,' he told Bea. 'And tell the bride and groom congratulations, best wishes, et cetera, et cetera, et cetera.'

When he had left, Bea looked at her watch again. 'Should I call her?'

'Call who?'

'Phoebe, stop woolgathering,' Bea said with annoyance. 'Call *Molly*.'

Phoebe coloured.

'She's sick again,' Bea said. 'She's miscarrying, this time for good.'

'Oh, Bea,' said Phoebe plaintively, for she was tired of

nursing the woman's anxieties, 'pour yourself a drink and *relax*?'

It was twenty past one when Nick finally persuaded Molly to get dressed; after all, they were to be married in less than an hour. Molly turned back the covers and swung her legs out over the edge of the bed, carefully planting both feet firmly on the floor. Then she stood up; she put on her underwear, her liner socks, then her heavy Ragg socks; she put on the long satin slip. But when she picked up the wedding dress from its heap on the floor she couldn't bring herself to step into it. Suddenly the lacy panels seemed to be even more frayed, more yellowed, more shapeless than ever. The dress simply didn't fit; it had been made for a femininity of long ago, for a body with large bosoms and a tiny corseted waist – a far cry from the way Molly was built to begin with, let alone the way she was now, two months pregnant. She was silly to have insisted upon wearing it. When they were young she and Phoebe had been allowed, on special occasions, to play dress-up with the gown; and later, as a sixteen-year-old filled with romantic notions of a Victorian-style wedding in a buttercup field overlooking the sea, she had promised herself that she would wear that dress, and no other, when she got married. But it was an outdated promise, and she was wrong to have blindly stuck with it. Now the idea of stepping into that tattered antique dress for this afternoon's ceremony struck her as forced, affected – and because it was in so many places beyond repair, quite depressing.

'Aren't you getting dressed?' Nick asked, coming in from the bathroom, tucking his white shirt into dark-grey trousers.

Molly didn't reply; she carefully put the wedding dress on a hanger and hung it over the edge of her closet door.

She opened her bureau drawer and selected a pair of corduroy slacks, clay coloured, with pleats in the front. Nick had bought them for her last Christmas, and they had always been a little big for her, but now she appreciated the roominess of the waist – especially after sucking in her stomach all morning in order to prevent the buttons on the lace dress from bursting. Then she picked out a bulky turtleneck sweater, one that she had knitted for Nick but which had turned out too small for him. She smoothed out her hair and looked at herself in the mirror: her face was drawn and puffy from crying, but the outfit suited her, a little plain, a little stodgy, but far more appropriate than the ratty-looking heirloom wedding dress.

Nick seemed to understand – or rather, if he didn't quite know why she had suddenly decided against wearing the dress, he did nevertheless sense that it would be wrong of him to show a lot of surprise over her decision.

'You look nice,' he told her, standing beside her in front of the mirror and knotting his tie. 'You would have frozen to death in that dress.'

'It was too tight anyway,' Molly said.

'Tight where?'

'Tight here,' Molly said, circling – or rather, trying to circle – her waist with her hands.

'Wow,' said Nick, standing back to look at their reflections in the mirror. 'We're really going to do it, aren't we?'

'Are we?'

'Do you want out?' Nick said.

'No. Do you?'

'No.'

'So we're going to do it, then,' Molly said, pressing at the puffiness under her eyes with the cool tips of her fingers. 'Of course, there's still time to elope,' she said.

'Do you want to elope?'

'When I look like this, I want to elope,' Molly said. 'Don't give me any rubbish about how nobody will notice I've been crying.'

'You look beautiful to me,' Nick said.

'Yeah,' Molly said, '*right*'.

'You do,' Nick said. He placed his hands on her shoulders and drew her to him. He kissed her eyelids, first one, and then the other; Molly kept her eyes closed, and pulled him hard against her.

'I'm sorry about all this,' she said. 'Getting all worked up the day of our wedding – I could have chosen a better time to have an adolescent identity crisis.'

'It's not adolescent,' Nick said softly, 'and it's not a crisis.'

Maybe not, Molly thought. But then why was she feeling like she was eighteen again, trying to come up with a college major, trying to *be* someone? And what had happened to all that anger she'd felt towards Phoebe during yesterday's argument?

'My wife,' Nick murmured. 'My beautiful wife.'

'Not wife,' Molly said, wincing. 'Don't say wife.'

'Why not?'

'It sounds so . . . so *old*,' Molly said.

'Nick,' she whispered after a while.

'What?'

'I really love you, Nick.'

'I know,' he whispered back.

As they left the room the memory of a certain sensation flashed through Molly's mind, a physical sensation she'd had just recently but which she'd been too preoccupied to notice, or to think about. Now she thought about it: it was a feeling of warmth, of fuzzy softness.

'You put the flannel sheets on,' she said glancing back at the unmade bed. 'When? Last night?'

'I got cold,' Nick confessed. 'It was lonely without you.'

Molly felt a pang go through her; she, too, had lain chilled all night long in the twin bed up at the farmhouse, though until now she hadn't realized that it was Nick's absence that had kept her so cold. What a stupid idea, for them to spend the night apart. At the same time she found herself thinking with a bit of reproval that it was a little early for flannel sheets; she tried to remember when they had put them on the bed last year. Wasn't it after Thanksgiving? As one born into a northern climate, Molly was leery of giving in to the cold too soon; there was a subconscious fear that if you started piling on the layers of warmth too early you would use up all available layers as the weather got even colder and thus be without a trump card against that final deep plummet of the mercury in mid-January. Yet it was cold and damp *now*. What did it matter *when* they had put the flannel sheets on the bed last year? Or whether anyone else in Winslow had already put them on?

What's astonishing, Molly marvelled to herself on their way out of the house, is the amount of trivia that I've got to break away from. She wondered if Phoebe had managed to rid herself of all these folklorish rules that could make life miserable: waiting until after Thanksgiving to put the flannel sheets on, for example, or keeping the thermostat set at sixty regardless. What would it be like to be free from this Yankee culture?

Phoebe would know. But Molly sadly realized that she probably wouldn't be able to ask her oldest friend about any of this.

# 14

Phoebe had to admit that overall the wedding was a fine affair. Molly appeared calm throughout the ceremony, though her face looked wan, a little – and was this ridiculous? – older? yes, older, than Phoebe remembered, and it made her wonder what precisely had upset Molly earlier to make her take off so suddenly for Winslow in Bea's Saab. Whatever it was, Phoebe was surely responsible; and she would have liked to retreat upstairs with Molly to the twin beds of Molly's old bedroom, where they could lie against the ruffled pillows the way they had when they were children, and she could undo all the wrongs she had ever done. But her desire was based on the faulty assumption that she and Molly would be able to talk with each other about touchy issues. And that just wasn't possible; it was clear from their talk in front of the fireplace that they both needed time away from one another to sort things out, to glean what perspectives they could on the things that had been said. Besides, it was, after all, a wedding, not a therapy session, and Molly deserved to let the celebration of her marriage take priority over everything else that afternoon, including the preservation of an old friendship.

As Molly and Nick made their promises Phoebe stood to one side of the fireplace; when she had handed Molly the ring – Molly smiled, that same shy smile that Phoebe knew so well – Phoebe stepped back into the cluster of guests to join Cindy Ann and Andrew. Cindy Ann was wearing a red muu-muu; tears rolled freely down her cheeks until Elaine, anaemic and weedy-looking in a colourless boat-necked dress, handed her a tissue. After the ceremony there was an awkward moment when Phoebe, as the maid of honour, was expected to make a toast. She coloured, but quickly managed a laugh, saying she'd always been terrible at making toasts (and she was) . . . so, well, here's to the bride and groom. It wasn't much of a speech, but Molly would understand. Anything more, in fact, would have probably seemed too uncomfortably cheerful to both of them.

Later she apologized to Leo for having snapped at him over the phone on Friday night. 'I was under a lot of pressure,' she explained. 'Don't hold it against me.'

'Of course not,' Leo said. 'I know exactly how it is.'

Oh no you don't, thought Phoebe, smiling politely at Leo's feet. Leo was wearing wing tips.

'I hear you work for a senator – '

' – Senator Gove.'

'Ah,' Phoebe said, and thought for a moment. 'Is he a Democrat or a Republican?'

Leo stared at her, then exhaled a laugh of disbelief. 'The Senator is a *Democrat*,' he said. 'One of the neoliberals, as the press is so fond of saying. What, did you miss the write-up in *Esquire*?'

Phoebe decided not to ask what state Senator Gove represented. She also realized that Leo had bad breath. 'Excuse me,' she said, 'but I'd better stop my son from eating all the carob chips off the wedding cake.'

'Catch up with me before I leave,' Leo called as she left him standing by the sofa. 'We should exchange numbers.'

'Is that silk?' Elaine cried, fingering her sleeve as she headed towards the buffet.

Phoebe turned her head to avoid the cigarillo smoke. 'Rayon.'

'Do you mind?' Elaine said, and she rolled back

Phoebe's collar to inspect the label. 'Hollander,' she said to Stan. 'Remember that name. I never wear prints,' she said to Phoebe, 'but there's something about that one, I bet I could get away with wearing a pastel like that – it's not really purple, sort of a mauve, wouldn't you say? It gets so difficult when you're my age,' she said, sighing; 'you want to look young but not *too* young – I remember when everyone was wearing miniskirts and you'd see these fat old matrons walking around with their dresses halfway up their thighs and the skin would be all mottled and dimply and solid cellulose, I mean it just looked disgusting and I swore I'd always try and look my age but what do you think, could I get away with something like this?'

'Why not?' Phoebe said pleasantly, surveying Elaine's deathly shoulders and neck and thinking that nothing after all could make the woman look any worse.

'You're Molly's oldest friend, that's what Nick tells me,' Elaine said. 'And you're a lawyer out in Los Angeles?'

'San Francisco,' Phoebe said.

'Oh, that must be so ex*cit*ing,' Elaine warbled. 'What kind of law do you do?'

'Litigation, mostly,' Phoebe said. 'I'm working on an antitrust case right now.'

'Antitrust!' Elaine shrieked. 'Stan, come over here and talk to Molly's friend! The one who's a lawyer! She does antitrust, Stan! Stan does a lot of antitrust,' Elaine informed Phoebe. 'He's always having to fly down to Washington to meet with the Justice Department over this or that. Though with the current administration, well, you know how lax they're getting, I'm sure you're right on top of what the Antitrust Division thinks about all these mergers, letting them fly right on by – Who did you say you worked for?'

'Judson and Day,' Phoebe said. The smoke from Elaine's cigarillo was bringing out violent instincts in her.

'I've heard of them – they're a very top-notch firm, aren't they?'

'I don't know how you'd characterize them,' Phoebe said. 'Excuse me, but my son – '

'Oh, but they *are*,' Elaine said. 'You're very lucky to be working there – do you like it?'

'No,' Phoebe said flatly. 'I hate it.' She left Elaine standing there cocooned in her cloud of smoke and made her way over to the buffet table, where Andrew and Dave were playing a game of bluff. Andrew held out his palms, on which Dave rested his own; then Andrew whipped his hands around in time to slap the tops of Dave's hands, shrieking with laughter at Dave's none-too-exaggerated grimace.

'Andrew,' Phoebe said from across the table, 'go easy on Mr Adams, this is just a game, you don't need to slap him so hard.'

Andrew turned back to Dave, and held out his palms again. 'Come on!' he said. 'I get another turn!'

Phoebe left them to their game, and refilled her champagne glass. Over by the fireplace Bea was lining up the members of the wedding for pictures; when she spotted Phoebe, she insisted that Phoebe pose for one picture with Molly and Nick and Leo, and then another with just Molly and Nick, and then one with Molly alone. Phoebe found this final pose difficult. She was afraid of the camera's eye, for one thing: what it could see, what it could tell about their relationship at this particular moment. But she also harboured a sort of primitive fear, that if they allowed their image to be captured on film today, their rift would be forever fixed.

'Phoebe,' said Bea, '*smile*!'

('I'm not saying you should offer her a *job*,' Phoebe

heard Elaine say to Stan afterwards. 'I'm just saying you ought to talk to her and find out why she doesn't like that law firm. She might be able to offer you some *insight*.'

'Elaine?' said Stan wearily. 'I'm on vacation?')

Phoebe stayed at the wedding until six, then said goodbye and took Andrew back to the Martin farmhouse to give him a bath before bed. She had a headache from the champagne, and she had eaten too much of Bea's wedding cake, which seemed overloaded with unidentifiable grated vegetables – courgettes, probably; maybe some carrots; perhaps even a little pumpkin. It had been a long day, and she was glad to be alone. She was impressed with the cheerful front she had managed to keep up – and it *had* been a front, for unlike Molly she had had nothing more momentous to overcome the sadness that underscored the afternoon for her. She had felt out of place much of the time, a ghost among revellers.

But now, with the wedding over, the remaining week of her vacation stretched before her like a cold white space, seven long empty days to fill before it was time to go back to California. Phoebe wanted very much to think that with such a long block of time she would be able to mend things with Molly – but what if she couldn't? How could she face that? And she hated to admit it, but she was tired of being on vacation; in a perverse way she wanted to get back to the drudgery of her day-to-day life. Which shouldn't have been all that surprising, actually, given the fact that up until now the vacation had been a continuous series of crises: first Molly's near miscarriage, then the lost document, then her fight with Molly. So that she was entitled to feel tired, to want to return to a more normal routine.

Yet she couldn't change her plans, not now, not without a good excuse. She had to stay. But what to do? Last month, sitting in her office surrounded by haphazard stacks of unreadable corporate memoranda, two weeks in Vermont had seemed like barely enough time to do all the things she wanted. All the people to visit, the places to rediscover, the childhood memories to unearth with her oldest friend, along with all the catching up they had to do – she would never have time to do everything in just two short weeks, she had thought. And yet now it seemed as though she had seen everybody and gone everywhere that she wanted; and as for Molly – well, everything was on hold until who knows when.

Seven days. Phoebe couldn't remember having had such a stretch of unscheduled time since before law school. There was that one trip to Mexico with Rusty, before Andrew was born, but Rusty had been so hell bent upon filling up the day with planned events – snorkelling, aquaplaning, a day trip up into the mountains. Even their relaxation time was scheduled: Now we're going to have Margaritas, he might have said at a point too early in the day for her to want to face another Margarita; and then we can go make love – Phoebe? Are you listening? Not once during that entire week did she have any time to doze on the beach with a stack of magazines and paperbacks too trashy to pick up; not once did she have any time just to daydream.

Well, there certainly wasn't any Rusty around during this vacation to devise an itinerary of back roads that had to be explored. There also wasn't any legal work that she had to do; somewhere along the line all that reading material she had brought back in her briefcase had lost its urgency. And Andrew seemed to have developed an attachment towards Dave that made her feel a little secondary some of the time. When Andrew was a toddler the idea of 'time off' had caused Phoebe to just roll her eyes (because if she wasn't billing hours at the law firm she was pouring Andrew grape juice, or wiping it up, or scrambling after him as he headed towards the steep hill of Marin Avenue on his tricycle; time off from work was merely time on with Andrew); yet she was now learning something she should have learned a little earlier: that her almost-five-year-old son didn't require all of her attention all of the time.

So. She had seven days of vacation during which to enjoy herself. *Maybe* at some point she and Molly would find it easier to talk to one another; *maybe* they could apologize, and start over; but in the meantime she could get to know the Winslow that Molly knew, and perhaps by doing so could come to understand her friend a little better. She could visit Max; and she could spend some time with Jack and Cindy Ann: they could go to Joe-Ray's this Tuesday, and listen to guitar music. She could catch up on her sleep, and read some spy novels; maybe she would even go down to Barnet's Pond, and see what Duncan Crane had done to the Caleb camp. (Though she doubted she would go; she felt a little shy about seeing Duncan, for some reason, and also didn't want to exert the energy needed to get acquainted with a stranger.)

Seven whole days, Phoebe thought – seven whole days to do anything you want. That's nice, isn't it? An entire week, all to yourself?

But Phoebe still felt qualmish about having all this time. Aside from her general fear that she and Molly might *not* be able to patch things up, she also had a terrible feeling that because of her work schedule she had forgotten how to enjoy herself, how to take advantage of free time, slow down, relax. She didn't know if she could stand not being busy.

Mum, she heard herself whining, what can I *do*?

Thus Phoebe spent the next several days proving to herself that she did know how to relax, that she did know how to enjoy herself. She forced herself to slow down, and made a promise that each day she would try to rediscover something new about Winslow, something she might have been inclined to overlook until now. Though the woods were off limits because of hunters – Phoebe didn't even feel comfortable in one of Jack's fluorescent orange windbreakers – she took long walks down the dirt road, up into the sugar bush. Sometimes she took these walks by herself, in the early morning, before breakfast; but often – because she resented the idea of being secondary – she would convince Andrew that there was something that *he* could discover: a granite wishing well, an unkempt cemetery; or a haunted house – the ramshackle Patterson place, its living room littered with World War II magazines, and upstairs, a rickety carved piano. Listen, she would whisper, *spooks*; and as he froze, gripped in his mother's fantasy, she would run her fingers over its chipped-off keys, releasing from its innards a tinny arpeggio of doom which filled the room like a swarm of black bees.

Andrew was most interested, however, in bundling up in one of Phoebe's old jackets and riding around in Louise's jeep with the top down. They made a ritual of driving up to the quarry to stare down the steep cliffs of granite into the stagnant leaf-littered water below, and then they would head down into Winslow, and call on the Poultneys in their general store, where Carl would invariably have a different maple-syrup shape for Andrew, or an ice cream cone, or a T-shirt with a map of Vermont on its front. 'Say thank you,' Phoebe would have to remind him, and then she would wander about the store, marvelling over the price of a five-pound jar of unfiltered honey, a small wheel of Cabot cheddar, a simple cast-iron skillet, a slab of marble for cooking taffy. As she browsed among the wares she fantasized that she had a farmhouse up the hill, a little white cottage with a garden of perennials in back; she was down here now to stock up the cupboards and had an unlimited budget to spend on wild honeys and maple syrup, long sausages that she would hang from the rafters in the pantry, gallon-sized jugs of tangy apple cider. She and Andrew would drive back in the jeep with their groceries in boxes, and when they got home she would fire up the iron cookstove, put on a griddle, and make thick, buttery grilled cheese sandwiches, which they would eat at a simple wooden table sitting on simple wooden chairs. Oh, what a San Francisco lawyer's salary could buy back here! How warm they would be all winter long with little stoves crackling in their bedrooms, great downy coverlets on their beds, soft woollen scarves to keep the icy wind from ripping into their chests! How healthy they would be, living on this whole-grain bread from Canada, fresh eggs, and raw milk from the dairy farm up on top of the hill! And what classy dinners she would give as spring arrived and with it the wild asparagus, the fiddlehead ferns, that they would gather by the marshes!

But then Ida would shuffle in from the back room, and ask her once again to describe the flowers out in San Francisco. Her fantasy of buying a winter's worth of staples for her cottage on the hill would dissolve as she remembered her plane tickets, the weight limit on her luggage, and she would put off for another day indulging in the frivolous decision as to which one of those staples – cheese, honey, maple syrup – she would have room for in her suitcase.

Often during these trips to the Winslow General Store Carl Poultney would take Andrew out back to demonstrate an ancient tool, or to give him a small wooden figurine that he might have carved the night before; and it was during those times that Phoebe would lean against the counter and chat with Ida. Ida could remember a Winslow of long ago, a Winslow whose mill was operating and whose streets were all of the same dark oil-packed dirt as the road up to East Winslow was today. They had their own crowd of young marrieds, as she called them, and the men would go off to work in the mill or up in the quarries while 'the girls' would get together for whatever club was meeting on that particular day of the week. Monday was sewing club, Ida informed Phoebe, Tuesday garden club, Wednesday whist; Thursday they all stayed at home to catch up on housework and then Friday they met again for knitting club. And they buckled down, too, she declared; one year they got together and knitted one hundred ski sweaters on commission. 'I did sleeves,' Ida told Phoebe, 'one sleeve right after the other tills I got so's I knew the pattern by heart.' And the money they earned? 'Oh, that was ours to keep,' Ida said emphatically, 'and I bought myself this blue suit over to St Audie with hat and gloves and shoes to match. Carl couldn't get over it!' She laughed, letting her head fall back, searching the rafters for a sharper memory of the expression on her husband's face forty years ago. 'He says to me, "Ida, what do you need yourself a blue suit for, when're you going to get all dolled up in an outfit like that? How come you didn't buy yourself one of them new electric mixers?" And I says to him, "Carl, you want me to have a mixer, *you* buy it, but I'm going to have me a good set of clothes."' And did she ever get the mixer? Ida's face lost its glee, as though she had been reminded of her bad hip. 'Oh, I got the mixer eventually,' she grumped, 'so's Carl could have his mashed potatoes every night.'

Ida had also played the fiddle as a young woman, and she told Phoebe about the year she won the Fiddlers' Contest. 'I was thirty-one,' she said, 'and I was seven months pregnant but that didn't stop me – I got up on the stage and when I finished they didn't stop clapping until I played it all over again!' What was the prize? 'Prize?' Ida exclaimed. 'Why, dearie, there wasn't any prize, I just got the *title*. I won, that's all.'

Phoebe could tell that Ida enjoyed telling her these stories that she had packed away in her memory, and Phoebe enjoyed listening to them. But Ida's fate – watching *Dallas* every Friday night, dreaming of a jewelled ranch in sunny Texas – made Phoebe ache for the elderly woman. She wished that somehow she could convince Ida that she wasn't really missing anything – that even Texas had its cold spells, and while LA might be warm year round the air would make you sick. 'I don't care,' Ida would staunchly reply; 'long's I don't have to put me on a sweater every day of the year I don't care if the air's like poison.' 'Oh, but Ida,' Phoebe would argue, ' – think of autumn, think of all the colours! We don't get anything like autumn foliage out in California!' And Ida would just sniff, shake her head, and keep on rocking in the maple rocking chair with its printed patchwork cushion: 'All them colours mean but one thing to me,' she would declare, 'and that's that I got to get Carl's long underwear out of the trunk and wash it up all fresh for him so's we can go another month without having to turn the heat up.'

There seemed to be no way to convince Ida that she wouldn't be better off in Texas, or southern California, and Phoebe began to feel a little disingenuous as she raved on and on about the vibrancy of the autumn foliage, or the crystalline beauty of an ice storm. After all, the changing of the leaves and the coming of winter were nothing but carefully nurtured memories for her, had nothing to do with getting a cord of wood stacked, or putting on storm windows, or hoping that a pair of Dr Scholl's liners would, as advertised, keep her feet wondrously warm in those old boots that still had another year's wear left. Who was *she* to be giving Ida a pep talk when in another week she'd be on a plane back to California, back to sunshine, back to flowers? Phoebe felt ashamed; her attempts to console Ida were no better than those that a snotty-mouthed John Dunn could have conjured up. This place is *just* so outrageously *beautiful*! John would marvel, his visit miraculously coinciding with a break in the August heat wave, or the peak of foliage season, or the heaviest snowfall Killington had on record. But John Dunn would always leave before the snow turned black and crusty. He was safe. Phoebe was safe. And Ida, who would spend the evening stitching in a new elastic waistband on Carl's woollen underwear, was not safe.

And yet, although Phoebe felt a little insincere, there was also a part of her that felt justified in everything she said to Ida. To be sure, after her run-in with Molly she was probably bending over backwards to focus on the more positive aspects of life here in Winslow, and maybe she was going overboard with Ida. But so what? She was just trying to appreciate the town, that was all. And no, she wasn't thinking of calling up Carl Poultney's 'lady lawyer' over in St Audenbury to talk about job possibilities; she was still quite clear about not wanting to move back to Vermont. She just wanted to understand this place a little better. Through Ida. Through Carl. Through long walks along the dirt road. And to that end, she felt she was entitled to gush.

During this week, as she filled her days with long walks and visits to the general store, Phoebe had no contact with Molly. She tried to explain away this troublesome fact by telling herself that it was because Molly was busy with school, but she knew that wasn't the case; if last week had turned out a little differently, Molly would be taking one of her sick days right now, and the two of them would be going to antique shops, perhaps, where Molly could pick out the wedding present that Phoebe had not yet bought for her. She then tried reminding herself that they had both seemed to want to sort things out alone – but did that mean they weren't even going to speak to each other for the rest of the vacation? Finally on Wednesday she promised herself that she would stop down at Molly's that afternoon – but when Louise happened to mention that she was driving into St Audenbury to do some shopping, Phoebe decided that she couldn't do without a pair of gloves from the factory outlet over there, and since she was also low on toothpaste and Andrew needed some nose drops, she guessed she'd better go with Louise.

'I thought you were going down Molly's,' Louise said.

'I'll go tonight,' Phoebe said.

But she didn't.

Not that Molly was stopping by to visit *her*, or calling *her* up to suggest that *she* come down for dinner. Phoebe began to settle into the disheartening realization that the rest of the vacation might very well go by without their patching things up. This possibility had, of course, crossed her mind several times, but it had always been tempered by the security of having eight full days ahead of her, or seven, or six, during which somehow, one way or another, they would find a way to mend things so that the two of them would, in Bea's words, be giggling teenagers again. But as the days passed, and nothing happened, Phoebe's doubts about the likelihood of a reconciliation grew until one night when she said to herself: Okay. So you're not so close any more – it's not the end of the world. Some friendships last; others serve their function and then retire. This one's retiring – don't let it bother you that much.

But it did. This wasn't just any friend; this was her *oldest* friend. And she couldn't help but feel that it was a shortcoming on her part that had allowed this stalemate to occur. Why was she procrastinating? Was she afraid of another argument, that all-out cat fight that never took place? Phoebe didn't think that was the reason; they were beyond another major argument at this point. No; what was really holding her back was a growing sense of inferiority towards Molly. Her friend's tendency as a child to be so quietly agreeable now seemed to have matured into a calm inner confidence that she herself lacked. It didn't matter that everyone else was going to law school, medical school, business school; Molly simply wanted to weave, and so weave she would. And her confidence seemed to keep her on top of things in a way that Phoebe could only dream about. Molly never would have lost the Schein memo, for example – but if she had, she would have known right away how to placate Herb while in the meantime making arrangements to find the document. Under better circumstances Phoebe might have said that she admired Molly; but right now she only felt intimidated by her friend; she was all too afraid that since last Sunday Molly, in her clear Yankee vision, would have put her finger on so many ways in which Phoebe's life was lacking that there would never be time for her to even *begin* to explain it during the remaining days of this visit.

All this Phoebe found quite shameful, of course. Here she was, avoiding Molly just because Molly had things a little bit more *together*? Hardly the behaviour one should expect from a woman her age. By Thursday her shame gave way to a panicky realization that there were just four days left before she was due to go back; and so she arranged for Andrew to spend the afternoon with Cindy

Ann, who was baking chocolate chip cookies, and drove down into Winslow alone. As she turned into Molly's long driveway she found it blocked halfway up by a recently dumped heap of cut wood. She backed out, parked the car on the street, and walked up the driveway to where she met Nick, who was coming from the back porch for another armload. He had already stacked up a neat wall of logs along one side of the porch, and was halfway through the second layer.

'Where've you been all week?' Nick asked her, fitting logs into the crook of his arm. He was wearing a blue flannel shirt with bleach spots on its front tails. 'Haven't seen you since the wedding.'

'Oh, around and about,' Phoebe said. She didn't know how much Nick knew, or how firmly he had taken Molly's side. 'Where's Molly?'

'She had a meeting after school today,' Nick said over his shoulder as he headed towards the porch. Phoebe counted seven logs in his arm.

'What time is she supposed to be back?' Phoebe asked him.

'I don't know,' Nick replied. 'She said something about Doris being ticked off, so she could be there until six.'

'Maybe I should come back,' Phoebe said.

'Oh no you don't,' Nick said, handing her a dungaree jacket.

'What's this for?'

'To keep that fancy sweater from getting full of wood chips while you help me get this wood stacked,' Nick said.

So Phoebe spent the next hour traipsing back and forth from the driveway to the back porch, managing at most four chunks of wood in one trip but usually three or even less. (One of these days – after the trial – she had to join a gym. This was ridiculous.) Woodpiles meant spiders to

Phoebe, and before picking up a log she would give it a good kick and roll it about to make sure that any spiders would run off to another log in the pile. Nevertheless she was edgy the entire time; each armload that she managed to transport from the woodpile to the porch without some giant clam-bellied black *thing* scurrying up her arm to bite her on the neck she considered a major triumph.

'Not bad,' said Nick when the last log was neatly in place. 'Three stacks deep – that should last us until February.'

Phoebe brushed wood chips off her arms, and wondered if any spiders had got into her hair. 'How much wood is that?' she asked him.

'Oh, about a cord.'

That's all? Phoebe thought.

'Come on,' Nick said. 'We deserve a beer.' She followed him into the house, which smelled of curry and woodsmoke; while Nick uncapped two bottles of Molson she took off the jacket and ran her fingers through her hair, then went over to warm her hands by the woodstove. Nick handed her a beer, and as she took the first sip she felt for one brief second like some kind of road-construction worker: tired and sweaty and entitled to as many of these as she needed to revive herself.

'Hard work, I'd say,' Nick said. 'I don't imagine you stack a lot of woodpiles out there in California. Do you have a fireplace where you live?'

'Yes,' Phoebe said. 'Though I don't get around to using it very often.'

'How much does a cord of wood go for?' Nick asked.

'I don't know,' Phoebe said. 'I've never bought one.'

'Then what do you burn?'

'Duraflame,' Phoebe confessed.

Nick laughed.

'Hey, look, even Andrew can build a fire with

Duraflame,' she joked, then hastily added, 'Not that I actually let him, of course.' After all, she didn't want Nick to think that she went around letting her child build fires; he might mention something to Molly, and Molly would get the impression that she didn't care if Andrew played with matches – Oh, stop it, she scolded herself. Stop being so paranoid about Molly's opinion of you as a mother!

She realized that a silence had fallen over the room, that Nick was looking at her thoughtfully. As their eyes met he brought his bottle to his lips, tipped it upward, set it back on his thigh. Phoebe suddenly had a terrible vision of them having a few more beers and ending up in bed together, making love underneath one of Molly's quilts. And even though she knew that this would never happen, even though she wasn't even attracted to Nick in a way that she might *wish* for it to happen, nevertheless she already felt that the sin had been committed. Just by imagining it. In a setting where any mature adult in his or her right mind would have imagined it.

'So where are you going to apply to law school?' she asked him, in order to focus her thoughts on less unnerving matters.

'We haven't decided,' Nick said, and Phoebe smiled to herself over his use of the word *we*.

'You were lucky,' he went on, 'getting into Boalt.'

Phoebe wrinkled her nose and gave a shrug; but she couldn't help recalling her elation the day she heard from Berkeley. She had had a string of rejection letters from Yale, Chicago, Harvard (none of which had really surprised her; but they did make her realize how she had built her hopes up); then Stanford and Columbia. She was getting gloomier and gloomier, convinced that if she didn't get into what was viewed as a top ten school, her chances of ever finding employment would be nonexistent. She began to think about going into journalism. She began to think about moving to Washington, DC. She began to hate the idea of moving to Washington, DC, and began to think about moving to New York City. And then came that wonderful letter from Berkeley admissions, so personally warm that she felt as though she were being welcomed into a large family.

(Ah, yes, I remember feeling that way myself, she heard Janice say. How quickly we learn otherwise.)

'What was it like for you?' Nick asked her. 'Was law school really as bad as it's made out to be?'

Phoebe didn't know quite how she would answer that. She didn't want to discourage him, but on the other hand should she paint a falsely rosy picture? It was too bad that he hadn't asked her that question when she had been in law school; back then she would have reassured him that it wasn't bad at all – a little boring, maybe, but no, nothing like *The Paper Chase*. Yet the longer she was out of law school the more her recollections soured. What a bunch of nerds the first year of law school had turned them into! It didn't matter whether or not you had a Professor Kingsfield, happily willing to crucify you in front of a hundred other students; Professor Kingsfields weren't the problem – in fact they probably even did you a little good, in their own sadistic way. The problem was the nerd mentality that permeated the halls of the law school like a contagious disease. You'd start out the semester and look around you and see a few molish-looking weirdos carrying around their clunky plastic briefcases, trying to keep their yellow shirts tucked in; but you'd band together with the more normal-looking types in their jeans and T-shirts and you'd all talk about public interest law and government service, maybe joining the Alameda County Public Defenders' office, maybe going up to Alaska to work with Legal Services. But then something happened: the men started getting haircuts, and shaving their beards; and the women went out and bought a few preppy-looking jackets, started wearing nylons under slacks; and lunchtime discussions focused on Promissory Estoppel, or the Rule Against Perpetuities, or Specific Intent. So that by the time second-year interviews rolled around and the scent of money hung heavily in the air, the only distinguishable factor between you and that nerd you had shied away from on the first day of law school was that he was still sitting up in the front row with one arm perpetually raised and you weren't. Beyond that, you were one and the same.

Not only that, but law school seemed to have stolen her sense of humour; looking back she saw a dreary-minded soul who took her work so seriously: studying nights and weekends, outlining her notes, briefing cases. And now she wished she could have been a little more relaxed about everything, wished she could have laughed at herself: for agonizing over which particular outline to buy, for furiously highlighting entire pages in yellow. She wished she could have let herself have fun at her moot court argument instead of standing there, board stiff, terrified, in front of a panel of acting judges. She wished she could have realized that none of this mattered, in the long run.

Yet how much of this should she disclose to Nick? And who was to say that her perspective was any better these days? Maybe she still had it all wrong.

Nick had opened up two more beers as he waited for her answer. Phoebe took the bottle and brought her chair a little closer to the stove.

'No,' she finally said, 'it's not as bad as it's made out to be. There are just a lot of jerks you have to deal with. And it will depend a lot on where you end up going too;

some schools are better than others in terms of the competitive environment.' She didn't think she sounded very convincing; but what else could she say?

'What about courses?' Nick asked her. 'Say I wanted to do environmental law when I got out – should I try and find a school that has a lot of good environmental law courses?'

Phoebe shook her head. 'It doesn't matter what courses you take, in the long run.' She thought of Janice, with her sixty-eight in Wills and Trusts, taking over the estates work at Judson and Day now that Francis Clapp had been asked to leave. 'Go to the best school. Do law review. Publish a note, be an editor – that's what will count, not whether or not you took a course in environmental law.' She turned to look at him; he had hoisted his legs up on to the kitchen table, and was tipping back in his chair. 'Is that what you think you might want to do, practice environmental law?' She found it hard to ask that question without sounding cynical – because everyone started out wanting to practice environmental law, or something along those lines – and she hoped her cynicism didn't show.

'Maybe,' Nick said. 'I'm not sure what I want to do – maybe I won't even end up practicing, it's a good degree to have even if you don't – but if I *do* practice, I'd like to feel as though I were doing something constructive, something good, rather than just helping corporations keep their asses clean.'

Phoebe smiled. 'Like me?'

'I didn't mean it that way,' Nick said. 'It's just that I don't really care a whole lot about making money – '

Phoebe smiled again.

'Oh, shit, I didn't mean it that way either!' he exclaimed. 'This is coming out all wrong!'

But Phoebe let the smile linger in her eyes. He wasn't

offending her; he was just saying what any prelaw student would have said. At that stage they were all full of optimism – and why should Nick be any different? It was all ahead of him, all so simple: next June he would become a father, and next autumn he would begin law school, and he would have been sufficiently forewarned so that he would manage to stay sane, and not catch nerd fever, and not fall victim to the lure of corporate practice. He would go forth and do good.

Phoebe wondered if he would really be so lucky. Maybe he would; maybe she had just screwed up, had just made too many wrong decisions along the way. Such as taking the job with Judson and Day as a way of keeping her options open. (How had she kept her options open, anyway? Hadn't she really narrowed her options? For if she ever left Judson and Day, she would have to take a job that was at least respectable: because a Judson and Day background wasn't anything to be squandered; it was to be used with a vengeance.) But would Nick make these mistakes? Something told her that he wouldn't, that in five years he would in fact be practicing environmental law, or perhaps using his law degree for something else but in any event doing good. Maybe it was because of his spirit. He seemed less malleable than most law students; and besides that, he didn't seem to have the built-in belligerence, the ambition to nitpick to death every last detail, that destined so many of them to end up at a firm like Judson and Day, professional advocates who saw everything in black and white. Nick seemed to see the world in shades of grey. He seemed to see the middle ground. And for this, she realized, he might not end up being the best lawyer – whatever field he chose – but he would be a lot more interesting to spend an afternoon, a day, a week, a lifetime with.

Molly, Phoebe realized, was very lucky.

Not that she was giving in to an attraction to Nick. It just didn't exist – or if it did, it was too deeply buried underneath layers of scruples. Yet as Phoebe sat thinking about Nick, she couldn't help but wonder what her life would be like with someone like him to come home to every night. Someone – and she wasn't trying to glorify the guy, but Molly certainly hadn't made that curry – someone who might have cooked fine meals for her a couple of times a week. Someone to look at houses with, and plan for vacations; someone who in better wisdom might have helped her realize a long time ago that perhaps she was in the wrong line of work.

There was no doubt about it. Molly was very, very lucky to have Nick. And Phoebe wished there were some way that she could communicate this to Molly. But how? It was bound to come out all wrong.

'You're awfully quiet,' said Nick.

Phoebe coloured.

'Environmental law, not caring about money,' he mused. 'I bet is all sounds pretty naïve to you, doesn't it? Like who is this dope?'

It doesn't sound naïve,' Phoebe lied. 'It sounds enviable.'

'Well, it *is* naïve, but what the hell. Tell me more about your job,' he said. 'What made you decide to work for that firm?'

'Hah,' said Phoebe. 'Beats me.'

Nick looked at her. 'I knew you weren't crazy about it, but is it really that bad?'

Phoebe thought for a moment, then quickly decided that she wasn't going to worry about discouraging him with respect to law firms. 'It sucks,' she said flatly.

Nick laughed.

'I'm serious,' she said. 'Do you know what happens to

me when I think that next Tuesday I'm going to be back in the office?'

'What?'

'My heart starts pounding,' she said, 'and this hot little core of anger that sits in my stomach all the time begins to flare. I think of my boss and it flares a little hotter. I think about putting in a few all-nighters and it flares even hotter still. Then I think about working evenings and weekends and holidays and being expected to pretend that Andrew doesn't exist, to put him out of my mind because he's doing fine with the baby-sitter or he's doing fine with Rusty, and by now I've got a regular furnace going in me, just at the thought of going back to work next Tuesday.'

'Evenings and weekends,' Nick said, and he winced. 'Holidays too – you really don't have a lot of time off, do you?'

'Not when you're doing litigation,' Phoebe replied.

'This may sound a little simplistic, but why don't you get out of litigation? There are other things to do, aren't there?'

'Sure. The problem is that litigation is at least more exciting than a lot of other areas. For all the time pressures, at least you're always busy; at least you're not stuck in an office going over someone's will.' But as she spoke these words, they did not ring true. It was someone else talking, not Phoebe – some other hotshot young associate, a John Dunn, a Nut or maybe even a Bolt, but in any events someone who really wanted to spend the next thirty years preparing for trials, rushing from pretrial conference to court and then back to the office to sign the latest brief that was spitting out of the word processor. But she didn't want to do that! Who had duped her into thinking that she did? And besides, for someone at her level what was so great about litigation? It was just another file drawer of documents to be reviewed, at best another brief to be drafted – but even then, it would have to be written under so much pressure that she'd never feel proud about the finished product. It wasn't exciting – it was mentally monotonous and physically exhausting.

'Sounds like a no-win situation,' Nick said.

'Up until now, yes,' Phoebe said. 'But I think things are going to change.'

'Oh? How?'

'I don't know,' Phoebe said. 'But they have to.'

By now it was five-thirty, and Molly still wasn't home. Nick rose from his chair and lifted the cover to the pot on the stove; steam swirled up into his face, and the sweet heavy aroma of the curry thickened in the room. 'Got plans for dinner?' he asked her. 'There's plenty of food.'

Phoebe would have liked to stay here with Nick, talking into the night; he was so easy to talk to. That was not, however, why she had come down here; she had come down to see Molly. But Phoebe suddenly felt too tired to see Molly, to confront the awkwardness that would invariably arise as soon as Molly walked in the door. Maybe tomorrow. She could call Molly, and they could make dinner plans, perhaps.

'I really should get going,' she told Nick. 'Andrew's probably eaten all of Cindy Ann's cookies by now.'

'Better Andrew than Cindy Ann,' Nick said cheerfully. 'Well, you have to admit,' he added defensively, seeing the look of surprise on Phoebe's face, 'the girl's gotta lose a little weight one of these days.'

Phoebe laughed. She never would have dared to say it out loud.

'Will you answer a question?' she asked him.

'That depends.'

'How angry is Molly with me, for the things I said?'

Nick puckered his lips in a frown, continued stirring the stew.

'Don't answer if you don't want to,' Phoebe said. 'I probably shouldn't have asked.'

'No,' Nick said, 'I'll try to answer. But I want to think about what I say before I say it. I don't want to make things worse.'

Worse. It was a hard word to hear from a third party, because it confirmed that things really *were* bad between the two of them.

'I don't think she's angry,' Nick said after a while. 'I wouldn't say she's feeling very close to you these days, but I don't think she's angry.'

Phoebe waited; she sensed a qualification on the edge of Nick's thoughts: she's not angry *but* –

'Molly's going through a rough time,' Nick finally said.

A rough time? Molly?

'Maybe it has something to do with the baby,' he said, 'or maybe with the fact that we'll be moving next year. Or maybe also with seeing you, and what you're doing, I don't know exactly. But I think she's feeling vulnerable, and I think on Saturday you managed to hit her where it hurt.'

Molly vulnerable?

'Oh, hell,' Nick sighed. 'Look, I guess I'm not really all that comfortable talking about it – I'm trying to tell you how she feels, and something may be getting screwed up in the translation, and then – then I'm in deep shit.'

'I'm sorry,' Phoebe said, colouring, shaking her head. 'I shouldn't have asked, I shouldn't have put you on the spot.'

'You didn't,' Nick said. 'I'm just going to draw the line right now.'

'Of course.' Phoebe stood up. 'I should be going, anyway.'

'Let me ask *you* something.'

Phoebe waited.

'Do you mind if I tell her you asked me if she was angry?'

At a gut level she did mind. The child in her didn't want Molly to know that she was dwelling over the issue. It was a bratty defensive instinct deeply rooted within her, a refusal to cry uncle, to break down until the other side did. But that was embarrassing enough for her to acknowledge to herself, much less admit to Nick. A more adult reason for not wanting him to say anything was that it would only emphasize how inept Phoebe was at working things out with someone face to face – yet she and Molly had implicitly agreed, in front of the fireplace on the morning of the wedding, that on this issue they each needed to sort things out on their own.

'I don't mind,' she said. 'How can I?' She slung her bag over her shoulder and started for the door.

'Sure you don't want to stay?'

'I'm sure.' It wouldn't be fair to Molly, who would return home from a long taxing meeting with Doris only to find Phoebe sitting by the stove in her kitchen. Hi, it's me again. Time for a little more verbal combat – I was thinking this time we could go for rock bottom, what do you say?

'I think it's better that I leave,' she said. 'I don't want to put Molly on the spot.'

Nick smiled. 'Actually, I was a little surprised myself to see you pop in here this afternoon. Though to be honest,' he added, 'I do keep waiting for things to fall into place for the two of you while you're back here.'

'Well,' Phoebe said, 'maybe. And if not this visit, then maybe the next.'

'The next visit may not be for a long time,' Nick

reminded her. 'Don't you think they'll fall into place before then?'

Phoebe looked at the floor, then gave her head a shake. 'Nick,' she told him, 'you are *very* much the optimist, you know that?'

'I am,' he confessed. 'But I think I have reason to be, in this case.'

'Why?'

'Because I don't think you two are so far apart after all,' he said.

Phoebe felt her eyes fill with tears when he said that; she quickly looked down at the floor, and turned to open the door.

'Drive carefully,' Nick said. 'And hey – thanks for helping me get all that wood in.'

Phoebe managed a laugh, though it was a sad laugh, and she sensed that the sadness was audible. 'Thanks for the beers,' she said. 'And the company. If I don't see you before I leave, good luck with the law schools.'

Nick smiled.

'We'll keep you posted,' he said.

# 15

Molly was, as Nick told Phoebe, going through a troubled time these days. Granted, it was a relief to have the wedding over with; she felt liberated from all those trivial doubts that might have nudged her towards backing out at the last minute: like the way Nick never cleaned the bathroom, or the fact that he always came home with name-brand groceries. The vows had been made; there was no turning back. And besides, she didn't want to turn back; it felt *good* to be married. Having been with Nick for so long, she had thought it wouldn't feel much different; but it did; and though she couldn't yet say just why, she liked the way it felt.

But apart from that, most everything else about her life seemed as bleak and gloomy as the damp grey November sky. Here she was, about to turn thirty – and what had she done? She was a schoolteacher who spent her spare time doing crafts. Cute. Very cute. And while it was nice to be pregnant (Count your blessings, she heard her mother say), she couldn't help but feel a bit of a panic over the thought of motherhood. What if she woke up one morning and realized that all this time what she had really wanted to do was to become an architect, say – what then? How would she ever manage to become an architect if she had a toddler to care for? And if she put it off until the child was in school, she'd be thirty-five, too old to start anything. Molly was convinced that life had passed her by, that she'd missed her chance; and that it was all her own fault.

She would have liked to talk about all this with Phoebe,

would have liked to forget everything that had been said between them and sit down and pour out her misery. She wanted to hear her old friend Phoebe argue with her, comfort her, convince her that it was never too late to do anything. Come on, half the women in my law school classes were over thirty-five, she wanted to hear Phoebe say. What do you mean, you've missed your chance?

But Molly couldn't forget Phoebe's words to her that Saturday morning: You're wasting your life out here in the sticks. And as a result she was afraid that if she poured out these gloomy feelings, these self-doubts, to Phoebe there wouldn't be that pep talk waiting for her; there would instead be too many I-told-you-so's, more than she could bear to hear right now. They were in the midst of a cold war, and it would be unrealistic to hope for any sympathy from Phoebe.

Which, of course, only darkened her spirits. Her oldest friend, back here for her wedding – and they weren't even speaking to one another. How on earth had this come about? Was it her fault? Maybe in her isolation she had forgotten how to open up to women her own age? Molly thought back to her apprehensiveness before Phoebe's arrival. 'Phoebe's going to steal the show,' she had cried to Nick in the middle of the night. And yet that hadn't turned out to be the problem; Phoebe hadn't stolen any show, she had just come back a different person, a woman Molly no longer knew – and who no longer knew Molly. And because of their history they had gone along trying to pretend to one another that they were still the best of friends that they had been five, ten, twenty years ago. When in fact they weren't. Too bad they couldn't have just introduced themselves all over again, Molly thought sadly, let a new first impression form and then take it from there. Maybe they wouldn't have ended up liking each other – but then again, maybe without the shackles of the past they could have relaxed a bit more and let a new friendship grow.

To add to her general malaise Molly was also finding herself increasingly irritated by her life in Winslow. Little everyday matters that previously comforted her suddenly began to vex her. Winterization, for instance: formerly a kind of art form to her northern spirit, it now became a tedious series of rituals – putting on storm windows, closing off the second bedroom – merely designed to corner her into a tiny suffocating cubicle. A trip to the town library, once a cosy place to spend a late rainy afternoon sitting by the fire in one of the worn leather chairs, suddenly seemed like a sad joke as she perused its limited selection of historical novels and spy thrillers. The Poultneys' store she avoided altogether. She was tired of its cheddar cheese; their lettuce was always wilted; and everything cost twice again as much as it did at the IGA. Besides, Molly was afraid that there might be some kind of a magnetic lure to Ida Poultney's rocking chair, and if she wasn't careful she might fall asleep, like Rip Van Winkle, and wake up twenty years from now to find herself rocking away, methodically knitting on another carrot-coloured cardigan.

And the people at school! Today Doris had called an afternoon meeting to discuss the problem of 'The Unauthorized Usage of the School's Computer.' There was only one Apple, Doris reminded the faculty, and the policy was that it was available only to those students with a B average or higher. And yet, Doris exclaimed, her face reddening, in the last week alone she had found four D students playing video games on the machine! Molly had sat silently, watching with disgust as the Barrington Union High faculty plotted its offensive against these overly eager but, unfortunately, below-average students. Brad Kenshaw proposed that they issue access keys to qualifying students. That wouldn't work, Doris countered; the students would just lend the keys – or sell them, on some kind of black market basis – to their unqualified friends. Susan Mitchell then suggested that they issue photo-ID cards to the qualifying students; these cards would have to be presented to whatever faculty member was on guard at the time. Everyone seemed to favour this idea, especially Brad Kenshaw, who had always wantcd to bc somc kind of a guard, and also Mrs Welch, whose son had a Polaroid and who would probably be willing to make up the ID cards for a minimal fee. Everyone but Molly, that is, who finally exploded.

'For heaven's sake, just buy them a second computer!' she exclaimed. 'These kids might not be D students if they had something to motivate themselves with!'

'We can't afford another computer, Mary,' Doris promptly responded. She was obviously irritated. 'Where do you think the money would come from?'

'From raffle tickets and bake sales, the same place that it comes from for their trip to Washington,' Molly said. 'In fact why don't we just bag the annual trip to DC; it's just one big beer blast anyway.'

Doris Conran pursed her lips. Susan Mitchell took out an embroidered handkerchief and blew her nose. Brad Kenshaw undressed her with his lazy grey eyes. And Mrs Welch's head bobbled about as though the world had suddenly accelerated on a road with too many curves and too many bumps for her ageing internal shock system.

These are my peers? Molly thought grimly. These are the people I spend seven hours a day with, five days a week?

Even her students were getting to her. When they

found out she had got married that weekend they kept calling her Mrs Ulrich, until she told them that she had kept her own name – and then they insisted upon calling her Mrs Adams. *Ms*, Molly wanted to shout, MS! – is it really such a hard word for you to say? Then, on Wednesday morning, she had walked into her classroom to find a large square box wrapped in white tissue paper with a silver bow on top. Oh, lord, Molly thought, trying to control her expression – I know I'm supposed to be touched by this but it's exactly why I wanted to elope. She tried to set it aside but at the students' insistence she was forced to open the gift; from inside the box she lifted out a mammoth cut-glass punch bowl, its cavity packed with twelve tissue-wrapped cups to match. Molly thanked them politely – no, no, she already had two blenders, this was a much better idea – and told herself it wasn't so bad; her mother could find some use for it. Nevertheless she felt inescapably depressed to think that the students had this notion of her as having metamorphosed into some kind of a cheerful gracious hostess overnight, a matron with an insatiable appetite for formal entertaining and an index file stuffed with family wassail-bowl recipes. The Mrs Nicholas J. Ulrich. In monogram.

As Molly left the school after Doris's meeting that Thursday afternoon, she wondered if perhaps it would help if she got away, even for a couple of days. Maybe she and Nick should give themselves a honeymoon of sorts – after all, they had just got married, and when was the last time they had taken a vacation together? They could go up to Montreal this weekend, stay in a fancy hotel, spend the evening in the old section, singing French folk songs in a crowded bistro. Why not? Molly suddenly felt as though she couldn't make it through the next week without a weekend escape; it was as if it were already March, and she were suffering from a severe attack of cabin fever, only the cabin wasn't her house but rather everything about this quaint-little-village-by-the-river.

Then go, she told herself. What's the problem?

The problem, of course, was that with Phoebe scheduled to leave on Monday, this weekend was their last chance to make some kind of a gesture towards reconstructing their friendship. Molly wasn't sure whether such a gesture would actually come about (and if so, who would make the first move); but she did know that it would look like a pretty harsh snub if she were to take off, just like that.

Wait another week, she told herself. Sure you need to get away; sure you deserve a vacation; but it's not going to kill you to put it off for another weekend. Besides, if you go, you'll always wonder if there was something you could have done or said that would have thawed the ice crystals that seem to form whenever you and Phoebe get together in the same room. Time is short; this is your last chance. Molly suddenly thought how terrible it would be if Phoebe and Andrew drove off on Monday morning with things the way they were right now. She could lose touch with Phoebe for ever. And losing touch with Phoebe meant losing touch with a part of herself; for while they weren't, admittedly, best friends at the moment, they would always be oldest friends, and if Phoebe disappeared she would take with her the missing link to ancient memories, memories that would then remain buried for ever.

Thus by the time she got home, Molly had decided to broach the idea of a weekend in Montreal to Nick, but suggest that they go during the weekend after next, or maybe over Thanksgiving break. From the car she could see the dogs waiting for her, as usual, in the window seat in the kitchen. Nick was standing over the stove. On her way into the house she noticed the newly stacked woodpile. That was nice of him, she thought; then she flashed on waking up the next morning to find the front porch, the back porch, even the bulkhead, all piled high with wood, closing off their access to the outside world.

You really do need to get away.

Molly pushed open the door to the kitchen; an acrid metallic smell brought a surge of nausea to her throat.

'What smells so bad?' she said to Nick, who was running cold water into a pan in the sink.

'Rice.'

'It doesn't smell like rice.'

'*Burned* rice,' Nick said over his shoulder, 'all right?'

Molly left him and went to change her clothes. When she returned to the kitchen he had set a new pot of rice going, and was working the crossword puzzle to *The New York Times*. 'Sorry for snapping,' he said. 'How was your day?'

Molly told him of Doris's pressing concern over who was using the computer. 'These people are idiots,' she said. 'They should have become cops, not teachers.'

'Well, you only have to deal with them six more months,' Nick said. 'You can start counting off the days.' His words were meant to comfort her, but instead she felt her stomach tighten. Next year. Where were they going to be? And what was she going to be doing?

'By the way,' Nick said, 'Mrs Burgess called about you doing some sweaters for her grandchildren for Christmas.'

Molly looked at him.

'She said she knows it's a little short notice but she wants to give them all ski sweaters this year and she's too busy to knit them herself.'

'And I'm *not* too busy?'

Nick shrugged. 'Call her,' he said. 'I'm passing on the message.'

'Ski sweaters,' Molly said, nodding. 'For all her grandchildren?'

'That's what she said.'

'Do you know how many grandchildren Mrs Burgess has?' Molly tried to keep her voice calm.

'No,' said Nick.

'Seven,' Molly told him. 'And do you know that they're all giants?'

'No,' said Nick.

'Well, they are,' Molly said. 'They're inbreds. Either that or they've got some kind of a glandular disease. Now, what I'd like to know is why she thinks that I've got time to knit seven giant sweaters for her seven giant grandchildren.'

'She doesn't expect you to do it for free,' Nick said.

'Well I might as well do it for free, at the rate she'll pay me!' Molly cried. 'Why doesn't she get Ida Poultney to knit the goddamn sweaters? Why does she think *I* want to knit them?'

Nick looked puzzled. 'You've always been knitting sweaters for people,' he said. 'Ever since high school.'

'So why should they all presume I want to *keep* knitting sweaters!' Molly shouted. 'Just because I've done it since high school doesn't mean I want to do it any more! I'm turning thirty! And I'm sick of knitting sweaters! I'm sick of making quilts, I'm sick of my looms and sick of my yarn and sick of everybody in this town oohing and ahhing over my work and never giving me a chance to do anything else!'

'There isn't much else to do here,' Nick reminded her.

'Well then, all the better reason for us to move away,' Molly said furiously. 'As long as we stay here I'm never going to be anyone other than little Molly Adams, the knitter, the weaver, the Winslow girl cranking out quilts one after the other just because it's expected of her.'

'Nobody expects it of you,' Nick said.

'Oh yes they do,' Molly said. 'If I threw out my loom and started programming computers they'd come to visit one by one to see what was wrong. Oh but Molly, your sweaters are so gorgeous. Oh but Molly, your quilts are heirlooms. Oh but Molly – yeah, well fuck you too!'

Nick looked puzzled.

'Nick,' she sighed, 'I want to get away from this town.'

'We will,' he said. 'I'm certainly not going to go to law school here in Winslow.'

'I don't mean next year,' Molly said. 'I mean right now.'

'Right now?'

'On a vacation,' Molly said. 'A honeymoon. I was thinking we could go up to Montreal. I need to get away, Nick; I'm going to go crazy if I don't get away. I'll do something stupid at the school, I know I will. I have to get away.'

'Then we'll go away,' Nick said. 'We'll go away this weekend.'

'Not this weekend,' Molly said. 'Next weekend.'

'Why not this weekend?'

Molly shook her head. 'We can't,' she said. 'Not while Phoebe's still here.'

'Ah, yes,' Nick said, tipping his head back and narrowing his eyes. 'Speaking of which.'

Molly waited.

'She was down here this afternoon,' Nick said.

'What for?'

'To visit.'

'Who, you?'

'No, Molly,' Nick said. 'You.'

'Are you sure? Maybe she just wanted to see you, to talk to you about law school.'

'Molly,' Nick said, 'she came here to see *you*.'

Molly was silent. No longer could she make the first move. She had waited too long, and now Phoebe was the one with the good heart, the forgiving heart.

'I tried to talk her into staying for dinner,' Nick said. 'She said she had to go pick up Andrew.'

'See?' Molly said quickly. 'She didn't really want to see me, or else she would have stayed for dinner. She's angry,' Molly said. 'She's permanently pissed.'

'Molly?' said Nick. 'Like will you knock it off?'

Molly sighed. Nick was right; she was searching for a way to pin the blame for their continuing discord on Phoebe, when in fact she herself was still feeling quite uncomfortable with the idea of seeing Phoebe face to face. She tried to imagine what it would have been like to return home this afternoon to find Phoebe sitting in *her* kitchen, talking with *her* husband, and she did not imagine that she would have reacted very well. Maybe she did want to clear the air, maybe she did want to reconstruct their friendship – but not tonight. She felt too vulnerable tonight.

'So what time did she come?' Molly asked lightly.

'Three-thirty,' Nick said.

'And what time did she leave?'

'Five-thirty,' Nick said.

'Two *hours*?'

Nick shrugged.

'What did you *do* for two hours?'

'Stacked wood,' Nick said. 'Had a few beers, talked about law school.'

'Oh? And what did she have to say about law school?'

Nick shrugged. 'She said it's not so bad. She said not to worry so much about which courses to take; what it boils down to, she said, is where you went to school and whether you did law review. That kind of stuff.'

'Oh,' Molly said. 'So she was telling you to go to the best school you get into, regardless of where it is.'

'Not exactly,' Nick said. 'She didn't put it to me in those terms.'

'Still, though,' Molly prodded, 'if the best place you got into was in Chicago she'd probably tell you to go to Chicago even if we didn't want to live in Chicago, right?'

'Molly, take it easy,' Nick said. 'You sound as though Phoebe's out to make you as miserable as she can. All she said was, go to the best school, do law review. That doesn't mean she's telling me to drag you off to some godforsaken place next year where we'd both be miserable.'

'*You* won't have time to be miserable,' Molly said. '*You'll* be busy with law school.'

Nick closed his eyes, ran his fingers through his hair.

'So,' Molly said, leaning back in her chair. 'What else did you talk about? Did you talk about me?'

'As a matter of a fact, yes.'

Molly sat up. 'You did?'

'Yes, we did.'

'What did you talk about?'

'Phoebe asked,' Nick said slowly, 'whether you were angry with her.'

Molly waited.

'And I told her you weren't.'

Molly didn't say anything.

'I told her you weren't angry, you were just going through a rough time,' Nick said.

'Hey, *thanks*.'

'Well, what *should* I have said? That you *were* angry with her?'

'No,' Molly said. 'You didn't have to say anything. You could have just said, Why don't you ask Molly if she's still angry with you?'

'I'm sure that's just exactly what you'd like me to have said, I can see how eager you've been all week to get together with Phoebe, face to face.'

Molly shrugged.

'Well, it doesn't matter, does it,' she said after a while. 'It's all water over the dam. But it sounds like you had quite a talk, the two of you, sitting in here by the stove drinking beer all afternoon.'

'She's an interesting woman,' Nick said. 'And she's an easy person to talk to.'

'I'm sure she is, for you,' Molly retorted. 'You've got so much in common, after all – I'm sure you could have talked well on into the night, if it weren't for the fact that I was due to come home.'

'Oh, Christ,' Nick said. 'You know what, I think you're jealous.'

Molly forced an exaggerated laugh.

'You are,' he said. 'You're jealous of your best friend.'

'She's not my best friend,' Molly said sharply. 'She's just my oldest friend.'

'Whatever,' Nick said. 'You're jealous.'

'I am not.'

'You are too.'

'I am not.'

'Admit it, Molly; you *are*.'

'Nick,' Molly said, 'you are so unbelievably stupid, did you know that?'

'No,' Nick said.

'Well you are,' Molly said. 'You are the stupidest human being that I know. I can't believe how unbelievably stupid you are, that you would think that I was jealous of Phoebe.'

'Okay,' Nick said. 'I'm stupid.'

'I'm glad you can admit it,' Molly said. 'You are even

so stupid that you have just burned the second pot of rice. Did you know that?'

'No,' Nick said.

'Smell it?'

'Yes,' Nick said.

Molly shook her head. 'You are just so unbelievably stupid,' she told him. 'I'm not hungry any more. I'm going to bed. And don't talk to me. I don't want to be reminded that I've just married such a stupid human being.'

'All right,' Nick said.

'Thank you,' Molly said. 'Now, good night.'

'Good night.'

'Nick,' Molly said.

Nick groaned.

'Nick,' Molly said, 'wake up.'

'What time is it?'

'It's morning.'

'It's still dark out.'

'It's November, it's morning. Nick,' she said, 'I don't really think that you are stupid.'

Nick sat up in bed. He looked at the clock; the clock said five-fifteen. Nick groaned again.

'Nick,' Molly said, 'I am not jealous of you-and-Phoebe. Do you know what I mean by that?'

Nick nodded.

'And you understand that?'

Nick nodded again, and slid back down under the covers.

'Don't go to sleep,' Molly said. 'I need to talk to you about this.'

'Why couldn't you have talked to me about it eight hours ago?' Nick demanded. 'Why do you always have to go off and sulk and *then* talk to me about it?'

'Because I am a sulker,' Molly said. 'And you married me knowing that I was a sulker. So quit complaining.

'However,' Molly went on, 'and this is very hard for me to say so you have to promise not to jump on me and tell me it's about time I admitted it. Do you promise?'

'I promise.'

Molly was silent for a while, then said, 'I *am* jealous of Phoebe. I'm jealous of what she's done with her life. And I'm jealous of your opinion of her.'

'What do you mean by that?'

'You admire her,' Molly said. 'And you should. I admire her. Everybody here admires her. But I wish that I had accomplished something so that you and everybody else would admire me as much as you admired her.'

'Don't say that,' Nick said. 'Don't feel – '

'Shut up,' Molly said, 'and let me say it. If you don't let me say it I will keep it bottled up inside until one day you'll come home from law school and find little bits and pieces of me all over the living room. So let me say it.'

Molly paused; she listened; Nick seemed to have stopped breathing.

Molly continued: 'But as it is, I haven't accomplished anything.'

Nick was silent.

'I weave, but so what,' she said.

'And knitting sweaters is a drag,' she went on.

'And only morons get off on helping hick adolescents dissect frogs,' she finished.

Nick was silent.

'See?' she said. 'You even agree with me. By all objective standards my life is a complete waste. I am a nobody. I am an intellectual zero. I am about to become a baby machine and nobody in the world will ever admire me.'

Nick sighed.

'Don't interrupt,' she said.

'Now you are thinking, it's just because Phoebe's here that Molly's getting so down on herself; as soon as Phoebe goes home Molly will relax, she'll be her old self.

'Uh-uh,' Molly said. 'It's not going to work that way. Phoebe's made me see things differently. I can't admit that to her, of course; but it's true. You know,' she said, and her voice suddenly softened, 'I should have known this would happen.'

'What do you mean?'

'I should have been able to foresee that when Phoebe came back she would call into question every decision I'd made since she left,' Molly said. 'But I'd forgotten what it was like to be with her. I mean, you grow up with a friend who challenges you on everything, you're bound to feel a bit of relief when she finally moves away, because you're no longer under the gun all the time. But really what happens is you get soft on yourself. You stop pushing yourself. You stop questioning yourself. And then when that friend comes back for a visit – well, everything you thought you were sure about gets thrown to the wind.

'And yet all I can do is blame her,' Molly finished. 'For all the things I haven't done.'

'Don't be so hard on yourself,' Nick said. 'Phoebe's life isn't any bed of roses; she's the first to admit that.'

'To you,' Molly said. 'But not to me.'

They lay in silence for a while; outside the wind picked up, and a spidery branch tapped at the window.

'Maybe things will fall into place this weekend,' Nick said. 'As I told Phoebe – and I hope you don't mind – I don't think you two are so far apart.'

But Molly shook her head. 'You may be right, but I don't think anything is going to come together this weekend. I thought it might, earlier this afternoon, but I was wrong.'

Nick shrugged. 'I don't understand, then.'

'You don't have to,' Molly said quietly. She thought for a moment, and then said, 'I think I want to go to Montreal this weekend.'

'What about Phoebe?'

Molly turned on her side, and brought her knees up. 'She'll undersand. She ought to, anyway. Remember, it's mostly because of what she said that I'm feeling this need to get away.'

'Are you sure she won't think you're trying to spite her?'

Molly thought for a moment. 'No.'

'Why not? How will she know?'

'I'll tell her,' Molly said. 'I think I can manage that much.'

You do understand, don't you? Molly heard herself saying to Phoebe. That this isn't to spite you? That I just need to get away – from Winslow, my God, *you've* got to understand that – and that I need to get away right now? And of course I wish this visit had turned out differently, wish I could talk to you about everything that's been running through my mind – and naturally it also makes me feel terrible – after all, I asked you back, you came three thousand miles and here I go and run off to Montreal on your last weekend, like what a waste of a vacation you must be thinking – but you do understand, don't you?

Molly shook her head. Do you really think that you're going to be able to confide in Phoebe about how sorry you are that you can't confide in her any more these days? Don't you think that's expecting quite a turnaround? Come on, you know damn well that you're going to see her and freeze up. Maybe you can talk to Nick about your feelings – but not to Phoebe.

Maybe you should just make light of it, she thought. Guess what! she would bubble. Nick's taking me to Montreal this weekend for a *honeymoon*. Hey, that's great, Phoebe would exclaim; a honeymoon – and *Montreal*, what a beautiful city. Hey, let me treat you to a night at the fanciest hotel you can find, okay? As a wedding present? Someplace where they bring you champagne and strawberries for breakfast, what do you say?

But Molly knew that if they had that kind of exchange they might as well call it quits, for ever. Two old friends having nothing in common any more, gushing with phony cheer while keeping saccharine smiles pulled tight across their faces – it would in fact be a recognition of doom. For both of them.

I don't know what I'm going to say, she thought as she parked Nick's jeep in the Martins' driveway that Friday afternoon. Oh, well. I'll play it by ear. Maybe that's the best way anyway. I shouldn't worry about it so much. That's probably been the problem all along.

She walked up the back steps and opened the kitchen door; Andrew was sitting at the kitchen table, colouring with a purple felt-tip pen on a yellow legal pad.

'I'm working,' he told her.

'I see,' she said. 'Where's your mum?'

'Gone for a walk,' Andrew said. He drew his page of scribbles over the top edge of the pad and down behind, and continued on the second page with a green pen.

'Where'd she go?' Molly asked him.

Andrew glared at her. 'I'm trying to *work*,' he told her.

'I'm sorry,' she said. 'I just want to find your mum.'

'Well, I told you, she's gone for a walk,' Andrew said.

'And you don't know where?'

'No.' He drew up the second page, and began on the third page with the blue pen.

'How about your grammy?' Molly said. 'Where's your grammy?'

Andrew didn't reply.

'You're not here all alone, are you?'

'My gram's taking a nap,' Andrew said. 'If you keep talking to me like this I'm not going to get any work done.'

My God, Molly thought; this kid doesn't fool around with his playtime. 'Can I ask you one more question?' she said.

'What?'

'Can you lend me a piece of paper?'

Andrew carefully tore a sheet from his pad.

'And can I borrow one of your pens?'

Andrew handed her the black pen.

'Thank you.' Molly sat down at the kitchen table. She wasn't sure what to say in her note to Phoebe. Maybe you shouldn't leave her a note, Molly thought; maybe you should wait for her to come back. But Nick was waiting for her down at the house with her car packed and ready to go; it was a three-hour drive to Montreal, and they wanted to get there in time for dinner.

You planned it this way, she accused herself. You knew that there was a chance that Phoebe wouldn't be here, and you purposely allowed yourself no extra time.

Molly shrugged. So what else was new? It was par for the course, the way things were going these days.

Now: what was she going to say in the note?

'What are you doing?' Andrew said.

'I'm trying to write your mother a note,' she told him.

'Oh,' he said. 'Why aren't you writing it, then?'

'Because I'm not sure exactly what to say.'

'Oh,' he said. 'My mum writes lots of notes,' he told her.

'Is that so,' Molly said.

'Yes,' Andrew said. 'She writes them to my dad, and gives them to me, and I give them to my dad.'

'Ah,' said Molly.

'Then my dad reads them, and he writes her notes, and gives them to me and I give them to my mum,' Andrew said.

Andrew the go-between. Molly felt as though she were being offered a glimpse into her friend's life that she was not, at this point, entitled to.

'I hate doing that,' Andrew said.

A sudden surge of helplessness, of inadequacy, overwhelmed her when he said that. What perspective could she offer, she who barely knew him, she who had never been touched by the trauma of divorce? And at the same time she hated herself for being so rational, so unmotherly, for not just kicking aside her inadequacies and drawing the child into her arms to give him whatever insufficient comfort she could offer. Who cared if she barely knew him? Who cared if she'd never gone through a divorce?

She didn't have much time, though, to dwell on this; Andrew had already turned to a new page, and with the orange pen he had begun a new drawing. And so Molly began to write.

It was easier than she had expected. It always was, writing as opposed to talking, and as she wrote she imagined them striking up a new correspondence – this note would serve as the first letter – in which they would be able to say in letters everything they couldn't say to one another in person. A sort of old-fashioned reacquaintance through the mails.

This is the letter that Molly wrote:

*Phoebe – I stopped by to see you but Andrew tells me you are out for a walk. Actually, I stopped up to say good-bye; Nick and I are taking off to Montreal tonight – a honeymoon of sorts, I guess you'd call it. We'll probably be back late Sunday night. Please forgive me for not waiting around but we want to get an early start so that we don't completely lose the evening.*

*Listen: it hasn't been the best of visits, and I don't want you to think I'm trying to get back at you by taking off like this. I kept thinking, No, we shouldn't go away this weekend, it's Phoebe's last weekend here and I should really stick around and try and patch things up with her. But I think you know as well as I do that that probably won't happen. Not this weekend, anyway. Maybe later. And what I need to do now is get away from this place.*

*And I'm sorry for the urgency. (Couldn't she have waited, for Christ's sake? you are thinking.) Perhaps it's avoidance on my part, not knowing quite how to deal with you; if so, I'm sorry. I will say this much: A lot of the things you said to me have been weighing pretty heavily on my mind – what I'm doing, or not doing, with my life, etc. Who knows; maybe I have been wasting it, as you said. In any event I feel this need to get away. Not that one short weekend is going to give me an entirely new perspective that will change my life, but it might help. Besides, I don't think we're really ready for one another yet, do you?*

*Anyway, I hope you understand. Thanks for coming back; maybe the next time we get together things will be different. Have a good trip back. And good luck with your trial – try not to let your boss get to you. Easy for me to say, of course, but he has no right to dump on a woman like you.*

*Love, Molly*

'What's it say?' said Andrew.

Molly folded the note in half, then in half again, wrote

*Phoebe* on the outside, and propped it against the cut-glass spoon holder on Louise's lazy Susan.

'It says good-bye,' she said.

'How come you're saying good-bye right now?' Andrew said. 'We're not leaving.'

'But I am,' Molly said. 'Want to give me a hug?'

Andrew climbed down from his chair and wrapped his arms around Molly's neck, pressing his cheek against hers. The gesture took Molly by surprise; she hadn't expected him to be so forthcoming with affection. But when she tried to prolong it he pulled away. He went back to his chair, turned to a fresh page on his legal pad, and began drawing again.

'Andrew?'

'I'm trying to work now.'

'I know you are, but will you do me a favour?'

Andrew waited.

'Make sure your mum gets the note?'

Andrew nodded.

'Thanks,' Molly said. 'See you later.'

''Bye,' said Andrew.

Outside a warm damp wind swept fallen leaves across the lawn. She started up the jeep, rolled down the window, and backed out of the driveway. Having said what she wanted to say in the note she found herself wanting to be gone now before Phoebe got back. She headed down the dirt road with the warm wind blowing against the side of her face. As she passed the dairy farm at the crest of the hill she glanced in her rearview mirror and saw someone in a red jacket coming out of the farmer's back door with a package in her arms. It looked like Phoebe, but she couldn't tell for sure.

# 16

'Yolks like that,' said Mrs Cutter. 'You don't see 'em that colour orange if you buy them down to Poultneys'.'

Phoebe smiled.

'Well go ahead and eat it,' Mrs Cutter said. 'What are you waiting for?'

Phoebe ate a slice of the hard-boiled egg that Mrs Cutter, the dairy farmer's wife, was offering her on a plate. After swallowing it she gave her head an obligatory shake of disbelief, and smiled again. 'Wow,' she said.

'See?' said Mrs Cutter. 'You eat a yolk like that and you'll never be able to settle for anything less, I guarantee. How many do you want?'

'Oh, a dozen,' Phoebe said.

'Get two dozen,' Mrs Cutter said. 'You should eat more eggs, I can tell by looking at your hair.'

Phoebe touched her hair.

'You see? It doesn't shine like it should. You eat more of these eggs and your hair will shine like mine. Now. You want some milk.'

'Yes,' Phoebe said.

'Then come along,' Mrs Cutter said. She waddled across the kitchen, past Phoebe, out of the kitchen door, and across the yard to the milk room. Phoebe followed. Everything in this tiny cubicle was in stainless steel: the counter, the sink, the heavy refrigerator door set into the wall. Mrs Cutter yanked open the refrigerator door and took out a squat, gently curved bottle of cream. Phoebe hadn't seen cream in such a bottle since she was a child; it didn't look real.

Mrs Cutter took a tea cup from the shelf, prised off the top to the bottle, and poured the cream into the cup. She handed it to Phoebe. Phoebe took the cup, and held it.

'Go ahead!' Mrs Cutter said, waving her arm in front of Phoebe's face. 'Drink up!'

Phoebe held the cup to her lips, and sipped the cream. It tasted like butter.

'Drink it all!' Mrs Cutter said. 'Did you ever taste cream like that before?'

Phoebe shook her head. Was she really supposed to drink a half-pint of cream? Straight?

'You need more cream,' Mrs Cutter said. 'I can tell by looking at your skin, you got pockets under your eyes already.'

Phoebe frowned.

'You drink more cream and you'll get rid of those pockets under your eyes,' Mrs Cutter said. 'You look *terrible* for a girl of your age!'

Phoebe took another sip of cream.

'Now,' Mrs Cutter said, 'how much milk you want?'

'Oh, a quart,' Phoebe said. She set the cup of cream on the counter and began fumbling in her purse to find her wallet.

'Get two quarts,' Mrs Cutter said. 'I tell you, you got to drink more milk and cream, you got to start worrying about your skin. You drink milk, don't you?'

'Oh yes,' Phoebe said.

'Every day?'

'Oh yes.'

'You have to drink more milk,' Mrs Cutter said. 'Girls don't drink enough milk these days. They grow up, they think they don't have to drink milk and I tell them they're going to shrivel up when they get old and they don't believe me, they think a glass of milk is going to make them fat.'

Phoebe gave a cluck of disapproval.

'Now, how about some butter,' Mrs Cutter said. 'You need some butter too?'

'No, thank you,' Phoebe said. 'How much do I owe you for the milk and eggs?' She wanted to leave before the farmer's wife made her eat butter. Besides, it was getting late, and she wanted to call Molly and ask her to have dinner at the water-wheel restaurant tonight. A time for them to talk. Alone.

'No butter?'

'No butter,' Phoebe said. 'Just the milk and eggs.'

'Two dollars, then,' Mrs Cutter said.

As Phoebe counted out the correct change Mrs Cutter put the eggs and the milk into a used paper bag. 'How're you going to fix these eggs?'

Phoebe felt as though she had just purchased a crown roast for a holiday dinner, rather than a staple such as eggs. 'Maybe make an omelette with some of them,' she said. 'They're mostly just to have on hand.'

Mrs Cutter shook her head. 'You *scramble* them,' she said. 'And don't add any milk, that'll just make them runny, you drink the milk plain. All right now?'

Phoebe smiled, and took the bag.

'All right now!' Mrs Cutter exclaimed. She tightened her apron and held the door open for Phoebe. 'You hurry on home now,' she said. 'You feel that wind? You feel how warm it is for November? There's a storm coming,' she said. 'You hurry home.'

'I will,' Phoebe promised.

'You want me to drive you? It's a long walk back.'

'No, really,' Phoebe said. 'I need the exercise. But thanks.' She headed down the driveway.

'And be sure to scramble them with butter!' Mrs Cutter shouted after her. 'Don't mess 'em up with oleo!'

'I won't!' Phoebe shouted back. She waved good-bye

and started down the hill. She walked quickly – Mrs Cutter was right, the air was too warm, uncomfortably warm, and the low yellow-grey clouds looked like rain. After a quarter of a mile she had to stop and remove the heavy woollen jacket she was wearing. She was hot, but it felt good to be walking, especially after drinking all that cream.

At the bottom of the hill she crossed a narrow one-lane bridge, then continued on the road as it entered the sugar bush. The property had been posted with no-trespassing signs long ago, but a decade of winters had frayed the edges of the signs and bleached the once-bold lettering to shades of pink and grey. What a shame that all of this is going to waste, she thought. She had heard Dave talking to Stan at the wedding about his plans to tap the grove in exchange for a percentage from the old banker, and she imagined bringing Andrew back a few years from now to help out with the sugaring. (You tell me how *that* would stack up against a trip to Vail, she wanted to say to Rusty.) She envisioned Andrew helping Dave pound the spigots into the trunks; they would hang the wooden buckets around each tree, and the days would be warm, and the nights cold, so that the sap would be running at its peak. Then the two of them, Dave and Andrew, would drive the jeep through the woods to empty the buckets of sap into the large metal cans which they would bring back to the sugarhouse, where Phoebe and Molly and Louise and Bea would be tending the evaporator pans, their faces glowing from the sweet-smelling steam of the sap in its various stages of reduction. And when it was all done they would hold a sugaring-off party; Andrew himself could pour the hot honey-coloured syrup directly on to a pan packed with fresh white snow and watch it harden into glossy Rorschach shapes.

Phoebe shook her head and shifted the bag of eggs

and milk. She had to stop romanticizing everything. It wouldn't happen that way at all, she told herself. Dave would have modern plastic tubing, none of these old-fashioned wooden buckets – and shame on you for situating all the women in the sugarhouse, tending the fire! Wouldn't you be out there in the woods, too, right alongside Andrew and Dave? Or shouldn't you be?

Still, though, it was a nice thought.

Soon the trees thinned out, and she found herself looking beyond the stand of willow trees and across the fields to the two farmhouses. Already the light was fading, and the fields, in this late November dusk, held a sense of gloom, an English sort of gloom of the moors, Phoebe thought. It was the type of gloom that came on schedule, every November, and once again, as she had done when she was a child, she found herself taking comfort in it. Why? Partly because of its punctuality, but also because it was the type of gloom that turned on yellow lights in farmhouse windows, that served up bowls of stew and pans of biscuits, that stoked the fire and thereby lent a sense of well-being to the simplest of surroundings. It had been so long since Phoebe had actually seen and smelled and tasted this gloom, this comforting November gloom of the Northeast, that she had forgotten that it existed; but as she walked along the dirt road towards the farmhouse she realized that it was so permanently programmed into her that every year in late November, when the western rains had begun to pour upon the urban hills of San Francisco, she had subconsciously been searching for that yellow light, and listening for that snap of a dry log catching fire – and she never, of course, had found it. Certainly not in downtown San Francisco; certainly not in the hills of Berkeley. Rather than give any of this much weight she had always passed it off as some kind of *déjà vu*; but now she realized that all these years when people had repeatedly asked her what she missed about Vermont and she had repeatedly answered, 'Oh, not a whole lot, maybe the foliage in October, maybe a blizzard around Christmas' – she was off base. For what she really missed about Vermont was the comfort, the security, of this gloom. And only in November, and only in the late afternoon, and only in Vermont, would she ever find it.

'How come you took so long?' Andrew demanded.

Phoebe put the eggs and milk into the refrigerator, then hung up her jacket on the rack in the back hall. 'It was two miles down and two miles back,' she said. 'That's a long walk.'

'How come you have to take these long walks, then?' Andrew said.

'Because I like to see what there is to see,' Phoebe told him. 'And because I never get a chance to just take a walk when we're out in California.' She picked up the yellow legal pad and flipped through his drawings. 'Hey, I like that one,' she told him.

'That's our house,' he said.

'That's good,' she said. 'Why don't you draw a picture of Grammy's house too? What's this?' she said, picking up the note that Molly had left.

'That girl was here,' Andrew said.

'Molly?'

'I was trying to work,' Andrew complained. 'She talked all the time.'

Phoebe unfolded the note and skimmed it. She sat down. She skimmed it again, to make sure she understood it correctly; and then she read it closely, word for word.

Molly was gone.

I blew it, was her first thought. I procrastinated too long.

But anger quickly blackened over her remorse. Why couldn't she have waited! Phoebe thought. Jesus, I come back for the first time in six years and she decides to just up and split three days before I go back? What does she think – that I came all the way back just to visit Ida Poultney? Mrs Cutter?

Phoebe closed her eyes, breathed deeply, relaxed her jaw. She went into the pantry and poured herself a glass of wine and returned to the table to reread the letter. Yes, that's what it said: Nick and Molly had taken off to Montreal tonight.

So. Molly was gone. They weren't going to have dinner tonight; they weren't going to see each other again, not for a long, long time. Right now, as she sat at her mother's kitchen table, Molly and Nick were northbound; tonight, as she tucked Andrew into bed, they would have checked into a downtown hotel, would be having a drink by a sparkling indoor waterfall. Well, touché, Molly; and Phoebe couldn't help but recall their childhood game of goose, whereby they each fought to give that final cuff to the other. Gotcha last, echoed Molly's voice, laughing as she sped towards the Canadian border.

Yet the letter said otherwise. Phoebe's fury began to subside as she reread Molly's words. *I'm not trying to get back at you by taking off like this*, Molly insisted; and Phoebe told herself that she was being unfair. Obviously Molly had agonized – or at least debated – over whether or not she should leave. She knew the risk, knew how Phoebe would react, and yet she nevertheless decided to go. Okay, so she wasn't trying to get back at Phoebe. And anyway, what's so surprising about the departure? Phoebe asked herself. The two of you have had five days together – and have you? All right, then. Sure you went down to visit Molly yesterday afternoon – but you didn't stay for dinner, did you? You could have called Cindy

Ann, she would have been more than happy to keep Andrew for dinner – but no, you chose to leave just in time to miss Molly. So come on. Quit acting so holier-than-thou. And quit acting as though this weekend would have been any different. Did you really think the sun was suddenly going to come out and the two of you would go skipping off into a field of flowers together? As Molly said, you're not ready for one another yet.

Phoebe went over the letter again. *A lot of the things you said have been weighing pretty heavily*, Molly wrote; *who knows, maybe I have been wasting my life*. Reading those words, Phoebe's heart suddenly ached with all the regret she'd been denying since last Saturday. You shouldn't have listened to me, Molly! she wanted to cry. I didn't know what I was saying, I was tense and angry about dealing with Herb! You should have written off what I said as total bullshit; I do it all the time, mouth off as though I'm an authority on something – it's the way I've been trained. But you should have known better – you grew up with me, you should have known not to listen to me. Really, if anyone's wasting her life it's me, just as you said – me, working day and night in a job I hate, wondering what trick Herb Sullivan is about to pull next. How could you have given me any credibility?

Oh, shit.

She thought back to her conversation with Nick the day before, when he had told her that Molly was not angry with her but rather was going through rough times, was vulnerable. It had surprised her to hear that; and she had passed it off as a bit of overprotectiveness on Nick's part; but this letter confirmed it all. Phoebe felt sick with remorse; she felt it was urgently incumbent upon her now to call every hotel in Montreal until she managed to locate Molly so that she could somehow make it clear that whatever turmoil she was going through was completely unnecessary – of *course* it was, given that it stemmed from heated words, spat out when Phoebe'd been angry at the world, angry at herself.

Oh, *why* hadn't she held her tongue?

She winced, thinking again back to their argument that Saturday morning. What had she said, exactly? Something about Molly weaving her little fibre-arts trinkets out here in the sticks? Yes; and she had baited her, too, asked her when she was going to go out and make something of her life. Why did she have to say all that? Molly's craftwork was obviously professional, obviously beyond any category of 'fibre-arts trinkets.' (Oh, come on, Phoebe scolded herself; don't be so restrained; Molly's got a sense of design that puts your taste in the category of Ethan Allen. You look down the road five or ten years and Molly'll probably be selling her work in some gallery in New York, if she can just plug herself into the right network.) And as for the other accusation – well, Phoebe couldn't, in all honesty, say that she suddenly viewed Molly's entire situation as ideal; but it had become increasingly clear to her over the past week that what Molly was making of her life was apt to yield more happiness, in the long run, than what Phoebe was making of hers. Don't go out and change your life! she wanted to cry out from here to the Canadian border. I didn't know what I was talking about!

And yet there was nothing she could do.

She could, of course, write Molly a response and leave it at her house, slip it under the door, a similarly casual note on a piece of yellow paper. Yet that just didn't seem proper. It was all right for Molly to have done so; she had come up to say good-bye in person, and, upon finding Phoebe gone, had done the next best thing by dashing off a quick message. But for Phoebe to respond now with another note reminded her too much of all the notes she and Rusty hastily scribbled back and forth when they didn't want to deal with each other. Molly deserved more than just a reply note; she deserved a long thoughtful letter; and while she might be able to write it this weekend and leave it for Molly, it might be better to write it once she got back to California, when she could give it a little distance. Phoebe was aware that this might be yet another way of procrastinating on her part; but even if it was, maybe the extra time would put things in a better perspective.

As she folded up the piece of paper she saw once again how Molly had signed it with the word *Love*. How much that one closing word controlled the meaning of the note, she thought. Molly could have signed it *Take care*; she could have left a few dashes, with an *M*; she could have just signed it *Molly* – all of which would have lent a sense of finality to what Molly wanted to say to her. But by signing it *Love* Molly seemed to be asking for her own thoughts on the matter – and also letting Phoebe know that from her perspective there was no ill will at the core.

Phoebe sighed. So perhaps all was not lost, she thought; perhaps as her mother had said, things would change, given a little time. Maybe at forty they would be close again; maybe they, too, would be clucking away in some far-off kitchen about the Beatles and menopause and the horrid way that their children were wearing their hair. And maybe at seventy, or eighty, they would even talk about that time long long ago when they were turning thirty, when nothing seemed to click between them. Time is short, they would say, gazing through cataracts, reaching out to one another with gnarly fingers: let's talk about that week in November. Remember how we fought? Remember how we couldn't talk to one another? Remember how silly it all was?

* * *

Phoebe stayed at home the next day; she had thought she might drive Andrew over to New Hampshire to show him the Old Man of the Mountains and perhaps take him up Cannon Mountain on the tramway; but the rain had settled in, and so instead she helped Louise sort through the junk that had accumulated on the shelves in the basement. Most of it consisted of knickknacks from an earlier era – Depression glass, martini mixers, a box of beaded necklaces – and Phoebe thanked her mother but told her to go ahead and give it to the thrift shop. Then Andrew joined them, which made things more difficult; he spotted a ceramic rabbit-pitcher whose lifted paw served as a spout, and insisted upon taking it back to California. Phoebe gave in; it was not worth the fight. Besides, she glimpsed in her mother's face a hint of pleasure when she saw that her grandson wanted something from her basement shelves, which made Phoebe wonder if she had been too quick to reject the rest of her mother's offerings.

During lunch Cindy Ann called to remind them of the square dance scheduled for that night. Phoebe hadn't planned to go; it had been organized by a couple who had just moved up from Philadelphia, and she wasn't in the mood to meet new people. But Cindy Ann, who drove up later that afternoon to show them the skirt she had made – a bright red dirndl, with an embroidered yellow border around the bottom – couldn't conceal her disappointment. 'No, course you don't *have* to come,' she said. 'I just thought Andrew might think it was fun.'

'Andrew might,' Phoebe said, 'but I'm not into square dancing. It's been too long; I've forgotten how.'

'Oh, come on, Phoebe,' Cindy Ann said. 'You'll have a good time! Look – I bet it's because you don't have anything to wear.'

'That's not it,' Phoebe said. 'I swear.'

'Because you can always borrow something of mine,' Cindy Ann went on. 'We can just pin it together at the waist.'

If I end up going, I'll go in jeans, Phoebe thought. Don't think for one moment that I'm going to dress up in some Slavic outfit from the bottom of your trunk so that I can blend in with the rest of the crowd as we all do-si-do around the room.

'Well, then, if you really don't want to go, could I take Andrew?' Cindy Ann asked. 'I'd bring him home by ten o'clock, and wouldn't let him out of my sight – '

'All right.' Phoebe sighed. 'I'll *go*. But if it turns out that I want to just sit on the sidelines and watch, don't make a big stink and drag me into it, all right?'

Cindy Ann laughed, and tousled Phoebe's hair. 'I certainly *will* make a big stink,' she said. 'You don't go to a square dance to sit on the sidelines!'

Actually, despite her initial reluctance Phoebe found herself looking forward to the square dance. There were still a lot of people who hadn't seen Andrew yet, and she confessed to wanting to show him off a little more before returning to California. Besides, everybody else in the family was going; that being the case she had no basis for making Andrew stay home, and did she really want to spend her last Saturday night here alone in an empty farmhouse?

As Phoebe changed from one pair of jeans to another, she thought about Molly and Nick – who, if they hadn't taken off to Montreal, would probably be going to this square dance. She wondered what they were doing instead on this Saturday night up in Montreal, wondered if they were treating themselves to a holiday. They certainly deserved it.

She thought back to Molly's note again, and wondered what kind of perspective Molly would be able to get in a foreign city three hours from Winslow. Would she perhaps be able to see Phoebe's words for what they were, cheap shots, verbal digs, baseless accusations meant for shock value? Maybe Nick could help her out? There was a part of Phoebe that still felt obligated to locate Molly somehow and order her to forget everything that she had said. But there was another part that was content to let things ride for now. Molly was smart. Molly was reasonable. Molly had a head on her shoulders – more of a head than I do, Phoebe thought – and she could be trusted to ultimately realize what kind of foolishness Phoebe had conjured up that Saturday morning.

And it was with this trust that Phoebe found herself approaching her last few days at home. In a way she felt freer than she had at any point during her visit, for the pressure was off. She didn't have to go visit Molly; she didn't have to pretend that they were as close as they'd once been; she didn't have to wonder whether and how she was going to patch things up. To be sure, they weren't very intimate right now, but as Nick said, they probably weren't very far apart either. It really was just a matter of time, and letters; maybe another visit a few years from now would be entirely different. As she fluffed out her hair Phoebe realized she felt much the same way she used to feel when, in the midst of agonizing over a particular decision, Rusty would raise the startling possibility that she didn't have to make the decision right then and there. So don't decide, Rusty would say with a shrug. So let it rest.

The square dance was held in the grade-school cafeteria; it was crowded and hot, and Phoebe could barely make herself heard over the music blaring from an old phonograph. 'No, I'm divorced!' she shouted.

‘Sorry to hear that!’ Brad Kenshaw shouted back. ‘Some guy sure made a big mistake!’

‘Hey Mum, watch!’ Andrew and Cindy Ann had teamed up for this dance; as Phoebe waved from the sidelines Cindy Ann, bent at the waist, began spinning him around and around. ‘Now-circle-forward-to-the-right!’ the caller’s voice twanged out; but the record was old and badly scratched, and as a result the dancers missed their cue, so that they all kept on jostling and spinning with their partners until suddenly, like a flock of wild birds, they fell into another formation, joining hands and circling a couple that had, by no choice of its own, ended up in the middle.

‘Did you see that, Mum!’ Andrew shrieked as he skipped on by. ‘Did you see me do that!’

‘I saw you!’ she shouted back to him. ‘Keep going! How’s your teaching these days?’ she shouted to Brad.

Brad didn’t answer; he was looking at her chest with glazed eyes.

‘I said, how’s your teaching!’ Phoebe shouted again. ‘Are you still teaching history?’

But before she had to shout again the song had stopped, and Brad raised his glance. ‘You want to go take a spin?’

Phoebe had to make an effort not to stare at him in disbelief. Take a *spin*? So that – what, they could go *make out* or something?

‘What do you say,’ Brad said. ‘You’re a big girl, you’re out of high school.’

Yes, but you aren’t, she thought. ‘I actually have a date,’ she told him.

‘Yeah?’ said Brad. ‘Who’s that?’

‘My son,’ Phoebe said. ‘Andrew, come over here and meet Mr Kenshaw.’

‘Did you see me do that, Mum!’ Andrew cried. ‘Did you see me go under everyone’s arms?’

'I saw you!' Phoebe exclaimed. 'You were great!'

'Cute kid,' Brad remarked, looking loftily about the room. 'Don't know why the old lady's got such a bee in her bonnet.'

Phoebe ignored him. Doris Conran had just come in, wearing a dark-brown skirt with a matching dark-brown sweater. As she headed towards Phoebe she looked like the bearer of bad news.

'Phoebe Martin,' she said. 'I heard you were back in town.'

'Hello, Mrs Conran,' Phoebe said. 'How are you?'

Doris Conran frowned. 'I'd be better if it weren't so damp out,' she said. 'My back hurts in this kind of weather.'

'I'm sorry to hear that,' Phoebe said.

'Yes, well,' said Doris. 'You know, when Mary told me you were coming back I thought you'd at least have time to come and say hello to all of us over at the school.'

'Well, you know how busy things get,' Phoebe said. 'Have you met my son?' She drew him against her, tousling his hair.

'Who's that?' said Andrew.

'That's my principal,' Phoebe told him. 'Say hello to Mrs Conran.'

Doris waited.

'He gets a little shy sometimes,' Phoebe finally explained, when Andrew didn't say anything.

Doris regarded Andrew as though he were an insolent pupil; then she turned to Phoebe. 'As a matter of fact, Phoebe, I waited at the school several afternoons, thinking you'd stop by.'

Phoebe smiled politely, tried not to look at the whiskers on Doris's chin. 'Are you going to do the Virginia reel?' she said pleasantly. 'I think that's the next dance.'

Doris turned and surveyed the crowd with a pained

expression on her pinched schoolteacher's face. 'Dancing doesn't agree with me,' she said.

What *does* agree with you? Phoebe wondered. She was thankful to see everyone gathering in two straight lines, and she excused herself from her former principal. 'Hope you have a nice evening,' she said.

'I'm afraid that's not on the agenda,' Doris replied. 'My mother's sick and I've got to get back to the house and sit with her. It's not easy, you know, taking care of a woman her age.'

'I'm sorry,' Phoebe said.

Doris sighed. 'It just makes me wonder, though, who'll be taking care of me when I get to be her age. Or rather, knock on wood,' she said. ' – *if* I get to be her age.'

Phoebe suddenly felt as though the air around Doris might be diseased. She stepped back, then took Andrew's hand. 'Give my best to your mother,' she told Doris. 'Tell her I hope she feels better.'

'Well, she won't be feeling better,' Doris was saying as Phoebe turned away. 'She's too old to feel better.'

There's one good thing about running into Doris, Phoebe thought, purposely taking a position in the line as far away from Doris Conran as she could get; and that's that I can rest assured that at least *all* of my perceptions about this town weren't off base. What a witch! She glanced back; Doris had rooted herself to the floor, her neck jutting forward in a permanent posture of stern disapproval. Somehow it was impossible for Phoebe to imagine that Molly knew a different Doris. I'm trying, she wanted to say to Molly; I've spent hours with Ida and Carl, and Mrs Cutter's got a wonderful heart, but as far as Doris Conran and Brad Kenshaw are concerned, I'm having a *very* difficult time seeing any redeeming value in their contributions to this world.

Then the music began, and Phoebe forgot about Doris

and Brad. She lost herself in the gaiety of the dance, missing her steps, scooting along to catch up, clapping to the music as the mismatched couples one by one skitted their way from one end of the line to the other. When it was over she was sweaty and breathless; she made her way over to the refreshment table, where she quickly drank two glasses of a 7-Up punch. As she caught her breath she looked about at the crowd: there was Cindy Ann with Jack, fanning herself with a handkerchief that matched her skirt; there was Louise, chatting with Bea and Dave over by the door; there was Brad Kenshaw, still without a dance partner; and there was Doris Conran, fingering her whiskers and looking for someone to scold. And all the rest strangers. Phoebe looked at these people, all dressed in their navy blues and forest greens, basic practical colours; and she suddenly felt an emptiness overcome her. It was as though the wattage in the lights had dimmed, or a draught had blown in from an open window. Her first thought was that it was loneliness; Molly should have been here, and yet she wasn't; and Phoebe flashed on how it could have been: they might have stashed a six-pack of Molson out in the car, maybe a few joints, and every so often they'd duck out for another beer, another few tokes, then come back inside to crack up over all these silly ridiculous people trying to *square*-dance, of all things.

But this emptiness she was feeling went beyond loneliness, beyond missing Molly. She recalled how she had felt a week ago at Molly's wedding, so out of place, and though there had been other reasons for her estrangement that day she realized now that she just didn't belong here any more. This wasn't her home any more. She was a visitor, a guest, another John Dunn who from now on would only be an observer of quaint traditions, a collector of old memories. She could take her long walks down the dirt road, and visit the Poultneys, and buy her milk and eggs from Mrs Cutter, and even dance the Virginia reel at the local Saturday-night square dance. But she no longer belonged here. She was, like everyone else who moves away for good, a stranger in her hometown, an alien from a foreign land; her visits would always have a beginning and an end, and in her bag she would always have a return flight ticket with a weight restriction.

Phoebe was about to recapture Andrew from Cindy Ann and leave – it was almost ten – when she noticed Duncan Crane standing alone by the far wall. He was wearing his leather bomber jacket tonight, along with jeans and cowboy boots; and his sandy blond hair lay at odd angles, as though he had just pulled off a tight cap. Phoebe wondered how long he had been there, whether he had joined in any of the dances; she also wondered whether he had seen her. Had he decided against saying hello?

Phoebe herself felt an obligation to go over and talk to him as he surveyed this crowd of Yankee merrymakers, these devoted legatees of barn raisings and quilting bees and baked-bean suppers and, of course, square dances. After all, she should apologize for not having made it down to his camp; and they did have something in common, Duncan being another outsider, though of a newcomer sort. Yet the shyness that had prevented her from going down to his camp this past week began to resurface, and with it embarrassment, for she really had no excuse for not having taken him up on his offer. And obviously, it was too late now, for she would have to spend tomorrow packing, getting ready to leave on an early-Monday-morning flight.

But Phoebe didn't have a lot of time to ponder these issues, for Duncan had spied her, and was heading in her direction. She smiled, and gave a silly little wave with one hand, a gesture of would-be jauntiness.

'Where were you last week?' Duncan asked. 'I kept expecting you.'

'I got tied up,' Phoebe answered lamely. Duncan waited; she gave a shrug and went on. 'First one thing, then another – I'm really sorry, though; I'd have like to see what you've done.'

'You could have seen more than that,' Duncan said. 'If you'd come down on Thursday you might have seen the moose that lumbered right up to my back door.'

'A moose?'

'Scared my pants off!' Duncan laughed. 'I'd just finished lunch and was on my way out to put on some new shingles and suddenly there's this big pair of nostrils at the window.'

'I grew up here and I've never seen a moose,' Phoebe said. 'How big was it?'

'*She*,' Duncan said. 'And she must have weighed over a thousand pounds. We stood there staring at each other – I couldn't move, though my nuthatches didn't like it, they got all upset, flew away on me – anyway, she finally lumbered off again, and by the time I got my camera out and the flash attachment loaded she was too far away, even for my zoom. Plus I would have had to take a picture of her butt and I didn't think that'd be too respectful.'

'No,' Phoebe agreed.

'But that's what you missed,' Duncan said. 'Where's Molly tonight?'

'Up in Montreal,' Phoebe said. 'She and Nick took a honeymoon of sorts.'

'That was kind of sudden,' Duncan said. 'Nick didn't mention it to me.'

Phoebe shrugged. 'Well, that's where they are.'

'Huh,' Duncan mused. 'You two ever get back on track?'

Phoebe started.

'Nick said you weren't having the best of reunions,' he said. 'Like you weren't on the same wavelength any more.'

'We've had closer moments,' Phoebe said cautiously. What had Nick told him?

'I imagine it was quite a letdown, coming back and getting excited about seeing your best friend and then finding out you don't have anything to say to each other.'

'Oh, we had plenty to say,' Phoebe said. 'It wasn't all too nice either.'

'And now you're feeling guilty,' Duncan said.

Phoebe looked at him curiously.

'Don't,' Duncan said. 'How could you expect things to be the same? Two friends grow up together, one takes off, the other stays home – the balance is bound to be off, at least until you both straighten out your priorities. In the meantime, though, I'll bet you've been going around with your nose up in the air thinking how terrific you are for escaping, and Molly's been acting like a total bitch, making jabs at you for being Ms Hot Shit Lawyer, and you're both saying to yourself, Oh, I'm such a shit, what's wrong with me, boohoo, I'm such a failure at keeping my women friends, I'm rotten, I'm evil – '

Phoebe burst out laughing.

'Don't worry about it,' Duncan said. 'You *are* rotten, you *are* evil, but so are we all.'

Phoebe continued to smile, and found herself wondering what had led her to think she would feel so shy with him. Suddenly he seemed to have stories to tell, wisdom to give; and she wished she had made more of an effort to get to know him.

'Where are you from?' she asked him.

'I'm from here.'

'No,' she said. 'Before that.'

'Before that, Baltimore. Before that, Hershey, Pennsylvania. You know, the town with all the little chocolate kisses on the streetlamps?'

'Why'd you come up here?' Phoebe prodded. 'Why Winslow?'

'My family used to have a place up here,' he said. 'We'd come up summers, and then my father started bringing my older brother and me up every autumn. We'd go deer hunting, which was great until I discovered I had a fear of rifles, so then my father made me stay at the camp while he and my brother went out alone. I had to fix dinner, so we lived on beans and hot dogs,' he told her. 'Made me go bald at the age of fifteen.'

'What were you doing in Baltimore?'

'Going to school.'

'Where?'

'Johns Hopkins.'

'What were you studying?'

'Engineering,' he said. 'What is this, a deposition?'

Phoebe coloured. 'I was just curious,' she said. 'I just wondered what someone like you would see in a place like this.'

'Ah-ha, I can tell we have here a displaced person, the Winslow girl who's seen faraway horizons and tasted foreign foods and the home turf never seems quite so satisfying any more, right?'

'No,' Phoebe said. 'I like Winslow.'

'But you wouldn't be caught dead living here.'

'I wouldn't put it that way,' Phoebe said. 'But I like living out in California, yes. If I had to move back here for some reason I certainly could do it, but I don't think' – she paused for a second – 'I don't think there's a lot of room for me to grow here.'

'Course there isn't,' Duncan said. 'If you were raised here you're never going to be able to see it the way others do. But let me tell you, that's too bad; because this is one fuck of a beautiful neighbourhood, this Northeast Kingdom. It's a good thing I wasn't born and brought up here,' he said. 'I'd hate to miss out on getting a virgin perspective through my adult eyes.'

Phoebe found herself searching his face, as though he could at this last minute in her vacation impart some of that virgin perspective to her, give her one last door to unlock before she left; and then she realized that he was searching her face, too, and that the two of them were staring deep into one another's eyes, and had been, for almost a minute. Phoebe felt a heat wave rising in her cheeks; she averted her eyes.

'Some dance, isn't it,' she remarked, after a moment.

'Sure is,' Duncan said.

'Do you come often?'

'Oh, no,' Duncan said. 'I hate dancing.'

'What brought you here, then?'

'You,' said Duncan.

Which stopped Phoebe dead in her line of questioning.

'I really was expecting you to come down to the camp,' Duncan said.

Phoebe opened her mouth, then closed it.

'I thought of calling you,' he said, 'but I didn't want to intrude. Also there was another factor,' he said.

Phoebe waited.

'I don't have a telephone,' Duncan said.

Phoebe smiled.

'Then I thought of writing you a letter,' he explained. 'But I realized it wouldn't get to you in time. And besides, I wouldn't have known how to sign it. *Hope to see you, exclamation point, exclamation point?* No, that would have sounded ridiculous.' He waited expectantly, but

Phoebe didn't know what to say. She couldn't reciprocate with tales of hopes and frustrations, for she hadn't really thought very much about Duncan over the past week. She'd had too much on her mind, really, with Molly and all.

'Look,' Duncan said, 'why don't you come down tomorrow? Bring your little boy along, we can have lunch out on the dock.'

Phoebe shook her head. 'I'm going to be doing laundry and packing all day tomorrow,' she said. 'I have an early flight Monday morning.'

'Then come back tonight,' Duncan said.

'Tonight?'

'Spend the night with me.'

For a moment Phoebe was speechless. When she had managed to collect her thoughts she said, 'Look, I'm not sure what you're proposing – '

'Yes you are.'

Phoebe coloured. 'Well, in any event, I've got a son, I've got to take him home and put him to bed, I can't walk out just like that.'

'Sure you can,' said Duncan.

'How?'

'Get your mother to take him,' he said. 'After two weeks he must be comfortable enough with his grandmother to let her put him to bed.'

Phoebe shook her head. 'Listen, thank you,' she said, 'and I'm really sorry I didn't get down last week, but I can't make it down tomorrow and I definitely can't just take off with you tonight. You'll have to understand.'

'I don't,' said Duncan.

Phoebe moistened her lips, crossed her arms, and looked out at the crowd of square dancers. What had originally begun as a casual conversation had now shifted into an entirely different gear. Her mind was already made up – of course she wasn't going to leave with him tonight! – but nevertheless she was at loose ends as to how to handle the situation with dignity. She felt dreadfully out of practice in this area; except for one disastrous blind date, she hadn't gone out with anyone since her divorce – a result primarily of her job: because there wasn't time to get involved with anyone when you were a member of the litigation department at Judson and Day. Any spare time was consumed by more urgent matters: grocery shopping, playing with Andrew, getting enough sleep. Oh, maybe she nurtured along a few fantasies, and occasionally fretted about the amount of time that had lapsed since she'd been with a man; but sex had become, by and large, a dead issue. Which shouldn't have been surprising *regardless* of any time factors: for who could get excited about sex when the pool of daily contacts was limited to the likes of John Dunn – styleless sexless on-track professionals, personal failures, victims of their own dutiful dreams of success? Why bother?

Not that she was any great shakes herself.

But now, here was this leather-jacketed Duncan Crane, inviting her down to his cabin late on a Saturday night, to spend the night with him. For a moment Phoebe stopped focusing on how to decline and focused instead on the merits of his proposal. What if she did go? What if she told her mother to take Andrew home and put him to bed and oh yes, not to wait up for her – what then? Phoebe shifted her weight, shook her head; such a rendezvous was out of the question. It would be, after all, just a one-night stand, no more, no less. And did she need any more emotional havoc? Absolutely not. Besides, her diaphragm was back in Berkeley.

No, she thought: taking off with Duncan Crane – it was something she might have done five years ago, ten years ago, during her more rebellious years; but certainly not today. She was beyond all that. She wasn't so reckless any more. She had a head on her shoulders, right?

Right.

How good she was.

'Mum,' Phoebe said. 'I have a favour to ask.'

Louise finished ladling out another cup of punch and handed it to Susan Mitchell. 'What's that?'

Phoebe looked at Susan Mitchell, who had turned to chat with Doris Conran; they were clearly within earshot. 'Could you get someone to cover for you?'

Louise looked puzzled, but she turned to Sally Higgins and asked her to tend the punch bowl. Then she untied her apron and moved away from the table with Phoebe. 'What's wrong?'

'Nothing's wrong,' Phoebe said, and she looked once again over her shoulder. 'I have a favour to ask.'

'You already told me that,' Louise said with a touch of impatience. 'You'll have to tell me what it is before I can respond, Phoebe.'

'Well, I was wondering . . .'

Louise waited.

'I was wondering if you could take Andrew home tonight.'

'Of course I can,' Louise said. 'I didn't realize you were having such a good time.'

Phoebe looked away. This was going to be more difficult than she had anticipated. For some reason she had presumed that her mother would know intuitively what lay beneath her innocent request; but Louise apparently had no idea that Phoebe was going to leave the square dance with Duncan Crane and go up to his cabin. For the night. Phoebe wondered how explicit she should be. She could merely confirm her mother's impression (Oh, yeah, I'm having a great time, see you later but don't wait up for me) but that seemed too misleading. Or she could spell it out for her mother: but spell *what* out? While she was fairly certain what would happen, she wasn't positive; you never could be sure; and why should she put her mother through unnecessary shock?

'I *am* having a good time,' Phoebe began.

'Good!' Louise exclaimed, and she cupped her daughter's face between her palms. 'You stay here as long as you want; I'm ready to leave soon anyway and I'll get Andrew tucked in and by the time you get back I'll have some Irish coffee ready, okay?'

Phoebe looked beyond her mother's beaming face, so full of plans for a late-night chat with her daughter, to where Duncan Crane was waiting by the door, arms crossed, leather jacket zipped up tight around his neck, his eyes laughing at this mother-daughter transaction that Phoebe was awkwardly negotiating. Phoebe looked back at her mother.

'Mum,' she said, 'I've met someone.'

Louise turned instinctively, as though Phoebe were about to draw that someone into their conversation.

'You probably know him,' Phoebe said. 'Duncan Crane?'

Louise lifted her chin with recognition as she turned back to Phoebe 'Yes,' she said. 'I know Duncan.'

'We're going up to his place,' Phoebe said. 'Don't wait up for me.'

Louise nodded, pursing her lips thoughtfully.

'Now, about Andrew,' Phoebe said. 'I told him he could stay for a few more dances with Cindy Ann and then he was to go home with you. I said I'd see him in the morning,' she confessed.

'Also – make sure he has Binky,' she went on. 'And maybe you should give him a few nose drops, he's been pretty clogged up.

'And oh yes – if he wants his door open that's okay,' she added. 'Sometimes he needs the hall light on to get to sleep.'

'I know,' Louise said.

'Well, see you later.' Phoebe paused, then gave a helpless jokey shrug. 'I probably won't be too late, you know. In fact, I'll probably be home within an hour – I just didn't want you to worry, you know?'

And Louise, who was trying to keep back a smile, merely nodded.

'Well, see you.' But Phoebe had just turned away when her mother spoke her name. She turned back.

'For heaven's sake, Phoebe,' Louise said, her face set with the sly pride of a parent whose child has just broken a long-standing taboo, 'have *fun*.'

And thus Phoebe made what she knew was a conspicuous exit with Duncan Crane. By way of protection she forced herself to become both deaf and blind to anyone who might be observing as she walked out; and only when the door clanked shut, muffling music and laughter, did she allow herself to look around, to hear the sounds of the night. Later, though, like a long-lost echo, Doris Conran's dark-brown voice rebounded up from the bottom of her memory. 'Will you look at those two,' commented Doris as Phoebe left with Duncan. 'I'd have thought that motherhood would have settled that girl down but obviously not, she'll probably keep her poor mother waiting up all *night*.'

# 17

Despite her mother's blessing, Phoebe found it hard to relax as she settled into the front seat of Duncan's Scout. She barely knew this man; what was she getting herself into, what kind of a fall was she setting herself up for? She'd done fine without a man in her life for the past several years; she'd found a comfortable plateau, a safety zone where work and motherhood relieved her from the burdens of dating – why rock the boat?

Phoebe didn't have a ready answer to that question; all she knew was that earlier that evening, as she debated how to respond (oh yes with dignity, of course) to Duncan's proposal, as she nudged herself towards a sensible, responsible reaction, she suddenly felt so overwhelmingly dutiful, so sickeningly *good*, that she wanted to scream. Why shouldn't she go? When was the last time she'd done something a little bit irresponsible? When, for that matter, was the last time she'd had herself a fling? And did she think the stars were going to align themselves like this again in the near future? Here she was on vacation, she had a built-in babysitter, Duncan was attracted to her, she was attracted to him – why not? And besides, one night with a man was not going to turn her into a basket case of neediness.

Duncan, in the meantime, had fallen uncharacteristically silent as he waited for the Scout to warm up; he concentrated on the rpm's, adjusted the choke, wiped the inside mist from the windscreen with an old dishcloth. Phoebe wondered if he, too, was having a few last-minute qualms: what to talk about, how to orchestrate the rest of the evening. On the other hand, maybe not; maybe he did this regularly. And as a twinge of self-doubt caught her stomach, she couldn't help but laugh at herself, for she realized how nothing ever changed: whether nineteen or twenty-nine, all it boiled down to was this: Am I really someone special? Or am I just another head of curls on his pillow?

As Phoebe was wondering how to tell Duncan that this wasn't something that *she* made a habit of doing, Duncan gave the engine a final rev, backed out of the parking lot, and took off through town, around the village square, past Molly's dark and empty house, and then up the steep hill towards East Winslow. Instead of trying to initiate an awkward conversation Phoebe sat back and watched out of the window: haunting evergreens silhouetted against a night sky; a mobile homestead, the owner's Rambler perched on cinder blocks; an abandoned school bus off to the side of the road. They reached the crest of the hill and passed the Cutters' dairy farm; but then, instead of continuing down the main dirt road another mile to where they would hit the turnoff – another dirt road – into Barnet's Pond, Duncan braked, swung the wheel abruptly, and made a sharp turnoff on to what looked at best to be a makeshift track into the underbrush.

Phoebe grabbed the armrest with one hand, the dashboard with the other, as the Scout hit a ditch. 'I don't remember this road!'

'It's a short cut!' They charged down into a gully, the Scout lurching from side to side as Duncan sought to avoid a rock here, a fallen log there, and all along the way branches slapped against the windows. Phoebe sought to map out in her mind the route they were taking, to determine when they would intersect the road she rememberd. How long were they going to continue this exercise in trailblazing?

But then the branches cleared away, and the beams of the headlights showed two muddy tyre tracks leading up out of the gully. Duncan picked up a little speed as they approached the hill, and Phoebe assured herself that as they crested the top they would see the familiar well-oiled road leading down to the small lake.

'Keep your fingers crossed,' Duncan said with a chortle; 'I always get stuck on this hill.' Phoebe held on tightly as the Scout began its climb, up and up; but sure enough, suddenly its tyres began to spin in the muck. Duncan stepped on the gas, but as the wheels spun faster and faster they lost all traction, and the Scout slowed to a stop about halfway up.

Duncan laughed. 'I knew this would happen!' He let the Scout roll back down to the bottom of the gully, then backed up about thirty feet, put it in first gear, and charged forward again. This time they were three quarters up before the tyres started spinning; but by keeping his foot on the accelerator they inched their way to the top, where the Scout, its wheels suddenly on flat firm tracks, shot forward with unexpected speed.

'Had you worried, huh?' Duncan said, grinning, shifting.

'I wasn't worried,' Phoebe said, brushing her sweater, as though she had been out behind, pushing.

'See? You *are* worried, you think we're lost, you think we're never going to get down to the camp. Like what's this turkey trying to prove, anyway – right?'

'Wrong,' Phoebe said. 'I know where we are, I'm just wondering when we're going to join up with the other road.'

'What other road?'

'The main road.'

Duncan laughed.

'What's so funny?'

'I told you, this is a short cut; it takes us straight to the camp. I built it myself,' he told her proudly.

'You built this road?'

'Resurrected it, actually,' he said. But before Phoebe could reply the Scout lunged down on Duncan's side, as though its left wheels had fallen off the edge of the earth; and Phoebe, who had relaxed her grip when they'd reached the top of the gully back there, was thrown across the seat against him – just as Duncan, in an attempt to level the Scout, jerked the steering wheel sharply to the right, in the process knocking Phoebe in the cheekbone with his elbow.

'Sorry about that!' Duncan braked to a stop as Phoebe hoisted herself upright, pressing the heel of her palm to her cheek. 'Are you all right?' he asked.

Phoebe swallowed.

'Let me see,' said Duncan, but Phoebe shook her head.

'I'm fine,' she said, though she had received quite a sharp blow, and if she were alone, she would have let the tears come.

'God, I'm such a klutz!' Duncan laughed. 'Are you sure you're all right? Take your hand away, show me the damage.'

'I'm really okay, don't worry.'

'You're sure?'

'I'm *sure*.'

'Good,' Duncan said. 'Then you won't sue me?'

Phoebe gave a dry laugh and shook her head. 'No, I am not going to sue you. Let's get going, I'm kind of cold.'

'Did you ever think about how you could support yourself by getting into a bunch of minor little accidents?' Duncan said as he steered the Scout through another thicket. 'God, what a life – you let yourself get rear-ended, hopefully the guy's a little drunk so there's no question as to liability, you end up with whiplash, which is a pain, sure, but not debilitating – and so you sue! You figure one a year, each one bringing in maybe six or seven grand – you could live on that amount up here, you know.'

But Phoebe, whose cheek was beginning to swell, and whose own neck had suffered some kind of a snap as they bounced through the gully, was not amused by this. 'It's a fine idea until you happen to get mutilated,' she said, annoyed. 'Besides, it's a royal pain in the ass dealing with insurance companies.'

'You don't deal with insurance companies,' Duncan said. 'You get yourself a lawyer, and then he – oops, *she* takes care of everything – '

The Scout stalled.

'Hey, what's the matter?' Duncan demanded of his instrument panel. 'Damn engine,' he told Phoebe, on the verge of another laugh. 'It hasn't got used to this northern air.' But when he tried to start it up again it turned over once, sputtered, then stalled again. Duncan frowned, hunched over the steering wheel, turned the ignition key, and listened as the engine pulsed but did not catch. He turned the ignition off, then tried again, staring blankly out of the windscreen. Still no luck. Finally he sat back and crossed his arms.

'What is it?' Phoebe said, though she knew.

Duncan set his jaw.

'Are we out of petrol?' Phoebe asked.

'No,' Duncan said. 'We are not out of petrol.' He climbed out of the Scout and walked around to the back, where he opened up the rear door and flung the blankets about. Then he slammed the door shut and hit the side of the Scout. Phoebe waited; in another minute he walked around to the driver's door and climbed back in.

'We're out of petrol,' he told her.

'Oh.'

'I thought I had a can in the back but I don't,' he said.

Phoebe shook her head and stared out of the window.

'Damn petrol gauge,' Duncan said.

'Is it broken?'

'No.' Duncan laughed. 'I forgot to check it.'

Ha ha, Phoebe thought. Very funny.

'Maybe you're not out of petrol,' she said, after a moment. 'Maybe you got some water in the tank coming up the hill. Try it again,' she said.

Duncan tried it again; the engine merely whined. He sat back. 'I don't mean to rush the evening but we might as well start hoofing it,' he said. 'How are you set for shoes?'

Phoebe was wearing clogs. 'All right,' she said. 'How far are we?'

'From where?'

'From your camp.'

'I don't know,' he said. 'A couple of miles, maybe.'

'Because we could go back to my mother's,' Phoebe said. 'Maybe she has a can of petrol.'

'We're probably farther from your mother's than we are from my camp,' Duncan reminded her. 'And besides, I know I've got a can of petrol down there, in fact I know where it is, it's right on the porch where I almost tripped over it this afternoon.'

So Phoebe, resigning herself to an hour-long hike through the woods, opened her door and climbed out – stepping into several inches of muck. A wet chill ran from her toes up to her scalp and back down her spine, settling in her torso, which was unprotected by the loosely knit fisherman's sweater. It was so *cold* As she edged along the side of the Scout, evergreen needles breathed against her neck; she stumbled forward in momentary fright. These woods had once belonged to her, light and familiar and dapply warm; but in the darkness of the night they seemed cursed, full of decay and malignant growth, humus gone bad, a breeding ground for bats and snakes, for genetic wild cards.

She wished she had boots.

They had walked less than a hundred yards when Duncan stopped short, and roughly grabbed her arm.

'What *now*,' Phoebe said.

'Hear that?'

And Phoebe, who was wanting to make time, said, 'No.'

'Wait,' Duncan said. 'He'll do it again.'

'Who?'

'Ssshhh!' They stood together like statues, waiting, listening, and then from far away came a series of short muffled hoots.

'There!'

'What is it?'

'It's an owl. Listen again.'

In several seconds the owl hooted again. 'Hoohoo – hoohoo . . . hoohoo – hoohooaw!'

'Wow,' Duncan whispered. 'This is incredible.'

'I guess,' Phoebe said absently, bending down to roll up her trouser legs, which were soaked to her knees.

'No, really,' Duncan said. 'They're usually not hooting at this time of year, they usually hoot in the spring.'

Phoebe, however, wasn't particularly impressed by this fact; straightening up, she started to move on, but Duncan caught her arm. 'Wait,' he whispered, and then he loosened his grip, twitched his shoulders around, lifted his head, and froze. Suddenly a strange alien cry rose from his throat, a soft alto series of hoots; he waited, and in a moment the owl hooted back. Duncan paused, then repeated his hoot; again in a moment the owl hooted back.

Phoebe shivered, though not from the cold; this was *weird*. And she felt a sudden delight: it was as though she had made her way into another era, into a murky prehistoric world where man, bird, and beast were all one species, calling out to one another, warning, testing, inventing signals for the years to come.

She even forgot about being cold. 'Hoohoo – hoohoo . . . hoohoo – hoohooaw!' called Duncan. 'Hoohoo – hoohoo . . . hoohoo – hoohooaw!' called the owl in return.

It was Duncan who broke the spell; he suddenly relaxed his stance, and turned to her. His eyes shone as he unzipped his jacket; Phoebe sensed he had begun to sweat from concentration. 'Let's go,' he said softly. 'Pretty soon he'll catch on to me.'

'Where'd you learn to do that?' she asked, as they started making their way along the road again.

'I spent a year in the woods in upstate New York,' he told her. 'There was this owl who lived behind my house – he taught me.'

'Is it hard?' Phoebe couldn't imagine her vocal chords creating such a sound.

'It's not hard calling them,' he said. 'What's hard is getting them to call back.'

Phoebe was impressed by Duncan's skills; and to be sure, his calling to the owl evoked in her a long-lost sense of wonder for the world of nature, a world her day-to-day life so rarely intersected. But as she continued along beside him she found herself wondering how an objective description of Duncan would come across to Janice. Well, let's see, he's a dowser, she would have to say; and he lives alone in this cabin by a lake, and hoots with the owls – Phoebe imagined Janice narrowing her eyes in amusement, type-casting Duncan as perhaps a holdover from the sixties, an unambitious sort, happily self-supportive, content to let the rest of the world make deals, and settle cases, and worry about the economy. And I bet he wears Birkenstock sandals, Janice would say, with Ragg socks, and baggy woollen trousers, and lumberjack shirts, no?

And how would Phoebe respond? Would she be able to defend him? And what if Duncan were to show up in California? She couldn't imagine Duncan mixing very well in her lawyers' circle; and Phoebe realized that whatever happened with Duncan tonight she would probably want to keep him well separated from her life in California. Which filled her immediately with a sense of shame. Was she really so spineless?

They trudged along. By now Phoebe was chilled through all over; too proud to ask Duncan for his leather jacket, she hugged her chest tightly, and thought of sun, sand, warm tropical waters. But it didn't do much good, and as they crested another hill and still there was no sign of Duncan's camp, or Barnet's Pond, Phoebe admitted to herself that although she had grown up in this region, and although she had weathered frigid winters and knew how great the human body's capacity was for exposure, she was scared. She was scared that they were lost, that this hand-hacked road would lead nowhere, that they would be spending the night in the woods and nobody would think to come looking for them. Though the sky had cleared and the moon was out she was scared of a sudden arctic storm; and she was scared of hypothermia setting in, of death raising its ugly gnarled roots from the undergrowth, causing her to stumble, and Duncan, too, the two of them lying back with exhaustion – just for a minute – as their body temperatures continued to drop and flakes of snow began to dust their souls.

* * *

What Phoebe didn't realize that evening was that they *were* a little lost. After abandoning the Scout Duncan had led her along his road for a half-mile or so, but having worked on the road himself he knew of all its twists and turns, and thought he could shorten their journey by cutting up over this one knoll that his road encicrcled, and then meeting up with the road again on the other side. He misjudged distances, however, or else veered off too far to the north, because the road they intersected was the wrong road, and though he didn't let on to her, they ended up backtracking a good mile before getting back on course. So that by the time the underbrush thinned out and the moonlit waters of Barnet's Pond sparkled through the shoreline cedars, Duncan himself felt the relief of a lost hiker.

The road followed a ridge, high above the water, and soon they reached Duncan's camp, where a steep series of steps descended the embankment, passing Duncan's log cabin and continuing on down to the shoreline. The steps were made of old logs, split long ago and grown over with moss in some places, strewn with wet leafy debris in others. Duncan led the way, cautioning Phoebe to watch her step, unless she felt like taking a late-night dip, in which case he'd advise her just to jump off the dock, it'd be a lot less painful than bumping down these steps into the pond.

Phoebe grasped the fibry-barked railing with both hands, turned sideways, and cautiously made her way down the steps like a toddler, aligning both feet on each log before taking another step. She had lost all sense of time; it could have been twelve, or one, or even two o'clock; and she had long ago abandoned all notions of any romance developing between Duncan and herself. All she was concerned about was getting warm again. She looked down upon the mossy shingles of the cabin's roof, the great stone chimney rising up along one side, and with each step she imagined a new delight waiting for her within: a blazing fire, thick woolly Hudson Bay blankets, a snifter of brandy.

Thus her heart sank when upon entering Duncan's cabin she found it colder within than it was without. Not only that, but the cabin was as far from any notions of cosiness as she could have imagined. Duncan had knocked out all the walls, so that it was just one stark open room; and one quarter of this room was taken up by stacks of lumber, rolls of insulation, and giant sheets of plasterboard. No rugs covered the raw plywood floor; instead it was spattered with unswept trails of sawdust, littered with bags of nails and hand tools and stacks of books. The cabin's back side pressed so close to the embankment that tree roots clawed at the window, and all along this wall stretched a long counter of unfinished particle board, which housed in its middle a chipped porcelain sink, its grey-coated underbelly and pipes exposed below. Several bird feeders, half-filled, sat upon the countertop, and at one end a sack of birdseed lay on its side, spilling forth its mixture of sunflower seeds and cracked corn and millet. On the floor below the counter Duncan's bare mattress lay at an odd angle, his electric-blue sleeping bag piled in the middle; this mattress, along with a rocking chair that he had positioned in front of the picture window, were the cabin's only furnishings.

As Phoebe tried to control her shivering, Duncan set about building a fire. When it was blazing he loaded up an armful of wood and disappeared out of the back door. In his absence Phoebe hovered as close to the fire as she could, roasting first her front side, then her back, then her front again; but it wasn't enough. Unable to exorcise the chill, she looked for a blanket, but all she could find was Duncan's sleeping bag. Any inhibitions that might have earlier restrained her now gave way to more primitive instincts, and when Duncan returned several minutes later he found Phoebe by the fire in the rocking chair, mummified in his sleeping bag, her clogs and socks on the hearth, her mud-splattered trousers hanging from an iron hook that jutted out from the stone chimney.

'Good for you,' he said. 'I would have suggested it but I didn't want to sound like an old lech. How are you doing?'

Phoebe nodded grimly.

'Let's see the cheek,' he said. 'Uh-oh, yup, you're going to have a shiner. Sorry. Do you want to put some ice on it?'

Ice! The very thought sent chills throughout her body. She shook her head.

'Well,' Duncan said, 'how about something hot? Tea, maybe? Constant Comment?'

'How about some brandy?'

'Nope,' Duncan said. 'That's a myth. It'll make you feel warm at first but all it does is lower your metabolism. I'll make you some tea first.'

Phoebe turned back to the fire. No wonder he and Bea get along so well, she thought. Next thing he'll probably offer me is a bowl of oatmeal.

'So what do you think?' Duncan asked, as he set water to boil and began rinsing out mugs. 'Great potential here, wouldn't you say?'

Phoebe hedged. 'It certainly is rustic,' she said. 'And you must like spending a lot of time alone.'

'Mostly, yes,' Duncan said. 'Though there are days when I'm ready to climb the walls, and that's when I usually make up a grocery list, or go up and borrow some tools from Dave Adams.'

'What are you going to do when winter comes?' Phoebe

asked. 'Are you really going to stay warm enough with wood heat?'

Duncan handed her a mug of tea. 'Something tells me this kind of life isn't exactly up your alley.'

Phoebe allowed a smile; cupping the hot mug between her palms was like plugging her spirit into sudden heat, and she began to feel a little less grouchy. 'I'm a wimp,' she admitted. 'I'd put in a furnace, and I'd need to be closer to civilization, to people. But apart from that – oh, I don't know, I might be able to get into it. What happens if you have an emergency, though? What happens if your appendix bursts?'

'It already did,' Duncan said. 'Twenty-eight years ago.'

'You know what I mean.'

'You're right,' Duncan said. 'Which is why I've got to get a phone down here. But you can't worry about those things.'

'You have to,' Phoebe said, 'when you're a parent.'

Duncan raised his eyebrows. 'So you do,' he said. 'So you do.'

They fell silent. A log snapped, sending sparks; Duncan brushed them back into the fireplace, then turned the logs with a long iron poker.

'Have you met many people since you moved up here?' Phoebe asked, after a while.

Duncan laughed. 'Is there anybody I haven't met, that's the question,' he said. 'All it took was one night at the band concert last July and the whole town knows my middle name, knows my grandfather had gout, you name it. It was great,' he said. 'All these grand notions of moving to the backwoods and being a hermit get shot to pieces within the first month. Not that anyone comes to visit me out here, but they all seem to know that I've moved my bed into the kitchen, or that I'm putting up a new railing, or that I drank too many beers the night before. You know, they all make fun of my dowsing but I bet you half of them stand in the middle of their living rooms every night and ask their Y-rods: Is Duncan's dock about to fall into the pond? Does Duncan need to eat more steak? And has he moved his mattress again?'

Phoebe laughed at Duncan's mimicry.

'These people, they're great,' he went on, 'they really are. They all know everything about you – believe me, I'm going to get the third degree about you coming down here tonight – and they've all got advice to give. No kidding!' – and he shook his head – 'I was in the clinic over in St Audie a while ago for – shit, all right, for a urinary infection, and the next day Ida Poultney's telling me to drink cranberry juice. And then I run into Susan Mitchell coming out of the high school and she tells me her husband gets them – *them*, mind you, no name for it, just *them* – chronically. And then Doris Conran follows right behind her, all curious, wants to know my symptoms, you can just see her start worrying. God, that Doris, she cracks me up!'

'Doris never cracked me up,' Phoebe said. 'Doris Conran is one of the reasons I left town.'

'Oh, she's a softie at heart,' Duncan said. 'All you have to do is tell her she's looking like Katharine Hepburn today and from then on she doesn't have a complaint this side of Lake Champlain.'

'Katharine Hepburn?'

'Or Bette Davis,' Duncan said. 'It doesn't matter, she just wants someone to notice the new shade of purple lipstick she's wearing.'

'She probably has a crush on you,' Phoebe said.

'I certainly hope so!' Duncan exclaimed. 'Not everyone has a standing invitation for bourbon on the rocks, Saturdays at four. Ever been in her house?'

'Are you crazy?' Phoebe said. 'Of course not.'

'God, you should see it, it's full of all these hokey black velvet paintings, you know, the kind you see in Juarez or Tijuana, and in the middle of her dining room there's this goddamn shrine to her cat, flowers and pictures and tufts of hair, I guess it got hit by a car or something – anyway, she sits me down in her parlour and serves me bourbon with stale cheese popcorn or Cheez Doodles, sometimes it's those orange marshmallow peanuts she thinks taste great with bourbon. But who am I to complain, the bourbon's great. Course I blew it one week,' he said. 'My sister was visiting and I took her along and Doris dried up and poured us half-jiggers and didn't say more than five words. And then when I went alone the next week she made me rearrange her living room and put up the storm door and finish raking the leaves, the sole reward for which was one rum ball! What a lady,' he laughed. 'Really, isn't she something else? I've got to start teasing her about those shoes she wears, those awful tie-up clodhoppers – see if I can get a rise out of her.'

Phoebe couldn't imagine her own self teasing Doris Conran about the shoes she wore. But she could imagine Duncan teasing her, and probably underneath her outrage Doris would be so flattered that she would go into St Audenbury the next Saturday morning and buy herself a pair of high-heeled pumps.

What a different place this is for him, Phoebe thought. Duncan with all of his charms would probably come out of these Saturday-afternoon bourbon hours with a library of taped conversations in which Doris got her mother, a Russian immigrant, to talk about the Ukraine – stories that everyone knew deserved to be carefully heard and recorded but that had never had a chance to be told because nobody wanted to mess around with Doris. But Duncan wasn't afraid of Doris's ornery nature; Duncan would be able to make Doris laugh. And if Duncan ever did anything wrong in Doris's eyes, her rebuke would never get the best of him, as it did Phoebe; it would just give him something else to tease her about.

Duncan suddenly excused himself and went outside again. Phoebe thought he had gone for another armload of wood, but in a few minutes he returned and announced, 'Two hundred degrees!'

Phoebe frowned, puzzled.

'You might think my homestead has very few amenities,' he told her, taking two towels down from a shelf above the sink, 'but one amenity it isn't lacking is a first-rate sauna.' He handed her a towel. 'People talk about woodstoves and insulation and getting your storm windows up,' he said, 'but this is how you really survive the cold.' He disappeared into the bathroom and came out seconds later, wrapped in a towel. 'See you in a bit,' he said. 'There are a couple of lanterns hanging from the trees; follow them.'

'Wait a minute,' Phoebe said. 'I hate to bring this up, but what about the Scout?'

'What about it?'

'Well, we did just leave it back there in the woods,' Phoebe said.

'Yeah, so we did.' Duncan said, and gave a laugh. 'Guess we'll have to flip to see who lugs the can of petrol back tonight. But we can deal with that later,' he told her. 'Now go change.'

Phoebe, barefoot and wrapped in a towel, made her way along a spongy root-lined path, through the pines, to a tiny boxy hut set against the steep side of the hill. She tightened her towel, opened the door, and squinted from the sudden blast of heat. Inside Duncan was sitting up on the top bench, slumped back against the wall, oily and slick with sweat. Phoebe gave the door another push to close it tightly, then sat down on the bottom bench.

'Come on up,' he said. 'You won't get a sweat going down there.'

'In a minute.' The thermometer near the ceiling said one ninety. Two local points on each side of her neck immediately began to burn; she had forgotten to unfasten her gold hoops, and she did so now, carefully laying them in the corner, where bench met wall. The she hoisted herself up on to the upper bench. The rise in temperature was enough to make her grimace; it hurt to breathe, especially through her mouth, and so she took in air through her nostrils, in quick shallow breaths. Beads of sweat were fast collecting across her chest; she touched her finger to her skin, and felt a sudden rivulet flowing down between her breasts and into the crease of her belly. She tightened her towel again and sat back beside Duncan, closing her eyes. When she opened them the temperature had risen to two hundred. Could it really be that hot? It didn't matter; it felt wonderful.

On top of the tiny woodstove was a tray of rocks.

'Ready for steam?'

'Surrre.'

Duncan leaned over and dribbled water from a pitcher on to the rocks; they sizzled furiously as the steam rose, and in a moment it was as though a hot Turkish towel had smothered her. She choked, held her breath for a moment, then breathed in a tiny bit of air, and then a tiny bit more.

'This,' she murmured, 'is heaven.'

Duncan poured more water on to the rocks. This time, however, the blast of steam was too hot for her; she dropped down to the bottom bench and bent forward, her face between her knees. When she straightened up she found Duncan sitting beside her. 'I overdid it,' he wheezed. 'I think I just scalded my lungs.'

'What's the hottest you've got it?'

'Boiling point,' Duncan said. 'Without any steam, though. Want to give the upper bench another try?'

They climbed up; this time, instead of sitting beside one another, they sat at opposite ends of the bench, legs outstretched, facing one another. On the wall above Duncan's head was a picture of Finns in the sauna, beating each other with birch twigs.

'Back in San Francisco I go to the baths a lot,' Phoebe told him sleepily. Her voice seemed thick and slow, drugged from the heat. 'I go with this other attorney, Janice.'

'Nice image,' Duncan murmured. 'Phoebe and Janice, shedding their suits, kicking off their high-heeled shoes . . .' He eyed her lazily through waves of heat, and touched his foot to hers, then moved it away, suddenly shy.

After a while she found herself waking up as her body adjusted. 'I hate it, you know,' she said to Duncan.

'Hate what?'

'What I do,' she said.

'Oh,' Duncan said. 'I knew that,' he said.

'How?'

'That afternoon, up at the Adamses',' he said. 'You had this edge to your voice, you sounded as though you wished I hadn't brought the subject up.'

Was it really so obvious?

Duncan splashed a little more water on to the rocks. 'Why do you hate it?'

Phoebe hesitated. She hadn't intended to get into the details, but suddenly she wanted to tell Duncan all about it. And so she told him about Parco-Fields, and the hours it demanded of her. She told him about the stacks of documents she faced every day. She told him about her colleagues, the enthusiastic Nuts, the alienated Bolts. And she tried, as best she could, to give him an impartial portrayal of Herb Sullivan.

'Nobody's that evil,' Duncan said.

'That's what I thought,' Phoebe said, 'until I worked for him.'

'Oh, come on,' Duncan said. 'He's got his soft spots too.'

'One,' Phoebe said. 'M&M's. Every day at four o'clock, there he is, pulling the M&M knob on the candy machine. One bag, no more, no less.'

'Where'd he go to law school?'

'University of Virginia,' Phoebe said, 'and he's been sulking ever since about not getting into Harvard.'

'You see? There's another soft spot. Now: think of Herb having sex.'

'He doesn't.'

'Don't act like his daughter, of course he does.'

'Then don't make me think about it,' Phoebe said. 'It's too revolting.'

'Think about Herb having sex,' Duncan went on, 'and then think about all the problems he has. He probably can't get it up very easily,' he said. 'And he's probably uptight about going down on his wife.'

'Can we stop this?' Phoebe said. 'I believe I'm feeling quite nauseous.'

'And now think about his kids,' Duncan said. 'Think about Herb in the delivery room.'

'Herb wouldn't have been in the delivery room,' Phoebe said. 'Herb would have been squeezing in a last-minute argument before the Ninth Circuit.'

'And think of him holding his newborn son,' Duncan continued, 'all wet and blue and bloody and as the baby cries Herb starts to cry too – or maybe it's been a

Caesarean, some kind of an emergency thing, and his wife's life is on the line and then everyone pulls through like a Hollywood movie – come on,' he said, 'this guy's just another Doris Conran, he laughs and cries and what he probably needs most is to be teased about the colour of his tie.'

'I tease him about his tie,' Phoebe said, 'and it's all over.'

Duncan ran his fingers through his hair, which by now was dark and stringy and wet. 'All right, all right,' he said. 'So maybe he is a jerk. Maybe he does make life miserable. But he doesn't have to; he doesn't own you.'

'Yes, he does,' Phoebe said, though it was a nice thought, Herb not owning her, and she tucked it away for future consolation.

'Then leave,' Duncan said.

'I plan to,' she said. 'As soon as my trial's over I'm going to find another job.'

'What?'

'I don't know,' Phoebe said.

'Something in law?'

'Oh, probably. What else?'

'That edge,' he said. 'There it is again.'

Phoebe shrugged. 'I don't know what else I'd do,' she said. 'Besides, I like law,' she said. 'And I have to admit, I like the money.'

'Don't we all,' Duncan said.

'Then what about you?'

'What about me?'

'You're an engineer,' Phoebe said. 'You could be out there making tons.'

'Tons of nothing,' Duncan joked. 'No,' he said, 'I didn't do too well in school, I'd have trouble getting a job. And anyway I like living here. For now, anyway. I have my cabin. I have my pond. I have my sauna and my books and every kind of bird imaginable lives in these woods and when spring comes, oh God, I can't wait, that wonderful moment when the ice begins to crack and then the loons are flying low over the water – well!' he said, 'it wins hands down.'

As he spoke Phoebe gazed across the tiny cedar-walled room at him. In the last minute she had suddenly drifted so far away from everything: from Judson and Day, from Janice, from her home in the Berkeley hills; from her mother and Molly, even from Andrew. All that existed for her right now were the four walls of this dimly lit cubicle, the infernal stove, the sweat tickling her neck, her breasts, the insides of her arms. And Duncan, of course. By now he was drenched in his own sweat, and she had a vision of him on a hot summer day, shirtless, swinging an axe to fell a tree, all the muscles in his shoulders and back working together, fresh-smelling sweat and grime collecting in the shallow fatless folds of his stomach – and then breaking when the tree was down, whisking off his hat, wiping his brow, guzzling a beer.

Then, just as quickly, that vision was replaced by another, more immediate one: that of Duncan on top of her, about to enter. She shifted her hips, involuntarily, as though to accommodate him, and for a second she caught her breath, so suddenly full she felt. She looked over at him. He had fallen silent, as though waiting for a response. She uncrossed her legs, pressed the balls of her feet against his. He pressed back. He closed his eyes, and she closed hers, and there they sat, fusing.

Later, lying naked side by side on the blue striped ticking of Duncan's mattress, bodies spent, fingers interlaced, they listened to the tall pines creaking in the wind. Embers glowed in the fireplace; and moonlight shone through the wide picture window, casting grey shadows of branches across the floor. Until now Phoebe had been radiating enough heat from the sauna so that she was comfortable lying there with nothing on, but she was growing chilled again, and she reached for his sleeping bag.

But Duncan stopped her. 'You're not cold,' he said. By his side was a kerosene lantern he had taken from one of the trees on their way inside; he held it to her body, examining her. Phoebe shivered.

'Phoebe,' he said softly.

'What?'

'Nothing,' he said. 'In the spring, the phoebes will be calling your name. Phoe-be,' he said, and then he smiled, embarrassed, as though catching himself in a moment of silly sentimentality.

Phoebe turned on her side. 'When I was a girl my mother used to tell me they were calling me to come outside,' she told him. '"Hear the phoebes?" she would say. "Run along and see if you can find them!" It was a ruse,' she told Duncan. 'She just wanted me out of the house so she could get her spring cleaning done.'

Duncan smiled.

'Though Molly was jealous,' she said. 'For there were never any birds calling her name. I think I probably lorded it over her too,' she added. 'Maybe that's been out problem all along, me lording everything over her.'

'Are you tired?'

'No,' Phoebe said. 'I'm cold.'

'We can go back in the sauna,' Duncan suggested. 'We never did make it into the lake, you know.'

'The lake?'

'You have to close your pores up,' he said. 'You have to plunge into cold water.'

'You,' Phoebe said, 'are crazy.'

'Get your towel,' he said. 'I'll go throw more wood into the stove.'

'I'll get my towel,' Phoebe said, 'but I'm not putting my big toe into any lake in the middle of November.'

And yet she did. Phoebe would never forget that experience, trotting naked in the dark along the path from sauna to steps, tripping down to the water's edge, wavering as Duncan splashed ahead and whooped in shock, throwing moonlit drops into the air; then charging ahead into the water herself: the unbelievable blow to her chest as she plunged, the terror of black ice water, the panicky delight of running back to shore, the exhilaration of a second plunge. Afterwards they sat, numb and exhausted, on a bench between two trees, the light from another lantern illuminating the swirls of steam that rose from their bodies. She would never forget it; and years later, when describing the night to Molly, she would swear that curls of ice had stiffened her hair, and drops of water had frozen on the tips of her breasts, like diamonds.

# 18

Phoebe awakened abruptly. A moment ago she had been fast asleep, dreaming, of all things, that she was back in law school; now she was wide awake. Duncan was nowhere to be seen. She sat up on the mattress; outside a smoky mist had settled over the waters of Barnet's Pond, and at the far end, towering up out of the cloud, rose the granite outcrop of Barnet's Ledge. It was the first mountain Phoebe had ever climbed – though mountain it wasn't; rock cliff was more like it – and she recalled the weakness that had almost buckled her knees as she stood on the edge, looking down upon the flat slate-coloured expanse of water below. 'Phoebe, get back from the edge!' Bea had cried; but Phoebe, unable to shift her stance for fear of lurching forward, remained frozen in place until Bea yanked her back from behind. 'Must you always give us such a *fright*,' Bea had grumped, handing out sandwiches.

Phoebe pulled the sleeping bag around her. Beyond the picture window was a small ledge where Duncan had placed several bird feeders; as she watched, tiny chickadees darted down from nowhere, selected sunflower seeds, and darted away again. Feeding stations, in fact, were everywhere; the miniature houses, the seedcakes, the bags of suet and strings of doughnuts hanging from the branches, lent a primitive, superstitious atmosphere to his woods, as though these offerings were meant to ward off evil spirits, like garlic scattered around a gypsy's camp. As Phoebe continued to watch, a brilliant red bird – a cardinal? a scarlet tanager? – landed on the ledge and began pecking at the seeds, then suddenly flew away, up into the trees.

Phoebe lay back and tried to place in chronological order all the events of the night before. First we took a sauna, she thought, and then we came back and made love, and then he built a fire – no, then we took another sauna, then we went swimming, then we came back and made love again – when did we get to sleep? she wondered. Her watch had stopped at five forty-five; it was light enough now to be eight o'clock, maybe nine, they still had to get the Scout, by the time she got home it would be close to noon, Andrew would be acting up, her mother would be worried – angry too –

Phoebe threw off the sleeping bag, scooted across the room, and pulled her trousers off the hook above the fireplace. When Duncan came in several minutes later he found her fully dressed, splashing cold water on her face. 'We should have set an alarm,' she said, blotting her cheeks with a dishtowel. 'My mother is going to be completely freaked – what time is it?'

'Quarter to eight,' Duncan said cheerfully. 'Good morning.' He set down his load of wood and kissed her.

'Good morning,' Phoebe said.

'How'd you sleep?'

'Wonderfully,' Phoebe said. 'I feel completely rejuvenated.'

'Course you do,' Duncan said. 'Did you think I put the mattress in the kitchen just to be eccentric?'

'Oh, come on, you mean I slept so well because there weren't any – what do you call them?'

'Noxious rays.'

'Right,' Phoebe said. 'Look, I hate to be a sceptic but I think my sleeping well had quite a bit more to do with our five-mile hike and our sauna and what followed the sauna.'

'As you wish,' Duncan said. 'I'm not out to convert you.'

'Good,' Phoebe said. 'Are you sure it's only quarter to eight? It seems a lot later.'

'What's your hurry?' Duncan said. 'You don't have to be at work this morning.'

'I have to get home,' Phoebe said. 'How long will it take us to get the Scout?'

'I already got it.'

'You did? How long have you been up?'

'Awhile,' he said. 'She started up just like that,' he told her. 'Sorry about all the inconvenience it caused. Let's see your cheek.'

Phoebe touched the top of her cheekbone; it was tender, but not painful.

'The sauna'll cure everything.' Duncan started scooping birdseed out of the sack and pouring it into a cylindrical feeder. 'Though if anyone sees you today the whole town is going to think that I assaulted you.'

Phoebe remembered him loosening her towel, pulling her with a long-forgotten urgency down on to his mattress. 'You did,' she said softly.

Duncan turned to gaze at her over his shoulder. Then he turned back and began filling another feeder. 'We could debate that,' he murmured. 'Who assaulted whom.'

But Phoebe's debating instincts had been baked away by last night's sauna, or else softened by lovemaking. She stood behind him and kneaded his shoulders. 'Some other time,' she said. 'If you tell me where you keep the coffee I'll get some going,' she offered.

'I don't drink coffee,' he said. 'But there's all sorts of tea in the bottom cupboard. Try the Morning Thunder,' he suggested. 'It's got a pretty good kick. There,' he said, 'the chickadees will be in seventh heaven.'

While the tea steeped Phoebe rinsed out their mugs

from the night before; she would have one quick cup, then ask Duncan to drive her back. She could be home before nine – before Bea, or Dave, or Cindy Ann, or Jack happened to stop by. It wouldn't be so bad walking into the kitchen and facing her mother and Andrew, just the two of them; but if Cindy Ann were there she would make all sorts of loud gawky references to sunrise services, aren't they beautiful, all the while giving Phoebe exaggerated winks, hoping for a minute-by-minute report later on. Which she wouldn't get. Dave himself might not have noticed her departure the night before; but Bea certainly would have, and she would greet Phoebe with a wave of judgement repositioning all the muscles in her face as she stood to leave: she had things to do, she was sure she'd see Phoebe before tomorrow but if not it was wonderful for her to have made it back for the wedding and isn't Duncan doing a nice job on the Caleb place?

'Thinking about Herb again?' Duncan asked.

Phoebe laughed. 'No,' she told him, 'I was thinking about what Bea Adams was going to have to say about all this.'

'All what?'

'This!' Phoebe exclaimed. 'You, me, taking off last night and then me not getting back until nine o'clock this morning.'

'Nine?' Duncan said. 'That's in a hour.'

'Or thereabouts,' Phoebe said.

'Stay the morning,' Duncan said.

'I can't,' she said. 'I told you last night, I have too much to do today.'

'So do I,' Duncan said. 'It can wait.'

'Maybe your work can,' Phoebe said, 'but I've got a plane to catch tomorrow morning. I'd love to stay,' she said, 'but I can't.'

Duncan waited.

'I really can't,' she said.

'Then forget about the tea,' he said, and he traced her jawline, first one side, then the other. 'We've got time.'

But it wasn't so much a matter of time that made Phoebe reluctant to lie down with Duncan on his mattress again; it was more a matter of unspoken family protocol. For some reason she felt fine facing her mother so long as what had happened with Duncan had happened last night; but she felt uncomfortable with the idea of walking into the farmhouse kitchen with her face still flushed from Duncan's caresses. It was as though she would simultaneously be flaunting both bad behaviour and good fortune.

Besides, unless he had another packet, they had used what appeared to be the last of his condoms the night before; and a skipped menstrual period was one memento she could do without.

Phoebe locked his wandering hands at the small of her back; then she reached up and drew her fingers through the strands of his hair. 'Duncan,' she said. 'I'm glad we spent the night together. And I'm glad to be with you right now,' she added.

'But?'

'But I need to go home,' she said. 'I need to see my son. Oh, I could probably give you some convoluted psychological explanations about not wanting to mix roles – mother, daughter, lover – so quickly, but why go into all that, why not keep things simple?'

'Simple,' he said. 'My lawyer girlfriend's telling me to keep things simple.' He may have meant only to tease her, but the laugh lines that last night seemed so permanently etched into his eyes abruptly vanished, leaving his face with a sad scoured look. Phoebe suddenly sensed that an imbalance existed, that Duncan's vulnerability this morning was greater than hers: he had no child to tend to, no clothes to pack, no travel plans to knead away the cramp of loneliness in his heart. Not that she herself would be able to banish him completely from her thoughts; yet it was true that her mind would be occupied by more pragmatic matters this afternoon: rounding up Andrew's toys, reconfirming their reservations, finding room for all the blocks of cheese, the cans of maple syrup she wanted to bring back. The magic of their evening – and the realization that it would not happen again – would probably hit her on the plane tomorrow; but right now she had other things on her mind; and knowing this gave her an uncomfortable sense of power. She turned away without answering him, troubled.

'All right,' Duncan said. 'As you wish.' He finished pouring seed into the house-shaped feeder, then took it outside. Phoebe tried to ignore her guilt by busily picking up her things; then she took another sip of tea and set her mug in the sink. Outside the air was scented with spruce, a smell that reminded her of the pitchy gum they used to pick off the trees down here, its terrible turpentine taste overshadowed by the thrill of finding a wild food.

Duncan was perched on a ladder, hanging the feeder from one of the lower branches of a pine tree. Already a flock of tiny brown birds was fluttering around him. 'Ready?' he said, climbing down.

'I'm ready,' said Phoebe.

'Okay, then,' Duncan said. 'Got everything?'

'I think so.'

'Too bad.'

'Why?'

'Because you don't,' he said.

Phoebe frowned. 'What'd I forget?'

Duncan grinned, wiped his hands on the seat of his trousers, and started up the long steep stairway that led to the road above, where the Scout was parked. 'If I told you,' he said without turning around, 'then I wouldn't have anything to lure you back with, would I?'

But Phoebe, annoyed, checked her bag. She had her wallet, her chequebook, her Swiss army knife (which they had used the night before, to open a bottle of wine). She was fully dressed; she hadn't worn a hat, or gloves, or a scarf –

Forget it, she told herself. Whatever it is, you can do without it.

This morning Duncan took the familiar dirt road back rather than the short cut, and Phoebe was surprised at how quickly the trip went: within fifteen minutes they had reached the other main road. She found herself a bit disappointed: perhaps a part of her had been looking forward to an hour-long journey; – or maybe she'd even been wishing for another mishap: a flat tyre, say, something out of her control that would have given them a little more time together. But sooner than not they were heading down through the sugar bush, then following the stand of willows, and it was at exactly five to nine that Duncan veered his Scout into Louise's driveway. He braked to a stop and put it in neutral.

'Well – ' said Duncan.

'So – ' said Phoebe at the same time.

They laughed,

'Good luck with your trial,' he said.

'Good luck with your cabin,' she said.

A long silence passed, and Phoebe wondered if her mother was watching from the kitchen window.

'The sauna was wonderful,' she said. 'I can still feel the heat.'

'I can still feel you,' Duncan said. 'I can still feel your knees shake.'

Phoebe coloured, found herself wanting for words

again. One thing about Duncan, he didn't beat about the bush. Out of the corner of her eye she saw a curtain fall back into place.

'Listen,' Duncan said, 'nobody likes long good-byes, so we'll cut this short. You take care.'

'You take care too,' Phoebe said.

'But I really mean that,' Duncan said. 'You've got the beginning of an ulcer, you should slow down, you should find some way to combat tension.'

'I don't have an ulcer,' Phoebe said.

'You're going to,' Duncan said. 'If you keep this up.'

'What are you talking about?'

'I dowsed you,' he said.

'You what?'

'Last night,' he said. 'While you were sleeping. Look,' he said, and he held his left palm over her stomach.

'So what!' Phoebe laughed. 'That doesn't tell me anything!'

Duncan shrugged, and removed his hand. 'It tells me a lot. See a doctor,' he said. 'Let me know what he says.'

Phoebe laughed again, and shook her head. 'You're crazy.'

'Crazy,' Duncan said, 'but right. There's your mother,' he said, 'watching us from the upstairs window. Come on, let's get her heart rate up into the target zone.' He took her in his arms and tried to press a long kiss to her lips; but Phoebe's self-consciousness checked any passion she might have otherwise felt, and she responded with a tight puckery kiss, cheerful and brusque as a distant aunt's.

'Good-bye,' she said. Duncan himself said nothing, though, and as she walked towards the house and Duncan backed his Scout out of the driveway, she wished she hadn't said it with such finality.

* * *

Seated at the head of the kitchen table, Louise announced that Andrew had got sick in the middle of the night. 'It was all the excitement,' she said. 'Plus I don't think anyone was keeping an eye on how many cookies he ate, or how many cups of punch he drank.'

'Did he throw up?' Phoebe asked.

'Four times,' Louise reported. 'Actually, I was relieved; the way he was hollering I thought he might have had appendicitis.'

'Where is he now?' Phoebe asked. 'Sleeping?'

'Oh, no,' Louise said. 'He ate a good breakfast and then Dave stopped by and the two of them went down to the beaver pond.'

Phoebe wondered what kind of an explanation Louise had given Dave as to her whereabouts.

'Well?' Louise said.

'Well what?'

'Well did you have a nice time!'

'Oh,' said Phoebe. 'Yes.'

'Very nice?'

Phoebe poured herself a cup of coffee. Was her mother really asking for details?

'Phoebe, for heaven's sake, stop acting like you're sixteen again, clamming up whenever I ask you a question. Did you sleep with him or not?'

Phoebe spilled hot coffee on to her wrist. 'Ouch!' she said. 'Yes.'

'Thank heavens,' Louise said. 'And congratulations.'

'Don't congratulate me, Mum,' Phoebe said. 'It's not that big a deal.'

'It is; and besides, I had money on this.'

'You what?'

'Bea and I made a little bet,' Louise confessed. 'I said you would and she said you wouldn't.'

Phoebe sat down.

'She said she hoped I won, though,' Louise said. 'She said as soon as she saw you that first morning she could tell that you were spending all your time working, either at the law firm or taking care of Andrew, and that what you needed most was a little romance in your life.'

'A little romance,' Phoebe said.

'But ultimately she thought you'd chicken out at the last minute,' Louise said. 'And I said she was wrong.'

'Well, Mother,' Phoebe said, 'you were right. What time will they be back?'

'Who?'

'Andrew and Dave.'

'Eleven or so,' said Louise. 'Was it good?'

'Was *what* good!'

'You know,' said Louise. 'With Duncan.'

'Pretty good,' Phoebe said, aggressive in her curtness. 'What else do you want to know?'

'Are you going to see him again?'

'See him again!' Phoebe exclaimed. 'When would I have time, I'm leaving tomorrow!'

'I'll take care of Andrew tonight,' Louise offered. 'Why don't you have dinner together?'

'Where, at the water-wheel restaurant, where the whole town can see us? I don't need that,' Phoebe said.

'My dear daughter, the whole town saw you leave together last night. I don't think you'd raise too many eyebrows by going out to dinner with him.'

'Well, I don't have time,' Phoebe said. 'Besides, we've said our good-byes.'

'Are you going to keep in touch?'

'Who knows,' Phoebe said. 'I'm not planning on anything.'

'What did you really think of him?' Louise asked, leaning forward. 'Bea thinks he's the most wonderful thing that ever set foot in the Northeast Kingdom.'

'He's nice,' Phoebe said.

'Nice? Is that all?'

'Mum,' Phoebe said, growing more agitated, 'I don't know how to describe him. He's nice, that's all. We had a good time together, maybe we'll stay in touch, maybe not. Don't make this out to be more than it really is.'

Louise sat back and lifted her chin defensively. 'I'm not,' she said. 'I just thought – '

'I know what you thought,' Phoebe said. 'It sounds to me like you were hearing wedding bells as soon as I walked out of the door last night.'

'I certainly was not!'

'You were too – and you were probably wondering when Duncan would get the Caleb place finished up so Andrew and I could move back.'

'I was thinking no such thing,' Louise said indignantly. 'I just wanted you to have a good time. And if things work out . . . well, they work out.'

'Don't hold your breath waiting,' Phoebe said. 'I had a good time, but that's that. Besides, Duncan's too much of a purist for me. He and Bea think along the same lines. No coffee, no brandy – and he believes in this water-witching stuff.'

'And you found that all very intriguing, didn't you!' Louise demanded.

'What do you mean?'

'He's a far cry from anyone you might meet at your law firm,' Louise told her, 'a far cry from all your lawyer friends.'

'Yes,' Phoebe admitted.

'And you liked that, didn't you?'

'Yes,' Phoebe admitted.

'Well! There you have it.' Louise sat back smugly. 'I bet you'll miss him more than you think.'

That's all I need, Phoebe thought. 'I won't have time to miss him,' she told her mother. 'Not with my trial.'

'Yes you will; you'll get back there and find yourself with all these other lawyers and there won't be one of them, not *one,* that you'll be interested in and you'll think to yourself, Gee, I had a good thing with Duncan back there in Vermont.'

Phoebe rolled her eyes.

'See? You're already missing him,' Louise said. 'You're just a little scared, though, and so you're pretending not to care. You know I'm right, you should listen to your mother – '

Phoebe held up her hand. 'All right, all right,' she said. 'Maybe I will miss him, but I don't really expect that much is going to come of this. We had one nice night together but three thousand miles is awfully far.'

'He's getting a telephone,' Louise reminded her. 'Bea told me so.'

'It's still awfully far.'

Louise fell silent, then gave a melancholy sigh. 'Of course it is,' she said. 'And I know it was just one night, I know you're going home, I know you won't be back for a while. But you worry me, Phoebe, you really worry me!'

'Why?'

'Because there's more to life than work and Andrew!'

Phoebe began to fume silently. The last thing she wanted from her mother was a speech on the many ways in which a man could solve her problems. It was okay for Phoebe to let herself privately envy Molly for having Nick, it was okay to tangle her life a little for one night with Duncan Crane – but it was *not* okay for her mother to end what had been a wonderful visit with a prescription for a second husband.

'Don't get me wrong,' Louise said. 'I'm not saying a man is going to solve your problems.'

'Thank you,' said Phoebe.

'Don't get testy,' Louise said.

'Who's getting testy?'

'You are,' Louise said, 'because I'm about to give you a lecture. Now where was I?'

'Prince Charming,' Phoebe said. 'You were denying your conviction that he was a panacea.'

'Which he is not,' Louise said emphatically, missing – or ignoring – Phoebe's twist. 'And I am also not telling you to thwart your ambitions – lord, I'm the last one to give you that advice, my generation, Bea and I, we got the raw end of the deal on that note, nobody ever urged us to become lawyers, or doctors – so I want you to be a good lawyer, the best you can, if that's what you want. But not if it means shutting out a Duncan Crane who happens to walk through your door.'

'You seem to be implying that I'm turning them down right and left,' Phoebe said. 'You know, I don't meet a lot of interesting people, you said yourself: the guys in my life are litigators, patent lawyers, tax lawyers – they don't look too good to me, and I'm sure I don't look too good to them.'

'All I'm saying,' Louise said firmly, 'is – let me begin again. I think the only reason you let yourself take off with Duncan last night was because you were on vacation.'

'So what?'

'So I bet if you ran into someone like Duncan back in California you never would have let it happen.'

'That depends,' Phoebe said. 'If he were someone very special I'd let it happen, I probably wouldn't have too much to say in the matter.'

'That's my point,' Louise said. 'Last night, did you think that Duncan was someone very special?'

'No,' said Phoebe. 'I thought he was nice.'

'Exactly,' said Louise. 'And because you were on vacation you were willing to let yourself be a little bit more carefree than you normally would.'

'And you're saying that's good?'

'I'm saying that's good,' said Louise, 'and I'm also saying that you might be a little happier out in California if you let yourself be as carefree back there as you were last night.'

'Lower my standards, then,' Phoebe said.

'Don't lower your standards,' Louise said. 'You just don't have to be such a perfectionist.'

'Obviously I'm not,' Phoebe said, tapping her finger on the table. 'Look at the guy I married.'

'You did what anyone else would have done,' Louise snapped. 'You were in love with Rusty and you married him and it didn't work out and so you got divorced. Don't hold yourself forever responsible for that.'

'I'm not holding myself responsible,' Phoebe said. '*He's* the one who was screwing around. No,' she said, 'all that taught me was that I don't have very good judgement.'

'And so in the meantime you're waiting to meet someone who will knock you off your feet,' Louise said, 'someone whom you will be one hundred per cent sure about from day one, while all the time turning your eyes away from any Duncan Cranes who might walk by, because while they may be nice, and funny, and you may have a good time with them, they're not perfect and therefore not worth your valuable time!'

Phoebe realized she was pursing her lips furiously; she tried to relax, and took a sip of coffee, but her hands were shaking. She had thought she might get a little grief for having stayed out all night – but instead her mother was essentially berating her for not doing this more often. Could she not do anything right these days?

'In Molly's view I'm wasting my life at the law firm,'

she said sarcastically. 'In your view I'm too picky about men. What's Bea's view?' she asked. 'Maybe we can get her input on all of this.'

'That's not fair,' Louise said. 'I'm just telling you this because you're my daughter and I love you.'

'Well, I don't see you following your own advice,' Phoebe returned. 'Daddy's been dead for more than twenty-five years and I don't see too many men in your life. Maybe I get my high standards from you,' she said. 'Maybe I'm just following your example.'

Louise's eyes darkened when she said that, and Phoebe quickly looked away. She'd gone too far, way too far. She'd broken the rules. Never had she brought her father into an argument, at least never with such viciousness.

'I'm sorry,' she said, after a terrible moment. 'I shouldn't have said that.'

'No,' Louise said, drawing herself up, 'you shouldn't have. But since you did let me tell you something.' She paused, fixing her eyes on Phoebe, and when she spoke again her voice had lost its snap. 'There was a man,' she said, 'another man, whom I met several years after your father died. I don't think you would remember him. I liked him. He was fun. He made me laugh. But I didn't love him, not the way I loved your father. And so I let him go.' She paused again. 'Why? Because I thought that to let myself really get involved with another man he would have to make me feel just like your father made me feel, when I was nineteen and young and full of passion and head over heels in love. This man didn't make me feel that way. But you know,' she said, 'I wish – *look* at me, Phoebe! – I wish he were around these days. I wish I'd been more patient to see how things might develop, rather than holding him up to a standard he couldn't ever meet.'

Phoebe sought but could not find any words of comfort;

she wanted to cry but something had plugged her up. Her mother's regrets sat on the table like a broken plate. She recalled an earlier moment during this visit when she had suddenly sensed that her mother was getting old, and now she realized what this meant: that time was running out for both of them: for Louise to have her second chances, for Phoebe to learn from her mother, who knew. And she felt deep within her a mixture of love and terror and hate: love for the woman, terror and hate for the pain her death would cause.

Phoebe closed her eyes. She reached across the table, seeking her mother's hand; when their fingers locked, pressing hard against each other, she felt as though they were two blind people, grieving for light.

Andrew and Dave appeared shortly before lunch, both of them wearing red woollen jackets and the orange John Deere caps. Andrew dropped his jacket on the floor and climbed into Phoebe's lap while Dave waited in the doorway.

'See any beavers this time?' she asked, smoothing out his hair.

'Yeah, it was this big!' He held his arms apart to demonstrate. 'I got sick last night,' he told her.

'I heard,' she said. 'I'm sorry.'

'I threw up ten times,' he said.

Phoebe braced herself for the inevitable question – How come you weren't there? – but Andrew started squirming instead. 'I'm starved,' he said.

'You wait until lunch,' Phoebe said. 'I think Grammy has some soup for us.'

'Ick,' said Andrew.

'Don't say ick,' Phoebe said. 'You'll hurt Grammy's feelings. Thanks for taking him down to the pond,' she told Dave.

'Glad to do it,' Dave said. 'I have to admit, I'm going to miss the little fella. I'll take care of him tonight, if you want to spend a little more time with your new boyfriend before you have to leave,' he offered, winking.

Phoebe set Andrew down. Last night she had found herself wishing she'd taken Duncan up on his invitation earlier in her visit; but now she was grateful for the fact that she only had to endure one day of everybody's nosiness. Maybe Duncan liked living in a fishbowl; she didn't.

'Thank you,' she said, with as much politeness as she could muster. 'But I'll be around tonight. I've got a lot to do here.'

'Did you get him to demonstrate his dowsing rods?' Dave asked. 'Did you get him to find a new well on the Caleb property?'

Phoebe stiffened.

'The guys's a nut for that stuff,' Dave told her. 'Sometimes I think he's got a few screws loose up here.' He twirled his finger at his temple.

'I don't think you should jump to conclusions,' Phoebe said. 'Maybe he's on to something that you and I don't know about.' I *did* sleep well, she thought. And I *have* been having stomach problems.

'Bah,' said Dave. 'How's his sauna working, anyway?'

'Fine.' Phoebe wondered if Dave planned to ask how Duncan had performed in bed; and she imagined giving him an answer that would keep him quiet for the next five years.

But Dave didn't ask that; instead he set about to give Phoebe yet another piece of advice. 'I bet you're worried about how it's going to work out, three thousand miles apart,' he said.

Phoebe stared in astonishment. 'Not really!'

'Let me tell you how Bea and I handled it,' Dave went

on, as though he hadn't heard. 'I was in the service, of course, and she was back here, and we wrote each other these letters that would have burned the eyeballs off the US Postal Service, you know what I mean?'

Phoebe was speechless.

'So what I'm saying is, keep the smooching going through the mails,' he said. 'You wouldn't believe the spice you can write.'

Phoebe looked to her mother for help; but Louise just returned a smug smile. Phoebe turned back to Dave. 'Things are kind of up in the air,' she said.

'They won't be, after a couple of months of letters,' Dave said, winking again. 'If you ask me, Phoebe, he's a pretty good catch,' he said. 'Even if he's got a few screws loose he'd be something to brag about back in San Francisco. Especially since as I understand the situation there aren't a whole lot of guys available to a girl like you since they're all busy dating each other, if you know what I mean.'

'Whatever,' Phoebe said. 'Like I said, things are up in the air. Isn't lunch ready, Mum?'

'Would you like to stay?' Louise asked Dave, ignoring Phoebe's look of betrayal.

'Unfortunately I have to get back, we're taking Bea's parents out for Sunday dinner,' he said. 'Hey, sport, I guess this is good-bye,' he said to Andrew. 'See you tomorrow.'

'See you tomorrow,' Andrew said.

'I have this thing about saying good-bye,' Dave explained to Phoebe. 'It's too final, you know?'

'I know,' Phoebe said.

'It just makes it easier if you keep the pretences up,' Dave said.

'I see,' Phoebe said.

'Well,' and Dave tugged his hat down over his forehead, 'see *you* tomorrow. And remember what I said about those love letters.'

'What'd you guys do this morning,' Phoebe asked her mother, when Dave had left. 'Sit around making bets on which one of us was going to switch coasts?'

Louise lifted her chin as she set out place mats, soup bowls, the jar of peanut butter. 'It wasn't my idea,' she said haughtily. 'It was Dave's. And don't think I put my money where my heart was wanting it to go,' she added. 'Between East and West don't think I don't know which coast would win out.'

That afternoon Phoebe went about the house, listlessly gathering together a sweater here, a toy there, in an effort to get their suitcases packed by evening. Her mother's words to her that morning had flattened her spirit, in a way; not that she was dwelling on thoughts of Duncan, but her vulnerability seemed to have arrived a little ahead of schedule; and she no longer felt that sense of power she had felt earlier that day. She found herself composing silly scripts in which Duncan would show up to drive them to the airport tomorrow; or in which, upon unlocking the door to her apartment, the phone would be ringing, and it would be Duncan, calling her from the pay phone outside the Poultneys' store. She even imagined a dozen red roses arriving at the law firm, with all the secretaries squealing and cooing and demanding a description.

And you have the nerve to get on your mother's case? she scolded herself. You might as well be placing bets yourself: who will be the first to write, how long before he gets a phone installed.

Phoebe crammed a folder of unread memos into her briefcase. It astonished her how much work she thought she would get done back here; and there was a sense of satisfaction in knowing it had gone untouched. In fact one thing she felt quite proud about was that during this second week of the vacation she had, apart from griping to Nick and Duncan, pretty much succeeded at putting aside all thoughts of her job, of Herb, of the upcoming trial. Not once had she lain in bed fretting about the state of the documents; not once had she awakened with a knot in her stomach, worrying about upcoming depositions. The little flame she had described to Nick had stayed low; and she could honestly say that she had had herself a vacation.

But as she tugged at the zipper on her briefcase the little flame began to flare up. She thought of John Dunn patronizing her with his system for organizing documents. She thought of Herb lecturing her for misplacing the mismanagement memo, informing her that this little incident would undoubtedly resurface in her annual review. Then she thought about Christmas, and how in their condo at the base of the mountain Rusty and Shirley and Andrew would be zipping up in their carefully selected bursts of colour – red, yellow, royal-blue – and by now the furnace within her was going full force.

Phoebe took a break from packing; she went downstairs and started to pour herself an early glass of wine, then remembered Mrs Cutter's warning, and had a glass of milk.

How are you going to handle it when you get back? she asked herself. What are you going to do when you walk through the doors of the Barracks and there's Herb waiting to scream at you and there's John Dunn looking so cocky and there's Janice, dead with apathy as she draws up another will?

Phoebe didn't know; but she somehow sensed that it was going to be easier. He doesn't own you, Duncan had said of Herb last night; and she realized how different the next six months would be if she could approach her job from that perspective. Well, why not? It is true, he doesn't own you, he doesn't have a claim on your life; all he has is a right to your billable hours. And if you can keep that in mind it will change the way you deal with Herb, it will change the way you deal with John Dunn, it will change the way you make it through the upcoming trial, with its guaranteed all-nighters, its guaranteed theft of your weekends and holidays. And after the trial? After the trial you leave.

Phoebe took comfort in this approach; it was as though the nature of the flame within her had changed from a dull orange to hot white, as though it were fuelled now not by a few old newspapers but rather by a precious elemental gas. Of course, she still wasn't sure where she would go after leaving, what kind of a job change she would make. But whatever it was, it wouldn't be litigation. Maybe it meant going with a smaller firm, or setting up practice on her own; maybe it meant taking a step down in the eyes of all the John Dunns and becoming corporate counsel somewhere. It didn't matter, though. Things would fall into place.

It was later that night, while towel-drying her hair, that Phoebe noticed her gold hoops were missing. She paused, frowned into the mirror, and then she remembered that she had left them on the bench in Duncan's sauna.

Phoebe felt a stone drop in her stomach. The earrings had been a Mother's Day gift from Andrew – his first, her first, picked out by Rusty four years ago. Though Andrew had no recollection of the purchase itself – he'd been sleeping in the carrier on Rusty's back – he loved being reminded that he had given them to her, and since Phoebe wore them frequently he seemed to have grasped the pleasure of giving a cherished gift. And now they were gone.

Phoebe wanted to cry. She felt that an ugly punishment was, in the end, being meted out, that some puritanical spirit far far removed from the jocular bets of her mother and Bea and Dave was getting in the last word for her sins of the night. Why hadn't she remembered the earrings? And how could Duncan have done this to her, holding them as some kind of bait to get her back to his cabin in the pines? How childish of him! She would have to write and tell him to send them back. He wouldn't like it, he would think she had no sense of romance, no sense of humour – but for Pete's sake, Phoebe wanted to cry out to him: those earrings don't belong to your heart, they belong to Andrew's!

That evening she scribbled a quick note, trying to keep her anger in check but none the less making it clear that he had to send them back. Just writing the letter put her mind at rest, and she slept well that night. But later that next week, when a small brown packet would arrive at her house in Berkeley express mail, with no note, no return address, Phoebe wouldn't end up feeling quite as much at peace about the matter as she had assumed. In fact it would turn out to be quite the opposite. Holding the earrings in the palm of her hand, she would feel undone, as though a link had just been cut; and contrary to expectation she would find herself wishing that Duncan had ignored her note, and kept those hoops of gold waiting for her on his windowsill.

# 19

Phoebe stepped off the lift on the thirty-third floor, cheerfully greeted the receptionist, and strode through the heavy double doors into the Barracks. There was Janice, standing by the coffee machine, waiting for the pot to finish brewing. Phoebe walked up behind her, set down her briefcase, and tapped her on the shoulder. 'Hello there.'

Janice turned and gave a shriek, nearly knocking her mug off the table as she threw her arms around Phoebe and hugged her tightly. 'This is very unlawyerly,' she cried, drawing back, then hugging her again, 'but Jesus, it's good to have you back!'

Phoebe laughed, and tousled Janice's hair. 'It's good to *be* back,' she said. 'Hi, Linda,' she called out to her secretary. 'Hi, Stella, hi, Maureen.'

'Welcome back, have a doughnut,' Maureen said, offering her a Winchell's box. 'I won the football pool this week, so it was my turn to buy.'

'How was your trip?' Linda asked. 'How was the wedding?'

'Oh, fine, fine,' Phoebe said. 'Hi, Laura.' She waved to the fourth secretary in the pool. 'You got a perm, it looks great.'

'Tell her the news, Laura,' said Maureen.

'*Big* development while you were gone,' said Linda, nodding.

'Tell her, Laura,' said Stella. 'Don't keep her in the dark!'

Laura smiled. 'I'm pregnant.'

'You are? That's wonderful!' Phoebe exclaimed. Laura was thirty-eight, and unattached; in the past she had made it no secret that she was looking for someone to father a child for her – with no strings, of course, she would always emphasize.

'Come on,' said Janice, 'get another doughnut and pour yourself some coffee and come into my office, I want to hear all about your trip. What are you doing for lunch? I thought we could go to the baths – I haven't been since you left – '

'Well well well, look who's back.'

Phoebe glanced up from the cup of coffee she was stirring; John Dunn, his tie loose, his shirt-sleeves rolled up, had just handed Laura a handful of yellow pages. Purplish half-moons drooped under his eyes, and his forehead had broken out in adolescent pustules.

'Hi, John,' Phoebe said. 'Actually I was just about to come down and find out what was happening with Parco-Fields.'

'You don't want to know,' John said, and before Phoebe could answer he turned to Laura. 'These are the inserts that go into the insert on page 4-b. Then take out the old section two and move up section five to before section three and after section four, which you should already have moved to section one. Okay?'

Laura sighed.

'THIS ISN'T FUNNY, LAURA, THIS THING HAS TO BE FILED TODAY!' John screamed.

'Yes, John,' said Laura, clipping his yellow pages together and lifting herself from her chair. 'I'll be down at the WANG if you need me.'

John screwed up his face and rubbed the back of his neck.

'What are you filing?' Phoebe asked him.

'I am filing,' John said, 'a motion to compel the

production of certain additional documents that we have just discovered our dear plaintiff still insists on holding back.'

'John's been working his ass off,' Janice explained. 'Herb's had him here for – how many, John? How many all-nighters have you pulled in the last week?'

John glared at Janice.

'Lots,' she told Phoebe 'Be nice to him; Herb threw a tantrum yesterday because the motion didn't have a section on some case – '

'*Rowan*,' said John. 'And *Rowan*'s not even on point in this situation.'

'But you know how Herb is,' Janice said.

Phoebe gave John a sympathetic look. Nut though he was, she felt sorry for him right now, she really did. 'Can I help?'

'I want you to get me off this case,' John said. 'If I have to deal with Herb Sullivan every fucking day for the next six months I quit.'

'Oh, now, come on,' Phoebe said, 'it's not going to be that bad. Show me what you have so far and then go get yourself some breakfast. Soon as you eat something you'll feel better. Take a nap too – you look like you need some sleep.'

'Sleep?' said John sullenly. 'What's that?'

Phoebe looked at Janice, then back at John. 'Really, go get some food and rest. Now: it has to be filed today?'

John nodded glumly.

'Okay, we have until four-thirty, five if we get really desperate,' Phoebe said. 'Are there any exhibits?'

'The exhibits are all ready,' John said. 'Eddie's in charge of exhibits.'

'Eddie's been wonderful,' Janice told Phoebe. 'He stayed here three nights in a row digesting Schein's deposition so that John could prepare for the next round. Eddie's gold.'

'Eddie's about to become an honorary member of the goddam bar,' John said.

'Go on,' Phoebe said, handing him his jacket. 'I'll take care of things; you go get a good meal.'

'What if Herb comes looking for me?' John said. 'What's my excuse?'

'Vital functions,' Phoebe said, giving him a push. 'Now *go*.'

Thus Phoebe spent her first day back, not organizing her office, not going through her mail, not going to the baths with Janice and telling her about Duncan Crane's sauna, but rather hurriedly proofing pages as they spat out of the printer and reassuring John that they would indeed make the deadline. And they did; at four-fifteen Herb scrawled his signature on the last page ('I want a word with you when you get back,' he told her, capping his pen); at four-twenty Phoebe hailed a cab to the courthouse, and at four-twenty-nine she hand-delivered their motion to the clerk, who stamped the magical date on the front page.

'Just tell me, yes or no,' said John when she got back.

'Yes,' Phoebe said.

John closed his eyes.

'John,' Phoebe said, 'I told you we'd make it – you shouldn't let yourself get so worked up over these matters.'

John glared at her. 'Easy for you to say, all mellowed out after a two-week vacation in Vermont. How many hours of sleep did you get back there, all totalled? One hundred? Two hundred?'

Phoebe didn't answer. What could she say? How could she begin to explain that if things weren't getting to her like they used to, it had nothing to do with the amount of sleep she had been able to catch up on?

Just then her buzzer sounded. It was Linda. 'Herb left a message for you,' she told Phoebe. 'He's tied up the rest of the afternoon but he wants to see you first thing tomorrow.'

'Thanks.' Phoebe hung up. She wished she could say something to John that would erase the frown lines from his brow.

'I can just see it,' John went on, 'waking up to the smell of bacon, frost on the mountaintops, clean fresh air – I wish *my* best friend had decided to get married back in Vermont two weeks ago; then I wouldn't have been around for Herb to draft me, I'd have been in some log cabin popping open a bottle of champagne.'

'Well, if it'll cheer you up I wasn't drinking a lot of champagne while I was back there,' she told him. 'It was more like Gallo Chablis.'

'Chablis,' John said, and his eyes began to glaze over. 'Pouilly-Fuissé, Chassagne Montrachet – did I ever tell you about my trip to Burgundy after the bar exam? Did I ever tell you about some of the wines I got to taste? Wow. Nothing to do all day but eat and drink and sleep – '

'John.'

John let himself slump into a chair. 'Did you ever feel like murdering someone?' he asked her. 'You know, I could murder Herb just like that. I really could. I wouldn't think twice, I could do it in cold blood.'

'Take it easy, John,' Phoebe said. 'Remember, you've got a lot of friends when it comes to dealing with Herb. Probably ninety per cent of the firm feels the same way as you do.'

'Yeah, but ninety per cent of the firm doesn't have to work for him.'

'Well, *I* do, so you've got a friend right here,' Phoebe said. She surprised herself by saying that, but she realized that working with John wasn't going to be anything like she had anticipated. 'Look, if it makes you feel any better, I've got to go down first thing tomorrow and get chewed out for losing that document. How pissed was he, anyway?'

John was staring at her telephone – still dreaming about Burgundy, Phoebe imagined.

'Like how hard is he going to come down on me?' Phoebe asked. 'I just want to be prepared.'

'John?' she said when he didn't reply.

John blinked, and looked at her. 'Huh?'

'Like how upset was Herb about that Schein memo?'

'What Schein memo?'

'The one I lost,' Phoebe said.

John frowned.

'Remember? The one about mismanagement?'

John shook his head blankly.

Phoebe began to wonder if she had dreamed the incident. 'Don't you remember, when Herb put you on the case he gave you a stack of documents to read for Schein's deposition and one of them, the one that dealt with mismanagement, I had lost? Remember? And Herb had had to go and find it himself?'

'Oh, right,' said John. 'Was that just a week ago? God, it seems like all that happened a year ago.'

'Well?' Phoebe said. 'How mad is Herb?'

John shrugged. 'I don't know, I think he's forgotten about it by now.'

'I doubt that,' Phoebe said.

'You never know,' John said sullenly. 'Every day he's got something new to be pissed off about. He wakes up and says, Oh boy, a new day, who can I jump on today?'

'I doubt he's forgotten about the memo,' Phoebe said. 'In any event I'll find out tomorrow morning.'

John yawned.

'Tell you what,' Phoebe said. 'We got everyone served, right?'

John nodded.

'Well, look, Herb's tied up with something else, he's not going to come prowling around – why don't you take off? It's almost six anyway, that's not a totally unreasonable hour to be leaving – go home and get a good night's sleep; I'll wrap up loose ends, what do you say?'

'Six? Hey, the night is young, I'm just getting cranked up,' John said. 'Oh, all right, I'll take you up on your offer.'

'And here,' Phoebe said. 'Take this home for dessert.' From her bag she took out a maple-sugar man, lying in state in its souvenir box. John held it in his hand and gave a weak smile. 'Forget dessert,' he said. 'This'll be my dinner, I'm out of Stouffer's.'

Phoebe didn't stay too late that night herself; after John left she brought the stamped copy of the pleading down to Eddie for him to file, then superficially tidied up her office. At seven o'clock she switched off her light, left the firm, and drove back across the Bay Bridge to Berkeley, changing lanes by rote to end up on the right freeway. Landmarks seemed both familiar and foreign to her: the sculptures in the tidal flats, for instance, seemed to have reproduced themselves while she'd been in Vermont; their scrappy shapes of wood and iron stretched on and on, silhouetted against the city skyline like lost toys. She exited the freeway and drove up Solano Avenue, then up the steep hill, up and up and up to where she veered her car into the driveway and shut off the ignition.

Andrew was with Rusty tonight; her apartment still held a close musty odour from an absence of people coming in, going out, coming in again. She kicked off her heels and stripped out of her suit, rolled off her pantyhose, and pulled on a pair of sweats; then poured herself a glass of wine and went out on to the balcony. Far away a foghorn hummed its deep sigh, and beyond the Golden Gate Bridge the lights of a freighter inched through the darkness.

It was good to be back.

Not that she wasn't well aware that the next six months were going to be brutal. She couldn't help but be aware of that, just by watching John today – why, in ten days he seemed to have undergone a complete transformation. In fact, if she thought it mattered, she might even have reclassified him as a Bolt, the way he'd been talking. Was working for Herb really that bad?

Oh, yes.

Phoebe straightened up and took a deep breath, already anticipating the reprimand she would receive tomorrow morning. That's okay, she told herself; you actually deserve a reprimand; you shouldn't have lost that document. Even if he goes overboard and rakes you over the coals, don't let it get to you. Phoebe felt once again that hot white anger steadily burning deep within her and reminded herself that things were different now. Remember what Duncan said? He doesn't own you. And if he doesn't own you, she thought, then he can't hurt you.

Herb rocked back in his stately leather chair, clasping the back of his neck with one hand and holding the phone to his ear with the other. When he saw Phoebe in the doorway he nodded and pointed to a chair in front of his desk, and continued with his conversation.

Phoebe sat down and crossed her legs, positioning a yellow pad on her lap. Herb seemed to stare through her as he talked, and she averted her gaze. His corner office looked out over the Bay, but the view was obscured by fog this morning; the Transamerica tower several blocks away was barely visible. On the wall opposite his desk was a collage of black-and-white portraits: Herb's children, she supposed, two girls, preschoolers, wide eyed and toothy, with wind-whipped hair. Phoebe didn't recall having noticed these photographs before, and she thought back to Duncan, prodding about Herb's soft spots. Perhaps this was evidence, and she wondered how long ago the photographs had been taken. Were these the faces that waited for Herb every evening as he commuted back to Marin in his Porsche? Or were his girls older now, Valley Girls, with posters of Michael Jackson over their beds? And what about photos of his wife? Where were they?

'Give us Peterson on the fifth,' Herb was saying, 'and we'll give you Bunker next week.'

So he was talking about deposition schedules. He would hang up and maybe before reprimanding her for losing the document he would assign her to one or the other; he would remined her of the various issues to be covered, the type of testimony they would be looking for. She would nod and make a few suggestions herself; she would laugh at any jokes that he might make. But as she waited for him to finish his conversation she found herself imagining how different her life would be if instead of scheduling depositions Herb were to be negotiating a settlement right now. What if he were to hang up and hold out his palms and say: Whelhp – that's that. No more Parco-Fields. She would be able to go to the baths with Janice that day; she would get home by seven, maybe even six-thirty. Her entire game-plan could change: she could call a headhunter this afternoon, mail out her résumé tomorrow without the burden of pulling a Grossman. She could even work it that she would start a new job after January first, and take a vacation at

Christmastime – maybe get her own condo at Vail, so that she could spend part of Christmas Day with Andrew. Maybe they could even have Christmas dinner all together, Rusty and Shirley and Andrew and herself. Certainly at the very least she could devote the next month to Christmas shopping: finding something very special for Andrew, getting her Vermont presents mailed out on time, for once.

But a negotiated settlement was about as farfetched as the idea of eating a pleasant Christmas dinner with Rusty and Shirley. 'We're going to litigate this case to the eyeballs!' Herb had once said; 'We're gonna be going round the clock, guys!' And so it would be for the next six, eight, ten months of her life.

'Welcome back.' Herb hung up the phone and leaned forward in his chair. 'How was your trip?'

Phoebe smiled politely. 'Fine.'

'Vermont, right?'

Phoebe nodded.

'Nice place,' Herb mused. 'I went to college in Vermont, did you know that?'

'No,' Phoebe said.

Herb nodded. 'Middlebury,' he said. 'Pretty in the autumn, but the winters were a son of a bitch. Don't ask me how anyone lives there.' He looked out of the window and flipped a pencil around and around on his blotter. Phoebe waited.

'How did Schein go?' she finally asked. She might as well bring up the subject; Herb was going to get around to it himself anyway.

But Herb didn't start reprimanding her for the document, as she had expected; he just rolled his eyes and shook his head. 'Gave us the usual runaround,' he said. 'We'll have to do him again after he gets back from

Tahiti. Jesus,' he said, 'everyone's going on vacation except me.'

Phoebe glanced at her pad. She had doodled a succession of fireworks across the top of the page.

'Well, maybe next summer,' Herb said. 'Ever been to Japan?'

'No.'

'I'm thinking of taking the kids over there,' he said. 'Strikes me as an educational venture, wouldn't you say?'

Phoebe nodded.

'Though I hate raw fish,' Herb said. 'I hope that's not all they serve.'

Phoebe waited. Why had he called her down to his office, anyway? To talk about Vermont? His kids? To gripe about the lost vacation opportunities? Maybe it was a ruse to get her to open up and confess to him how frustrated she was with the firm, with litigation. Maybe he was baiting her, to see how committed an attorney she really was.

She flipped the top page over to a fresh one, wrote the numeral 1 and retraced it, over and over, waiting.

'Well, back to business,' Herb finally said. 'You're going to Houston next week.'

Phoebe blinked.

'You and McManus,' Herb said, referring to a junior partner on the case. 'We've got depositions to defend.'

Houston? Next week?

Herb shrugged. 'Don't jump for joy,' he said. 'Somebody's got to stand up for Bunker and Lowe. Look, it could be worse, I could have sent you to Detroit,' he said. 'Would you rather go to Detroit? I was going to send John Dunn, but if you want Detroit it's okay with me. You want Detroit?'

Phoebe shook her head. Her ears were ringing.

'How long will I be gone for?' she finally asked.

Herb shrugged. 'Depends,' he said. 'Maybe two days, maybe two weeks. You'll have to allow for some prep time too. Talk to McManus, he'll brief you.'

Phoebe realized she was losing control inside; it was as though somebody had poured petrol on to her quiet white fire of confidence. She slipped her bag over her shoulder and stood up.

'And by the way, Phoebe,' Herb said with a wry smile. 'Try and keep the documents together this time, huh?'

Phoebe nodded.

'Okay then,' he said. He picked up his phone and buzzed his secretary, swivelling around to face the window.

'What's the problem?' asked the managing partner, a short pudgy man with too serene a look on his face for Judson and Day. 'I thought all bright young associates like yourself were chomping at the bit to get some litigation experience.'

'I have a son,' Phoebe said, her voice trembling, 'a four-year-old son, and I can't be hopping on a plane to Houston for two weeks on the spur of the moment.'

The managing partner frowned. 'Well, Phoebe, you must have had some idea of what the job would entail when we originally assigned you to our litigation section. Didn't you?'

'Yes,' Phoebe said.

'Then you can't let us down now by asking to be taken off the case just like that,' he said, and snapped his fingers. 'Parco-Fields is big stuff; you've been working on it for – how many, three? – three years, and the trial's coming up next spring. We can't let you off; you're an indispensable member of the team.'

Bullshit.

'Look,' he said, 'I'm sorry, I know it's rough on your

family life, but it's rough on everyone's family life. That's the way litigation is. But I personally would consider it an honour to be in your shoes.'

It was useless. Nothing she could say was going to change his attitude. Come what may, she was going to be checking into a hotel in downtown Houston next week (*was* there a downtown Houston?) with a dolly full of document bags.

The managing partner swallowed the rest of his Coke. 'Now if,' he said, 'when this is all over with, you decide that litigation is not the field for you, then come see me again.' He squeezed the can, crumpling it in the middle. 'But you can't jump ship like this in the middle of the storm.'

'Tear it up,' Janice said. 'Right now, before anyone else sees it.'

Phoebe folded her letter of resignation in thirds and slipped it into a crisp white envelope. She was still shaking. She sealed the envelope and placed it with care in the centre of her blotter.

'Phoebe, you have to cool off,' Janice said. 'It's ten o'clock. You got the news half an hour ago. Sit on it until after lunch, at least.'

Phoebe shook her head. She couldn't talk. The fire within her was raging out of control now, thick clouds of black industrial smoke billowing up before her eyes.

'It's really not all that bad,' Janice said. 'I mean, Houston's not so great but Detroit's worse, and it's only for two weeks at most – Rusty can take Andrew, can't he?'

Phoebe levelled a look of hate at Janice.

'Okay, okay,' said Janice. 'But just wait until after lunch. Come on, we'll go to the baths and you can make sure this is what you really want to do, what do you say?'

Phoebe picked up the envelope and tapped its edge against the blotter. Then suddenly she crumpled it in her hand and slammed her fist against the wall. 'Houston!' she cried. 'On one week's notice!'

Janice stood back.

'I could be down there for two fucking weeks, three, four!' she cried. 'And then where are they going to send me? Cleveland? Pittsburgh? Cairo? And this is going to go on for the next six months? I CAN'T TAKE IT!' Her eyes filled with tears, and she dropped her head down into the crook of her elbow, on her desktop. 'I can't take it, I can't take it,' she kept crying, over and over. 'I thought I had a handle on it, after being back in Vermont; I thought I could stick it out, I thought it wouldn't get to me but I was wrong,' she sobbed. 'I was wrong, wrong, wrong.'

Janice edged behind her desk and gently laid a hand on her shoulder as she continued to sob. 'I thought I could get through just by knowing that when it was all over I'd change jobs,' she said, weeping. 'Knowing that I'd find something that would give me more time for Andrew, more time for myself. I thought I could get through just by knowing that Herb doesn't own me. But he *does* own me. No matter what I do he owns me! God; how could I have thought I'd be immune from him?'

Janice didn't say anything; after a while Phoebe picked up her head and took the Kleenex that her friend was holding for her. She blew her nose and wiped at her eyes, and swivelled around to face her window in case anyone walked in. Across the street, construction workers sat on a steel beam, thirty-three storeys above Market Street, drinking coffee.

'And yet it's not just Herb,' she said miserably. 'It's everything about this kind of work. Everybody talks about litigation as though it's the chance of a lifetime, the only worthwhile thing for us lawyers to do. Litigate to the eyeballs, guys – we're going round the clock!' Phoebe gave a bitter laugh. 'Hah. What's so great about hitting the road for six months, defending depositions in Houston one week, Detroit the next? What's so great about pulling all-nighters until you're ready to drop? What's so great about working every weekend for the rest of your life?'

Just then her buzzer sounded; it was John Dunn, and Phoebe cut him off. 'I'm tied up right now,' she told him. 'I'll buzz you back in a few minutes.' As she hung up she happened to glance at a snapshot of Andrew propped against her Dictaphone. It was a recent picture, taken this past summer, and she thought once again of the collage of photos on Herb's wall, those toothy grins, those dancing eyes; and of Herb's plans to take his children to Japan next summer. Would he ever make the trip? Possibly; but would he know the little girls whose hands he held as they stepped off the plane?

'And it sucks for everyone, you know,' she said. 'It might be different if you could make it to Herb's position and then sit back and contemplate how you're going to enjoy your millions. But it doesn't even work that way: you make it to where Herb is and you're still busting ass, still coming in on weekends – maybe not like the grunts, but it's no holiday. Do you know what Herb said to me in his office this morning?'

Janice waited.

'He said, "Everybody's going on vacation except me,"' Phoebe said. 'He knows what a mess his life is. He's got two little girls and do you think he gets to spend more than five minutes a day with them?'

'Do you think he cares?'

Phoebe reached for another Kleenex.

'This is Herb Sullivan we're talking about,' Janice reminded her. 'The guy who you once said had had an emotional lobotomy?'

Phoebe sighed. 'Well, it would probably take twenty years of analysis for him to realize how much he cares,' she said. 'But he does care. Down deep.'

For a while Janice didn't say anything; then she reached for the crumpled envelope. 'So can I have this?'

Phoebe looked at the envelope sadly. Whatever she'd said in the letter, it would have to wait. There was something impotent about resigning in a burst of rage, something that would make her look both vulnerable and silly. It would be Herb's victory, not hers.

And thus she knew that she would stick it out. Realizing that, she thought she might feel a bit of satisfaction, for not giving Herb that victory; but she didn't feel any satisfaction; instead she felt that no matter what she did, or thought, or felt, Herb would always be the victor, the winner of an ongoing game of goose.

'Take it,' she said to Janice. 'Just don't throw it away here; you never know who might go through the rubbish.'

'I'll take it home,' Janice said. 'I'll keep it in my top drawer – it might make things more palatable for you, just knowing it's there.'

Phoebe smiled, a tired, comfortless, worn-out smile. 'Maybe,' she said. But she doubted it.

That evening she stopped at Rusty's to pick Andrew up. Shirley had just taken him out for ice cream, however, and while she waited for them to return she told Rusty the news about Houston.

'Well, at least you don't have to worry about Andrew,' Rusty said. 'I can take care of him for as long as you have to be down there.'

'That's not the point,' Phoebe said. 'What kills me is having to just up and leave like this. I'm a *mother*, not just a lawyer; I can't do this!'

'So quit.'

Phoebe gave him a weary smile. What if Rusty had been in her office earlier that day, instead of Janice?

'I can't quit,' she told him. 'Not now.'

'Yeah, maybe you're right,' Rusty said. 'But God, that's mature of you. How was your trip, anyway?' he asked. 'Was it good to see Molly?'

Phoebe looked at him; for a brief second it was Nick standing there in his flannel shirt with its bleach spots and his hiking boots all covered with wood chips, and he was asking her if she had any new thoughts on the way things were with Molly, now that she was back in California. Then it was not Nick but Duncan beside her in the grade-school cafeteria, recasting everything that had happened with Molly in his slapstick light. She almost started to tell all that she knew, but then the vision snapped, and it was her ex-husband in front of her, his collar open, his tie draped around his neck as he uncorked a bottle of wine. There were only so many things that she and Rusty could talk about, and Molly was not one of them.

And so she merely said, 'Yes, it was good to see her.'

'That's nice,' Rusty said. 'You want a glass of wine while we're waiting?'

Phoebe shook her head. 'I've got pockets under my eyes,' she told him. 'See?'

'Huh?'

'Here,' she said. 'I have to drink more milk and less wine.'

Rusty gave her a queer look as he poured red wine into a glass.

'Rusty,' she said, 'why does it get to me so much? You're a public defender, you litigate, you seem to do all right – what's wrong with me?'

'Nothing's wrong with you,' Rusty said. He swirled the wine around in his glass and breathed in the aroma. 'Look, don't think it's a snap for me,' he said. 'I pull enough all-nighters too – I just pull them here at the kitchen table rather than on the thirty-third floor of a downtown high-rise.'

'Then why doesn't it get to you?'

'I'm not working for a guy like Herb,' Rusty said. 'And besides, it does get to me, only in different ways. How do you think it feels to stay up all night helping some rapist stay out of jail only to find out the next week he's gone and done it again?'

'So what else would you do?' Phoebe asked him. 'Go work for a firm? A corporation?'

'I don't know the answer to that,' Rusty said. 'I haven't thought that far ahead. But it'd sure be nice to have a sunny office,' he said, 'with new furniture, and new carpeting. Or a secretary, all to myself,' he mused. 'Imagine that.'

Later that night, while putting Andrew to bed, she told him that she had to go away on a business trip. 'Just for a couple of days,' she promised him, hoping it would be true. 'And I'll call you every night.'

'What about me?' he said.

'You'll stay with Daddy,' she said. 'Daddy'll make you banana pancakes, I bet.'

Andrew said nothing, and Phoebe feared he was going to become sullen and withdrawn over the thought of her absence. She wondered if there would be any way to explain to him: depositions in Houston, pretrial preparation, Herb. It'll change, she wanted to reassure him. It won't always be this way. And we *will* take that trip to Disneyland next summer.

But Andrew had rolled over and raised his head on his elbow in what struck Phoebe as an alarmingly adult manner.

'Know what?'

'What?'

'Know who I miss?'

'No,' she said. 'Who?'

'That man,' he said.

Phoebe frowned.

'You know, that man in the garden with the orange hat who bought me all the candy,' he said. 'Hey – did you remember to bring my hat back?'

'What hat?'

'The one he *gave* me, Mum,' he said. 'Did you forget it?'

'I'll have Grammy send it,' she said quickly. 'You'll have it by next week.'

Andrew lay back and stared at the ceiling for a moment, then rose up on his elbow again.

'You know that fat lady?'

'Aunt Cindy Ann,' Phoebe said. 'Not "that fat lady."'

'But she is fat,' Andrew said.

'That doesn't matter,' Phoebe said. 'What about Aunt Cindy Ann?'

'You know what she did?'

'What's that?'

'She made a monkey face and picked bugs out of my ear and ate them.'

Phoebe pictured Cindy Ann going through her theatrical antics with Andrew, and tried to imagine her sister-in-law with a child of her own.

'She's pretty dumb, isn't she,' Andrew said.

'No, Andrew, she's not dumb,' Phoebe said. 'She's just trying.'

Andrew lay back down and squinted one eye shut. 'Bet I can sleep like this, Mum,' he said. 'Think I can?'

Phoebe leaned over and kissed his forehead. 'Maybe,' she said. 'You try, and then tomorrow morning you can tell me what you saw during the night.' Andrew fell silent, and levelled his one-eyed gaze towards the foot of his bed.

Oh, my son, she thought, my Little Two Eyes: what do you see with your one eye open and your one eye shut? What does it mean to you that I will go to Houston next week, that you'll be shuttled off to your father's?

And what will all of this mean to you, years from now? How long will it take for you to forgive me?

Perhaps because she had resigned herself to getting through the next six months; perhaps because of a need to reestablish credibility after the document mishap – but whatever the reason, Phoebe's efficiency over the next several days surprised not only John, Eddie, and Pete McManus (who had been forewarned of Phoebe's propensity for losing documents), but also herself. She organized her office; she prioritized stacks of reading material, and made it through the first two tiers; she consulted with John over the remaining issues to be covered during the second Schein deposition. ('You go,' said Phoebe. 'No, *you* go,' said John, 'I went to the first one.' 'Which is exactly why you should go to the second one,' said Phoebe. 'Oh, *fuck*,' said John, 'why do I always end up with the raw end of the deal these days!') On Thanksgiving Day – Rusty had Andrew – she sat out on her balcony, sunning herself as she read through depositions, took notes, reviewed files; and late in the afternoon she drove over to the City to meet Janice and Stu, and the three of them went out to an Italian restaurant, where Phoebe, feeling deprived after two weeks of Vermont cooking, ordered two courses of pasta and a side dish of gnocchi. 'It's Thanksgiving,' she said, shrugging when the waiter frowned.

In fact, she felt so far along with her work that when Janice half-jokingly suggested on Friday morning that they go to the baths that afternoon while the rest of the firm (or rather, most of it) gathered in the conference room for the TG party, Phoebe thought it was a wonderful idea. 'For all I know it may be my last chance until after the trial,' she told Janice. 'Why not?'

As they were leaving, John Dunn came out to refill his coffee mug. 'A Parco-Fields associate has time for the TG party?' he asked, pouring sugar.

Phoebe looked at Janice, and Janice looked at Phoebe.

'Actually, we're not going to the TG party,' Phoebe said.

'Then where are you going?'

'To the baths,' Janice said.

'A Parco-Fields associate has time for the *baths*?'

'It's my lunch break,' Phoebe said.

'So what?' John said. 'Who gets lunch breaks these days?'

Phoebe looked at Janice again; she wanted to get out of the office before Herb happened to come looking for her.

'Oh, all right, I'll lay off,' John said. 'But tell me: what do you guys do at the baths, anyway? Sounds rather kinky to me.'

'We talk girl-talk,' Phoebe said. 'We yak it up in the tub.'

'You might consider it yourself,' Janice said. 'Maybe Eddie would like to go to the baths.'

'No thank you,' John said, drawing up his shoulders. 'One thing I am *not* interested in is going to the baths with Eddie.'

'Well,' said Phoebe, 'see you later.'

'You'll be back?' said John.

'Of course I'll be back,' Phoebe replied. 'It's Friday night, what else would I be doing on a Friday night?'

Because they were short for time, they took a cab, and

even then they almost missed their reservation. The front lounge was heady with dampness, and the attendant took their money and handed them their towels as though annoyed by their patronage. The walked down the mirrored hallway to the staccato beat of New Wave – Phoebe couldn't have identified the group – and went into their room.

'You surprised me,' Janice said as they settled back in the tub, their foreheads beginning to glisten from sweat and steam.

'Why?'

'Taking off like this,' Janice said. 'If Herb – '

Phoebe held up her hand. 'I don't want to talk about Herb,' she said. 'I don't want to talk about Parco-Fields, and I don't want to talk about Judson and Day. For the next half hour I want to veg out.'

'Good idea,' Janice said. They sat in silence for a while, and Phoebe felt her pores opening up, letting out the poisons that had been accumulating since she walked through the doors of the Barracks on Tuesday morning. She thought back to Duncan's sauna, to the four walls of that tiny room, their race down to the water; she wondered if she would ever feel so cleansed again.

'You didn't say very much about the trip during dinner last night,' Janice finally said. 'How did things end up with your friend? Did you get over that barrier?'

'Not really,' Phoebe said. Now that they were alone – she'd found it difficult to talk about Molly with Stu present – she told Janice about their off-key visits, about their caustic words on the day before the wedding, their week apart, and then the remorse she felt while reading Molly's farewell note.

'Ouch,' Janice said, when she had finished. 'That must have been pretty heart-wrenching.'

'It was,' Phoebe said. 'And I'd give anything not to

have said the things I said – especially about her wasting her life. *She's* not the one who's wasting her life.'

Janice took a sip of water.

'And yet I guess it needed to come out,' Phoebe went on. 'You wouldn't believe how tense things were getting; something had to snap. And anyway, I have a feeling we'll work things out over time. I don't know how, but we will. For one thing, we're going to write – or at least, *I'm* going to write; and I think she'll write back.' Maybe this weekend I'll have some time, she thought. No, I've got to prepare for the Bunker deposition. Well, maybe after Houston. Christ, she thought, I don't even have time to write a letter.

'Of course, I haven't even told you about another significant development,' she said.

'You got a job,' Janice guessed. 'You're moving back to Vermont.'

'Guess again.'

'You turned on to Jesus,' Janice said, irritated. 'Come on, Phoebe, don't play games.'

'I met someone,' Phoebe said.

Janice sat up, sending waves across the tub.

'I kind of,' Phoebe said, 'you know . . . had an affair.'

'Jesus Mary and Joseph,' Janice said.

'It's no big deal,' Phoebe said casually. 'I mean, it's not like I've fallen in love or anything, but, well, you know, it's been, shall we say, quite a while?'

'I'm in shock,' Janice said. 'I just don't know what to say.'

'Congratulate me,' Phoebe said. 'That's what my mother did.'

'Well *tell* me about it!' Janice exclaimed. 'Who is he, what does he do, what's he like, how did it all come about?'

And the presentation that Phoebe had planned, with

all its emphasis on Duncan's more traditional qualities (his engineering degree, for instance), its omission of his various eccentricities (his dowsing). dissolved as Phoebe tried to describe what happened. For one thing Janice, with her lawyer's inquisitiveness, asked a lot of direct questions: 'When did you first meet?' 'When did you next meet?' 'What was he doing down there in the field?' 'What was he dowsing for?' And for another, Phoebe found herself *wanting* to tell Janice everything about him: about his hooting to the owl, his mattress in the kitchen, his sauna, his birds – as though by telling her she could recapture some of the magic of that evening.

'So how did you leave things?' Janice demanded.

'Open,' Phoebe replied.

'*Open!* Why?'

'What do you want me to do? Start up a long-distance relationship? He doesn't even have a phone,' Phoebe said. 'Besides, like I said, it wasn't all that big a deal. It really wasn't, you know.'

'The very fact that you got involved was a big deal,' Janice said. 'And he doesn't sound like any old Joe Blow either.'

Phoebe said nothing.

'In fact he sounds like a breath of fresh air,' Janice said. 'For one thing, he's not a lawyer; that shows he's got a lot of common sense.'

Phoebe felt a knot tighten in her stomach.

'Also, you said he's rebuilding this place from the bottom up? And knows about birds, knows how to get an owl to hoot back to him? And on top of that he's literate and funny and straight? God, Phoebe – why didn't you just phone in your resignation and move in with him?'

The knot turned into cramp, and Phoebe once again heard her mother's voice back in her Vermont kitchen: 'I wish I hadn't held that man up to a standard he couldn't meet.' But it wasn't that she was holding Duncan up to too high a standard, was it? Wasn't it more a matter of pragmatics – Duncan living back there in Vermont, Phoebe with her job in San Francisco? Really, what could she do? There was no way to let things develop, no way to give it a chance; and she'd be crazy to start fixating on him, to start scheming, plotting out vacation time.

'Ah, Phoebe, you are more of a fool than I thought,' Janice said, shaking her head.

Phoebe didn't reply; her mind had suddenly been overshadowed by the foreboding sense that she had made a big mistake whose visible consequences were thus far just the tip of the iceberg. She ducked her head under the water, to melt it all away.

'All right, so I'm a fool,' she said when she had risen up out of the bubbly froth. 'But there's nothing I can do about it now, so why cry over spilt milk? I'm here, he's there, and that's that and I'm not going to dwell upon it. What I *would* like to dwell upon are the good things that came of this vacation.'

'Like what?'

'It put a lot in perspective,' Phoebe said.

'It doesn't sound like that to me,' Janice said. 'You let a guy like that slip through your fingers, I have to admit it sounds like things have got completely *out* of perspective.'

'Well what am I supposed to do!' Phoebe cried. 'Quit my job and move back there on the basis of one night?'

'No,' Janice said. 'Just don't write him off as no big deal.'

'What'd you do, talk to my mother?'

'No,' Janice said. 'Oh, Phoebe, don't get upset. Come on, I'm sorry. I shouldn't have cut you off like that. *How* did the trip put things in perspective?'

'I don't know,' Phoebe said. She closed her eyes, and saw Duncan in the trees, nailing up another bird feeder.

'I'll bet it put a lot into perspective about working here,' Janice offered. 'It must have been kind of nice to spend two weeks with people who don't care about depositions and trial dates and probate court.'

Phoebe looked at her friend gratefully, for Janice had just salvaged all the optimistic thoughts that Duncan's image had made a mess out of. It *was* nice to see once again how the rest of the world lived, to spend a few weeks with people who were neither Nuts nor Bolts, people for whom a lost document would be allotted no more personal anguish than a lost credit card: Hey, you make a few phone calls, you do what you can, you don't kill yourself over it.

'Let me ask you something,' she said. 'What if we were to start up our own firm? What do you think it would really be like?'

'I think we'd be busting our asses.'

'But it'd be different, wouldn't it?' Phoebe said. 'Working for ourselves as opposed to Herb – don't you think it'd be different?'

'I don't know,' Janice said. 'I have to admit, things have got a little more comfortable now that Frank's gone. I don't feel like there's such a rush to leave – maybe I should even hang on until they kick me out. Why deal with it now? Why not keep drawing a paycheque?'

'But think of the freedom we'd have,' Phoebe said. 'We could go on flexitime, we could do job sharing, we could even arrange for six-month sabbaticals – what do we have to lose?'

'Our paycheques,' said Janice. 'Which may be all right for me, but you have a kid to support.'

Phoebe wondered if perhaps her mother would put up some money.

'And anyway,' Janice went on, 'you're too disorganized to start up your own firm. You'd probably misplace the name and number of the first client who walked in the door.'

'But I'm getting more organized,' Phoebe said. 'Look at what I accomplished in the last two days. And besides, if we hired Eddie we'd be in great shape.'

'Phoebe, not only are you a fool, you're also a dreamer,' Janice said.

'I'm not a dreamer,' Phoebe said. 'I just don't want to wake up twenty years from now and wonder what I've done with my life.'

Just then the attendant knocked on the door. 'Five minutes!'

'These guys,' Janice complained, looking up. 'They're getting so obnoxious.'

'I bet we could do it,' Phoebe said later, reaching under her skirt to adjust her blouse. 'Other people do it right out of law school; we've got three years' experience on them.'

'If you call what we've done experience,' Janice said. 'I'm not so sure.'

'We could start out with contingency fee cases, personal injury stuff,' Phoebe went on. 'And then maybe we could handle some divorces – we may not get rich, but we'd bring in a decent income after a while.' She pulled out the misshapen bow she had just tied on the front of her blouse and started over.

'If I can only get through the next six months.' She sighed. 'Things are going to change like you wouldn't believe.'

# 20

That afternoon at the baths Phoebe promised herself that she would write to Molly as soon as she got back from Houston; maybe she didn't know what – if anything – to do about Duncan Crane, but at least she could work on her relationship with Molly, a relationship which was tangible, which had a history, which had more of a context. But as it turned out, Phoebe never got around to writing that letter; in fact, she never got around to doing anything, besides her work, over the next six months. After the Houston trip there was the Denver trip, and then the week in LA, and then it was Christmas, which she spent working on another brief, conscious of the holiday only when she called Andrew in Colorado and heard Christmas music in the background. A rainy January, February, and March passed with no days off; she began to keep a change of clothes at the office, and even brought her pillow in for those frequent occasions when she had to spend the night. One afternoon in early April she left the office briefly for a hair appointment, and as she walked outside she was shocked to see a miniature bed of tulips in full bloom. Why, it's spring, she thought with astonishment; and she realized that for the past several months the only significance of the calendar date had been its proximity in time to the upcoming trial date. Which on that afternoon was less than two weeks away.

But despite a judge who had tried very hard all along to keep things relatively on schedule, the trial date was postponed, first once, and then again, and then one afternoon in May rumours of a last-minute settlement hovered like whispers in the halls of the Barracks. That afternoon Herb was said to be spending all of his time on the phone with the other lead attorneys on the case, and Phoebe, editing an evidentiary brief, found herself doodling in the margins, unable to finish, unable to focus on perfecting her line of argument. Her right arm felt heavy, as though wrapped with wrist weights; and it suddenly seemed as though everyone on the team were pacing along on a treadmill whose motor was about to be cut. And yet nobody was allowed to believe it, and so they all continued to go through the motions of editing their briefs and organizing their exhibits as though the trial would, in fact, begin next week.

It didn't. That Thursday afternoon at four-thirty Herb called the Parco-Fields staff into his office and announced that a settlement had just been reached. Hearing this, Phoebe felt that champagne was in order, and indeed, she and John Dunn exchanged barely repressed looks of anticipation, for they had hidden a bottle of Mumm's in Phoebe's bottom desk drawer, behind her extra shoes, and if they could get it chilled in time they could have their long-awaited celebration today. But as Phoebe glanced around from face to face she noticed that several of the other associates actually appeared crestfallen: they had been eagerly looking forward to the trial experience, and a settlement was not, by their standards, cause for a celebration. (They were the last remaining Nuts on the case, of course; over the last several months Phoebe had been forced to reclassify most of her colleagues – beginning with John Dunn – as Bolts, because working for Herb had revolutionized them all, in a way: no longer did they bother keeping their wingtips shined; no longer were they looking forward to a noontime jog with a junior partner, once the case was over. They were looking to leave.)

Back in her office she and John slapped palms; then John proposed that they plan a real celebration for the next afternoon: he would get some caviar, perhaps, to go with the champagne. And so, for the first time in almost a year, Phoebe left the office before six. In fact, she even hit rush hour on the Bay bridge, which cause her to joke out loud to herself that here was proof that there was at least one benefit to working late all the time. (Another benefit, Phoebe would discover when she finally sat down to examine her bank statements from the past six months, was that litigation had saved her quite a bit of money: there had been no time for shopping sprees, movies, or other entertainment; and since Christmas, almost every single dinner – though it might have been no more than a carton of yogurt – had been paid for by Mr Parco, or Mr Fields.)

Back in Berkeley – it was still light out, she marvelled – she picked Andrew up at the babysitter's, and took him out to a Mexican restaurant for a celebration dinner of their own. As they ate their burritos she kept drifting away, though – with the pressure suddenly off it was as though her mind had, without any warning, collapsed – until Andrew would shout, 'MUM!' at which point she would snap back, shake her head, laugh, and say incredulously, 'It's over.'

'What's over?'

'Parco-Fields, Andrew – it's all over!'

At home she gave him a bath, found his last remaining pair of clean pyjamas, tucked him into bed, and read him the first chapter of *The Wind in the Willows*. She would read a chapter a night from now on, and then she would read *Charlotte's Web*, and *Tom Sawyer*, and *Robinson Crusoe*. When Andrew had fallen asleep she switched off his light and wandered about the house, not knowing quite what to do with herself. In the living room dust kitties had balled up in the corners; cobwebs laced the wrought-iron ceiling lamp, and the Miró print hung at an angle. She straightened the picture, and pledged to give the apartment a thorough scrubbing-down that weekend, one that would pass even her mother's inspection.

And she did. Saturday morning she cooked a big breakfast; after reading the paper she ran a load of laundry and vacuumed the living room. She was just about to start in on the bathroom when the mail arrived: the telephone bill, *Newsweek*, a couple of flyers, and then a long white envelope postmarked WINSLOW, VERMONT. It was addressed to her, in Molly's careful script. Phoebe sat down on the sofa. Oh dear. All this time had passed and all she'd done was to jot Molly a postcard telling her she would write her a longer letter at some point.

*Oh, dear.*

*Greetings,* Molly had written. *I have been sitting here for half an hour trying to find a way to begin this, and finally figured that I might as well begin with a birth announcement.*

*I have a little girl.*

*Her name is Sarah.*

*She came a little early – May 4, after a short labour – and only weighed six and a half pounds; but she is getting fat now. She is a happy baby, so far, and I feel blessed, especially after hearing from my mother how much of a screamer I was. We have taken out baby pictures of both Nick and myself; she looks like me, though when she sleeps her mouth forms a kiss, as Nick used to. (Elaine, of course, is convinced that she is a spitting image of herself as an infant. God help me.) I'll send pictures as soon as we get reprints; right now everything is still too disorganized.*

*Another piece of news: we are moving to LA this summer; of all the schools that Nick got into – and there weren't a whole lot, as it turned out; there must be an awful lot of hotshot prelaw students out there – UCLA was the best. It took me a while but I'm slowly adjusting to the fact that my child is going to learn to say 'palm tree' and 'surfer' before she learns to say 'blue spruce' and 'cross-country.' I myself am looking forward to running into Jane Fonda at the supermarket; and people tell me the smog isn't all that bad, as long as you stay in west LA. I must say, though, that I'm not too keen on living in some one-storey ranch house and spending half my life on the freeway. But I will cope.*

*Do you ever get down to LA on business? We won't have a lot of extra money so I doubt it will be very easy for us to get up to San Francisco. But maybe you and Andrew can get down for a visit once in a while. It would be good to see you.*

*Which brings me to the third purpose of this letter. I'm sorry for taking off like that to Montreal. I feel I left you in the lurch, and I wish I hadn't. As it turned out, the trip was a total disaster – we ran out of petrol, the hotel was five times as expensive as we'd thought, and to top it off I ate some bad shrimp. But it was a needed break. (You did get my note, didn't you? I left it on your mother's kitchen table?) I'm not sure how much of a 'new perspective' it gave me, but when I got back I immediately packed up my loom and put all my yarns into storage; it lasted until March, and then I unpacked it all and ended up doing three wall hangings, better work than I've ever done – sold two and received three orders to do on commission. I guess I shouldn't fight that part of me. I have to admit that sometimes I wish it were a little more glamorous – it's home oriented, and thus lonely – but then again I've never been the social butterfly. In any event I'm looking forward to letting a little California imagery creep into my work; those back here in Vermont are getting a bit stale, I think.*

*Well: I've caught you up; now it's your turn. In a way*

*you've become such a mystery to me, Phoebe. When I hear you 'talking law' I'm inclined to categorize you as another one of those 'young upstarts,' but then I think of the girl I grew up with, and* then *I think of the woman who married this man named Rusty, and had a child by him, and then divorced him; who is now trying to raise the child while practising law, preparing for trials, keeping track of documents . . . and suddenly it's impossible for me to put it all together. It's as though I have a warp all set up on my loom but no wool for the weft, so that while I may have an idea of what the finished tapestry could look like, it will never take form.*

*I'm sorry for the way I acted when you were back. Not so much with respect to our argument (that 'little tiff,' my mother keeps calling it, prodding for an explanation); but rather for being so defensive the entire visit and tossing all your accusations against me back into your court. But it was hard for me; all you had to do was stand there in my driveway that first night and you managed to call into question everything about me. I'm sorry, though, for clamming up. I wish I could have foreseen my emotions a little more clearly, wish we could have brought things out into the open a little earlier.*

*Ah, yes.* If only. *If only I were a little more mature. If only I had in my hands a ready script that would tell us how to take it from here, would bring us as close as we used to be and might now be if we had continued to grow together, which we obviously haven't. But I don't have that script. And in truth I hesitate to say how it will really be, living in Los Angeles, five hundred miles from you and your life as an attorney up there in San Francisco. Maybe we'll get together quite often; maybe we won't. I think we owe it to ourselves, though, to wipe out the expectations, and start from scratch. You are, after all, my oldest friend.*

*Sarah is awake; it's feeding time. (By the way, I'm sure you realize that despite all my talk about weaving I'm hardly doing any work right now.) Don't feel compelled to write back immediately; I'm sure you're incredibly busy, either with your trial if it hasn't happened yet, or with some other big project if the trial is already over. Did you put on a witness? What about that guy you were working for – has he dropped dead yet? (Maybe I could arrange for it?)*

*Do write back, though, at some point. (I feel a little awkward writing all this, and worry that perhaps I should let it sit for a day or so and then edit out certain parts, but I think I'm going to just stick everything into an envelope and mail it.) Give me your view, your thoughts, your feelings, about the visit. About us. About me.*

*Everybody here asks about you, of course. Nick wants to know if you think it'll be necessary for us to live near the campus; he sends his love. My parents are fine; their project this spring is to solarize the house. Duncan Crane had been working with Nick this winter. He is talking about going camping out West during July and August. I asked if he was going as far as California and he got very vague and mysterious but I wouldn't be surprised if you got a phone call from him; according to Nick he's always dropping references to Bay Area attorneys.*

*And I'll send you our address when we get one.*

*With love from*
*The LA Kid*

*P.S. One print I did happen to have lying around was the picture my mother took of us the morning of the wedding, when we were sitting by the fire. As for what to make of the expressions on our faces – I leave it up to you.*

Phoebe sat for a long time on the sofa with Molly's letter in her hands. A little girl named Sarah . . . Duncan working with Nick . . . Los Angeles . . . if only I were more mature. She suddenly wondered where she had put the wall hanging that Molly had given her. Had she tucked it in the back of her closet? Under her bed? In her memory the colours didn't seem quite so sad, quite so dowdy, as they had last November, back in Vermont; and she decided that later today she would find the right place for it: possibly the front hall, where visitors could admire its gentle furry textures.

Phoebe reached for a yellow legal pad on the coffee table, and curled back up on the sofa. She would begin by thanking Molly, once again, for the wall hanging, and at some point in the letter she would pass on a casual greeting to Duncan. Outside on the balcony Andrew was teaching Marilyn, the professor's daughter, how to play Go Fish; from downstairs the notes of the Bach fugue clashed as the professor's wife practised her piano lesson, trying to mesh treble with bass. One of these days, she would get it right.